Storm Warning

A Sonny Marshall Thriller

Terry R. Bacon

Stagnant Millpond Publishing

ISBN-979-8-9880748-0-9

ISBN-979-8-9880748-1-6

Cover design by: My Custom Book Cover, LLC

Library of Congress Control Number: 2023911859

Printed in the United States of America

To learn more about Sonny, visit www.sonnymarshall.com.

www.terry@terryrbacon.com

www.Stagnantmillpondpublishing.com

For my wife Debra

My heart and Soul

With deepest gratitude to Fritz Geisler for his undying friendship and support and to many family members and friends who read the manuscript and provided invaluable suggestions.

Thanks to Petra Hincke, who offered considerable expertise in Spanish and was an excellent proofreader. Thanks also to the many martial arts masters who offered their knowledge of Aikido and Krav Maga and to the saxophone and blue musicians who were and continue to be an inspiration.

Man is a rope stretched between the animal and the Superman—a rope over an abyss.

Friedrich Nietzsche

Blues Comin' Down Like Rain

Woke up this mornin', ain't feeling no pain
Then you walk out, baby, blues comin' down like rain
Yeah, yeah, momma, blues comin' down like rain.

Chorus:
Gotta hole in my soul, since you ran away
Like lookin' for sunshine on a rainy day
Cause you ran away, cause you ran away.

Wind blowin' through leaves, Devil callin' my name
Since I lost my sweet woman, blues comin' down like rain
Yeah, yeah, momma, blues comin' down like rain.

Chorus

Ain't no place that's safe, ain't no cure for pain
Ain't no place to hide, blues comin' down like rain
Yeah, yeah, momma, blues comin' down like rain.

Chorus

Blues comin' down like rain, blues comin' down like rain
Don't matter it stop rainin', Devil comin' just the same
Devil comin' just the same, he comin' just the same.

Lijah Washington, 1948

Storm Warning

1

I learned about the missing girl in a bar in San Francisco. I could have let the matter drop. Thousands of children go missing every year. One more adds to the statistic. I'm a musician, and Erin Hightower was none of my business. Neither was the fight in Cactus Jack's that night. I've been up to my elbows in alligators many times, and I ought to know better, but I can't seem to stay out of the swamp. When someone's in trouble, I plunge in, alligators or not. I don't know if that makes me a Good Samaritan or a fool, but it's the decent thing to do.

Cactus Jack's is an upscale bar and grill with an adequate stage and a dance floor large enough for forty people. Sunday is locals' night at Jack's, and on stage the first and second Sunday of every month is the Storm Lake Blues Band—Xavier McQueen on bass, Garth Wyman on percussion, K.C. Vaughn on keyboards, Eric Young on guitar, and me, Sonny Marshall, on sax. During our first set, the crowd had been dancing to songs from our debut album, *Storm Warning*, and when we took our first break, my throat burned like hot sandpaper. The bar at Jack's sits along one long wall of the cavernous main room. A cluster of small round oak tables and chairs fills the rest of the room to the dance floor, and I saw only a few empty tables. The bar is the brightest part of the room, lit by red cones suspended above the mahogany bar top. It was crowded, but I found one open stool and waved at the bartender, Joe Warfield.

Joe raised his chin at me. "Same?"

I nodded and glanced in the mirror behind the bar. It was the usual mix of San Franciscans partying before the work week began, but a few feet away were two guys in a tense exchange. I couldn't hear them above the crowd, but a guy with a greasy black mop for hair leaned into the other and poked him in the chest. The greaser had the vacant eyes of a drunk or a stoner. The guy being poked was bald and barrel-chested. His jaw was clenched, and he was flexing his right hand. With each poke, his face grew more florid. He looked like a car whose driver had slammed on the brakes while flooring the accelerator. I imagined smoke pouring from his ears and admired his restraint. I wouldn't have tolerated someone poking me like that. The issue was apparently a backwater blonde with limp curls who sat beside the greaser. Her mouth was drawn, and beads of moisture lay on her forehead and upper lip. She looked down at the bar, tugging her companion's sleeve, but he ignored her.

"Here you go," Joe said, handing me a tall, ice-cold club soda with two slices of lime. A long drink puckered my mouth and cooled my throat all the way down. I set the empty glass on the bar, and Joe refilled it. When he handed it back, I cocked my head toward the trio down the bar.

Joe frowned. "I'm watching them," he said, flinging a black bar towel over his shoulder and rubbing his face with one hand, his fingers lingering on the stubble across his chin. Joe is solid but has packed on forty pounds since retiring from the Air Force fifteen years ago. He has long white hair and the pleasant face you'd expect on someone playing Santa Claus. He smiled at me, puffy cheeks reddening, and asked how my leg was doing.

"S'all right," I said. "Maybe someday I'll buy a new one." I'd been in a bad motorcycle accident eleven years ago. Three operations later, my left leg still bothered me. When the pain in my knee was most severe, it felt like the bones were being crushed. But tonight, I had only a dull ache, a reminder of the agony my knee could inflict if I abused it. I made a mental note to sit on a stool during our next set.

I drained the last of my club soda when I saw McQueen headed back to the stage. As I slid off the barstool, I felt a tap on my shoulder, glanced in the mirror, and smiled when I saw my old friend Fetch and his wife, Stephanie. I've known David Fetchenheir since second grade in Pasadena. He was the gangly kid always picked last when we were choosing sides for baseball, but the girls liked him. He was nice-looking and smart and had an easy way around people. His wife is an attractive brunette with eyes that sparkle like a rhinestone necklace catching the sun. Her skin is polished marble, and thick hair cascades around her shoulders in such perfect waves you'd think she was a model for L'Oreal instead of a high school chemistry teacher.

"I know you have to go on stage," Fetch said. "But I need to talk to you. We visited Steph's family last month, and I saw something that's bothering me."

"I keep telling him it was nothing," Stephanie said, her eyes drifting away.

His face sank momentarily, forehead knotted. Then he looked me in the eye. "No. I'm right about it."

Garth hit a few warm-up beats on his snare drum, and I cocked my head toward the stage. "I'll catch you at the next break."

Cactus Jack's is on a block of Pacific Avenue once known as Terrific Street, so named because the saloons, brothels, dance halls, and music clubs that crowded this street a century ago brought ragtime, blues, and jazz to the West Coast. According to local wags, the quality of the music was terrific. Al Jolson and Sophie Tucker performed here. So did Eubie Blake and Jelly Roll Morton, who invented jazz. In clubs like the Hippodrome, Nymphia, and Spider Kelly's, pretty waiter girls swung above the dance floor, their tiny silk skirts billowing in the breeze, revealing to gawkers below that they weren't wearing bloomers. But in the Whale, the wickedest saloon on the Barbary Coast, the whores wore nothing but fishnet stockings and feathery plumes, and they would perform whatever dance their customers paid for, their bare bodies bouncing to a thumpity-thumpity ragtime beat. It was dangerous music for a dangerous time.

After the earthquake of 1906, the Whale burned to cinders like the other hell holes on the Barbary Coast. If so much of the city hadn't been destroyed, you would have thought it was divine retribution for the harlotry, murders, thievery, and general wickedness of the area. As the city was rebuilt, there were attempts to restore the salacious appeal of Terrific Street, but they were doomed by San Francisco's metamorphosis from a gold mining town on the western frontier to a metropolis governed by gentry and laws the police actually enforced. Dance halls gave way to hotels, saloons to restaurants, and brothels to condos. An art supply store now sits where the Hippodrome was located, and the wickedest saloon in the west became Cactus Jack's.

During the heyday of the Barbary Coast, some saloons had slummers' galleries, catwalks above the main floor where for a dollar, the wealthy and privileged could witness the licentious behavior below without risking limbs, lives, or fortunes. To give them their money's worth, owners paid whores and ruffians to dance nasty or stage a fight that sometimes ended with a stabbing or garroting, the wounded victim displayed on the sawdust floor to give the titillated slummers their money's worth. But Jack's doesn't have a slummers' gallery, and what happened as we were starting our second set hadn't been staged.

I had my back to the dance floor and was letting my fingers fly up and down the keys when I was startled by an explosion of noise behind me. A bar stool screeched across the floor, and I heard the heavy thump of a body. I turned and heard chairs scraping as people backed out of the way. The crowd fell silent except for shocked murmurs. The air in the room felt dense.

"Get up, asshole," the greaser yelled. He stood over the other man, a glint of steel in his right hand. He waved the knife back and forth as the barrel-chested guy on the floor scurried away, all elbows and scrambling shoes. Joe raced around the bar carrying a small bat at the ready, but Joe was too soft and slow for a close encounter with a knife. Before I could think, I set down my sax and leaped off the stage, grabbing Joe's arm.

"Call nine-one-one," I whispered. Joe hesitated before running back around the bar. I faced the assailant.

"Stay the fuck outta this," he barked at me.

"Put the knife down."

"Fuck you."

"Come on, man. You don't want to do this. It's a party," I said, gesturing around the room. "Let's chill."

"Fuck you."

Yeah, right, I thought. *Fuck me. What the hell am I doing?*

Behind me, someone jumped off the stage, but I kept my eyes on the knife. It had to be the X-man, Xavier McQueen, our band leader and bass player, but I didn't want him distracting me. I waved one hand back to caution him away.

The guy hadn't attacked, so he was sizing me up. That was a mistake. He'd lost the advantage of surprise. He had a crooked smirk, the look of a man confusing bravado with courage. The knife had a thick handle and a five-inch folding blade locked open. It was a serious knife, so I reasoned the guy knew how to use it. He held the knife in the underhand position, the blade pointing forward, its razor tip positioned outside his trunk. If he got close, he could spill my guts with one sweeping arc of the blade.

I circled slowly to my left, and he countered by moving to his left. Behind him, people scurried away. I wanted his back to the bar, so it limited his movement, but he realized what I was doing, and his eyes widened in alarm. Then he sucked in a breath, raised his chin, and narrowed his eyes. He'd just made a stupid decision and was too drunk to execute whatever he planned. That didn't mean I wasn't in danger. It just meant his movements and reaction times were impaired, which gave me the advantage. Not that I wanted a fight. I just wanted to disarm this jerk before he hurt someone.

When the attack came, he didn't do what I expected. Instead of slashing from underneath, he raised his arm as he rushed me, stabbing down with his wrist turned inward. But he mistimed his footing as he rushed forward and lurched to his left. When his arm started down, I jumped backward and grunted loudly. The unexpected movement and noise startled him. I grabbed his wrist as it swung past and propelled his arm behind his back. At the same time, I pushed down on the back of his head with my other hand, and he somersaulted through the air, landing on his back with a sharp thud. As he hit the floor, he cried out, eyes bulging. The knife clattered away and spun in tight circles. Spitting mad, he rolled over, found the knife, and clambered to his feet, swaying wildly as he regained his balance.

He looked at me warily, lips trembling. A smarter man would have escaped while he could, but this guy was too macho, drunk, and committed to do anything but try to save face in front of the blonde at the bar. He switched the knife to his other hand and came at me again, swinging his knife toward my neck. I spun out of his way, my leading hand slamming into the back of his neck as he passed. It was an Aikido move I'd practiced a thousand times. He pitched forward and went down fast, face bouncing off the hard oak. He cried out again when he hit the deck, and his knife bounced across the floor.

He lay there, spitting blood. Then he shook his head and clawed after the knife, which lay a few feet away. Before he could reach it, the X-man stomped on the knife and snarled, "No fuckin' way." McQueen is six-three and weighs two-forty. He's got a shaved head and looks like an NFL lineman with a bad attitude. Never mind that he's really a teddy bear. When he snarls, he looks like he could bite your head in half, and no way would the greaser fuck with him. Instead, he lurched to his feet, spun wildly around, and hurled himself toward the nearest table. He grabbed an empty chair, spun back around, raised the chair over his head, and charged.

Chairs make clumsy weapons. They're too bulky to maneuver quickly and can throw the assailant off balance, but they're large and hard and will break your bones if one strikes you with enough force. I stood in a ready position, my knees and arms bent, then hurried two steps backward, my face a mask of fear. I dove into his shins when he drew closer and swung the chair down. The chair bounced harmlessly behind me as his feet jerked out from under him, and he flew forward onto his stomach, his face ricocheting off the floor again. I got to my feet, felt a stabbing jolt in my knee, and shook my head in disgust. The guy lay sprawled near the bar. I limped to him and smelled the coppery scent of the blood pouring from his nose and mouth. Then he threw up, filling the air with the acrid stench of bile and stale beer. He tried to push himself up, and I grabbed one of his wrists, pulled his arm over his back, and used my other hand to push his elbow toward his spine. It's a move that twists your opponent's arm in his shoulder socket. The more he resists, the more painful it becomes. I could control him by applying as much pressure on his elbow as needed to keep him on the floor just short of gut-piercing agony.

He muffled a cry and blurted, "Fuck, man."

I eased off and said, "Enough." Still not defeated, he tried to wriggle out of my grasp, so I pushed his elbow in more. He yelped at the sudden, sharp pain. I eased off again and said, "The more you move, the more it will hurt. You're done."

Two uniformed cops burst through the door a few minutes later. I dropped the guy's arm and limped away as one of the cops stood over the guy. Xavier picked up the knife by its tip and handed it to the cop. Joe told them what happened as I wiped my hands on a bar towel. The cop said he might need a statement from me, and I nodded. I limped back to the stage as they handcuffed the guy and led Joe and other witnesses outside. When I hooked my sax onto the neck strap, I felt another sharp twinge of pain in my knee.

I pulled up a stool and sat on it as the X-man approached the mike, grinning broadly. "Give it up for my man, Sonny," he crooned, peering around at me. The crowd burst into riotous applause like I imagine the slummers must have done a century ago. I settled back on the stool and put the mouthpiece between my teeth. We started the set with "Hang time," a blues number in B-flat with alternating sax and keyboard solos, and the dance floor was soon filled with rocking fans while one of Joe's barkeeps mopped up the mess in front of the bar. We made some fine music for another hour and a half and then took our break.

I found my way to Fetch's table as Joe rushed over with club soda and lime. "Christ, Sonny," Joe said. "You want anything else?"

"I'm good," I told him. But as he left, I slipped two Oxys out of my pocket and swallowed them with a long, icy drink. The pain in my leg now pulsed like a locomotive turning its big wheels, and I needed to head it off before it became a mind-bender. Fetch and Stephanie glanced at each other, but neither spoke.

Then Stephanie said, "That was impressive. The way you handled that guy."

I waved it off. "He was drunk. No big deal."

"It looked like a big deal."

"All part of the night's entertainment."

She gave me a porcelain smile while Fetch explained that I had black belts in Aikido and some other martial art.

"Krav Maga," I said.

Stephanie asked what those were. I explained that Aikido is a Japanese martial art based on blending with an attacker's motion and directing his energy away from you. Krav Maga is a self-defense discipline developed by the Israeli military.

"How long have you been studying those?" she said.

"Since I was twelve."

She arched her eyebrows, but I didn't want to explain, so I turned to Fetch. "What happened on your trip?"

He looked at Stephanie, anticipating skepticism, but she just pursed her lips. He turned back at me. "We took a family vacation. Drove to North Platte to see Steph's family. On our way back, we stopped for gas in Green River, Wyoming." He sipped his drink.

"And?"

"I saw a girl who went missing seven years ago."

I sat back, rubbing my aching knee, and studied his face.

"She was kidnapped, Sonny. In Sacramento. Seven years ago. She was never found. But I saw her in Wyoming four weeks ago."

2

As I waited for Fetch to continue, Stephanie folded her arms and glanced at her watch. She studied him, the corners of her mouth curled up in a look she might give twelfth graders who can't tell a hypotenuse from a hippopotamus. My mouth turned sour as I observed her out of the corner of my eye.

"Why don't you tell me what happened?" I said to him. Her eyes drifted away again.

"We were on Interstate Eighty in Wyoming and stopped in Green River for gas. I went inside to get something for everyone to drink."

"Where were you?" I asked Stephanie.

"In the bathroom with our girls," she said without looking at me.

"So you didn't see this girl?"

She shook her head and then lifted her wineglass to her lips with delicate fingers.

"It was a big convenience store," Fetch said. "Probably twenty people inside. But only one cash register was open, and maybe eight people were in line. Three or four people ahead of me were a dark-haired woman and a girl who looked about twelve or thirteen. They were facing away from me. Then the girl gazed around the store, and I saw her face."

He paused for another drink. The club had grown darker except for the blue lights above the stage, which filled the room with a blue haze. Fetch's face appeared to float above his dark shirt as though he were a character in a surrealistic film. It might have been my eyes adjusting to the darkness or the Oxys tripping through my brain. Whatever. My knee was numb, my mind buoyant.

"I saw her only for a moment," I heard Fetch say. "But I knew I'd seen her before."

"Did you recognize the woman?"

"No. I was trying to remember where I'd seen the girl when a name popped into my head. Erin. It came from some fog bank in my memory, but I still couldn't place her. So I said 'Erin' aloud like you'd call someone's name to get their attention. And she turned around, Sonny. She looked me right in the eye."

"Did she recognize you?"

He shook his head.

"Was she startled? Surprised at some guy calling her name?"

"More like curious. The woman wore a black coat and held some things she would buy in her left arm. Her right hand was in her pocket. After I called 'Erin,' she looked at me and then at the girl. She hesitated, took her hand out of her pocket, and grabbed the girl's hand. She said, 'Come on, Rachel,' She set the things she was carrying on the nearest shelf and led the girl toward the door."

"You think they left because you called the girl's name?"

"That wasn't her name," Stephanie interjected. She looked sharply at me, her nostrils growing wider. "The woman called her Rachel. Not Erin. Rachel. Maybe they left because the line was too slow. Or maybe she left her purse in the car. Or maybe she changed her mind and decided they'd eaten enough junk food on this trip."

Her alternatives were plausible, but I trusted there was more to it than a forgotten purse.

"So what did you do?"

"I left the line and walked toward the front door to see where they went. Then I noticed a guy watching me."

"A guy who hadn't been in line with them?"

He nodded. "He stood at a magazine rack pretending to read a magazine. When he saw me walking toward the door, he put down the magazine and moved in front of the door. He acted like he wasn't watching me but didn't move again until I stopped. A few seconds later, he turned and left. Through the windows, I saw the three of them enter a white van parked by the gas pumps. The van pulled away, and they headed east onto the interstate."

"David," Stephanie said, more gently than I expected, "you're reading too much into this." She wrapped thin fingers around his arm. "People see what they want to see. That girl was five when she was kidnapped. The girl you saw in the store was much older, and kids change as they grow up. Just think of our girls. Maybe the girl you saw had similar features. Maybe something about her seemed familiar, but the odds that you saw the kidnapped girl are infinitesimal. The guy with the magazine probably didn't even know you were there. His wife and daughter left, so he put down what he was reading and joined them. It has to be that simple. I'm going to the ladies' room."

As she left, I asked Fetch why he thought the girl had been kidnapped.

"I didn't. Not then. I didn't make the connection. But it kept bothering me. I couldn't get her face out of my mind. Then at work, I remembered where I'd seen her." Fetch is a videographer for KPIX-TV, the CBS station in San Francisco. He accompanies reporters into the field and shoots videos for stories that appear on Channel 5 Eyewitness News.

"Two months ago," he said, "Marcella Delgado did a feature story on missing children in California, and one of the cases she covered was Erin Hightower." He reached into his jacket pocket and handed me a three-by-five photograph. "It was her eyes. She has distinctive eyes."

The photo was grainy but clear enough. Erin Hightower was a beautiful child. She had long curly brown hair, a squarish face, and strong jawlines leading to a perfectly oval chin. Her upper lip resembled an archer's bow, and her nose was a tiny button of a thing but well-proportioned for her face. In this photo, her lips were open, and she had a small gap between her two front teeth. Probably still her baby teeth. She had a purple flower in her hair, but her most dominant feature was her eyes. They were green and shaped like teardrops. She had a look of wistful innocence. For her, the world was still enchanting. I could see why Fetch would find her memorable.

"We filmed a short segment with the police officer in Sacramento who has the case. That's how I learned that the girl I saw had been kidnapped when she was five. The story aired two months ago. I remembered it yesterday and got the file from the vault to watch it again. I printed that picture for you."

I gazed at the photo. "So this image was in the back of your mind when you saw the girl in Green River."

"It's her, Sonny. I don't doubt it. It's crazy, I know. The girl I saw in Wyoming is seven years older than when that picture was taken, so it took me a while to piece together where I'd seen her. She's now twelve, and Steph's right that children change as they grow up. But the eyes don't change."

It was time to start our third set. "Why haven't you gone to the police?"

"They wouldn't believe me."

If I'd known what was coming, I wouldn't have thanked Fetch for what he'd told me, but I didn't know, and it was late, the Oxys had kicked in, and warmth had spread through my body as the pain in my knee evaporated. I bid my friend goodbye and got up. The stage was clouded in a blue mist, and the guys in the band moved like shadows within it, and I could feel the music ahead, and it was fine. When I reached the stage, I strapped on my sax, felt my fingers slide onto the keys like touching all the warm, intimate places on a woman's body, and ripped off the opening riff from a Charlie Parker classic.

"Whoa, brother," the X-man crooned. "What are we doin'?"

"4-F Blues," I yelled. He nodded, and he and the other guys fell in with me. I don't know what happened to the next hour and a half. I gave myself to the music, passages flowing up from some well deeper than memory, flying off my tongue and fingers like lovers locked in a passionate embrace. We finished our last set with an explosive twelve-minute rendition of "Flame and Fury," the final song on *Storm Warning*. When we ended, I slumped back on my stool, my clothing stuck to my body, moisture oozing from my fingers, running down my golden instrument in rivulets. I came out of my trance and cleaned my sax while the other guys wiped down their instruments.

It had been raining outside. My car was beaded with rain, and the rain still fell. I stood at my car door for a moment, my face uplifted. The rain felt like drops of purity coursing down my forehead, into my eyes, and over my lips. As I drove home, the night rumbled with rolling thunder, and streaks of lightning flashed off skyscrapers like strobes from dozens of paparazzi cameras. The city's streets glistened, traffic lights, window lights, and neon signs reflected in shimmering waves on the pavement below. The Coppola Building glowed, so opulent and pearly white it looked like a multi-layered cake at a royal wedding. I drove slowly, still hearing the music in my head. My fingers drummed on the steering wheel, my eyes flushed with the whole phantasmagoria of San Francisco at night.

At the corner of Powell and 16th, some doped-up dirtbag bellowed madly, his voice splitting the air like flatulence. Something ragged that might once have been a trench coat hung dripping around his shoulders. His matted hair lay wrapped around his ears, and he wore army boots without laces. Whatever had scorched his brain left nothing but detritus. The whole underbelly of the city came alive at night—the hustlers, pimps, grifters, pushers, drunks, burnouts, freaks, junkies, gangbangers, and whores. Some scurried through the rain for shelter under eaves and in darkened porticos, tramping around the homeless, who slumped against buildings under soggy Goodwill coats or in shapeless cardboard boxes.

Other creatures of the night were clumped in alleyways or on street corners, picking at each other like sores, oblivious to the rain, lost souls trapped in a nightmare of their own creation, drugged up and dreamed out, living so far out on the edge that all they had left was an eternal now filled with needs that could never be met and days they would soon forget. They crept along in the shadows while around them, the city was ablaze with sparkling light. I drove through this radiant madness as though rowing past a beautiful garden along the River Styx.

My sanctuary is a top-floor condo on Broadway in Pacific Heights. It was still raining when I drove down into the garage. Mac's convertible was already there, beads of rain dripping from the sides, the black canvas top still wet. My girlfriend, Mac, is an associate fashion designer who was in New York for a show last week. She flew in late this evening, so I tiptoed into the condo, careful not to wake her, but I saw light in the bedroom. As I eased the door open, I saw her sitting on the bed, poring over clothing catalogs scattered on the comforter. She wore black silk pajamas, her long auburn hair lying easily on her shoulders, a pensive look on her face. She took off her black reading glasses when she heard the door open.

"Hey, you," she said brightly.

"Hey, back," I responded. We kissed as I sat on the bed beside her. "How was your trip?"

She threw her head back and gazed at the ceiling. She told me about a threatened stage workers union strike that could have shut down the show but didn't, about their frantic search for a replacement when one of their models broke her hand after tripping over a rug in her apartment, about making final adjustments to their new clothing line, dealing with producers and sewists and the press, scheduling interviews and dinners and then rescheduling everything at least three times, fending off the advances of practically every man she met, and feeling exhausted each evening. She told all that with a gleam in her eye and a mischievous smile on her lips. It was her world, and she loved it, and she'd waited for me because she wanted us to have a nice homecoming. We kissed again, and then I went to the bathroom to shower. I told her I'd be quick, and I was, but when I walked back into the bedroom, she looked at me with a knitted brow, the corners of her mouth drooping.

"You're limping," she said flatly. "Did you hurt your knee again?"

I've known Mac since she saw us playing at a club in Monterey three years ago. She was there with a tall blonde guy who wore a black leather sport coat, but as the evening wore on, we caught each other's eyes more frequently. During one of our breaks, she slid next to me at the bar and ordered a glass of Pouilly Fumé. She wore a green silk blouse and black jeans with rolled cuffs over black high-heels and had a gold bracelet with inlaid sapphires on her right wrist. She smelled like lavender and jasmine. I closed my eyes and was savoring her aroma when she turned to me and said, "I'm Marilyn. Marilyn Anne Crittenden, but everyone calls me Mac."

"Nice to meet you. Sonny Marshall." She offered her hand, and I shook it.

"I love the saxophone. I love its mellow sound. How come I've never heard of your band?"

I shrugged. "We're about to release our first album."

"What's it called?"

"Storm Warning."

"I'll look for it." She smiled, then brought the wineglass to her lips. As she sipped, we gazed at each other. Her eyes were the color of sable with tiny flecks of green. She had long lashes and lush eyebrows thicker at the bridge of her nose and tapered as they drew toward her temples. She had an angular face with a jaw shaped like the prow of a ship. Her lips were full and moist, leaving a pink trace on the wineglass when she lowered it. I'd never seen a more beautiful woman. I still haven't. During our next set, I watched as she and the guy headed for the exit. She paused to look back at me before leaving, and at that moment, my stomach twisted. But when the band finished for the evening and we were packing our gear, one of the servers handed me a slip of paper. It had a phone number on it and was signed "Mac."

When we began seeing each other, Mac and I vowed to always be honest with each other. She'd had two relationships that ended badly; the most painful was with a guy she hoped to marry. He was a vice president at Wells Fargo and seemed destined to rise in the social circles Mac aspired to join, but just before their engagement party at his parents' home in Sausalito, she discovered text messages on his cell phone from a woman in Nob Hill whom he'd been seeing on the side. She broke up with him during their engagement party in what her parents later confided was a horrific scene. So in keeping with our vow of transparency, I told her about the incident at Jack's.

Her face blanched as I told the story. When I finished, she stared silently at me and turned away, her hands clutching the comforter. Her brows lay flat across her face when she turned back, and her mouth grew tight.

"Are you out of your mind?" she hissed. "What were you thinking?"

"I couldn't let it go," I said quietly. "Someone might have gotten hurt."

"Yes! You! You might have gotten hurt. You could have been killed." Her face flushed. "I don't understand you. You're thirty-four, you have a bad knee, and you . . . you're a musician, you play in a band. What were you thinking?"

"Someone had to stop him."

"You're not a bouncer. You're not a cop. It's not your job, Sonny. Don't you get that? When some idiot in a nightclub pulls a knife, you call the police. It's not your job!" Tears welled in her eyes, and she stifled a sob. Her hand shook when she brought it to her face to wipe away a tear. "I love you, but I don't understand you. I can't come home some night and have a policeman knock on the door and tell me you've been killed. I can't do that. I won't. I can't."

"Mac."

"Shut up." She sobbed softly, wiping her eyes with one finger and then absently licking that finger as though tasting her salty tears would corroborate her anguish. As I watched her, the bottom dropped out of my heart, and my blood settled in leaden fingers.

"Don't ever do that again," she whispered. "Promise me you won't." Then she gathered her catalogs and set them on the floor. "I need some sleep." She pulled back the comforter and top sheet and slid underneath them, laying her head on the pillow facing away from me. I hesitated, then turned off the light and crept back into the main room, slowly shutting the door behind me. I know Mac well enough to know that more words now would be fruitless. When she feels wounded, the best nurses are solitude and time.

My condo has a large main room with a kitchen along the east wall. A long row of windows above the counter provides light and the warmth of the morning sun. I opened the liquor cabinet, found a bottle of tawny port, and poured a small glass. It was nearly three a.m., and I could see little activity outside my windows but an occasional car passing on Broadway. I sat on the sofa and sipped the port. It's a good port, but it tasted like toasty cough syrup tonight. I felt weary from guilt at having upset Mac. I understood Mac but couldn't have acted differently. Edmund Burke said the only thing necessary for evil to triumph is for good men to do nothing. If I hadn't stepped in, Joe would have faced that knife, and he was not equipped to handle it. What would be the greater guilt if I hadn't intervened and Joe had been killed? I set down my glass and lay back on the sofa. I closed my eyes and let my mind spiral down to a pinpoint as I sank heavily into my exhaustion.

I was swimming in a lake somewhere. A vast lake, cold water stretching to the horizon. Trees lined one faraway shore, a forest of cedars and Ponderosa pines. There was a beach behind me, but I couldn't see it. I wasn't afraid. I'm a good swimmer. It was a languorous day, the water perfectly calm, the sun shining brilliantly in the azure sky, warming my forehead and forcing my eyes closed against blinding sparkles of sunlight dancing in the water. Then I saw someone ahead, a man, struggling, his arms flailing, water flung into the air. He jerked up and fell backward, kicking frantically to keep his head above water.

I swam towards him in long strokes. My legs felt strong, and I was confident I could reach him quickly. I came within a few yards before tiring and moving like a motion picture projected one frame at a time. My limbs became turgid, legs no longer scissoring. They felt like they were bound by seaweed. I kicked but kept floating farther away. Then I saw it was not a man, but a woman. Long wet red hair was caked on her head. She was pale, gasping for breath, and had drops of water glued to her face. I redoubled my efforts but was knocked backward by a wave, then beaten by more waves, and I realized I wasn't on a lake but in the ocean. My mouth filled with salt. I retched but couldn't get the taste out of my mouth. The waves grew higher and denser. They towered over me, and I could hear the surf pounding and seagulls crying. No matter how hard I swam toward her, I kept slipping away. Then she began to sink.

I awoke with a start and bolted upright, my chest heaving, before recognizing the dream for what it was—my recurrent nightmare, one I've had a thousand times, not always in water but with a familiar theme and predictable outcome. In all these nightmares, I've never saved the drowning victim, pulled the falling person to safety, or found a way to prevent the harm I saw coming. I sat up in the dark, rubbed my eyes, and thought about Mac and our life together and the awful, sudden sadness of her homecoming, and I felt that if anything defined my life at this moment, it was a numbing sense of shame.

When I got home, I'd hung my jacket on a hook inside the front door. I got up and retrieved the photograph Fetch gave me. I lay back and stared at it, seeing the girl's face in the pale yellow glow of streetlights through the kitchen windows. She had an angelic face. Erin Hightower. I wondered if she was alive, if this child who'd been taken from her family had survived her ordeal.

"When you were taken," I whispered to the photograph, "you hadn't lost all your baby teeth. You still had the wonder of childhood ahead. What happened to you? If you're alive, where are you?" I stared until her image grew hazy and was eclipsed by darkness, but the lines and shadows of her face were etched in my mind, that broad countenance,

3

Mac had already left when I woke in the morning. The sun shone through the kitchen windows, assaulting my eyes until they became accustomed to the light. I found her note on the kitchen counter: *Sorry about last night. You worry me sometimes. We'll kiss and make up this evening. Love, Mac.* I rubbed the sleep out of my eyes and got coffee while I walked in circles, shaking my knee. I'd taken one sip when I saw the clock on the microwave. Nearly nine-thirty. I quickly pulled on jeans, a black t-shirt, and a gray corduroy sport coat and ran my fingers through my hair. Then I grabbed my saxophone and hurried down to my car.

When I was a kid, my father invested on behalf of my siblings and me, which enabled me to build a recording studio off Columbus Avenue near Washington Square. I was due there at ten. We recorded Storm Lake's two albums at the studio and were working on our third. I stuck my head in the control room and said hi to the crew before catching an elevator with K.C. Vaughn to the fourth floor, where we had two rehearsal studios. K.C. is a mountain of a man with a head like granite, big thick lips, and a round jaw covered with black stubble. He wears thick-framed black glasses that he constantly pushes back up his nose. His mahogany skin looks coarse but is soft, like a well-worn catcher's mitt. K.C. is one hell of a keyboard player and plays the organ at a Baptist Church on Sundays, but he has a substance abuse problem, his demon of choice being alcohol. This morning, though, he seemed firmly in command of his own ship.

Our band uses Studio A. We lease Studio B to other groups. When we got off the elevator, we saw Stuart Elgin, a mangy high-teens mutt, slumped on the floor outside

Studio B. Elgin, the drummer for Panic Attack, wears a permanent scowl and was staring across the hallway into what might have been another dimension.

"You good, bro?" I asked him.

"Fuck yeah," he said, as though that should have been obvious.

"Been there," K.C. muttered, and we went into Studio A. I said hey to the guys, and we shot the shit before jamming on two songs we were writing. Three hours later, we felt good about these two numbers, and I left for KPIX-TVs offices to meet Fetch and watch the video about missing kids. His hair was as boyishly neat as usual, and he wore a red plaid shirt and chinos. I told him he looked like an ad for Abercrombie & Fitch.

After giving me the finger, he said, "I need to warn you. Marcella asked who wanted to see it. I told her you're a friend interested in the Erin Hightower case."

"Fine. Let's see what you've got."

The story was a retrospective of California's most famous missing children cases. One girl had been found alive after years of captivity. Raped repeatedly by her captor, she'd given birth to two children. Others had been murdered, their bodies dumped or buried shortly after being kidnapped. The final case was the Hightower girl, who was abducted from a mall by a man in a security guard uniform. Grainy video from a camera outside the mall showed the guy lowering a small girl into the right rear door of a dark sedan. He ducked in after her and pulled the door shut. Investigators said he was the kidnapper, but the video didn't show him clearly enough for an accurate description. Then on screen was Erin's photo—the same image Fetch had shown me—and the narrator, Marcella Delgado, spoke of the toll the kidnapping had taken on the family. Her parents had divorced, and Erin's father had been arrested twice for DUI and had lost his driver's license and his job. Her mother lived alone in a gated community in Rancho Cordova.

Then there was a brief interview with the detective responsible for Erin's case. The text identified her as Det. Katrina Hastings. She was standing outside a police station, the wind whipping long strands of blonde hair across her face as she spoke. Hastings said what you'd expect—they'd never stop searching for the girl, the family shouldn't give up hope, and anyone with information should contact the Sacramento PD. After seven years, the case was cold, but they remained hopeful for new leads. The usual. When the story ended, I sat back, locked my fingers behind my head, and rocked back and forth while I gazed at Fetch. The chair squeaked every time I rocked forward.

"I'm not going to ask if you're sure that's the girl you saw."

"It's her."

"So what are you going to do about it?"

He held his hands out in front of him, palms up and fingers splayed as though trying to catch something. "I don't know. I had to talk to someone about it. I think about our two girls, if one of them went missing, how horrible that would be. Seeing that girl and learning that she'd been kidnapped made it personal. But I don't know what else to do."

"It's not much to go on," I told him and he nodded. "You didn't get a license plate number?" He chewed on his lower lip and shook his head.

The door opened and Marcella stepped into the room, flashing her patented on-screen smile, the corners of her mouth drawn up into rouged cheeks, perfectly white teeth framed between smooth pink lips. She extended a fashionably manicured hand. Marcella was working on becoming a celebrity reporter.

"David tells me you're interested in the Hightower kidnapping."

"I missed the story when it was first aired."

"You heard how good it was and had to see it?"

I nodded. "I've always been fascinated by your stories."

"That's a load of crap," she said, still smiling. "But thanks anyway. Do you know anything about the case I should know?"

"No more than is on the tape."

"Are you family? Family friend?"

I shook my head. She studied me momentarily, then gave me her best ingratiating smile. "David told me you're a performer."

"Saxophonist with the Storm Lake Blues Band."

"I love blues. Where does your band play?"

I gave her one of our business cards and told her she could find our performance schedule on our website.

"*Gracias.*" She fingered the card.

"*De nada,*" I replied.

"Meanwhile, if you learn anything, you'll come to me first, right?"

"You're doing a follow-up?"

"If there's more to the story."

"You'll be the first to know," I assured her.

"First and only?" she said, charming me with her cutest look, one arm akimbo, head tilted as she smiled. She handed me her business card as she left.

"She flirts with everyone," Fetch told me.

"I didn't take it personally. That woman's all business."

I told Fetch I'd be in touch. I walked back to my car, thinking about the video. At least two people were involved in the kidnapping. The guard put Erin into the backseat and climbed in beside her. Someone else drove away. I wondered if Erin was a random victim or if she was targeted.

I booted up my computer and googled Erin Hightower when I got home. There were thousands of hits, and I read a dozen articles and posts that seemed most promising. They quickly became repetitious. The best source was an article on *The Sacramento Bee's* website. I recalled what a major news story it had been, reported not only in the local paper but on CNN, other national news programs, and media around the country. Sharon Hightower had taken her five-year-old daughter to a mall in Sacramento late on a Saturday morning seven years ago. They'd gone into Macy's. Sharon was paying for a blouse when Erin wandered away. Surveillance video showed the child wandering through clothing racks and going out of sight behind one. A security guard stood nearby, cap covering his face. Investigators later said that he was of average height and weight, and the uniform was identical to uniforms worn by the mall's security force, although the mall did not employ the kidnapper.

While Sharon Hightower talked to the sales clerk, the guard walked behind the racks of clothing where Erin had disappeared, bent down, and stood up, carrying the girl in his arms. She wasn't struggling, and no one around them appeared to notice anything amiss. After he left Macy's, another video camera caught him turning toward the mall exit with the girl in his arms. He walked briskly but not fast enough to draw attention. In this shot, though, Erin's face was visible. Her eyes were closed, and she appeared to have something like a lollipop in her mouth. The getaway car was a green 2006 Chevy Malibu with California plates. Back in the mall, Sharon Hightower discovered that Erin was missing, and an alarm went out to mall security and the Sacramento police.

The Malibu was later found burning behind a warehouse near the airport and Interstate 5. By the time firefighters extinguished the fire, the vehicle had been reduced to a blackened skeleton. Police later matched plates on the burned car to plates in the mall surveillance video and confirmed that it was used in the abduction. The plates were registered to a pharmacist from Sacramento who had flown to Italy on vacation, but the vehicle's VIN revealed that the car belonged to Helen A. Babcock, a sixty-two-year-old widowed sales manager for a sporting goods store in Rosemont. The Sacramento PD traced her to her son's home in Mesa, Arizona, where she was visiting her new grandson.

Three days before the abduction, she'd parked her car in long-term parking at Sacramento International, and it had been stolen the morning of the kidnapping. The plates had been lifted from the pharmacist's Malibu parked in the same lot, but the lot's surveillance cameras showed nothing unusual.

The police and the FBI had waited for a ransom demand, but neither the parents nor the police ever heard from the kidnappers. In the months of investigative work that followed, Erin's extended family was scrutinized, hundreds of people interviewed, known sex offenders questioned, and surveillance videos enhanced and analyzed. Still, no suspects emerged and the case went cold as leads evaporated. On that Saturday morning seven years ago, five-year-old Erin Hightower simply vanished.

I shut down my computer, filled a glass with ice water, and went to my music room, a spare bedroom I'd soundproofed two years ago. I set the ice water on a table, pulled up my stool, soaked a reed, and put it on a gold metal Jody Jazz mouthpiece, which produces a bright, soft sound. I hung the sax on my neck strap and turned off the lights. In the darkness, I played up and down the blues scale in different keys, random musings as I thought about the missing girl. The flatted fifth on a blues scale produces a melancholy sound, the most dissonant interval in music. During the Renaissance, this interval became known as *Diabolus in Musica*, the Devil's Music. To the clergy and musicians of the time, it sounded ugly and unnatural, inappropriate in music meant to praise God. Bebop musicians in the 1940s and 50s adopted it as a way to distance themselves from traditional music. These days, you hear the interval in the alternating pitches of police and emergency vehicle sirens. Because the sound is so dissonant, it grabs people's attention. It's perfect for the blues, where it captures the despair of addiction, the anguish of dreams deferred, and the wickedness of someone you love doing you wrong. I played the blues that afternoon to open a window into the soul of men who would snatch a child from her mother and fathom what I could of the evil that must course through their dark hearts.

Half an hour later, I called Paul Fisher, my contact in the San Francisco Police Department. Paul is the lieutenant in charge of homicide. I met him three years ago after a man was murdered outside the KittyCat Club in North Beach. We were playing that evening, and the murderer was a guy I recognized from the club scene. The description I gave led to the man's arrest. After questioning me, Paul said he loved blues and had seen us performing at The Blue Room, so I gave him a *Storm Warning* CD. Two months later, I met him again when a hooker was beaten badly in the KittyCat's ladies' room.

A john had followed her in and was banging her head against a toilet bowl when he was caught by Derryann Tice, one of KittyCat's owners. Tice drew a Cobra derringer out of her ample bra and shot the john in the jaw, blowing out three of his teeth. No one was killed, but Paul caught the case when first responders discovered that the bleeding man was wanted for the murder of a tourist on Fisherman's Wharf. After he went off duty that evening, Paul returned to the KittyCat Club and caught our last set. Afterward, he and I drank shots of Balvenie until he left around three to check on the victim at San Francisco General.

Fisher is a lanky scarecrow of a man with thinning blonde hair, penetrating blue eyes, and a nose that could lead a parade. He always wears a black suit, a black shirt, and a narrow black tie. It makes dressing easier if you're color blind, he once told me. It's easy to spot Paul in a crowd, not only for his somber clothing but because he stands with his head bent forward, prominent nose aimed at the ground like a bloodhound locked on a scent.

I told him Fetch's story about seeing the kidnapped girl and added what I'd learned from Channel 5's video and my internet research. I asked if there was anything new on the case, and he said to give him thirty minutes. When he phoned back, he said, "Channel Five's news story generated a lot of leads, but none panned out. Whenever a case gets publicity like that, you get hundreds of calls from people who've seen the kid in a grocery store, like your friend, or say they know where she's being held, usually in their neighbor's attic, or had a vision and know where the body's buried. We waste time chasing crap like that, but we have to run it all down. Now and then, you get a lead that breaks a stalled case."

"What are the odds that the girl Fetch saw is Erin Hightower?"

"Not good. Let me tell you something. More than eight hundred thousand children are reported missing every year."

"Jesus. I had no idea."

"Well, the overwhelming majority are teenage runaways. Throwaways. Kids nobody wants. The kids know it, and some figure that whatever they're going to can't be worse than what they're leaving. Now, abducted kids. Most of them are taken by a family member. You know, the father who didn't get custody, the mom coming out of rehab who swears she's now straight, that sort of thing. Most are returned to the rightful parent within a week."

"A family member didn't take this girl."

"That's right. So across the country, about fifty thousand kids are reported taken every year by a non-family member, usually a babysitter or family friend, someone who knows the kid, but most of those incidents are benign. They were taking the kid out for ice cream or something and neglected to tell the parents. There are only about a hundred and thirty cases a year of stereotypical child abductions throughout the country."

"What are those?"

"That's where the child is taken by a stranger and is sexually abused or held for ransom. Or taken by somebody who intends to keep the child."

"How many of them are recovered alive?"

"Less than half. Around forty percent are dead within three hours."

"So, what do you think happened to this little girl? Erin."

"I'd say it's likely she was taken by someone who'd had contact with her, someone who knew her or had seen her, a repairman who'd come to the home, someone who saw the family at church, a teacher at her school. Someone local. Most kidnappers live within fifty miles of their victim. She was probably taken for sexual exploitation, and she's probably dead. Going by the numbers, that's the most likely outcome."

"But the guy who abducted her in Macy's wasn't acting alone," I reminded him. "There were two of them."

"I forgot that," Paul said. "Since there was no ransom demand, she was either taken by freaks who wanted to add a girl to their twisted idea of family or, more likely, by cooperating pedophiles."

"By what?"

"Child molesters working together. They may have passed the girl around before killing her, and she may have wound up on porn sites. When these pervs can't find a child prostitute, they sometimes snatch a kid and photograph or videotape the abuse. They sell it to child porn sites or pass it around the child porn underground."

My throat was dry, and I felt the sour taste of bile rising. "If the girl Fetch saw was Erin Hightower—"

"It probably wasn't."

"If it was—"

"Then whoever took her seven years ago probably abused her and disposed of the body. If she's still alive, and that's a big if, maybe they sold her to some crackpot who thinks he's God and wants young wives. That's rare but it happens. Or sold her to other pedophiles. These guys have specialized tastes. They prefer girls or boys of a particular age or type. If this girl was taken by a gang that likes five-year-old girls and kept her alive, when she grew out of their age range, they would kill her or sell her to other pervs who like them older. That's how it works. And they hook the kids on crack or smack. It's how they control them."

"Christ," I said.

"It can be a shitty world," Paul said. "The worst shit is what some parents do to their children. You don't believe it; come do my job."

"No, thanks," I told him. "I'm a musician."

He laughed. "I guess someone has to do that."

We were both silent for a moment, then he said, "Anything else?"

"Is anyone still looking for her?"

"It's an open case with the FBI and Sacramento PD, but I doubt the feds are actively working it. They don't have the manpower to investigate every missing person cold case. California alone has more than twenty-five thousand open missing person cases. The only person who might still be looking for her is the detective in Sacramento. Hastings. The one who caught the case."

I told Paul I'd seen her interviewed on Channel 5's news story and asked if he had her phone number. He looked it up. I thanked him and hung up. I glanced at the clock and saw that it was after four. I made a copy of the girl's photo and slipped it into my pocket. Then I grabbed my gym bag and drove to the Pacific Aikido Center on Stockton. It was a bright spring day with high clouds trailing across the sky. The air was damp from recent rain and had the sweet aroma of hyacinth and warm sourdough bread.

Our dojo is in a renovated brick building on a busy street. The interior is ultra-modern Japanese, with walls of yellow bamboo and red brick. A thick mat covers most of the floor. Along one wall is an imposing shrine to Morihei Ueshiba, the founder of Aikido. I practice here because Sensei Hisashi Miyamoto is the finest Aikido master in the Bay Area. I changed into my *karategi* and *hakama,* then greeted Sensei by bowing, hands in the Namaste position. After he returned the bow, I searched for Bai Tuo Rong. Bai is a high school junior, a wiry kid with thick black hair that towers over his head like the bearskin hats worn by Buckingham Palace guards. I spotted him across the room. Bai is a computer whiz, highly regarded, I'm told, in teen tech circles, and has already been accepted by Cal Tech. I showed him the photo of the missing girl. "She was five when this picture was taken. Is there a way to age this photo so I can see what she'd look like when she's twelve?"

"No problem," he said. "You want her thin, fat, chubby cheeks?"

"How about a range? Thin face, average, and overweight. And one showing what she'd look like if she's aged prematurely from crack."

His eyebrows lifted. "This kid's doing drugs?"

"Don't know. She was kidnapped seven years ago. Maybe she's been drugged. Maybe not."

"Sure, no problem. Tomorrow maybe. Or Wednesday. Thursday. Won't take long. I'll call you."

I thanked him, found a quiet place, and began stretching, bending at the waist and feeling the muscles relax in my lower back. My left knee ached, and I massaged it as I tensed and relaxed muscles in my thighs and calves. Aikido is a mental and physical discipline, and I focused on my breathing and the energy I imagined flowing through my body but found my mind drifting back to the missing girl. So I stood up straight with my eyes closed and slowed my breathing while I waited for Sensei to call us to the mat. I saw nothing at first. Felt nothing but peace. Then her face materialized, floating in the darkness, shimmering as though her image were painted on fabric wafting in a breeze. I thought, *if you're out there, I will find you.*

4

Four years ago, during the Monterey Jazz Festival, on a warm night filled with the aroma of sea salt and jasmine and the sweet pungent scent of marijuana, clouds of smoke floating over the crowd, I played with my eyes half closed, watching people's heads swaying to the music, some clapping, others undulating to the groove, and I noticed a striking woman in the audience. She had long, wispy red hair over a high forehead, a regal nose, and thick red lips, lips that begged to be kissed. Her companion was a tall, slender man whose narrow face, patrician nose, and small mouth gave the impression of a hawk poised on a branch contemplating its prey. His eyebrows arched over dark, knowing eyes, and he stood with his head angled slightly to one side, nodding rhythmically to each beat of the music. He wore a hint of a smile and whispered now and then into the redhead's ear. She responded by pursing those large red lips as though whatever he'd said electrified her soul.

She was Catherine Gauthier. A painter and Parisian now living in San Francisco with her partner, the hawkish man. He was Ari Kirakosian, owner of BiblioTech, one of the City's largest book stores, a quirky assortment of new and rare books, manuscripts, maps, recordings, and technology antiques in Lucite displays, including an Apple I, a TRS-80, and an Altair 8800. For geeks, BiblioTech is manna from heaven. It has free wifi and computers throughout the retail space where patrons can search the store's vast collection or download books. BiblioTech has five floors; the third is a huge social space with oak tables and chairs, a coffee bar, a wine bar, and scores of easy chairs where people can read or talk, which they do endlessly. It has the kind of hip ambiance San Franciscans love. On the fourth floor, at the back of Ari's historic brick building, is a secure area where he stores his most valuable collections. Behind that is a cozy room few people ever see, a room lined with bookshelves, tattered floor lamps, and dust balls that have been there long enough to have names. The room smells of aged parchment and leather, musty fabric, and stale cigarette smoke, and it has four overstuffed chairs that might be as old as the building itself.

As Ari and I became friends, he invited me to join him there for discussions with two of his other friends, John Sebastiani and Julien Kito. John is a former Navy Seal who became a Jesuit priest and was a first responder at the World Trade Centers during 911. Later disenchanted with the priesthood, he's now a security consultant. Julien is a retired professor of philosophy at Cal Berkeley. In his honor, we began calling ourselves the Philosophers Club, not without irony. We meet weekly to talk about everything from history and world affairs to the nature of the universe and the existence of God. Wine and spirits flow freely, and although we don't solve the world's problems or answer philosophy's most intriguing questions, we have a fine time bullshitting away the hours. Tuesday nights with these guys are sacred for me.

I didn't arrive at BiblioTech until six-thirty. Ari was the only one there. He sat in his chair, a comfy, gray old mare with a tattered Stanford University blanket across the back where the fabric was threadbare. He was in his classic pose—one leg crossed over the other, elbows perched on his thighs, a glass of red wine in one hand, a lit cigarette in the other. Smoke trailed over his head, regularly blown to chaos by a black circulating fan on the end table beside him, whirring quietly as it swept back and forth. His dark hair lay in a spiky tangle, which made him look boyish though he'd just turned fifty. When I came in, he crinkled his eyes at me.

"I was listening to Miles Davis today," he said as I sat opposite his chair. "Kind of Blue."

"The definitive jazz album. John Coltrane played the tenor sax, and Cannonball Adderley the alto. Jimmy Cobb was on drums."

He nodded and took a drag on his cigarette. "So what's new?"

I told him about the incident at Cactus Jack's and Mac's reaction. He grinned and said, "You're playing jazz, Sonny, but she's listening to classical. Have a glass of wine."

I did. "We made up last night," I told him as I returned to my chair. "One of those nights you remember for a long time."

"Congratulations," he said flatly as the door opened, and John Sebastiani ambled in. "How's that song going to end?" Ari continued.

"What song?" said John.

Ari almost imperceptibly shook his head, his eyes narrowing, and John caught the hint. He grabbed the wine bottle and a glass and plopped down in his chair, splashing the wine into his glass and gulping it.

"It's difficult to savor a fine wine when you chug it," Ari observed.

"True," John replied. Some wine ran down one corner of his mouth, and he wiped it with his hand. "But nearly every experience that isn't morally objectionable has some merit." He smiled broadly at Ari and refilled his glass. "And there's nothing immoral about swallowing good wine." John has dark hair that covers the tops of his ears and a short but unruly beard. He wore black leather pants and a white shirt under a trim dark blue sport coat made of some material that doesn't wrinkle. This evening he looked rakish and unkempt in a way I can imagine women being attracted to, but John is a chameleon. Some days he looks like he belongs on Saville Row; others, on skid row. It may be an act, but I don't think so. John makes up life as he goes along.

"Sonny's in need of absolution," Ari told him, raising his eyebrows.

John peered at me. "Weel! If it's forgiveness yer efter, y'ev come tae the wrong man," he said, feigning a Scottish accent. "Ah've gein up the absolution business."

"Aren't we better for it?" I quipped. He smirked and raised his glass in a toast. "I'm not looking for forgiveness from this group, but something happened Sunday night I want to tell you about."

Then the door opened, and in came the gaunt, silver-haired figure of Julien Kito. Julien bowed slightly and walked to his chair. He wore blue jeans and sandals, a black crew-neck sweater, and a gray cashmere muffler looped once around his neck. His long silver hair was parted in the middle and fell over his ears, and he wore black glasses whose lenses were perfect circles. When Ari offered him a glass of wine, Julien declined with a slight wave. He sat cross-legged, hands resting on his knees. Julien was born in Tokyo to Christian parents but became a Buddhist later in life. Though he's no longer a strict adherent, he has an air of tranquility and peacefulness that masks a penetrating intellect. He's recovering from throat cancer and speaks now, when he speaks at all, with a huskiness that seems ill-suited to a professor of philosophy. He sounds more like a seaman who's inhaled too much salt air, smoked too many cigars, and downed too many whiskies.

In deference to Julien's health, Ari stubbed out his cigarette in an ashtray on the end table and said to him, "Sonny's about to tell us a story." Julien turned expectantly toward me, and I relayed what Fetch told me at Cactus Jack's. I added what I'd learned from

Channel 5, internet research, and my phone call with Paul Fisher. Afterward, I took out the photo of Erin Hightower and passed it around.

As John studied the photograph, he said, "Green River was a waypoint."

Ari nodded. "Without a doubt. How was the girl behaving in the store?"

"Fetch didn't say. Just that she seemed curious when he spoke her name."

Ari took a sip of wine and gazed at the books on the shelves behind me. "She wasn't frightened," he observed. "She didn't scream or try to escape. She didn't appear to be captive. In short, there were no signs of distress."

"No," I said, "but after seven years of captivity or abuse, accepting her circumstances might have been normal. Maybe she was more afraid of making a scene than not making one. Or maybe she was drugged and chemically or emotionally dependent."

"If it was her," Julien rasped. "It most probably wasn't."

"That's bothering me, too," John said. "Why do you think your friend is right about seeing the kidnapped girl?"

I took a long sip of wine while I thought about John's question. "Did you ever play that card game called Concentration where you shuffle a deck and lay the cards face down? You turn over two cards. If they match, you take that pair from the table and get another turn. If not, you turn them face down, and it's the next guy's turn. The key to winning is remembering every card turned over and where it lay on the table. Whoever has the most cards at the end wins." They all indicated that they were familiar with the game. "No one could ever beat Fetch at that game," I continued. "Once a card was turned over, he always knew where it was. Fetch has the best visual memory of anyone I've ever known. If he says the girl he saw was Erin Hightower, I trust him enough to check it out."

John wrinkled his brow. "The girl he saw was a teenager. Or close to it. The girl in the photo is a child."

"He said her eyes were the same."

"That's a long shot," John argued. "It's different with adults. Their appearance doesn't change dramatically in seven years unless they've been seriously sick or hooked on meth. I agree with your friend's wife. A teenager looks a lot different from the child she once was."

"Granted," I replied, "so I gave a copy of that photo to a computer geek I know. He's going to age her face electronically. It won't be a positive ID, but if Fetch says that's the girl he saw, I'll believe it was Erin Hightower."

Julien sat in meditation, then said in his raspy voice, "Follow the probabilities. When you don't know what's true, ask what is probably true. Then try to eliminate the alternatives."

"It probably wasn't the kidnapped girl, Julien, but I can't let go."

Ari re-crossed his legs. "You're going to look for her, aren't you?"

I nodded.

"So let's play devil's advocate and assume your friend did see the kidnapped girl. Why did they take her? From what you've told us, this kidnapping did not appear random. The kidnapper wasn't a security guard but wore the uniform, so he planned the kidnapping. He followed the girl and her mother into a store and waited for the girl to wander away. Why her?"

"Key question," said John. "What's so special about her?"

"As far as I know, nothing," I said.

"Were her parents wealthy?"

"Apparently not."

"Why take a five-year-old," John continued, "especially from a high-risk place like a mall, with guards, security cameras, and witnesses, and not demand a ransom? What did they want with her?"

"That's the pivotal question, isn't it?" Ari said. "If you can answer that, you'll solve the mystery."

"Then ask what is most probable," Julien reminded us.

"Sex," John said. "Disgusting, yeah. Reprehensible. But I think your cop friend is right. If they didn't want money, they probably took her for sex."

"And they were probably local," I added. "I don't know how she wound up in Wyoming a month ago, assuming it was her. But she was probably abducted by two people living in or close to Sacramento."

Julien nodded. "Begin at the point of origin." He turned to Ari. "I'll have a small glass of brandy, please." Ari rose and left the room. Julien had been Ari's philosophy professor at Berkeley, and he's the only man I've ever seen Ari defer to. He returned a moment later with a small crystal of golden brown liqueur. Julien took it with a faint nod and continued: "The incident in Wyoming was a snapshot, but it's impossible to know where the people in Green River came from or where they went. So focus on the point of origin. Focus on the kidnapping and the most probable reason for it." That effort exhausted him. He sank back with a sigh and let his nose hover over the glass before putting his lips to it.

"If the girl Fetch saw was Erin Hightower, and they took her for sex, there's a high probability that she wound up on child porn," I concluded. "Paul said that's a likely scenario."

"Start with that assumption, then," Ari said. "If you're determined to pursue this, begin there and try to confirm it."

"Why are you so interested in this case?" John said.

He handed me Erin's photo, and I studied it again. "I'm intrigued by Fetch's conviction that this is the girl he saw. If he's right, John, no one is looking for her if she's still alive. The police have exhausted all avenues. They've moved on to other cases. Meanwhile, this girl was torn from her family and subjected to God knows what. Her ordeal continues if she's still alive, but no one is looking for her. Whatever happened to her is not right. That's why. It wasn't her choice, wherever she is and whoever she's with. That's why. Because someone has to care. Someone has to keep looking."

"Isn't that what Mac was upset about?" Ari said. "Someone has to keep looking, but it doesn't have to be you."

"It does, Ari. If not me, who?"

"I told you he needs redemption," Ari said to John. "He's atoning for what happened to his sister."

"Goddammit, Ari. This has nothing to do with Aileen."

Ari held his hands out, his palms facing me. "I'm not judging you, partner. But you need to understand why you're doing what you're doing. If you don't, you're liable to be blindsided."

I let the steam flow out of my cheeks. "No problem," I told Ari. "You're right. We're copacetic."

"Okay," John said, rubbing his hands together. "Game's on. How can we help?"

"One thing. I'd like you to talk to Fetch. See what more you can learn from him."

John nodded, a cocky grin growing on his bearded face.

5

Ari had coffee brought up after Julien and John left. A dark roast Columbian blend, it smelled like brown sugar and toasted nuts. Ari added a pinch of nutmeg to his and stirred it with a small silver spoon.

I said, "If pictures of this girl were posted on child porn sites, people who look at that crap might recognize her."

Ari sat in the chair beside me and set his cup on the table between us. He lit another cigarette, which dangled from long fingers. Resting his chin in the palm of his hand, he drummed his fingers on his lips. Dark locks of hair fell over his forehead. In profile, his nose looked as straight and sharp as a knife.

"You won't find them in the yellow pages," he mused. "Pedophiles are the scum of humanity. You can't even turn over the usual rocks and find them. But I know some people who might know some people. How badly do you want to talk to one of them?"

"I don't. I won't look at those sites myself. But if her picture appeared on a child porn site in this area, I don't know a better way to confirm it except to talk to a guy who trolls those sites."

"Even if pictures of her have been posted, the guy you talk to might not admit that he's seen them."

I shrugged. "Maybe not, but you miss every shot you don't take. If she's there, I'll track down the photographer."

"That'll be hard to do."

I nodded. "One step at a time."

"Okay. I'll see what I can set up. But understand; what these guys do makes them paranoid as hell. They won't meet with you unless there's something in it for them, something compelling enough to overcome their suspicion."

"Like what?"

"Like a kid. A connection. Videos. Something that feeds their disease. Something you're selling that they want to buy. The guy you meet may not come alone. He'll be nervous. He'll worry about entrapment." He sipped his coffee and flicked his ashes into an ashtray. "If he's working with anyone else, they'll come together. Don't go armed or carry anything that would alarm them. They'll check. They'll be looking for weapons or a wire."

"Got it."

"Be careful. These are vipers at the bottom of the pit. Sometimes they strike, and their bites can be fatal."

"Don't worry about me."

"That's what Achilles said during the Trojan War."

There was a heavy knock at the door. Ari opened it and stepped into the hallway. He left the door open, and the ceiling light down the hallway cast his dark shadow on an olive-green wall. I could also see Sana Houssian, BiblioTech's night manager, in the dim light. Like Ari, Sana is Armenian, and they're cousins. Both had distant relatives killed during the Armenian genocide in 1915 and are part of the Armenian community whose ancestors fled to California. Sana has a face like coarse sandpaper with deep lines etched around his eyes and across his forehead. He has a short, wiry black beard flecked with grey and thick black eyebrows over a long, broad, menacing nose. I've known Sana for years, but he rarely acknowledges me. His blank face hides whatever's happening behind those deep, dark eyes, making me glad I'm Ari's friend because Sana's blood ties with Ari are stronger than the steel cables holding up the Golden Gate Bridge. If I were in trouble and Ari asked him to help me, Sana would risk his life doing so.

But if Sana looks menacing, the next man in the hallway is flat-out scary. It was the shorter figure of Earl Zepeda, technically an employee of the bookstore but, in reality, the muscle behind Ari's broader business interests. Ari is a bookseller and a dealer in technology antiques, but he's also an importer/exporter, although what he buys and sells is largely a mystery. In his younger years, he was a programmer for Microsoft, then a consultant to technology start-ups. He wrote an uncannily accurate stock-picking program that enabled him to turn his modest earnings into a fortune and buy BiblioTech. But Ari primarily deals in connections. He knows a lot of people, some in the underworld, others on the fringes of legality, and he makes introductions and arranges trades but is known for his discretion, which makes him trustworthy to his connections but suspicious to the police and prosecutors, who think he's doing something shady but can't prove it.

Four years ago, a shipment for Ari arrived at the port in Oakland. He hired a shipping company to transport it to his warehouse next to BiblioTech. The shippers sent three men and a woman. They unloaded their truck but hadn't moved all the crates inside when quitting time came, and the three men left with the truck. Only the young woman remained, and she worked until nearly ten o'clock finishing the work her colleagues should have done. Ari was so impressed with her work ethic he hired her. Her name was Earlene Zepeda, and she was one of the hardest-working people Ari had ever met. She'd grown up on the mean streets of East San Jose and been a street gang member. Before she was sixteen, she'd been involved in drug and arms trafficking, extortion, auto theft, arson, burglary, robbery, and witness intimidation. She was a beautiful girl, and as she got older, her fellow gang bangers just wanted to fuck her, but being the gang bitch wasn't a role she was willing to play. So she fled to Oakland and moved in with an aunt and uncle.

A year after he hired her, Ari noticed that Earlene never wore feminine clothing, used makeup, or did anything to make herself conventionally attractive. She became increasingly sullen, a permanent frown etched on her face, and worked harder than anyone around her, as though needing to prove that she was worthy of the place where she found herself and the man who employed her. One evening when they were alone in the warehouse, they talked, and he learned what he'd long suspected—that Earlene was unhappy as a woman, didn't feel like a woman, and didn't want to spend her life as a woman. So Ari arranged for counseling and later her sex reassignment surgery. He paid for it and stayed with her throughout it. The Earl Zepeda that emerged was fiercely devoted to Ari. I don't doubt that Earl thinks of Ari as his real father.

The sullenness is now gone, but the figure I saw in the hallway still wears a challenge in the steely lines around his eyes and the tightness of his mouth, bearing himself along on a wave of testosterone like a jockey racing a horse. All the bravado and macho posturing tough young men grow up with emerged in a few short years in Earl Zepeda. He is fast, strong, good with a knife, fearless in conflict, and relentless in pursuing his mission. Ironically, of all the men I've known, he is the one I would least want to face in a fight. I would square off with him if my life depended on it, but otherwise, I would steer clear of the masculine madness that permeates every cell in his body. To say that he overcompensated when he became a man would be like saying that a nuclear blast is loud.

When they finished talking, Earl passed by the door and saw me. He stuck his head in and said, "*Quiúbole, compa!*" *What's up, partner?*

"*Nada, mi amigo.*"

He stuck his fist out in front of him, and we fist-bumped in the air.

"*Hasta luego,*" he said and walked away.

When I left BiblioTech that evening, the full moon shone like a spotlight, but the stars beneath it were disappearing behind a bank of dark clouds that soon eclipsed the moon and turned the city darker. The radio said there were storm warnings, and I could see white caps in San Francisco Bay even in the darkness. The barometric pressure was dropping, said the DJ. We're in for a spell of bad weather. Mac was working in her study when I got home. I kissed her, and she asked how my evening was. I didn't tell her all we'd talked about at Ari's place. I reasoned that some fights are not worth having, and I didn't know what would come of my quest to find Erin Hightower. If it died on the vine, I didn't want to upset her for nothing. But I felt ragged and dishonest and told her I was going to bed. On the way, I swallowed two Oxys to take the edge off, and I lay down, closed my eyes, and tried to sleep, but sleep wouldn't come. I kept thinking about what Ari said, that I'm acting like I need redemption.

When I was twelve, we lived in the Oak Knoll neighborhood in Pasadena. My father was an investor and my mother, a mathematics professor at Cal Tech. They'd done well, and we lived in an affluent neighborhood. My older brother, Angus, was away at UCLA. Aileen, my older sister, was a senior in high school, and Teagan, the youngest, was in second grade. On October 12, Teagan was at a sleepover with friends. Aileen and I were home with our parents, all sitting in the living room, when the doorbell rang. My father answered it and was knocked backward by a blow to his head. He stumbled and fell in the foyer with blood gushing from a wound on his forehead. Before we could react, three men burst into the house with guns and yelled for us to be quiet. Two of them—Jerrold Waite and Roy Buckhalder—carried my father into the living room and dumped him onto the sofa. The third man, Donald Reese, strode up to Aileen, forced her to her feet, and then ripped her blouse open. Aileen screamed, tried to cover herself, and fell backward into the wall, tears streaming down her face. Reese laughed and pinned her to the wall, pawing at her black bra. He squeezed the cups like he was crushing ripe peaches, then pulled the bra over her breasts and began rubbing them.

"She's got great tits, guys," he snickered. I ran at Reese, yelling for him to leave her alone. All I remembered later was the jarring impact of his fist and then falling toward our hardwood floor. When I woke up, I was lying in my blood. My face was hot where he'd hit me, and I could feel that side of my face swelling. The inside of my mouth was cut, and as I struggled onto my elbows, I spit out shards of teeth. My mother and father were on the sofa, their arms and legs wrapped with duct tape and tape covering their mouths. My father was slumped forward in defeat, blood dripping down his face. My mother looked at me with wild, fierce Irish eyes, imploring me to stay down. Aileen and Reese were gone. Then I heard her screaming upstairs and heard Reese slapping her repeatedly. Waite and Buckhalder were ransacking the house. They had duffel bags and were filling them with whatever looked valuable. I was determined to run upstairs and help Aileen, but the two thieves were in my path.

Minutes later, they walked away from the staircase, and when their backs were to me, I crept to my feet and eased toward the stairs, ignoring my squirming mother. They hadn't seen me when I reached the stairs, so I ran up. I turned the corner at the top and ran into Aileen's room, but she wasn't there. She cried out down the hall, and I ran to my room. She lay there on her back, naked on my bed, arms and legs tied to the posts with cut strips of a sheet. There was blood between her legs and down her thighs, and she looked at me with revulsion and horror, her face a mask of anguish. I could smell the coppery scent of blood and the stench of piss. Hearing a noise down the hall in my parent's room, I grabbed my baseball bat and ran toward their room. Reese came out as I reached the door and grabbed the bat before I could swing it. He tossed it away with a sneer on his face, grabbed my neck with a giant hand, and squeezed like a vise.

"You stupid little fuck," he snarled. He lifted me by the neck and drove me backward toward the railing at the top of the stairs. After slamming me into the railing, he picked me up by my crotch and set my butt on it. I could barely breathe, and my face felt like the skin was sluffing off. He glared at me wild-eyed, the smell of decay in his mouth and the stench of piss from his loins. Then he pushed, and I tumbled backward, tumbling head over heels, and slammed into the marble floor below, breaking both legs. He laughed and sauntered down the stairs while I lay there in agony. His laugh was eerily high-pitched, like a hyena. Every niggling screech assaulted my ears.

When he reached the bottom, I heard him say to Waite and Buckhalder, "Your turn with the little bitch. Ride her hard. She likes it rough."

But Buckhalder said, "Fuck, man, this is taking too long. We gotta split."

"Fuckin' pussies," Reese snarled.

After carrying the duffels to their car, they drove away. The police arrested them four days later when Waite tried to sell some of the stolen goods to a fence who was cooperating with the police so they would drop other charges against him. When my mother gave me the news, I was in traction, and I vowed never to be that helpless again. When I recovered, I told my parents I wanted to learn martial arts. I began with Aikido. Two years after earning my first-degree black belt, I started studying Krav Maga.

After that night, my relationship with my older sister changed. She felt guilty for what happened to me and needed years of therapy to overcome what happened to her, but I think she could never forget my seeing her naked and bloodied on my bed nor forgive our parents for not stopping it. I've carried the shame of that night since, and I feel like I owe Aileen a debt I can never repay. She says she doesn't hold me responsible, and the shrink I saw said no one could expect a twelve-year-old boy to defend his family against three armed men, but the rage in my heart said otherwise. Whether or not Aileen forgave me, I couldn't forgive myself.

Waite and Buckhalder got ten years for their part in our home invasion. They've been out of prison for that offense for over a decade, but both are back in San Quentin for crimes they've committed since. Donald Reese was sentenced to twenty years to life for raping my sister. He's been denied parole twice, but he's coming up for it again next year, and this time the prosecutor thinks he'll be released.

That's good.

I'll be waiting for him.

6

Thunder reverberating over the city woke me up on Wednesday. Deep rumbles waltzed across gray skies punctuated by flashes of lightning reflected on our bedroom walls. Steady rain thumped on the windows, which were open a crack, and brought the smell of clammy soil, flowers, and mist rising from wet roads. Somewhere a car alarm was going off, and I could hear the muted groaning of a truck engine. Mac stirred beside me and laid one arm across my chest. Her hair lay in a brown tangle. I turned on my side and buried my nose in her hair, which smelled like freshly cut peaches. I kissed her forehead, lips lingering on her skin. She pulled me closer, and my hand went to her waist. I kneaded her flesh, then lifted her t-shirt and caressed the soft mound of her breast. She responded by opening her eyes and lifting her face to mine. Then she took me in her hand and brought us together. As the storm outside continued, we made sweet love, nestled deep in the covers, our warmth and wetness trapped too soon in the afterglow of sex.

Breakfast was two cups of Kona coffee, which I drank black, and cold vanilla yogurt with fresh strawberries. Mac added a teaspoon of cream to her coffee. She showered first and rushed off to work. I put my sax together and practiced improvising in D minor for an hour. Then I showered, put on blue jeans and a Storm Lake t-shirt, and left for the studio. On the way, Ari called me.

"I set up the meet for you. A guy will call. I had to give them your cell number, but it was the only way. Don't know when it will happen, but be careful. He thinks you're a supplier."

"A what?"

"He thinks you sell children to pedophiles. As I suspected, my contact said the guy wouldn't talk to you unless you brought something to the table, something he wants."

"Christ."

"S'okay. Play it cool. Tell him you're making connections. You're entering the market in the Bay Area, and all you want now is to meet potential buyers. Show him the photo of the missing girl and ask if he'd be interested in a kid like that. Then ask if he's seen her before."

"Yeah, on a porn site. Got it."

"You need to come on like a player."

"Don't have the stomach for that, but I hear you."

"It's just an act, partner. You'll risk your life if this guy doesn't think you're legit."

"Got it. Thanks."

"Thank me if this works out. It's nasty business, Sonny. These people make cockroaches look good."

The band spent five hours in the studio jamming on songs in our set list for our gig that evening. Afterward, I left for the gym to practice with my Krav Maga club. Krav Maga is like the English language of martial arts—it borrows techniques from boxing, karate, Aikido, wrestling, judo, Wing Chun, and other martial arts, the way English incorporates words from other languages. The point of Krav Maga is to use realistic techniques to defend yourself and neutralize threats as quickly and efficiently as possible. At the club, I don't practice anything but Krav Maga techniques, but when I defend myself, as I did at Jack's the other night, I combine Krav Maga with the more graceful and spiritual practice of Aikido. I'm a practical guy. In a fight, I use whatever works. We were forty-five minutes into our practice, and I was sweating heavily when my cell phone rang. I had set it on my towel off the edge of the practice mat. As I walked to it, I wiped my hands on my sweatshirt. My clothes were damp, and the sour odor of sweat rose from my armpits. The call was from Paul Fisher, my friend at the SFPD. He said he needed a favor.

"What's up, Paul?"

"Annie's been arrested." Annie Porlier was a hooker Paul had taken on as a project. He'd put her mother behind bars when Porlier was fifteen, and he'd been looking after the kid since then. She was now twenty and in the fast lane for an early demise.

"What for?"

"Aggravated assault. She broke a guy's nose with a wooden coat hanger."

"Ouch," I chuckled. "Where was she?"

"In some fleabag in the Tenderloin."

"In other words, she beat up a john."

"That's what it looks like. Christ."

"I'm guessing he wouldn't pay her. So what do you need from me?"

"In my position, I can't get involved. You know that. I'd like you to bail her out. Can you do that for me?"

"Might be a good idea to leave her there, man. Make her sit this out and think about what she's doing with her life."

"I know, but I can't do that."

"She's a junkie, Paul, and a whore, and she's never going to straighten herself out if you keep rescuing her. But you won't take my advice on that, will you?"

"I already know what you're going to say."

"Because you've heard it a dozen times. Why bother? Fine. I won't waste my time repeating it. Where is she?"

"County jail."

"All right. What's the bail?"

"Two grand."

"I'll cover it and—"

"I'll pay you back, but she won't skip. You know that."

"I know my ass from my elbow, which is more than I can say about you when it comes to this kid, but I don't know if I'd trust her not to walk on this one. Aggravated assault. The prosecutor might decide to make an example of her. This is a dumb move, Paul. This kid's going to knock you on your ass."

"You said you weren't going to lecture me."

"Sorry. Couldn't resist.

"S'awright. I appreciate the help. Call me when she's out?"

"Yeah. I'll do that. And I'll drive her back to her place."

I took a quick shower, changed into my street clothes, and arrived at the Hall of Justice about twenty minutes later. She was being held in San Francisco County Jail number one, the intake jail, where the newly arrested are locked up. The reception area inside the door was crowded with uniformed cops and civilians like me, and the place smelled like stale farts and disinfectant. I wrote a check to cover her bail and then waited for Annie to emerge from lockup. They brought her out twenty minutes later. She didn't immediately recognize me, although she's seen me half a dozen times in clubs we were playing. When

I reminded her who I was, she said, "Oh yeah, I know you. You're Paul's friend. You play in a band, right?"

"Yeah."

"Cute guy with a goatee."

"That's my trademark," I said wryly.

Annie Porlier was a tall woman, probably five-ten. She had short brown hair tinted red, with long tufts that covered her ears like a cap with flaps. Her doughy skin had brown splotches like burned patches on grass, and she had a crooked nose with a small pearl in the crease of one nostril. A tattoo on her right shoulder read, "Life's a bitch." Whatever Paul saw in her escaped me, but I was seeing her through the lens of her addiction, not as a reclamation project.

"Yeah, well, thanks for bailing me out," she said.

"Thank your friend. He sent me."

"You don't like me much, huh?"

"It's not a question of liking you. You're a hooker and junkie, and you won't go straight, no matter what you tell Paul."

"I'm trying."

"Sorry, but that's bullshit. Stay in a program and get out of the life."

"Drug court keeps putting me in programs. They don't work for me."

"More bullshit. You don't want them to work. You'll keep hooking and snorting smack because it's easier than taking responsibility for yourself and cleaning up your act. And what really pisses me off is that you're using Paul as a sugar daddy."

She looked away, her lower lip trembling. I almost felt like a dick, but this wounded bird routine was part of her act. Junkies live for their next fix, and Annie Porlier was not going straight until she didn't have Paul to bail her out. Probably not even then. I've seen too many people like her spiral downward until there's nothing left but a carcass.

"You have a choice, Annie. You can turn your life around if you want to. Your life. Your choice," I said. I took her arm and headed toward the door. "Let me drive you home."

She shoved my hand away but followed when I pushed open the door and held it for her. It seemed unusually bright outside, the clouds having blown away. The harsh afternoon sun stung my eyes. I reached into my breast pocket and put on my sunglasses. They were the retro aviator kind with reflective lenses. All I needed was a white silk scarf and a pilot's license. My car was parked across the street. We were a few feet from it when I heard a scraggly voice behind us.

"Hey, bitch!"

Annie and I turned at the same moment, and she murmured, "Oh shit."

The guy approaching us wore blue jeans, a black hooded sweatshirt, and black motorcycle boots with steel rings on the sides. He had cruel eyes and a nose with a flattened ridge that had been broken at least once. His dark hair was shaved close to his head, and he had a wiry mustache and an anemic beard at the point of his chin. His mouth was crooked, one side raised while the other side drooped, an expression that might once have passed for a smile but now looked idiotic.

"Who is he?" I asked Annie.

"Derrick Sidwell," she whispered. "Thinks he's my pimp."

I looked hard at her and said, "What gave him that idea?" She averted her eyes as he sidled up to us, pointedly staring at her and ignoring me.

"Where you think you goin', girlfriend?" he said with the kind of lilt meant to sound friendly but came across as contempt.

"I—"

"What do you want?" I interrupted.

He turned slowly to me, his face a show of wonderment. "Tha fuck you care, man? This is my bitch." He reached for her arm, but I nudged her behind me.

"She's not going anywhere with you."

"Oh, now, see?" he said slowly, like he was talking to someone retarded. "That's tha kinda shit gonna get you fucked up, muthafucka."

He started to poke a finger at me, but I slapped it away and said, "How fucking stupid are you? You're going to pull some shit here in front of the county jail with, like, a hundred cops around? Do you even register on the IQ scale?"

That confused him. "What, man, fuck, no. What's this shit you layin' on me? All's I'm sayin' is you in some serious hurt you start fuckin' 'round with another man's bitch, know what I'm sayin'?" He tried to move around me and grab Annie, but I moved with him and held my hands out to push him away. He stopped with a snort, his eyes growing tighter. Then he tilted his head and stuck his face closer to mine. He smelled like stale tobacco and mold. "I'm gonna fuck you up, man."

I grabbed the front of his sweatshirt and jerked it up under his chin, twisting it against his windpipe. He was rattled, his eyes growing wide, his mouth gaping open, but he didn't resist. "This is how it is, dickhead. She doesn't belong to you anymore. You got that? You come near her again, and you won't believe the shit storm you're in." I released him and shoved him backward hard.

He stumbled before regaining his footing. Then he rubbed his neck and glanced around uncertainly before puffing himself up and trying to be hardcore. He strutted in place for a moment and then inched backward, throwing his arms out in front of him and flashing two middle fingers at me. "You come for me, muthafucka, I be ready for you. Count on it."

"It won't be me, dickhead. You'll be face down in a pool of blood before you know what happened. You won't see it coming, and you'll never know who did it. Now stay the fuck away from her. Am I clear on this, cuz? You need me to spell it out?"

He stood there numbly, unsure of his next move. I turned, took Annie's hand, and walked her to my car. Sidwell watched us and then swaggered off, mumbling to himself. But vermin like that never go away. They crawl into a sewer until it's safe to return.

"That guy's an asshole," Annie said as I opened the car door for her. "You better watch out for him."

I closed the door after she climbed in and then sat on the driver's side. I put my keys in the ignition and started the car, but before I put it in gear, I looked her in the eye and said, "Annie, he won't be a problem for me. He's a danger to you. He's a coward and a bully, and his pride's been wounded. You're his meal ticket, and I just threatened his livelihood. But he won't come for me. The guy's stupid, but he's not *that* stupid. If he doesn't back off, he'll come for you. He thinks you're weak, and your coke habit makes you vulnerable. So watch yourself and tell me if he threatens you. Okay? Because I can do something about it."

She nodded and then looked out the window at Sidwell as I drove away, wondering, I imagine, how her life got so screwed up. Paul told me she's from Phoenix. Her mom moved here for a job, and Annie attended school but dropped out before graduation. Then she fell in with a guy who promised her roses but made her eat thorns. She was now twenty going on fifty and had maybe five years to live if she didn't straighten herself out.

I dropped Annie off at the apartment in the Mission district she shared with two other women. The place had probably seen its best days in the 1940s. It was a turd-brown three-story wood building with paint peeling like sunburned skin and long trails of rust dripping from a scattershot of nail holes. It had a mini-mart on the first floor with a handwritten sign taped to the window welcoming gays and lesbians. A bicycle with no tires was chained to a lamppost in front of the store, and the windows were caked with several generations of grime. A sodden gray mass of old newspapers lay decomposing on the sidewalk.

"Thanks for getting me out of lock-up," Annie said.

I handed her a fifty-dollar bill. "Here. Get yourself something good to eat. Not at this dump," I said, nodding at the mini-mart. "I think there's a decent place a couple of blocks up."

"Yeah, I've been there," she said. "Thanks again." And she got out and walked straight into the mini-mart. *So much for my advice*, I thought. *Nobody's taking it today*.

As I drove off, I called Paul Fisher and told him I'd sprung Annie and had a cock fight with Derrick Sidwell, her pimp.

"You had a what?"

"A cock fight. You know, my cock's bigger than yours. Sidwell thought he was going to take Annie with him."

"I'll have him picked up on some pretext and warn him to leave her alone."

"He just got that advice from me."

"Maybe he needs to hear it again. Sidwell is a bad smell that won't go away."

"Whatever. I dropped her at her apartment building. When I left, she went into that Pakistani mini-mart for a gourmet meal."

"That place. They're due for a visit from the health department."

"Waste of time. Just send the Red Cross. I'll talk to you later."

"I owe you, Sonny."

"Damn right, you owe me. Later, man."

7

We played that night at Emil Washinawatok's Blue Room on Folsom, where it's blues and grooves seven nights a week. It's a crazy scene: two stories of neon lights in vivid primary colors; multiple dance floors, bars, and seating areas; heavy gold light fixtures that seem to float beneath the ceiling; and all bathed in soft blue light. It has room enough for hundreds of dancers, and when the place is rocking, we can barely hear ourselves on stage over the crowd noise below. The acoustics in The Blue Room are good, but a full house creates tidal waves of sound that rattle windows three blocks away. That night we were joined by Gemma Easton, a voluptuous brunette with long wavy hair and a high, lyrical voice. Gemma was a competitive swimmer in college and is still toned like an Olympic goddess. She was wearing a slinky purple evening dress and kissed the mike like she was giving it head, which drove half the audience wild—male and female. In years past, she and I went a few rounds together, but now it was strictly music.

While packing up at the end of the night, I checked my cell phone and found one message waiting. In voicemail, I heard a cigarette-inflected male voice.

"I hear we got a mutual interest," the recording said. "And you got something for sale. If that's true, meet me at one o'clock Saturday morning at the south entrance to Mt. Diablo. Come alone or it won't happen. No cops, no cameras, no wires, no weapons, no funny stuff. I'll check. Get outta your car and wait by the hood. I'll have on a Yankees cap. Name's Floyd."

Mt. Diablo State Park is east from the City across the Bay Bridge, through Oakland and Berkeley, and over the foothills to the western edge of California's verdant central valley, where much of the state's produce is grown. Mt. Diablo, the highest peak in the park, got its name from Spanish soldiers chasing runaway Chupcan Indians. The soldiers thundered after them on horses and had them in sight, but the natives vanished in the mountain's maze of towering sandstone rocks and forests of scraggy oak and brush. When the soldiers couldn't find a trace of their quarry, they called the area *Monte del Diablo*, the Devil's thicket. The setting sun can give the mountain an eerie red radiance, which adds to Mt. Diablo's mystique as a place where the devil dwells.

I arrived just after eleven on Friday night and parked on the shoulder. Crickets chirped in the underbrush, and leaves clacked in the warm breeze rising from the valley. The forest smelled of old wood and moist soil. When my eyes adjusted to the darkness, I walked to the gate and across the road to the trees beyond. Walking in a circle around my car, I paused every few steps to listen but didn't see or hear anything else. Back in my car, I took two Oxys from a vial in the glove compartment and swallowed them with lukewarm water. I wasn't afraid of the guy I was supposed to meet, but Ari's advice clanged around in my head like a broken rod in an engine.

At five minutes to one, I got out and waited by the hood. An owl hooted somewhere in the trees. The night had grown cool. I wore a down jacket and zipped it up as the chill penetrated my bones. Twenty minutes later, I wondered if anyone was coming. Then a vaporous figure emerged from the gloom on the road behind me. A thin man of average height and weight. He wore blue jeans and a sheepskin jacket. As he got closer, I saw long, stringy brown hair, a mustache trailing down the sides of his mouth to his chin, and a small tuft of hair beneath his lower lip. One of his eyelids hung lower than the other, making him look like he'd just slept off a lousy drunk. He appeared to be in his forties and wore a Yankees cap.

"Floyd," I said.

He nodded and shined a penlight in my face. I closed my eyes against the glare.

"You a cop?" he said. I shook my head. He pointed the penlight at a slip of paper in his other hand and read, "Are you now or have you ever been affiliated with any law enforcement agencies? Federal, state, or local?" I shook my head. "Did you bring or are you wearing any audio or visual recording devices?" I shook my head again. "You understand that if you are a member of law enforcement, you have to answer my questions truthfully."

"Got it. I'm not a cop."

He crumpled the paper and shoved it into a pocket. "Hold your arms out to your sides. I have to frisk you." Up close, he had the rank odor of garbage left in the sun for a week, a putrid mix of old coffee grounds, rotting fruit, and decomposing fish. The thought of him with a child was nauseating. He patted me down thoroughly. He'd obviously done it before. Then he told me to unzip my jacket and pull up my shirt. He shined his light on my chest and around my back, looking for wires taped to my skin. Then he felt in my jacket pockets and found the photo of Erin Hightower. He took it out, examined it, and tucked it into the back pocket of his jeans. After checking my other pockets, he removed my wallet and cell phone and shined his light on my driver's license.

As he started to turn away, I said, "I'll keep my things." He thought about it and handed the wallet back to me. "My cell phone?"

He shook his head. "This way." I followed him as he ducked under the gate and started up the dark road.

"Where are we going?"

"Up here a ways. Don't worry about it. But don't try nothin'. You're being watched."

Being watched? Is that bullshit? I wondered. As I listened to our footfalls on the pavement, I tried to recall where this road led. About a half mile ahead, I remembered, was an area of the park called Rock City, popular among rock climbers. I saw giant sandstone cliffs and boulders looming ahead in the dim light. Light from the moon and the cities below made the rocks glow red like they were heating over a fire. Floyd stopped just short of Rock City and told me to wait. He disappeared into a copse of oak trees to our right. I smelled burning wood but couldn't see a fire. When Floyd returned, he waved for me to follow. Thirty yards into the thicket, I made out the flames of a campfire. Closer still, I saw two men standing behind it. White smoke rising from the fire made their images flicker like evil apparitions.

The taller guy had a head like a honeydew melon and must have topped three hundred pounds. The rolls of fat beneath his chin looked like a stack of white bicycle tires. He wore dark slacks and a tan tent-sized parka that projected over his protruding gut. The other man wore blue jeans, black boots, and a black leather jacket. A biker. Closer to six feet, he had a ripped stomach, bulging biceps, and the tight torso of a weightlifter. Deep set in his cruel, unshaven face were black, wary eyes, not the dead eyes of a shark, but the alert eyes of a wolf. He studied me with the cocky assurance of a man who knows how to deliver a fatal blow, and I had no doubt he'd killed before. The fat man was twice his size, but this guy was a stone-cold primitive. It didn't look like his mental development was much beyond reptilian. All energy and impulse. A predator.

"What've you got for us?" the fat man said. Floyd showed him Erin's photo. The fat man fingered it and then looked at me. "This is it? The guy I talked to said you had a stable. Said you could lay your hands on five or six projects."

"Maybe she's like a sample," Floyd suggested.

"Somethin' ain't right," the predator said.

The fat man stuck out a hand to ward him off. "Just a minute. We were told—"

"You were misinformed," I told them. "She's not for sale."

"What the fuck, man?" the predator growled.

"I'm not here to sell children." The three of them glared at me across the fire like I'd just pissed in their soup. I don't know what the truth bought me, but I couldn't pretend I trafficked in children, not and live with myself afterward. "I just want to know if you've seen her before."

"If you're not a cop," the fat man said, "then who are you? You a private dick or what?"

"Yeah, who the fuck are you?" said the predator. "Definitely not SOL." He pointed a finger at Floyd: "You check this asshole?" Without waiting for an answer, he turned his dead eyes on me. "You got five seconds to tell me what the fuck you're doin' here. And if you brought the heat, motherfucker, I'm gonna cook your face in this fire."

Some hardasses are more bluster than balls, but this guy was the real deal. He looked dangerous as hell, but the truth was the only hand I had to play, and I was determined to keep playing it.

"The girl's missing. She was kidnapped seven years ago. I'm nobody. Just a guy trying to find her. She may have wound up on child porn sites. I only want to know if you've seen her on any of those sites. Then I'm gone, and I've never seen you guys. And what the hell is SOL?"

"You gotta be shitting me," the predator said. He shifted, moving his legs apart and tensing his body. It was a classic tell that says an attacker is preparing to strike.

"Sex offender list," said Floyd. "If you were one of us, you'd know that." He put his hands on his hips and shook his head in disgust. "Fuck!"

The fat man studied Erin's photo in the light of the fire. "I haven't seen her before. But she's real sweet meat. I'd fuck her."

Acid flooded my throat, and I wanted to hit the fat son of a bitch hard enough to knock his teeth into Nevada. I felt filthy just being in their presence.

"She didn't mean nothin' to me," Floyd said flatly.

"I'm tellin' ya, this guy brought heat," the predator said, but the fat man raised one hand, and I saw a cell phone in it.

"We would've heard," he said.

"Don't matter no how." The predator reached behind his back and came out with a dull black automatic. A Sig Sauer or a Glock.

"Hold on," the fat man said. "I need to think about this. Gimme a minute." He reached into a side pocket of his parka and handed a white plastic tie to Floyd, who came around behind me and tied my hands behind my back. I wouldn't have let him, but I wasn't faster than the Glock, and the predator was aching for an excuse to use it. Then Floyd kicked me behind my left knee, and I crumpled to the ground, my face barely two feet from the fire. Sharp pain sliced through my knee like a lance, but the Oxys made it feel like the pain was happening to someone else. The heat of the fire began to sear my face. I wanted to roll away from it, but I didn't know what the next play would be and had to keep my eyes on the gun.

"Time to waste this fucker," the predator hissed, moving around the fire and pointing the gun at my face.

"Bob," came a frightened yelp. They turned toward the voice. I twisted my head around and saw another man shuffling crab-like toward the group. He was shorter than the others and had a soft, round face and wire-rim glasses. He wore a gray down coat and stumbled forward, gut protruding and head angled backward. I tried to make sense of his posture when I made out an arm around the guy's throat and the body of another man behind him, forcing him ahead. The soft guy struggled to breathe. Then I saw the dark shape of a knife in his captor's hand. The business edge of the knife was pressed against folds in the soft guy's neck. It looked like a Marine KA-BAR combat knife with a seven-inch gray steel blade and a brown leather handle. It's a wicked knife, and I know only one civilian who carries a KA-BAR.

"Oye, *compa*," Earl called out. *Hey, partner.*

"What the fuck, Chuck?" the predator yelled.

"I couldn't help it," the soft guy cried. "He came up behind me. I didn't hear a thing."

"You a lame piece of shit."

"Back off, *puta*," Earl said to the predator. "I cut off his head."

The predator walked back to the fat man. "What'd I tell ya? Fucker ain't alone."

"All right," said the fat man. He held his chubby hands out in front of him like he was trying to stop traffic. "Slow down. There's a way outta this. You put away the gun. Okay? Then he puts down the knife. All of us walk away. No harm. No foul."

"Fuck that. I'm gonna waste this asshole," he said, waving the Glock at me. "If the burrito kills Charley, I'll make him wish his fucking mother never crossed the river."

"Jesus Christ! Don't do that," the soft guy moaned.

"Fuck you," the predator spat, walking back toward me and lowering the Glock. The shot came sooner than I expected and stung my forehead and cheeks, knocking my head backward. I was stunned but felt nothing except pricks of pain on my face. Then I realized I hadn't been shot. The bullet had hit the toe of the predator's boot, ricocheted off the ground, and spit rocks and dirt at my face. The predator had stopped in surprise and was gaping at the toe of his leading boot and the hole punched in the dirt directly in front of it. His face was frozen, a bewildered look in his eyes. He slowly turned his head and stared into the trees.

"The next one's in your ear," warned a voice from the darkness. "Don't move a muscle. Don't even breathe." I swallowed hard and then smiled as I recognized John Sebastiani's voice. "Drop the weapon," John said. "Ease it out of your hand." The predator didn't budge for a long moment. Then he opened his hand and let the Glock fall to the ground with a thump.

"Walk back to your buddies," John continued. "I don't wanna see anything else."

As the predator backed away, Earl shoved the soft man hard, and he tumbled into the fire stomach first, flailing his arms and screeching even before he hit the flames. The fire exploded when he landed on it, and I rolled quickly away as smoke and burning embers burst toward me. The man called Charley bounced up and scrambled away, rolling on the ground at the fat man's feet, flipping onto his back, swatting at the flames on his coat, and patting them out with a flurry of slap, slap, slaps. Afterward, Charley lay on the ground groaning, smoke rising from black splotches on his coat. The fire recovered, its yellow flames flickering even higher, its red embers glowing.

John emerged from the darkness. He wore camouflaged clothing and a black watch cap, and his face was blackened with grease paint. He carried an AR-15 assault rifle with a folded tripod and scope and pointed it at the predator.

"That was unnecessary," he told Earl.

Earl shrugged. "Sorry, *padre*. I push too hard." A fine sheen of sweat coated Earl's face, reflecting the dancing flames of the fire. The men across from it regarded him as they would a rabid animal. They'd gotten Earl's message that he was volatile. As John came around and covered them with the AR-15, Earl bent down, pulled back my hands, and slashed the plastic tie. Then he helped me to my feet. While I was rubbing my wrists, he picked up the Glock and handed it to me. I tucked it between my jeans and the small of my back and then had a head rush as feelings flooded through me—relief that John and Earl were there, grateful to still be alive, sick that I'd misjudged the threat, disappointed that they hadn't recognized the girl, or said they hadn't, and confused over what that implied. I was still certain she'd been kidnapped for sex, but I had no proof and was no closer to solving this puzzle than I had been hours ago. Shit and Shinola.

"What we do with them, *compa*?"

I wanted to flush them down a toilet, but that would return them to the sewer they crawled out of. I wanted to throw them into a pit and fill it with acid, but you can't obliterate the dark recesses of humanity by destroying a few evil men. I wasn't sure what to do with them, but I saw how something could come of this even if they hadn't recognized the kidnapped girl.

"I'm going to search them, *hombre*. You can motivate them to cooperate." I motioned Floyd to come to me, which he did hesitantly. Earl moved behind him, just out of Floyd's field of vision. With one hand, he scooped back Floyd's hair and then held the point of his knife under the man's right ear so a quick flick of his wrist would slice off the ear. I didn't think Earl would do it, but Floyd didn't know that. His lips quivered, and he mumbled something I couldn't make out.

"My cell phone," I said. He quickly reached into a shirt pocket and handed it to me. I turned it on and pushed the button for the camera. "Hold still." I raised the phone and took a picture of Floyd's ashen face. "Now give me everything in your pockets." He fished through them and gave me a set of keys, his penlight, a pack of smokes, a book of matches, and a wadded piece of paper with the questions he'd read to me at the gate. I tossed the paper and cigarettes into the fire and put the rest of his things in my pocket. Then I led Floyd away from the others and told him to sit down in the dirt.

The fat man was next. He also had car keys, along with a cell phone, my photo of Erin Hightower, and a dozen long plastic ties. I told him to stand still and raised my cell phone to snap his picture, but he was camera shy and needed some prodding from Earl before he would look straight at me. His face was devoid of the cunning I'd seen earlier. He now looked like a man who'd wagered everything he owned on a bet he couldn't win, and his heart sank as he waited for the debt collector. The predator was a defiant son of a bitch and didn't move as I took his picture. His face was a mask of hate. He glared at me like he was trying to memorize every detail of my face. He didn't change expression even when Earl patted him down and removed a folding knife from his back pocket. When I told him to follow me and sit beside the fat man, he obeyed but never took his eyes off me. I doubt he allowed a single thought to cross his mind except getting even for what we were doing.

When I got to him, the soft guy, Charley, had taken a flashlight and cell phone out of his pockets. Earl patted him down but found nothing else. Charley begged me not to photograph him, but a quick jab from Earl convinced him to shut up. As I took his picture, his lips and chin trembled, and his eyes blinked rapidly. I told him to follow me, but he didn't move. He'd gone somewhere inside and was wrestling with demons more ruthless than me, so I took hold of his arm and pulled him. When I did, his bladder released, and he whimpered. I could smell piss as it flowed down his pants leg. I led him to a small oak tree near the fire and told him to sit down on his butt, facing away from the tree. I motioned for Earl to bring the predator. I ordered him to sit the same way ninety degrees left of Charley, and tied his right hand to Charley's left using one of the plastic ties. Earl brought the others, and I tied them similarly, so the four men sat in a circle facing away from the tree, hands tied together. I pulled the ties tight.

"I'm gonna kill you for this," the predator assured me.

"You're about to have bigger problems than me." I stood up and crossed to John and Earl. "Let's go," I said, but Earl wasn't finished. He knelt in front of the predator, regarding him silently, then took out the predator's folding knife and clicked it open.

"Don't kill him, *hombre*," John warned. "That's not what *jefe* would want." *Jefe* was the code name we used for Ari.

Earl nodded at John and turned back to the predator. He held the folding knife under the man's chin and laid his KA-BAR knife on a vertical line down the man's face from the end of his left eyebrow directly down to his jaw. "*Pinche pervertido de mierda,*" Earl said with contempt. Then he jerked the KA-BAR down and sliced the predator's face open. The cut wasn't deep enough to be life-threatening, but his cheek lay open and would need stitching. Blood spurted from the wound and spilled down his neck. He howled in rage and jerked against the ties, eyes wide, tendons in his neck tense and thick. If he'd had the power to summon Satan, the intensity of his fury would have done it. He bucked against the ties, terrifying the guys on either side, who looked around in horror at the blood pouring from the predator's face. His body convulsed, flinging his blood in every direction.

John stood beside me with a disbelieving shake of his head and began to move toward Earl, but I put out a hand to restrain him. "For God's sake," he whispered to me.

"Leave it alone," I told him. "This is something he has to do."

After a minute, the predator's howling subsided. He sat silently, though his chest was heaving. Blood still poured from his wound. He glared ominously at Earl, and I thought Earl was now higher on this guy's shit list than I was. Earl pointed his bloody knife at the predator's eyes and said, "*Te condeno al infierno.*" Then he repeated the ritual with the next man in the circle, the wide-eyed, quivering fat man, cutting him deeply down the side of his face.

As that was happening, John asked me what Earl had said.

"He called him a fucking pervert. *Pinche pervertido de mierda.* After he cut him, he said, *Te condeno al infierno. I condemn you to hell.* Earl is settling accounts."

8

John and I walked down the long, dark road, our footfalls softly echoing on the pavement like distant drums. Earl Zepeda trailed as our rear guard. He paused now and then to peer into the gloom behind us. When we reached my car, I took two Oxys for my throbbing knee and drove down the South Gate Road. John had parked his car outside of Danville. As we left the park, Earl spotted a glint in the darkness off the road—the dim shape of two vehicles parked between trees. We investigated and found a blue Subaru Outback and a red Ford F-150. One of the sets of keys I took from the pedophiles had a key fob. I pushed the unlock button, and the headlights on the Subaru flashed. I tossed the other keys to Earl, and he opened the pickup.

"Take anything that will identify them," I said. The Subaru had temporary dealer tags, which I removed. I found the registration inside the glove box and a California driver's license issued to Robert T. Rayburn above the driver's visor. Behind it was a Wells Fargo VISA card issued to Rayburn. The photo on the license showed the fat man. Below was a Danville address. Beneath the driver's seat, I found a small manila envelope with something hard and small inside. I put everything in my pocket. The pickup yielded a registration slip and a wallet with Floyd Pruett's license. John found an empty shopping bag in the back seat of the Subaru. We dumped everything we'd found in it, and I tossed the bag into my back seat. We waited for Earl while he sliced the tires on both vehicles. Then I drove to John's car. We fist-bumped before they left, and Earl smiled at me, which was a first.

I arrived home just after four am. I locked the shopping bag and the Glock in a heavy safe I used as an end table in my music room. It came with the condo, the previous owner deciding not to move it. I didn't blame him. The thing must have weighed five hundred pounds.

Mac was asleep, so I took off my shoes and tiptoed into the bathroom. I took a shower and massaged my knee for ten minutes. Then I curled into bed beside her and savored her sweet perfume before I drifted to sleep. When I awoke around nine the following day, she was gone. Thankfully. I didn't want to explain about last night, and I didn't want to lie. I grabbed some coffee and a cinnamon roll and called Ari.

"Earl told me what happened," he said.

"Funny how John and Earl showed up just as I'm about to eat a bullet."

"One of life's amazing coincidences," Ari said.

"How'd you know where I'd be?"

"I didn't," he chuckled. "I knew where the pedophiles would be. One of my Armenian crew shadowed Pruett when he left his apartment. You guys left quite a mess up there. A fair amount of blood, I hear."

"Blame that on your surrogate son."

Ari laughed. "He told me. Earl's an independent thinker."

"Made me wonder if he was abused as a girl."

"That's something we don't talk about, Sonny. Having you think of him as a victim would wound his pride."

"That's okay. You answered my question."

"What question?"

"I can't remember. Back to last night. Were they gone by morning?"

"Um-hmm. My sources say the park rangers are puzzled."

"Best leave them in the dark."

"John says you didn't learn anything more about the girl."

"No. They claim they never saw her."

Ari paused. Then he said, "I could have Sana's crew pick up one of them. Earl would convince him to cooperate."

I thought about it. "Not now. I don't think they'd seen her before."

"Okay. Where do you go from here?"

"Sacramento. I need to talk to the detective investigating the girl's kidnapping. Katrina Hastings. Floyd Pruett has a Sacramento address. I don't know what's happening but still think there's a connection."

"Keep me in the loop."

"Absolutely. Thanks again for the air cover."

"Ciao."

Next, I called Paul Fisher, but he wasn't in. I left a message. Meanwhile, I opened my safe and dumped the contents of the shopping bag onto my kitchen table. I left the Glock in the safe.

Pruett's wallet revealed two recent pay stubs showing he worked for Sacramento's Department of Sanitation. A garbage man. Figures. He had some cash but no credit cards or insurance card. Nothing else but a grocery store coupon and a receipt from an adult bookstore in Sacramento. I googled his name and found him on the registered sex offender list for Sacramento, one of nearly eighteen hundred sex offenders living there. Unbelievable. *Eighteen hundred?* Pruett was forty-two, stood five-eleven, and weighed one seventy. He'd done a dime in North Carolina for indecent exposure, more time for possession of a controlled substance (meth), and child pornography. All in all, he'd spent half his life behind bars.

According to Rayburn's license, he was fifty-eight. He stood six-five and weighed two ninety. He wasn't registered as a sex offender and had no arrest record. But a google search revealed that he owned Rayburn Motors in Danville and an apartment building in Union City. The manila envelope contained two thumb drives. I put one in my laptop and opened it. The directory listed hundreds of files, but the file names were long random sequences of letters and numbers, and when I tried to open them, I was prompted for an encryption key. Same with the other drive. I was printing the photos I took of the four assholes when Paul Fisher returned my call. I asked for the conversation to be off the record. He said fine, as long as I hadn't committed a felony, and I told him what happened.

"That explains what I heard this morning," he said. "Two men showed up at a free clinic in Oakland with identical cuts down their faces. They claimed they'd been in an accident, but Oakland PD didn't buy it. They wondered if anything similar had happened in San Francisco."

"Who were the two guys?"

"Smith and Jones, and they paid cash. Sorry. No real names."

"No problem. But only two went to the clinic. The other two went someplace else. They would have needed treatment."

"If they did, I haven't heard about it. Meanwhile, you better watch your ass."

"I'm looking at it right now."

"All right, fuck you, wise guy. Talk to you later."

Before I called Sacramento PD, I looked up Bai Tuo Rong's phone number and dialed him. He answered after seven or eight rings.

"It's Sonny."

"Hi, dude," he said groggily.

"I wake you?"

"Well, shit, yeah, it's like, oh fuck, man, it's not even noon."

"Sorry about that."

"Don't you, like, sleep in Saturday mornings or what?"

"Sorry. I forgot you're still in high school."

"Well, yeah, dude, I'm, like, a kid. I need my sleep."

"All right, I won't call anymore until the afternoon."

"Righteous."

"I'm wondering about the photos you were going to age for me."

"Oh, sure, they're done, but I, like, you know, school and shit."

"Can I come pick them up?"

"Okay, no problem. I'll shove them in our mailbox."

"Later," I said, but he was already gone. Then I retrieved the number Paul had given me for Katrina Hastings and dialed. When she answered, I told her I had information on the Erin Hightower kidnapping and wanted to come talk to her. She didn't sound enthusiastic.

"I have a friend in SFPD," I told her, "who said you had hundreds of calls after Channel 5 ran that story on missing children two months ago."

"Five hundred sixteen," she droned. "Now five hundred seventeen. Why don't you tell me what you've got?"

"I need to see you in person. I have other information for you."

"What's that?"

"I'll explain when I see you, but I had a run-in last night with four members of a ring of pedophiles. I can positively identify two of them. I have photos of all four, and one lives in Sacramento."

"Okay," she said. "You've got my attention, but I'm off tomorrow. Make it Monday. What's your name?" I told her, and she said, "Monday. My office. Eleven o'clock."

"I'll be there."

9

Bai Tuo Rong's family lived off Clement in the Inner Richmond district, an area of homes, ethnic markets, laundries, hair salons, flower shops, banks, used bookstores, and Asian restaurants. I parked in front of a Vietnamese restaurant and walked two blocks to Bai's house. It was a neat, gray, two-story building with white trim and bay windows on the upper level—similar to every house on the block except for color.

I found a white envelope in their mailbox. Bai had penciled "Sonny" on the front. Inside were five photographs, including the original I'd given to Bai. The top photo showed Erin Hightower as she might look as a twelve-year-old. Her eyes had not changed, but her face was longer and her cheeks thinner than in the original photo. Her complexion looked warmer, too.

I called Fetch and learned he would be at work for several more hours. On the way to Channel 5, I drove through the Mission District. Just off Dolores Park, I parked, walked between two buildings, and knocked on the backdoor of a small clinic. A moment later, the door cracked open. One large eye on a black face peered at me. I said, "It's me, Shonnie." She was a woman of impressive stature, with braided black hair piled on her head like a giant pinecone and rainbow-colored earrings dangling like frisbees from her earlobes. She gave me a disapproving look, but that's Shonnie. "Is he here?"

"Where else would he be?" she droned. She waddled down the hallway and knocked on a pea-green door as weathered as an old barn. The thin man who emerged had the complexion of a raw chicken breast. Brown circlets of hair collided on his oversized head, and he wore a white lab coat stained with ink, blood, snot, and God knows what else. When he saw me, he ducked back into his office and returned in a few seconds with a dark brown bottle filled with Oxys. I handed him a thick wad of bills, and he nodded absently before backing into his office and closing the door. Good thing I don't come to him for his social skills.

Back at my car, I buried the vial in the glove compartment and drove to KPIX-TV. Fetch met me in the lobby, and I handed him Bai's envelope. He shuffled through the photos and rejected all but the one showing what the girl would look like if she were average height and weight for a twelve-year-old. He thumped the photo with one finger. "This one is closest. Except the girl I saw was more, I don't know, something, toned, I guess that's the word. Her cheeks and chin were better defined. I'd say she looked more athletic. But this is the girl I saw."

"Positive?"

"I'd bet my life on it."

I told Fetch about the guys I met with on Tuesday evenings at BiblioTech and said John Sebastiani offered to help him remember more of what he saw in Green River. I asked if he could join us Tuesday. He said he thought so.

Afterward, I drove home and spent the rest of the day practicing the songs we'd perform at The Malkin Lounge, that hip jazz club off Columbus in North Beach. That evening, before a small but appreciative audience, we performed mostly well-worn tunes I could have played in my sleep. After last night on Mt. Diablo, it was a mellow way to lose myself in the music. I was reminded all night of the old musicians' joke that jazz is better than sex—and lasts longer.

But my musical euphoria was short-lived. After I dragged myself home and fell asleep, I was rattled into consciousness by an alarm bell hanging next to my ear, clanging so loudly it hurt my teeth. I pawed it away and then swung, suspended by my feet, clasping someone's hand, a woman's hand, my sister Aileen. I held her with my right hand. I also wanted to grab her with my left hand but couldn't find it. Aileen swung above a blanket of clouds, the Earth out of sight far below. She wore a black dress with nothing underneath. I could see her breasts beneath the thin fabric and the red hair between her legs when the wind whipped the dress over her waist. She wept, her tears stinging my eyes. Then her fingernails cut into my wrist. I grimaced as her long nails sank deeper, and she grew heavier, and her nails began to shred my hand. I grasped her wrist tighter, which drove her nails into the bone, and blood flowed down my fingers and up her arm, long streams of red exploding in the wind, enveloping us both in a red mist. Then my hand was torn into long ribbons of muscle and tendon. She slipped away, taking part of my hand with her, and I watched her plunge into the clouds, tumbling and twisting until she disappeared into a grave of swirling white.

I awoke with a start, shivering, my t-shirt soaked, hands clutching the sheet. I pulled the blanket around my neck and closed my eyes. Mac lay quietly beside me. My heart beat so rapidly it felt like it might escape my chest. I calmed myself by listening to Mac's soft breathing, counting her breaths, and feeling the rhythmic rising and falling of her chest. Eventually, warmth returned, and I sank into the darkness and drifted unaware through the deepest part of the night.

Mac and I spent Sunday together, having brunch at a French bistro and strolling through the botanical gardens in Golden Gate Park. The day was sunny and clear, and the park smelled like redwoods and the sweet, spicy aroma of magnolias. We found an empty bench on Stow Lake and gazed across the green water at dragonflies flitting among the lilies and butterflies floating atop the flowers. Mac told me she had a quick business trip to LA. She'd be leaving early the next day and returning Wednesday or Thursday. I was relieved to hear she'd be gone and felt guilty. I didn't want my obsession with Erin Hightower to wreck our relationship, but I was keeping more secrets from Mac, and it felt like a distance between us.

As I sat with my arm around her shoulder, I wanted to give her the comfort she sought and be the man she wanted, but that obsessive part of my mind reiterated the commitment I'd made to myself: *if I can rescue this girl, I will.*

"What are you thinking," Mac asked.

I paused, clearing my mind of clutter. "That I'll be happy to see you when you get back," I told her, which was the truth, if not the whole truth.

That night the band returned to Cactus Jack's. I told Xavier McQueen I had to go to Sacramento on Monday and wouldn't be at rehearsal. He said fine, whatever; they had other things to work on. When I got out of bed Monday morning, Mac had already gone. I made coffee, retrieved the grocery bag with the items we took from the men on Mt. Diablo, and drove to Sacramento. It took two hours on Interstate Eighty.

I arrived an hour before I needed to meet with Katrina Hastings, but I had Floyd Pruett's address and wanted to check it out. I drove into a McDonald's drive-through and got another cup of coffee, which was bitter but gave me the jolt I needed. Then I entered Pruett's address into my car's navigation system and followed the directions to a two-story apartment complex built when Nixon was president and was now as tarnished as his reputation. The siding was crap-colored and water stained and had graffiti scrawled across the walls on the lower level. The grounds were overrun with weeds punctuated by rusted beer cans, styrofoam containers, discarded toys, dead potted plants, and other assorted debris. The centerpiece in this portrait of urban decay was a broken sink with rusted pipes that someone had probably tossed from a second-story balcony.

I parked next to the curb behind a green panel truck with a dented fender and sat watching the building. I don't know what I was looking for. I just wanted to get a feeling for the place and the man who lived here. While I sat there, a dark blue sedan inched past my car and pulled over in front of the panel truck. I hadn't seen the driver, but the guy in the passenger seat wore sunglasses and a black baseball cap. As they passed me, he glanced at me with studied nonchalance. I wondered if they were local cops or feds. Twenty minutes later, I set my navigation system for the address Katrina Hastings gave me and pulled away. The two cops in the blue sedan pretended not to notice as I drove past.

Hastings' office was in a large, three-story complex with gray walls and blue windows. The receptionist was a pudgy woman in her thirties with short brown hair who gave me a twice-over with cold, flat eyes when I said I had an appointment with Detective Hastings at eleven. "Sign in here," she ordered, pointing to the book on the counter. I did, and she pointed to a row of chairs in the lobby. "It's only ten minutes till, so you'll have to wait." Instead of sitting, I read items on their bulletin board. This was Child Safety Seat Awareness Month.

In ten minutes, I heard the clicking of a woman's heels behind me, and a voice said, "I'm Sergeant Hastings."

I turned and shook her hand. "I'm Sonny Marshall."

She was a tall, slender woman with a sculpted face and high cheekbones. Blonde, shoulder-length hair fanned out from her face and wrapped around her neck. Her nose was long and straight, and she had penetrating eyes the color of polished moonstone. Her lips reminded me of Ari's companion, Catherine Gauthier, who always looked like she wanted to be kissed. But Katrina Hastings' voice was all business, and she stared at me like I was the last person she wanted to see on a busy day. She wore black slacks, a red blouse, and a gray blazer with a necklace of black pearls. I could see a bulge on the right side of her waist.

"Have you got identification, Mr. Marshall?"

I showed her my driver's license.

"This says Torran Marshall," she said, her head cocked curiously.

"My real first name," I explained. "My father's Scottish and my mother Irish. They gave me and my brother Angus Scottish names and my sisters, Aileen and Teagan, Irish names. But Angus, who's eight years older than me, didn't like Torran, so he called me Sonny, and the name stuck. We Scots-Irish are great storytellers. I can share a lot more family history if you'd like."

That earned me a little loopy grin, the right side of her face rising higher than the left. "Tempting," she said. "Maybe some other time. Let's go to my office." She led me to a metal detector, and the officer there set the shopping bag on the belt while I walked through the detector. My left leg set off the alarm, and I got a pat down and a full left-leg massage as I explained that screws held my femur and tibia together. When I was cleared, I followed Hastings down a long hallway, and we took an elevator to the third floor. The interior of the building smelled like floor wax and gun oil. It bustled with uniforms and plain clothes cops. I heard telephones ringing and muted conversations as we walked down the corridor. Crime must be thriving in California's state capitol.

The sign on her door read, "Det. Sergeant K. Hastings." It was a small room with an imitation wood desk and matching bookcase. A window was open, and a glass wall divided the office from the corridor. Sunlight spilled in the window and brightly lit the room, and the cool air was refreshing. Her desk was piled with paper, her bookcase overflowing, but in one neat corner of this organized chaos was a framed picture of a dark-haired girl I guessed was her daughter. That led me to glance at her left hand; she was not wearing anything on her ring finger. Divorced with one child. I sat in the lone chair opposite her desk and asked how long she'd been with the Sacramento police.

"Ten years in July. Look, I'm busy. You said you have information on the Hightower case." I told her about Fetch seeing the girl in Green River a month ago and watched her face drop. "If that's all you've got," she said, "there's nothing I can do with it. Even if it was the Hightower girl, there were no other witnesses, and those places generally record over their surveillance videos after two weeks."

I had to admit the story sounded thin, but I stubbornly refused to give up. It's the Scots-Irish in me. I showed her the photos of Erin that Bai had aged, pointing out the one Fetch said was most like the girl he saw.

She scrunched up her mouth and nodded slightly as she studied the picture. "A credible job. Who did it?"

"A high school kid I know. Computer whiz."

"Aren't they all?" she said, smirking, her loopy grin giving her the appearance of a drunken wise-ass. "Can I hang on to this?"

"I made that copy for you."

She studied it again. "She might look like this if she's still alive. But odds are the girl he saw resembled Erin but wasn't her." She set aside the photo and looked at me. "I googled you. You're a musician. Why are you here instead of your friend?"

"He didn't think you'd believe him."

"He's right. But what's your interest in this case? Are you related to the girl's family? Writing a book on the case? What's your angle?"

"No connection, book, or angle. I just want to find her if she can be found."

"You should leave that to the police."

I shrugged. "It's been seven years. No one's looking for her now."

"I am," she protested loudly, tapping her finger on her breastbone. "I'm looking for her and will never stop looking. Don't get self-righteous with me. You don't know a damn thing. I've interviewed hundreds of people and spent months tracking down leads that went nowhere." She held out her hands, her fingers curled upward. "My hands and knees are raw from digging for any clue about what happened to Erin. I don't know why you care about finding her, but I can damn well tell you why I care."

I sat back in the chair to let the storm subside. After a minute, I said, "I read that wrong, and I apologize. My reasons for caring may not be clear to you. I'm not even sure they're clear to me. But I'm involved because a good friend is convinced he saw Erin. If he's right, she needs help. This may be your case, but it's not entirely your cause. Maybe I can help."

"Fair enough," she replied after a long pause, her demeanor cooling to a slow simmer. "But there are ground rules. This is a police investigation. *My* investigation. Don't interfere. If you learn anything, bring it to me."

"I hear you."

"You need to do more than hear me. You need to agree to these conditions."

"Okay."

"You have no authority here." She studied me for a moment, wondering whether I was being forthright with her. "You said on the phone you have information on some pedophiles."

"It's in here," I said, handing her the shopping bag. She emptied it on her desk and examined the cell phones and Pruett's wallet. "I know this asshole. We have him under surveillance. How'd you get his wallet?"

I told her I suspected the girl might have been kidnapped for sex. I know someone who connected me with Pruett and the others and met them on Mt. Diablo. She picked up the photos of the four men and said, "I don't know the other three. Who are they?"

"The only one I can identify is the big man, Robert Rayburn. You have his driver's license and a credit card."

She examined them. Then she opened the manila envelope and took out the thumb drives. "What about these?" she said.

"I took them from Rayburn's car. Underneath the driver's seat. The files on them are encrypted."

"Your high school friend couldn't crack the code?"

"I didn't ask." She put the drive back in the envelope.

"Interesting," she said. "How'd you come by this stuff?"

"Let's just say I asked them for it, and they gave it to me. They thought I was someone who trafficked in kidnapped children."

"That's why they met with you?"

"Yeah."

"How'd they get that idea?"

"Beats me."

She gave me a sidelong glance and lifted one eyebrow but let it go. "Pruett was photographed yesterday by one of our surveillance teams. He has a long white bandage down the left side of his face. Are you responsible for that?"

"Absolutely not."

She drummed her fingers on her desk. "Whatever happened, Pruett's panicking. You may have set something in motion that will force us to act sooner rather than later. Meanwhile, I suggest you return to San Francisco and play in your band. Leave the rest to us."

"Sound advice," I said, not intending to take it.

10

Tuesday was unusually warm for early May. By noon, the temperature passed eighty, and feathery clouds trailed across an otherwise deep blue sky. I'd awakened with a new riff, invented in my subconscious before I knew I was awake. I wrote it down before it slipped into the void. Then I had a hot cup of Starbucks dark blend coffee with a fruit-and-yogurt salad and thought about Mac, missing her warm smile, soft skin, and a dozen other things. I called her but got voicemail, so I left a message. Then I played my sax for hours, some Charlie Parker, some Stan Getz, some Storm Lake, and some musical meanderings untethered from everything except my funky mood. At eleven, I put on jeans, a B.B. King t-shirt, and a gray corduroy sport coat.

Ari and John and I had lunch at the Zuni Café on Market. We sat upstairs at a small table with a white tablecloth and chairs. "Rayburn's on the run," Ari told us. "My source says he married a Mexican and the two produced child porn. And performed in it. The word is they're headed south of the border. You really rattled his cage."

"That's good," I said. "Maybe the *Federales* will tie them behind jeeps and drag them through cactus."

"Don't count on it," Ari said. "It might be hard to cancel that guy's ticket. He's got the cash to grease a lot of palms, and there are enclaves of pedophiles in Mexico, Costa Rica, places like that. He and his whore might have a free pass."

"I don't care about Rayburn," John said. "Guy's got bad karma. One day he will cross the wrong person and get his nuts mixed in a blender. You can't be that evil for that long and get away with it. Sooner or later, the universe will deal him out."

"You think Rayburn was lying about not recognizing the girl?" Ari asked me.

I recalled Rayburn examining the girl's picture. "I don't think so. I wouldn't trust anything he said, but I don't think he was lying about that. He called her real sweet meat. Said he'd like to fuck her. My gut tells me he was seeing her for the first time."

"What did you think of that detective in Sacramento?"

I took a long drink of ice-cold water. "Capable. Definitely committed. She got pissed when I said no one was looking for the girl. But her leads have petered out. She won't find Erin on her own. She has nowhere to go, but she's too stubborn and hung up on procedure to accept help. She basically told me to fuck off and go play music."

"So she has a low flash point," John concluded, "but no clues."

"She came across as an officious twit. But she did tell me that Pruett is spooked. Sacramento PD's about to move on the guy."

"Have they ID'd the other two?" John said.

"Not as far as I know."

"Your friend is going to join us tonight?" Ari said.

I nodded. "David Fetchenheir. I call him Fetch." I asked John what he planned to do.

"Guided visualization. Kind of like hypnosis. I'll get him relaxed and take him back to that day and have him relive it. Maybe he can remember more than he told you."

"If he doesn't, I won't have much else to go on."

That evening, our meeting room seemed darker and mustier than usual. Ari had brought in a brown leather recliner that smelled like saddle soap. Fetch lay in it, eyes closed, arms by his sides. John sat beside him, peering at Fetch's face. His elbows were parked on his legs, hands clasped under his chin. Ari sat on the other side of the room, the familiar look of quiet contemplation on his face. Julien sat beside me.

"All of this is in the present," John told Fetch. "I want you to relive that incident, starting with you driving to Green River. You haven't stopped at the gas station yet. You're in your car on Interstate Eighty across Wyoming. Who's with you?"

"Steph and our girls. Amy and Stacy."

"Where are you coming from?"

"Nebraska. North Platte. Where Steph's family lives."

"What are you wearing?"

"Blue jeans. Yellow polo shirt. Windbreaker."

"What color?"

"Blue."

"What kind of day is it?"

"Sunny. Warm. A few clouds in the sky. I'm wearing sunglasses. It's stuffy in the car."

"Why do you stop in Green River?"

"We needed gas."

"Present tense," John urged quietly.

"We need gas. The girls are arguing in the backseat. I'm tired from driving. Everyone needs a break. I'm thirsty. They are, too."

"So you pull off the road."

"I see a sign for Exxon Mobil. I pull off on the exit. The station has four islands and a big convenience store. I see an opening next to a gas pump on the third island. I pump gas while the girls go to the bathroom. When I'm done, I replace the nozzle, put the gas cap back on, walk toward the store. I see a white van pulling in."

That got my attention. He hadn't mentioned that before.

"Are other vehicles there?"

"Yes. Twelve. Fifteen. Maybe more. It's busy. Some cars are parked off to the side. Three or four pickups."

"With all those vehicles around, why do you notice the white van?"

"They are pulling into the inside island. I have to wait for them as I walk toward the store. I don't know if they see me."

"Describe the van."

"The front is black across the bottom, the whole bottom half. Except for headlights. Above that is a white strip. Across the middle. A huge windshield. Tinted. The driver's side mirror is mounted on the front of the van, not on the driver's door. I've never seen that before. The van passes me. It's all white along the side. There's a sliding door in the middle."

"What shape is the body?"

"A big box, a long rectangle, but not boxy in front like a VW. The front slopes forward, from the top of the windshield to the headlights, making room for the engine."

"Do you see the driver?"

"No. Uh, yes, just a little. He's looking straight ahead. Twenties. Short dark hair. That's all I remember."

"That's all you see at this moment."

"Right."

"So you walk into the store." John led him through deciding what drinks to get and standing in line for the register. "You see a dark-haired woman in line ahead."

"Her back is to me. A girl is beside her. To her right."

"What is the woman wearing?"

"Black coat. Medium length. Goes down below her butt. High collar. Shoulder-length hair. Some tucked under her collar."

"She has dark hair. Black or brown?"

"Brown. Dyed, I think."

"Why do you think that?"

"Because it's too, uh, uniformly brown. Has a red sheen."

"What else do you notice about her?"

"Large nose. Very angular. Sticks out more than normal. She's carrying things in her left arm. A small box. A carton of milk. And a bottle of, maybe, orange juice. It has a red cap."

John led him through calling Erin's name and the girl turning and staring, but there was nothing new about these events. However, when he got to the woman's reaction, we learned something surprising.

"When the woman takes her right hand out of her pocket, something falls. It's white. Small. She doesn't notice. It falls to the floor as she takes the girl's left hand and starts to leave."

"Do you know what it is?" John said.

"Yes," Fetch responded. We all sat up in our seats, even Julien, who glanced at me with raised eyebrows.

"As the woman and girl head for the door, I walk to where they were standing. I see a folded slip of paper on the floor. A guy is almost stepping on it."

"What do you do?"

"I say 'excuse me' and pick it up."

"Then what?"

"I start to unfold it but worry about losing sight of the woman and girl when they leave, so I look for them and notice a man at the magazine rack watching me."

"Do you see what's on the paper?"

"No. I don't have it unfolded before I see the guy. I watch him watching me. I start walking toward the door, and he puts down the magazine, goes over, and stands in front of the door."

"How do you feel when this happens?"

"Uh, puzzled, uneasy. I've never been in this situation before. I'm trying to figure out what he's doing. I'm afraid to confront him."

"So what do you do?"

"I stop. After watching me for a moment, he turns and goes out the door."

"Where does he go?"

"To the white van. The woman and girl are already there. The woman slides back the side door."

"Is this door on the passenger side or the driver's side?"

"Passenger side."

"Where are you?"

"By the door. Watching."

"Okay, what happens next?"

"The girl climbs in, and the woman follows. She slides the door closed. The man at the magazine rack gets in the passenger side front seat."

"So that man's not the driver."

"That's right. The guy has a mustache and goatee. Wide face and dark hair covering his ears. Wearing a white shirt. Striped, I think. Thin stripes. The driver is younger and clean-shaven."

"Then what happens?"

"The van pulls away."

"Can you see the back clearly?"

"Yes."

"What does it look like?"

"All white except the rear window. That window looks black. There's a yellow license plate."

"Can you read the numbers on the plate?"

"No. The van leaves too quickly."

"The license plate is yellow. Bright yellow or dark yellow?"

"Bright yellow."

"Can you read the state?"

"No."

"Are there any noticeable designs or images?"

"Not that I can see."

"Which direction does the van go?"

"Back to the interstate, and I see them turn, uh, to the right, east onto Interstate Eighty."

"The direction you came from."

"Right."

"Okay, what do you do then?"

"I get back in line. I have to go to the back because I lost my place."

"What about the slip of paper? Where is it?"

Fetch fell silent. Then, in a bewildered tone, "I don't know."

"Is it still in your hand?" John said.

"I don't think so. I don't remember what happened to it. I think I was too, uh, shaken, by seeing that guy watching me."

"Could you have put it in your wallet?"

"I don't know."

"Why don't you check now?" Fetch did, but the slip of paper wasn't there.

John questioned him further, but he'd drained the tank dry. I was frustrated that Fetch couldn't recall what happened to the paper but was struck by two other revelations. I thanked Fetch and told Ari I needed to use a computer. He directed me to a second-floor office. What I needed took only twenty minutes. When I returned, Fetch had gone. Ari asked if I had found what I was looking for.

I sat in my chair and had a long sip of wine. "We've been assuming the kidnappers were locals," I said. "What if they weren't? What if they came from someplace else, kidnapped the girl in Sacramento, and took interstates back to where they came from?"

"Interstate Eighty goes through Sacramento," John observed. "And passes by Green River."

"On its way to New York," Julien added. "There are many states along that route. Your kidnappers, if that's who they were, could have gone anywhere."

"The problem is, we don't know where they were coming from," Ari said. "All we know is that they stopped in Green River and headed east when they left."

"And the girl was kidnapped seven years ago," John added. "If they were traveling on Eighty, they might have come from Sacramento, but why? Why risk taking the girl back there? It wasn't for a family reunion."

"I don't think they were in Sacramento," I told them. "They were someplace else on the west coast. I don't know why Erin was with them a month ago, but I don't think these people were locals. Seven years ago, for whatever reason, they targeted Erin Hightower.

Maybe for sex. Maybe something else. Whatever it was, they drove to Sacramento to grab her. They're not local, so they wouldn't run into people who'd recognize them. The Malibu was later found burning. I think they stole it to kidnap the girl, transferred her to another vehicle, burned the Malibu to destroy the evidence, then jumped on Interstate Eighty and escaped. They could have been gone even before the police knew she'd been kidnapped. I think it was a clean, professional job."

Ari nodded thoughtfully. "That's a plausible narrative that matches what we know."

"I think I know why they were on Eighty," I said. "Rural interstates are the safest roads in the country. I looked it up. Lowest accident rate per mile. They'd be unlikely to be pulled over if they drove at or just under the speed limit. And since rural interstates are safer, they'd also be less likely to be in an accident. They did everything they could to avoid being noticed while moving, and I'll bet they only used cash. No credit cards. No motel receipts. No tracks."

"I'm troubled by one thing," Julien said. His fingers were tented below his chin. "Who was the man at the magazine rack? What was his purpose?"

"A guard," I offered.

"But guarding what?" Julien said.

The four of us were quiet for a moment because the answer eluded us. Ari broke the silence: "I doubt he was protecting the woman and the girl from the people around them. They were at a gas station on an interstate in Wyoming A safe place."

I said, "Maybe he was there to prevent the girl from running or crying for help."

"Possible," Julien replied, "but it's been seven years. If she's stayed with these people all that time, she's lived more of her life with them than not. She wasn't distressed. She looked healthy, not wasted from drug use. She wasn't trying to get anyone's attention. I think a more reasonable assumption is that she was content."

Ari said, "Quite right, Julien. The most plausible explanation is that she wasn't in distress. She appeared healthy because she was healthy and comfortable with the people she was with. Whoever they are. Maybe it's that simple."

John shook his head. "Or, despite your wishful thinking, Sonny, the girl Fetch saw wasn't Erin Hightower. Maybe we're spinning a tall tale."

After a moment, Julien said, "I don't think so. I find three facts compelling. First, the girl immediately responded when David called her name. Next, the woman was troubled enough to take the girl back to the van. Finally, the guard. I can't think of a plausible reason for him to be there except to ensure that nothing happened to the girl. And where there's smoke, there's fire."

"Let's assume all that's true," John said. "But even if that was the kidnapped girl in the store, you have no idea where they were going."

"Actually," I replied, "I think I do." They looked at me as though I'd announced the discovery of Noah's Ark. "Fetch saw a yellow license plate on the rear of the van, right? But he didn't see one on the front. The bottom front of the van was black. Except for the headlights. He would've noticed a bright yellow license plate in front."

"I agree," Ari said. "He would have seen it."

"He didn't see a front plate because that van is licensed in a state that doesn't require front plates."

"An interesting assumption," Julien remarked.

"It fits with what we know. I googled a list of states that don't require front plates. There are nineteen."

"How many have yellow plates?" Ari said.

"Of the states with no front plates, four have issued yellow plates in the past thirty years," I replied. "Alabama, Pennsylvania, and West Virginia—but theirs were issued long ago. Only one state has issued bright yellow license plates since the year 2000. New Mexico."

"This is a huge leap of faith," John said.

"But a reasonable assumption," Julien argued, "if your friend is right and the van didn't have a front plate."

John shook his head. "Even if they were headed to New Mexico. That's a huge state."

I nodded. "Still, we know more than we did an hour ago. I think they drove east to Cheyenne, where they picked up Interstate Twenty-five and drove south."

"I don't know how that helps you," Ari said. "John's right. New Mexico has a lot of real estate. Where do you go from here?"

"I need to figure out the make and model of the van. Our drummer, Garth Wyman, is a motorcycle freak but also knows cars. He might be able to identify it."

"Sure," Ari said, "but whatever make and model it is, there'll be hundreds of them in New Mexico. Maybe thousands."

I shrugged. "We're closer than we were before. When you play music, you play one measure at a time. That's what I'm going to do. One measure at a time until I hear the melody. The melody is the story; like all stories, it has a beginning, middle, and ending. If I can discover the melody, I can find the girl."

11

Every large family has one kid who disappoints the parents by not following the path they want him to take. In my family, that's me. My brother Angus has a Masters in Accounting from UCLA. He became a CPA and is a partner with a firm in Los Angeles. My father and grandfather were in finance, so Angus followed the family tradition. Our parents are proud of him. Aileen studied art at Stanford and is a potter of some renown in Santa Fe. People say she's very creative. Our parents' collection of her pots is lovingly displayed at home. My younger sister, Teagan, has degrees in meteorology and broadcasting from USC and is the weather person for a television station in Seattle. She occasionally sends me clips of her broadcasts, and I see my gorgeous, grown-up baby sister, the meteorologist. Her style and charm make viewers feel good even when the weather's lousy. Our parents are proud of her, too.

In high school, I aced math, and my mother dreamed of me becoming a math professor like her, but I was drawn to music and loved playing the sax. I was good enough to attract the prettiest girls in school and woo them with soulful tunes. On the other hand, the math geeks spent most nights alone in their bedrooms playing with their square roots. So I went to UC Berkeley and graduated with a BA in music. Resigned to my musical obsession, my mother decided I should go to Julliard for a graduate degree and become a music professor, but I was the wild child of the litter. When I graduated, I bought a used 1998 Harley XL-1200C Sportster and took it to a place in Oakland I'd heard was *the* place, the *only* place in the Bay Area to have a Harley customized.

Oakland is not a Sesame Street kind of town. It's an adult dose. Some parts of the city are gritty war zones where rival gangs shoot it out. You can get your throat cut for wearing rival gang colors on another gang's turf, having the wrong tats, or screwing the wrong girl. Forget all the bullshit about racial harmony. Oakland is tribal, and the tribe everyone respects is the bikers who ride their Harleys into Wyman Bros. Motors in the industrial armpit near the Port of Oakland.

The first time I took my Sportster to Wymans, the lot resounded with the guttural roar of Harleys.   Thirty or forty bikes gleamed with chrome, one chopped Harley after another. Their riders were clad in black leather, faces harsh and defiant. They wore black watch caps, Nazi helmets, or greasy bandanas. Some openly smoked weed, which back then was like shoving your middle finger up DEA's nose. Many had knives hanging from their belts or chains wrapped around their waists. Everybody packed heat. They were filthy, bearded, and stank of oil and cigarette smoke and beer, and if you fucked with one of them, you fucked with all of them. Wymans was located in turf claimed by rival Latino gangs, but it was a free-fire zone because none of the gangbangers would tangle with the Wyman brothers or the tough sons of bitches who rode Harleys there. Even cops kept their distance. Especially the cops.

On my first trip to Wymans, three Angels lumbered over when I parked my Sportster and swung off it. I had wild-looking, long, dark hair and a mustache and goatee, which I still have. I was wearing threadbare jeans and a Grateful Dead t-shirt. Not Ivy League, so they didn't spit on me, but I wasn't in leathers and wasn't affiliated, which made them suspicious. I thought we might be headed toward something large, and I was ready to stand my ground. Then a twenty-something guy ambled out of the garage wearing black leather pants and motorcycle boots. He was slender but muscular and had long black hair held in place by a blue bandana. He was bare from the waist up. The skin on his torso and arms rippled with blue tats when he moved.

"What can I do you for?" he said, wiping his hands on a red rag.

"I'm looking to customize my bike." When he turned to look it over, I saw a pair of drumsticks sticking out of his rear pocket. "Hey, man, you're a drummer."

He looked back at me. "You play?"

"Sax. Jazz and blues. Some rock. I'm Sonny Marshall."

"Garth Wyman." We shook hands, and out of the corner of my eye, I saw the Angels easing away, which told me that in this tribal hierarchy, Garth was a high priest, if not a crown prince. "Where do you play?" he asked me.

"Here and there. How 'bout you?"

"Same."

"I'm looking to hook up with something steady."

"Yeah? Know a guy you should talk to. Bass man. Plays a Fender Precision. Guy name of Xavier McQueen. Blues man. I'll give you his number."

"Cool."

He looked back at the bike. "Ninety-eight XL twelve hundred," he said, running his hands over the bike like a sculptor examining a promising block of marble. "Ninety-fifth anniversary trim. Sweet. Frame's a little light. Can rattle at high speeds. Not a cruiser, but you can dress this up. What're you lookin' to do?"

That's how I met Garth Wyman, who later became the drummer for the band Mc-Queen and I started. Garth customized my bike. He told me I could find a better Harley for distance, but I liked the feel of the Sportster. I never felt more alive than when I was cruising down an open road seeing the country in three-dimensional Technicolor, the air smacking my face so fiercely that smells were rammed up my nose, nothing in my ears but the roar of the engine and the wind, body pulsing with the heart-pounding glory of freedom. In roadhouses from Yuma to Corpus Christi and from Memphis to Chicago, my chopped Harley and sax got me instant respect and a string of pretty women looking for a few thrills. During that time, I rarely slept in the same bed twice and only paid for a motel room if the new woman I was with couldn't take me to her place for one reason or another.

In August of the following year, a buddy and I were riding to the Harley rally in Sturgis, South Dakota, when a drunk pulled onto the highway. My buddy swerved around him, but I was too close. I braked hard and turned the bike sideways to avoid a head-on. Just before impact, I lept off the bike and might have cleared the roof of his car if I'd been able to lift my legs high enough. But I hit the car mid-thigh at forty miles an hour. The impact snapped my femur and shattered the knee in my left leg. I flew fifty feet before slamming into the pavement and skidded another fifty on my back. If I hadn't been wearing a helmet and leathers, I'da been DOA. As it was, I nearly lost my left leg. A year of reconstructive surgery hurt like a bitch, but I was damned lucky to be alive. My custom Sportster had to be deep-sixed in a junkyard. My sax was flattened and folded in half. It now hangs on a wall in my condo, a reminder of what happens when speeding objects collide. It's a shame about that sax. It was a Selmer Mark V, one sweet instrument.

But when I drove into Wymans this morning, all the bikers knew me. I waded through a phalanx of bumped fists and "What's up, man?" before I made it to the shop. As I was searching for Garth, my phone rang. It was Katrina Hastings, the detective in Sacramento, saying she had a meeting in San Francisco that afternoon at ICAC, the Internet Crimes Against Children Task Force, and asked if we could get together beforehand. She had some questions and wanted to update me on the pedophiles I'd told her about. We agreed on lunch at eleven thirty at Flore on Market, a funky cafe in the Castro.

I found Garth installing custom tailpipes on a new Harley Low Rider. It was royal blue and had more chrome than a Chevy auto assembly plant. The guys were finishing a complete custom treatment, and I told Garth I'd never seen a more beautiful bike. He flashed me a shit-eating grin, eyes shining.

"Hey, man. I need help identifying the make and model of a van a friend saw." I told him what Fetch said about the white van.

"Driver's side mirror mounted on the front?" he said.

"S'right."

"Boxy body, sloping front. Bottom third is solid black. That oughta narrow it down. Let's talk to Chris." We walked over to their auto body shop, where we found Chris Hendrix, a six-foot-six Neanderthal with long, stringy blonde hair and a mouthful of silver teeth. While I asked about the van, Chris spit tobacco into an Oakland Raiders coffee mug. I hoped he'd wash it before drinking out of it, but from the look of the guy, I doubt if he cared.

"Sounds like a Toyota Hiace," Chris said with a voice that sounded like a body being dragged over gravel. "Check the book." We followed him to an all-beat-to-hell office area in one corner of the shop. Shelves behind the counter were filled with hundreds of dog-eared, oil-stained manuals and reference binders. Chris pulled down a Toyota binder four inches thick and pawed through it until he found what he was looking for. Pointing to a photo, he said, "That it?"

The style and shape of the van fit the description. I'd have to confirm it with Fetch. "Could be," I told Chris.

"The Hiace had four or five generations. Yours is pro'bly a ninety-eight or ninety-nine, maybe two thousand. No later'n that."

I nodded. "Can I get a copy of this page?"

Chris snapped open the binder. "Ruthie!"

An older woman with gray hair like a Brillo pad stuck her head through the transom and yelled, "What?" After he handed her the page, she disappeared. A moment later, she thrust a copy back through the transom. I yelled thanks, but she had disappeared.

When I thanked Chris, he cocked a finger at me and pulled the trigger. I shot him back, saying, "Later, dude." Garth and I walked back through the motorcycle shop.

"So what's up with this?" he said, cocking his eyebrows.

"Looking into a kid's disappearance. The people who kidnapped her drove a van like this."

"Yeah? No shit. You need help, you know where to find me."

I was back home a little after nine. I scanned the photo and emailed it to Fetch. Then I drove to the studio to tape some riffs. At eleven fifteen, I drove to Flore on Market. Katrina Hastings was waiting at the bar. She looked damned good in a gray suit with a black blouse and a gold necklace. It was a warm, sunny day, so we asked for a table outside. She ordered an avocado salad, and I had the Cobb. We both drank iced tea. I asked about her meeting with ICAC.

"They're responsible for investigating child pornography, as you probably know, which today is mostly sold or exchanged on the internet."

"And the internet crosses borders," I said.

"Right. That pedophile case you dropped in my lap is about to bust wide open. The offense is federal, and ICAC comprises a bunch of different federal, state, and local agencies. We'd been watching Pruett because he matched the description of a guy who tried to kidnap a fourteen-year-old girl outside a Catholic high school in Sacramento. Turns out it wasn't him, but after the incident with you, we saw him emptying his bank account and pawning things."

"Preparing to run."

"Yeah. So we arrested him. Based on our surveillance and what you told me, we got a warrant to search his apartment, pickup, and computer for evidence of ICACs, and we found a mother lode."

"Like what?"

"Five big photo albums of child porn and a hundred and twenty-two CDs with movies of children being molested and raped. Some of them just infants."

"Holy shit," I said.

"It gets worse. I passed the photos you gave me around our office, and one detective identified the guy wearing glasses. Charles Buckallew. He's a criminal defense attorney in Fremont." She paused, looking at me, I guessed, for some sign of recognition.

"As I told you," I said, "I've never seen those guys before."

She stared at me for another beat and then said, "Okay-y-y. Anyway, we took Buckallew into custody yesterday. Oddly enough, he has a long cut on his face exactly where Pruett's face was cut."

She again paused, but I just gave her a blank look and took an innocent swallow of tea.

"When we searched Buckallew's home, we found a floor safe with documents showing that he negotiated contracts with people in LA and Miami to supply child porn to distributors in Asia and South America. We think he acted as the business manager for several child porn producers in our area, including R.T. Rayburn."

"The fat guy."

"Yeah. We have an arrest warrant on him and his wife, but they're in the wind. Besides his home, Rayburn owns an apartment building in Union City. We thought they might be hiding there, so we raided that building early this morning."

"They weren't there."

"No."

"I heard they might've skipped to Mexico. The wife is Mexican."

"Where'd you hear that?"

"Here and there."

"Damn it, Marshall." She threw her napkin on the table and fixed me with a glare. "That's not going to cut it. I need to know what you know."

"Like what?"

"Like how you managed to connect with those four scumbags. I'm still trying to figure out your role in this."

I thought about it for a moment. "I wanted to know if they recognized Erin Hightower's picture. I needed to find out if she'd ever appeared on a child porn website. I assumed that's why she was kidnapped."

"You didn't answer the question. How did you connect with them?"

"I have a contact who put them in touch with me."

"Who's your contact?"

"Nobody important."

She practically spit her next words. "This is a police investigation. What you're doing is obstruction of justice. You understand that?"

"Look, detective. When we met, you laid down some ground rules. I've got a few of my own. I'll help with your investigation because I want to find the girl as much as you do, but my sources are my own goddamn business, and if you press it, I will develop a terrible memory. You don't want my help? Fine. Solve the case yourself."

"Fuck you!" she snarled, slamming her glass on the table. She spun out of her chair and marched inside toward the bar. I sat glowering after her, the tips of my ears burning. The couple at the next table stared at me. "Lover's quarrel," I told them, but they didn't buy it. Turning awkwardly back to their table, they made a show of enjoying their lunch. Hastings had splashed tea all over the table, and I wiped it up with my napkin. Then I sat back for fifteen or twenty minutes and watched people passing on the sidewalk.

"Everyone calls me Kat," came a voice behind me. Her face was still flushed, but her features had softened. "Nobody calls me Katrina. Katrina was a hurricane."

As she sat back down, I said, "Yeah, well, that fits, too."

"Fuck you," she said, this time with her lopsided grin, which I had no clue how to interpret. Was she mocking me? She upended her glass and drank what was left.

"You want more tea?"

"No." She looked at her fingers and tapped the empty glass. "I want to close this case, and I'm not getting anywhere. Haven't been for years. That's why I agreed to be interviewed by Channel Five. And nothing came of it. Just a bunch of bullshit leads from crackpots. I don't want to retire someday and not know what happened to that girl." She looked at me and held her gaze, and I noticed that her eyes, tinged as they were with sadness, were perfectly oval and radiant. She was very easy to look at when she wasn't working so hard at being a detective. Except for that loopy grin.

"They were going to kill me," I told her. "The four pedophiles on Mt. Diablo. The one guy who looked like a predator. He was about to shoot me."

"We haven't been able to identify him."

"He was the badass of the bunch and might've killed me if two of my friends hadn't followed them and saved my ass. That's when their faces were cut, but I didn't do it. I don't use a knife."

"What do you use?"

"To defend myself? Hands and feet, elbows and knees. Surprise and misdirection. I have fourth-degree black belts in Aikido and Krav Maga. How about you?"

She pulled her jacket aside. "Beretta ninety-two FS. Nine millimeter. Twenty-round mag."

"You any good?"

"Three-inch shot group at fifty feet."

"Just for the record, I'm on your side."

She smiled, her loopy smile again, pink lips drawn up in the shape of a crooked heart, framing a row of very white teeth.

"I didn't finish telling you about the raid in Union City," she said. "All the apartments were rented except one on the first floor. Inside it, we found a movie set. Queen bed. Black drop cloth hung on three sides behind it. High-end movie cameras, stage lights, microphones. That's where Rayburn made child porn flicks. There were hundreds of DVDs and a machine for making copies. It'll take weeks for prosecutors to catalog the evidence. Rayburn participated in some films. He wore a black leather hood and beat children while he raped them. We have enough evidence to put him, his wife, Pruett, and Buckallew away for life."

"What about the fourth guy?"

"Don't have a clue."

"Did you find Erin Hightower's picture in anything?"

"No, but I didn't look through it. I can't look at that garbage. It turns my stomach. Federal prosecutors and the people at ICAC will have to do it. But I'm taking photos of Erin to ICAC this afternoon, including the one you gave me." She glanced at her watch. "Which reminds me, I need to go. ICAC has a database of hundreds of thousands of images of children who've appeared on child porn sites or publications. Their facial recognition software compares images in the database and flags possible matches. We'll know if Erin's picture ever appeared on those sites."

"You'll let me know?"

"Now that we're cooperating? Sure. I'll do that. But you have to promise to share with me, too. This may be your cause, but it's my case."

"Touché. I do have something before you leave. The van Fetch saw in Green River is a Toyota Hiace, a ninety-eight, ninety-nine, or two thousand. I think I know where it was headed after Green River." I filled her in on the yellow license plate that could only belong to a car registered in New Mexico.

She looked doubtful. "I wish we had more than that. Look, I have to go. But stay in touch."

"Sure." I watched her leave the cafe. She walked briskly, reminding me of the by-the-book police detective I'd met in Sacramento, but I thought my first impression of her might have been wrong. I wasn't sure what to make of her. Maybe she hadn't been mocking me. I paid the bill and retrieved my car. A few minutes later, I arrived at my apartment. We were recording another track this afternoon, and I had to grab some music.

As soon as I put my key in the lock and opened the door, I sensed something wrong. The main room wasn't how I had left it, and I was trying to figure out why when something struck the back of my head. I lurched forward into the room, legs buckling. As I watched the floor rise, the thought flashed through my head that Donald Reese, the man who'd raped Aileen, had gotten an early release and come after me. I wondered why no one told me he'd gotten out, but the room turned black before that thought could run its course.

12

I was walking on a pathway of soggy wooden planks through a forest of towering oaks and ground cover a hundred shades of green. The air was cool and damp. Moss grew over the edges of the planks—the forest slowly erasing evidence of man's intrusion. The gaps between the planks were filled with forest decay—shredded leaves, pollen, and desiccated remains of flowers. I was holding onto my sister Teagan's hand. The planks creaked and moaned beneath us. Though I was grown, Teagan was just five. That made no sense, but somehow I knew she would always be a child. She looked at me with wide, innocent eyes, dark hair framing her face, the prettiest of smiles separating her lips.

Hearing voices, I looked around but didn't see anyone.

Teagan pulled away, but I was transfixed by moss scaling ancient tree trunks and couldn't see where she'd gone. Then she cried from somewhere in the green maze. I tried to follow the sound, but it came from everywhere. Through the trees, I glimpsed an old house with dirty white shingles. A black-haired man with a scraggly beard pulled Teagan toward it, and they disappeared across the threshold.

Then I heard voices again. From somewhere in the darkness of the forest.

I ran toward the house, heart racing, and yanked open the front door. Inside was a foyer with doors leading to the interior. I sprang toward the first door, whipped it open, and raced into another room, larger, unfurnished with musty floral paper peeling from the walls. The house smelled like decay. There were more doors in this room, more in the next, and more in the rooms beyond that. The pungent odor grew stronger, the deeper I went. I heard Teagan's muted screaming but couldn't find her, no matter how many rooms I searched. The house seemed endless, door after door after door, room after room, and I kept hearing voices.

Something was pressing on my face, making it harder to breathe. I waded through the house with my face pressed against the walls.

Voices again.

Lord, it hurt. The back of my head. Throbbing. I wanted to move, but my limbs felt numb. I was . . . tired, too tired. Drifting in . . . and out of . . . the fog.

Forgive me, Teagan.

I lay on my side. Nauseous. Wanted to sleep. Wanted to touch my head where it felt wet. But my hand wouldn't move. Couldn't feel my left arm. Lying on it. My right hand. Behind my back. Tried moving it, but it wouldn't obey.

Voices again.

Two voices.

Where am I? I came home. For music. Something hit me. I'm on the floor. On my left side. Arms behind my back. Tied together. Head throbbing. Eyes closed. That's why it's dark. I know to keep them closed. Make the voices think I'm sleeping. *You shoulda'na hit him so hard*, a man's voice said. Then bang! Shock waves coursed through my brain. I wanted to cry out. Another bang. And more banging. Metal on metal. Christ, make it stop!

Fuck, one voice yelled. *Wait'll he wakes up*, said the other voice. *I'll make him open it.*

Lying on my left side. Can't open my right eye without them seeing me. But I can open my left. So I do. Slowly. Just a sliver. Something brown. Light brown. Shiny. I'm looking at a hardwood floor. In my main room. I see movement in the reflection off the floor. There's light behind them. They're in my kitchen. One of the dark shapes is very big. I know him. It's the fat man. It's . . . Ray. Something. Burn. Rayburn. A wave of nausea rushes through me. I want to throw up but know I can't. Can't let them know I'm awake.

Get those thumb drives and get the hell outta town, Rayburn says. *Kill these fuckers before we leave*, the other man says. His shadow is smaller. Can't see him clearly. But it must be, shit, it must be the tough guy. The predator. Now I really want to vomit. But I force myself to lie still.

When they know I'm awake, they'll kill me. But they want something first. That gives me leverage. If killing me was all they wanted, I'd already be dead. How'd they find me? Drawing a blank. A question for another time. If I survive.

I'm helpless while my hands are tied behind my back. Not handcuffs. Not rope. The fat man, Rayburn, likes plastic ties. They're tight. I try separating my hands, but my right one won't budge, and I can't feel my left. Have to get my hands in front of me. I know how but won't have much time once I start to move. Have to do everything right the first time. But with no feeling in my left hand, I don't know if those muscles will obey. Don't have a choice, do I? Okay, but then what? Get to my feet. Can't reason with them, so be ready for whatever happens.

"You're a John Doe," Rayburn whines. "But they know who I am. You saw the news. I gotta get those thumb drives and get the hell outta here."

"Not till I find the spic who cut me," the predator droned. "Motherfucker's gonna wish he'd died a hundred times before I cut off his fuckin' head."

"Shoulda'na hit the guy so hard," Rayburn said. He knelt by something. "Gotta get this goddamn thing open."

Get what open? This may be my last day, but if I'm going to die, I'll die fighting. Gotta rehearse my moves. Quick and fluid. Hands in front. Break the tie. Snap it on my knee. Fighting stance. Be ready. Defend while disabling my opponent. That's what they taught me. Do it without thinking. Thinking gets you killed. Quick, powerful moves. Textbook.

The problem is that your hands aren't tied together in martial arts training. Krav Maga requires two arms, one to deflect while the other counterattacks. Balance is critical in Aikido. You move fluidly with both arms. But the music to the dance I'm doing now hasn't been written. I'll be improvising.

I still couldn't see them clearly, but their voices were muffled, so I opened my left eye more. Mentally rehearsed my moves. Willed my muscles to relax. Took a slow, deep breath. Then as quietly but quickly as possible, I rolled onto my back and lifted my legs off the floor, slid my hands down and under my butt and up the backs of my thighs, past my calves and feet. My right hand did all the work. My left followed like a lazy cousin. When my hands were in front, I rolled backward over my right shoulder in a reverse somersault, pushed up with my hands, and was upright, staggering but upright, facing them, my head spinning. They turned and saw me, disbelief on their faces, the predator reacting quicker, the surprise on his face morphing into rage. I glanced at my wrists. They'd used two ties to bind them. Shit. I could break one but not two, and my wrists were bleeding, the ties were so tight. Bile forced its way up my throat, and my vision turned black.

I had enough presence of mind to feint toward the door. Rayburn fell for the misdirection and shuffled toward it while the Predator leaped at me with his knife. He was faster than anyone I'd ever fought. I was still reeling and stumbled backward when he grabbed my hair from behind, jerked my head up, and pressed his knife against my throat.

"Gonna kill you, motherfucker," he yelled. I knew he would, but not yet. My condo was a mess. They'd been searching while I was unconscious. My heavy safe sat in front of the kitchen counter. They'd dragged it from the music room and were trying to open it. I remembered seeing a large hammer in Rayburn's hand when he ran to the door. He'd been banging on the safe, thinking brute force would open it. Rayburn had a long bandage down the left side of his face, but the predator's wound was uncovered, a long, swollen ridge of red flesh, crusty scabs, and black stitches. It looked infected and must have hurt like hell. He'd be vulnerable there.

"What do you want?" I asked the predator.

"I want my Glock," he seethed. "I want money. Rayburn wants his thumb drives. And I want the name of that fuckin' spic that cut my face. I'm gonna roast him alive. Mostly I wanna kill your ass, but you're gonna answer my questions first."

"Asshole," I said. "I'm not telling you a fucking thing."

He jerked my head back and dug the knife into my neck. I felt blood flow, but he hadn't cut the artery. He wouldn't until he got what he came for.

"You think you're tough," he snarled in my right ear.

With my head bent so far backward, it was hard to talk, but I eked out a scratchy, "You're right. I think I'm tough."

Rayburn hadn't moved away from the door.

"You don't fuckin' get it, do you? Open the fuckin' safe. I'll cut your throat, and it'll be over quick. Keep fuckin' with me, and I'll take you apart piece by piece, one finger at a time. Then I'll do your toes, cock and balls, ears and nose, lips, tongue, and teeth. I'll do your eyes last 'cause I want you to see every piece of your body after it comes off. If you don't bleed out when your eyes are gone, maybe I'll let you live. You'll be a pathetic piece of shit, and you'll have a long time to think about how stupid it was to fuck with me."

"Can't talk," I managed, and then the Predator made a mistake. He pushed my head forward so I could speak. Before he realized his error, I jerked my head back into his face, slamming into the long gash on his face. At the same time, I spun away from his knife hand and escaped as he howled in rage, left hand covering his re-opened wound, blood pouring over his fingers. He looked at me with pure murderous rage and thrust his knife at me, a quick jab as he re-centered himself. It was a hunting knife, eight inches long, curved to a sharp point. The kind of knife you gut a deer with. Then he held the knife sideways in front of him, turning the blade back and forth, showing me its gleaming razor edge.

He was five feet away when I said, "I have a question. How'd your face get fucked up?"

His eyes went wide, and he lunged forward, his knife arcing so quickly it nearly reached me before I blocked it by thrusting my tied hands into his forearm, driving the knife away. At the same time, I lowered my head and launched upward into his face. The head butt sent a jolt of pain through my body, but the crown of my head connected with his nose and bleeding wound. His nose broke with a loud snap, and he bellowed in rage, sinking backward. Blood spurted from his ruined nose and the long cut down his face, which had burst open like a watermelon dropped onto concrete. He recovered and came at me again, plunging the knife downward. I threw my tied hands upward to block the blade, but he was too quick, and the steel tip sank into my shoulder before I could deflect it. Despite the pain, I propelled into him, anchoring my left leg on the floor and driving my right knee upward into the soft tissue between his legs. My knee caught him squarely on the balls, and he plunged to the floor writhing in agony, left hand covering his crotch, right still gripping the knife, which he repeatedly stabbed into the floor. We were covered in blood, and my shoulder stung like a bitch.

If the fat man had been stealthy, I might have died in the next instant, but I heard his shoes clacking on the hardwood as he lumbered toward me. I turned to see him just a few feet away, coming fast, the hammer raised. I quickly spun out of range but planted my right foot on the floor. He tripped over it and stumbled forward, slamming into a bookcase whose contents exploded. "Fuckkkkk!" he screamed. I threw myself at him with my elbows raised and jammed them into the lower left side of his back. The kidney blow knocked him to his knees, and the hammer clattered to the floor.

My instinct was to grab the hammer, but before I could bend over, an arm whipped around from behind me and jerked me backward. I was startled that the predator had recovered so quickly. He spat blood and howled in agony but still wrapped his left arm around my neck, brought his right arm around, and pressed the knife to my throat.

"Who's that fuckin' spic," he bellowed. "Where's that cocksucker?"

I felt the blade slicing into my neck. One jerk of his hand and I'd be dead. I quickly brought my hands up and grabbed his hand and wrist, then head-butted his broken nose, yanked down on his wrist, pulling the knife away, dipped my shoulder, and pulled my head under his right arm. The knife was now pointed at his side, and he was still applying force through that arm, so I lunged. The knife penetrated him just below his rib case. For a moment, his body tensed and grew still. Then he expelled a breath and seemed to implode. I let go and stepped away. Black blood seeped through his shirt, a growing torrent, and he gaped at the knife buried in his side, his own hand wrapped around the handle. But this guy was a freak of nature. He took a breath, glared at me with hatred, and started to pull the knife out. I kicked sharply on the side of his right knee, and he teetered for a moment, his face frozen in shock, then collapsed onto his right side, impaling himself on the knife. Blood poured from his wound, a pool of it spreading quickly. With a final shudder, his bowels released, and he lay still except for his left hand, which twitched for another few seconds. The room smelled like vomit and shit and heavy copper.

I'd all but forgotten about Rayburn. He walked gingerly toward the door, left hand clasped to his side. That kidney had to hurt like hell. I took three quick steps and launched a one-legged kick into the middle of his back. He plunged onto his stomach with a whoof of expelled breath and lay there trying to catch air. Before he could push himself back up, I straddled his back and put my hands over his head. My wrists were cut and bleeding, and the knife wound on my shoulder pulsed badly. I leaned back, and the ties binding my hands cut into his throat.

"This is for every child you fucked," I whispered. I leaned back until his gagging grew desperate. Then I leaned forward, easing the pressure on his throat. He choked and sputtered for a long minute, struggling to fill his lungs while I sat on his back.

"Please," he managed, his breath ragged. "I have money."

"Enough to pay for the lives you ruined?" I pulled back again, and the ties dug into his throat. He gagged and tried to buck me off, but I choked him until all voluntary movement stopped, and he lay still. He wasn't dead, but his brain, starved for oxygen, was in the void. I lifted my hands and pushed myself off his body. Standing on weary legs, my left knee and shoulder throbbing, I stumbled to the kitchen. Adrenalin had numbed my knee during the fight, but that natural anesthetic wouldn't last. Unless I took more painkillers, the howling agony I now felt was destined to become a brain burner when the adrenalin wore off.

I steadied myself, then leaned over and vomited into the sink. Spittle still dribbling from my mouth, I examined the bloody cuts around my wrists. The skin was worn away under the ties and stung like hell. My cell lay on the kitchen counter. Blood dripping from my fingers, I dialed 9-1-1 and told the operator I'd been attacked in my condo. I was injured, and one attacker was dead. She told me to stay on the line, but I clicked off after giving her my name and address.

I turned to keep an eye on Rayburn while I called Ari. He rushed from his office before we'd finished talking. My throat felt like a gravel pit. I craved water, but my hands were slippery with blood. Rayburn began to move, so I walked over and stomped on his head. Then I made one more call. I remembered the number and managed to dial it, although I couldn't see the buttons for all the blood. Kat answered on the fourth ring.

"What is it?" she said, irritated. "I'm still in the meeting at ICAC."

"Rayburn and Predator. Attacked me in my condo."

"Oh my God, Sonny. Are you all right?"

"Predator's dead. Rayburn hurt. I'm stabbed ... shoulder ... wrists, neck cut."

"For God's sake," she cried. "Tell me where you are." I did, and she said she'd be right there.

As I closed the phone, Rayburn was gasping, trying to push himself up. I dropped heavily onto his back. He grunted, reaching for me, but I slapped his hands away and got mine back under his head. He grabbed my wrists but didn't have enough leverage to keep me from choking him.

"Lemme go," he said with a raspy voice. "I have money. I'll pay you."

I leaned back just enough to shut him up. "Beginning ... your descent into hell. Child fucker. Gonna ride you ... all the way down. No charge."

I held him like that for what felt like an hour, but it was no more than a few minutes. Then I heard rushed footsteps outside. I eased my hands from under Rayburn's head and rolled off. I lay on my back with bloodied hands in front of me, pain radiating through every part of my body. Then I heard a loud pounding. An urgent voice yelled, "Open up. This is the police." I tuned them out but heard more pounding. Then a loud crash as the door splintered open. Two uniformed cops rushed in, guns drawn, and surveyed the carnage.

"Holy shit," I heard one of them say.

13

Ari arrived shortly after the uniformed cops and the paramedics and told them he was family. The paramedics cut the cable ties off my wrists, and Ari had them take us to the UCSF Medical Center, where he knew the director of emergency services. They stitched my shoulder, bandaged my wrists and neck, gave me shots for tetanus and hepatitis C, stapled my scalp, decided I had a concussion, did a neurological exam, gave me morphine, and sent me away with a prescription for antibiotics and another for Oxycodone, the first legit one I've had in years. Two hours later, we returned to my place and walked into a hive of activity. Rayburn was gone, but the medical examiner was inspecting the Predator's body. Crime scene techs dusted for prints, took photographs, and bagged evidence. Three detectives were in my kitchen talking to Kat Hastings and Paul Fisher.

Kat saw us first. She mouthed, "You okay?" I nodded. Paul wore his trademark black suit, shirt, and tie and had his nose buried in their conversation. When he saw us, he gave me a subtle head shake and tapped one detective on the arm. I must have looked as bad as I felt. They walked over, and Ari suggested we go to the den so I could sit down.

As I sat on the sofa, Paul extended a hand. "I'm Lieutenant Paul Fisher, San Francisco Police."

I played along and told him my name. Paul hadn't met Ari but knew him by reputation and was surprised to see him. I said Ari was a close family friend, and Paul nodded. The other detective introduced himself as Sergeant James Renicke and said he was leading this investigation. Renicke was in his forties with short red hair that lay flat on his head like a pencil eraser. He wore a black suit over a light blue shirt and a narrow red tie. The frown lines etched on his face said he didn't believe a tenth of what people told him. He took out a small blue notebook and asked me what happened. I told him, omitting some details of the fight.

When I finished, Renicke said, "I need to clear up a few things. You said those two guys knocked you out."

"One of them hit me on the head."

"Show me where," he said. I leaned forward and touched the staple on the back of my head. He examined it and wrote in his notebook. "They tied your hands with cable ties?"

"That's right."

"Um-hmm. I'm curious about why they tied your hands in front of you. Most guys would have tied them behind your back."

"They did tie them behind me. I managed to move my hands in front of me and roll off the floor before they could react."

"Yeah?" he said, his eyebrows raised. "How'd you do that?"

I explained how.

"That's a pretty neat trick," he said. "You must be an acrobat." He mimicked the moves I described. "I'm in good shape and couldn't do that."

"You get real motivated when someone's about to kill you."

"Um-hmm," he said, writing. "So it turns out these two guys are wanted for child porn. Did you know that?"

"Sergeant Hastings told me."

Renicke glanced at her, and she nodded.

"How were you connected with them?" he asked.

"I wasn't."

"You didn't know them?"

"No."

Kat explained that I'd been looking for a missing girl from Sacramento and had run into those guys during my search. I'd given her evidence of the child porn ring, leading to several arrests.

"Um-hmm. I'm still trying to understand why these two perverts, who were on the lam, took time to stop at your place. They were trying to break into your safe. Something in there they'd want?"

"They came looking for two thumb drives I took from Rayburn," I replied. "They tossed the place but didn't find them. They thought the drives were in the safe."

"Are they?"

I shook my head. "I gave them to Sergeant Hastings."

Renicke nodded, still writing. "Okay. Let's talk about the hunting knife that killed the guy in the other room. Yours?"

"No."

"You don't own any knives?"

"I have a complete set of kitchen knives," I said. "Forty-nine ninety-five on late-night TV. And they threw in a sharpener and eight deluxe steak knives."

He gave me a hard look. "So you think the dead guy brought the knife."

"I've never seen it before."

"Um-hmm. See, my problem is figuring out how this guy got stabbed in his side with his own knife. You say he brought the knife and intended to kill you with it."

"That's what he said."

"You never touched the knife? It didn't fall out of his hands? You didn't pick it up and stab him? I mean, that could be construed as self-defense."

"I never touched the knife."

"That's hard to believe." He mimicked holding a knife in his right hand and stabbing himself in the right side. "See how awkward this is? If I was gonna commit hari-kari, I wouldn't do it this way."

I shrugged. "You won't find my fingerprints on that knife."

"We'll check. Was the dead guy suicidal?"

I shrugged. "He didn't look happy."

"Um-hmm. I'm trying to imagine this guy saying he's going to kill you but instead slashes himself in the face and then commits suicide by stabbing himself in the side. I've been a cop for twenty-five years and seen a lot of suicides, but nothing like this. Why do you suppose he did that?"

I was tired of this. "Maybe he felt remorse."

"You always such a wiseass?"

"Only when I've been attacked in my home and treated like a suspect."

"Okay. So how'd this guy wind up with his own knife buried in his liver?"

I shrugged. "He came at me with the knife. I deflected it and broke his nose."

He consulted his notes. "With the top of your head?"

"Right."

"Then what?"

"He stabbed me in the shoulder, and I kicked him in the balls." Renicke wrote that down. "Then Rayburn came at me with the hammer. I tripped him, he fell into the bookcase, and I elbowed him in the kidneys. The dead guy tried to cut my throat, but I got away and, I don't know, there was a lot of blood on the floor. Maybe he slipped. Something like that. Whatever happened, he wound up with the knife in his side. Fights don't happen in slow motion. Makes them hard to reconstruct afterward."

"Um-hmm." Renicke continued writing. "Just one more thing. I saw your trophy case out there. You have black belts in two martial arts?"

I nodded.

"We had a short course on Krav Maga at the Police Academy. Pretty slick stuff. So, call me crazy, I'm thinking you used some martial art skills to take down this guy, make him turn the knife on himself."

"Now, *that* would be a neat trick," I replied. "Detective, the fight lasted two minutes. No more. I did everything a reasonable person would do to defend myself. He was hell-bent on killing me. The fact that he wound up dead is either bad luck or bad karma for him. What can I say? I went into that fight with a concussion and my hands tied together. My hands were still tied together when it was over, and I still had a concussion. But you know what? It was *his* knife. I never touched it. And, hey, shit happens."

"Um-hmm." He flipped his notebook closed. "That it does." He shot Paul a skeptical look and walked away.

"Asshole," I mumbled.

"He's paid to be skeptical," Paul said. He moved to the door but turned back, looked from Ari to Kat, and then me. "You won't have any problems here. They attacked you in your home. You had a right to defend yourself."

Kat watched Paul walk away and asked if he was my contact in the San Francisco Police Department.

With my best poker face, I deadpanned, "He would be a good one. Chief of homicide."

She gave me her loopy grin but didn't press it. Turning to Ari, she said, "We haven't met. Sergeant Kat Hastings. Sacramento PD."

"Ari Kirakosian." They shook hands, and Kat sat on the sofa.

"I assume Ari knows about the Hightower case," she said to me.

I nodded. "We're close friends."

Again, that loopy grin, which I now saw as a tell. When she had an insight, the right side of her mouth rose. "I have information," she said. "We could talk privately, but I'm guessing that Mr. Kirakosian will find out about whatever I tell you."

"As I said, we're close friends."

"This is sensitive police information. It needs to be closely held."

I nodded, and Ari said, "Understood. It will be."

She paused a moment, pushed a wave of blonde hair out of her face, then took out her iPhone and referred to it as she spoke. "The dead guy was Billy Luce. Got his name from his driver's license and a union card. Longshoreman in Oakland. I called Sacramento, and they've been checking records. Luce was born in Greenville, South Carolina, with a different name. Left at seventeen when his foster parents failed to return from a trip they'd supposedly taken to Massachusetts. Their bank accounts had been cleaned out, and they were never found. A few years later, he did a nickel in Georgia for attempted murder. After his release, he moved to Mississippi, where he beat an elderly man nearly to death but skipped bail and is still wanted on a fugitive warrant. The Texas Rangers think he was part of a car theft ring out of Dallas, but he vanished after a Ranger and three Mexican nationals were murdered in El Paso during a sting operation. In Oklahoma, he was arrested but never tried on child molestation charges, killed a man during a mugging in Arizona, and served a six-pack in Yuma for manslaughter. He was suspected of killing a seven-year-old boy in Las Vegas but was not charged due to insufficient evidence. That's what we know."

"I'm sure his death will be mourned," I quipped.

"He was a flaming, fricking psychopath," Kat offered, "and one mean son of a bitch. You're lucky he didn't kill you."

"Luck had nothing to do with it. It was years of training." She gave me a quizzical look, so I told them what Luce had threatened to do to me. "Luce tried to scare me to death, and that made him susceptible to a head butt he didn't see coming."

She flashed her loopy grin, and I wondered what insight she'd just had. Luce wouldn't threaten me again and wouldn't harm another child. In my moral universe, that's called justice. I didn't care what Renicke or anybody else thought.

"The bigger news," Kat continued, "is what we're finding on Rayburn's thumb drives." She glanced into the main room. Morgue attendants had bagged Luce's body and were lifting it onto a cart. The amount of blood smeared on the hardwood floor made the room look like a slaughterhouse.

"Sonny said the files on those drives were encrypted," Ari said. He leaned back in his chair and crossed his legs.

"They were," said Kat, "and nobody at ICAC could decrypt them. They don't have cryptographers on staff. DOJ contacted NSA and asked for emergency assistance. It took NSA five hours to crack just one of the files, and what they found is raising hairs on everyone's neck."

"There's too much buzz on the street for this to be a simple porn bust," Ari said.

"What do people think is going on?" I asked him.

Ari shook his head. "Nobody knows. Just that there's a lot of federal activity. My sources at the airport say more feds are flying in every hour."

Kat raised her eyebrows. "The FBI is sending dozens of agents to assist ICAC, but those guys fly incognito. You must have excellent sources."

"I try to stay informed."

She pursed her lips. "Well, some of the feds flying in are NSA. They're working twenty-four-seven to decrypt the rest of those files. The ICAC task force has issued forty-five warrants and made twenty-seven arrests. Before this is over, there could be hundreds of arrests nationwide. More around the world."

"What the hell's going on?" I said.

"Have you ever heard of MTO porn?"

"No," I said as Ari shook his head.

"Porn videos made to order. MTO."

It took me a moment to grasp the implications. I sat back in my chair and felt all the heaviness of the day. Thank God for Oxy.

"It works like this," Kat continued. "A customer contacts a porn producer and hires him to make a custom porn video. In this case, child porn. He specifies the situation, gender, age, ethnicity, and what he wants to see happen on the video—bondage, rape, seduction, fantasy, whatever. The producer finds the right child, kidnaps the kid if necessary, and shoots the video. Child porn made to order."

"That's disgusting," I said.

"It's horrifying," Ari added, looking as sick as I felt.

"Was that on those drives?" I said.

"Not the porn itself," Kat answered. "What they found were records of MTO orders and sales. Rayburn and his lawyer pal Buckallew were partners, and they were making millions. Prices for MTO videos range from a hundred to two hundred grand, and they had more customers than you would believe."

Ari closed his eyes and rested his chin on tented fingers. "Never underestimate the human capacity for depravity."

We sat in silence. I remembered how I felt when I learned about the World Trade Centers on nine eleven. Some news makes you question how you view the world and the people in it. It's always a sadder place afterward.

"How is it," I wondered, "that the ICAC people didn't know about this?"

"They've known about it for years," Kat said, "but have never located the producers. The world has three rings—here, Russia, and somewhere in Asia. But these people have sophisticated computer systems and top-notch security. They ship encrypted video files on thumb drives hidden inside a harmless-looking product and send the decryption keys separately. Those keys were listed in the encrypted files, along with customer IDs, product codes, prices, dates, and so on. But each file is encrypted with a different computer-generated key. It'll take months to decrypt them all."

"That's why Rayburn and the others agreed to meet with Sonny," Ari said.

Kat nodded. "They had urgent, open orders and hoped you could locate the children they needed. We learned that from Buckallew this morning. By the way, Pruett was just a flunky in their operation. Luce was the enforcer. When someone had to disappear, he handled it. No one cares that Luce is dead, but the task force was ecstatic to learn that Rayburn is in custody. Before they plant him in a deep, dark hole and stick a needle in his vein, they have lots of questions."

"I have one for you," I said. "Did they kidnap Erin for an MTO video?"

"It's possible, Sonny, but we may never know. We haven't found the videos. They're probably on a secure server somewhere in the Bay Area, but we don't have a clue where. With all the federal assets converging on San Francisco, and with the help of local cops like me, we'll find it sooner or later. When we do, we may learn why Erin was abducted—if Rayburn's group took her."

We were interrupted by a sudden commotion in the main room. We heard scuffling, and then a woman screamed, "Oh my God!" It was Mac. I jumped up and rushed into the room. She stood framed in the open doorway, eyes wide, blood draining from her face. She covered her mouth with shaking hands as she peered around. I ran over and tried to block her view.

"It's all right," I said, putting my hands on her shoulders.

"My God, Sonny, what happened? I saw the police cars." Her eyes widened when she noticed my bandages and the blood on my t-shirt. "Oh, no, what happened to you? Are you all right?"

"Some men attacked me when I came home."

"What? What men?" she stammered. "Are you all right?" Then she saw the morgue attendants with the black body bag on their cart. They'd wheeled it to the door and wanted past us. "What is that?" she cried. Then realizing, she brushed my hands away and stumbled backward into the wall beside the door, a look of revulsion on her face. "Oh my God, no. Oh my God, what happened?"

I tried to hold her, and for a moment, she let me, her eyes welling with tears. Then she saw blood smeared on the floor, and her mouth hung open. She struggled to breathe and began wailing, "No, no, no, no, no, no, no, no, no." She stumbled to the door, her arms trembling, and as she passed into the hallway, she said, "I can't be here. I have to go." I ran with her to the elevator and stood with her while it arrived, telling her it would be all right, but nothing I said helped. When the elevator doors opened, she said, "I'm going to my parents. Please let me go." She limped into the elevator and pushed the button. As the doors were closing, she looked at me, tears stained with black mascara streaking down her face, and cried, "What did you do?"

14

I stared at the outer doors of the elevator as it dropped, Mac's words seared in my mind. When the elevator stopped, the silence in the hallway felt unconditional. Morphine had smothered my pain like a down comforter. Now it was slipping away, and the sting of my injuries and the emptiness of Mac's flight radiated through my core.

Renicke startled me when he called from the door, "Who was that?"

"Mac. My girlfriend. She lives here."

"I guess you have some explaining to do," he said, turning away.

Fuck off, I thought. I returned to my kitchen and swallowed more Oxys with water. Renicke and Kat were talking quietly by my safe. Then John Sebastiani came through the door. He wore blue jeans, a white t-shirt, and a faded brown bomber jacket. "Ari called me," he said. "You okay, partner?" I nodded. He gazed at my bandages, shaking his head, and surveyed the bloody mess in the room. "You might want to pick up the place."

I laughed, despite myself. We went into the den, and I brought John up to date on what happened, adding what Ari and I learned from Kat. He listened thoughtfully, then gave me the concerned look a priest might give a parishioner who'd just lost his dog. "You need some help cleaning up your place?"

"I'll get a disaster recovery company to do it."

"I know people in the CIA who could make it look brand new."

"I don't doubt it. For an ex-priest, you have some interesting connections."

Kat walked over and said, "You've heard about the press?" I shook my head. "Word of the arrests is out. It'll be the lead story on tonight's news on the West Coast. And tomorrow's headlines in the Eastern papers. It's already online on CNN, although they haven't reported Luce's death. It won't take them long to put the pieces together. The story is rapidly gathering steam."

"I want to be kept out of it."

"Not an option, Sonny," she replied. "Rayburn's arrest is big news. Like it or not, your name is out there. SFPD Media Relations is being hammered with requests for information about you, and the media will google your band's website and find your bio and picture. That's how I looked you up before you came to Sacramento."

"I don't have to talk to the press," I said.

She chewed on that for a moment. "No, but you want some advice? It's better to be in front of a story than behind it—so long as your rendition fits the facts. It would be best if you shaped the narrative. Just tell the truth."

"All right," I said. "I'll talk to them, but on my terms. How will the police report this?"

"Watch the news tonight. Thanks to you, I'm the originating officer on the Rayburn arrest, so ICAC and the SFPD are having me front and center at the news conference." She glanced at her watch. "In about an hour."

Ari said, "You can spend the night at my place. I'll arrange for a crew to clean up here." The crew Ari talked about don't carry business cards and aren't for hire. They're in the Armenian underground in the Bay Area, friends of Sana Houssian, and they always owe Ari favors. I don't know what he does for them. Nobody asks and nobody tells.

On our way to BiblioTech, Xavier McQueen called, wondering why I hadn't shown up for the recording session. I explained, saying I needed a few days off. I had a message from Marcella Delgado, the reporter at Channel 5 News, wanting me to call her, along with dozens of other messages from reporters and news agencies requesting interviews. I didn't return their calls, but I did call my family. I didn't want them to learn about this on the news.

When we arrived at Ari's quarters above BiblioTech, Catherine Gauthier offered me herbal tea in a large ceramic mug. She had paint on her hands and wore a gray, paint-splattered smock over a pair of blue jeans and brown flats. Her long, red hair lay carelessly on her shoulders. She cupped my face with her hands and kissed the tip of my nose.

"You poor darling. What have they done to you?"

Not nearly as much as I did to them, I thought, but what I said was, "I'm fine, Catherine. I appreciate your concern."

Her thick lips were the color of rubies. She pushed them toward me in a pout that on the silver screen would have made grown men faint. "This tea is very soothing," she cooed. "You must drink some." It was strong and hot and smelled like flowers.

I lifted the mug in a toast. "Here's to beautiful artists with paint on their hands." She crinkled her eyes and gave me a luminous smile.

When she returned to her studio, I found my phone and called Mac's cell but got her voicemail. I apologized for the mess she had walked into and asked her to call me when she picked up the message. I was about to return Marcella Delgado's call when my phone rang. It was Kat, saying she'd just finished the press conference and I should watch the news.

"Have you interviewed Rayburn yet?"

"No, I'm headed to the hospital now with two FBI agents. We'll try to get a statement, but last I heard, he still couldn't talk. You bruised his throat pretty badly."

"I'm really sorry about that."

"I can tell. If Rayburn's smart, he'll confess and give up what he knows."

"You think he's that smart?"

"I think Rayburn's pretty much a steaming pile of shit."

"Very poetic."

"It's a gift."

I laughed. "Call me if you hear anything about Erin Hightower."

"Sure, but it could be weeks before we know anything."

I thanked her and was about to call Marcella when my phone rang. It was Fetch. I was a popular guy today.

"My God, Sonny, what happened?" His breathing was shallow and rapid.

"Are you hyperventilating?"

"Yes. No. No. We heard. An hour ago. It came over the wire. Marcella's been, uh, she's been trying to reach you. She wants an interview."

"Tell her I'll come to the studio tonight. Eight o'clock. She'll get her exclusive."

"I'll tell her. Jeez, are you all right?"

"Been better, been worse."

"Damn, Sonny, you could have been killed."

"S'okay, Fetch. I wasn't."

"Thank God for that." He paused and said, "By the way, I have something for you."

"Bring it to the station. See you there at eight. And catch your breath, Fetch. You sound like a fat man running a marathon."

Earl drove me to the station in a black Humvee and parked on the street. He wore black leather pants, a white wife-beater t-shirt, and spit-shined black combat boots. Two humongous silver rings were on his right hand. As he swaggered over to KPIX-TV's entrance, passers-by hugged the outer edge of the sidewalk and kept their eyes off Earl's menacing face. I didn't ask for a guard but smiled at his protective stance. When he'd seen my bandages, he spat a litany of Spanish curses faster than I could understand it, but the gist was that I'd been easy on Luce, and Earl was sorry the pig-assed mother humper hadn't found him first. I think that's what he said.

The interview with Marcella was predictable. She portrayed me as Superman without the costume. I said I was just lucky to be alive. She mentioned the Storm Lake Blues Band several times and closed by saying I'd recently prevented an assault at Cactus Jack's by single-handedly apprehending a knife-wielding assailant—and afterward played two more sets. She must have gotten that from Fetch. I made a mental note to strangle him.

Before I left, Fetch handed me a folded slip of paper. "After the other night, I checked the pockets in the windbreaker I was wearing. The woman in Green River dropped this when she grabbed the girl's hand. I must have shoved it in my pocket when I saw the guy watching me."

I unfolded the paper and tried to make sense of what I read. It was stamped "Salem, Oregon." Dated two days before Fetch encountered them in Green River. *Two* days before. About how long it would take to drive from Salem to Green River if they drove conservatively. "Son of a bitch," I muttered. "What the hell were they doing there?"

15

I woke up Thursday admiring those fictional tough guys who endure multiple beatings, are thrown through windows, leap from moving vehicles, escape by jumping three stories into a dumpster—and are ready in the next scene for more heroic feats. It doesn't happen like that in real life, not to musicians. I awoke with a throbbing shoulder, achy, itchy wrists, and a knee that felt like an elephant had crushed it. When I rubbed my left forearm, I discovered a painful bruise the size of a fist where I'd blocked one of Luce's thrusts. Only my head felt marginally better. As I lay there in ragged semi-slumber, I casually reached over to touch Mac. When I couldn't find her, I wondered if she'd already gotten up. Then I remembered how she'd left yesterday.

I wanted to sink into the pillow until the emptiness in my soul passed. Instead, I lowered my feet to the floor and gazed at the room. The bed occupied most of it. The walls were covered with graying floral paper. A lampshade had yellowed with age and had scarlet Victorian-era tassels festooned with cobwebs. The room smelled of dust and nostalgia. I made my way to the bathroom and took two Oxys and an antibiotic. Then I leaned against the medicine cabinet and stared into the sink. Rust stains trailed beneath both faucets, and mineral deposits had turned the sink's white surface scaly and dull. Breathing deeply and letting the air out slowly, I whispered to the sink, "I know how you feel."

Back in the bedroom, I pulled on jeans, a blue Monterey Jazz t-shirt, and loafers. The slip of paper Fetch gave me was in my front pocket. I re-read it, but my mind was slogging through quicksand, so I tucked it back in my pocket. My cell phone lay on a chest of drawers. I dialed Mac, thinking the call would go to voicemail as it was not yet seven, but she answered.

"Hi," I said. "How are you?"

After a moment, she said, "Terrible. I hardly slept last night."

"I'm sorry."

"You have every reason to be." I wasn't sure how to respond. After a beat, she continued. "I saw you on the news last night. And you're on the front page of the *Chronicle* this morning. They're calling you a hero."

"I could do without that part."

"Well, I'm glad they published those stories. I learned things I didn't know, which is surprising because after living together for years, I thought I knew you."

"Mac—"

"I don't want to argue over the phone."

"Me neither. Can we get together and talk about it?"

After a long pause, she said, "I suppose we should."

She didn't want to be around other people, so we agreed to meet at ten at the boat house on Stow Lake in Golden Gate Park. I closed the door and took out my sax. Putting the strap over my head, I rested my fingers on the keys and let the instrument hang from my neck. It felt like my oldest friend had come to visit. Closing my eyes and seeking music to match my mood, I played Sam Cooke's *A Change is Gonna Come*. I improvised around the melody but followed the melancholy pace of the song and then transitioned into Townes Van Zandt's *Waitin' around to die*. I lost myself in the music and didn't hear the door open. When I finished the Van Zandt song, I saw Catherine standing in the doorway, arms crossed, head leaning against the doorjamb. She looked lovely in a black sweater over gray slacks, her long red hair hanging in carefree tendrils around her face.

"I hope you don't mind," she said.

"Not at all."

"I've always loved to hear you play," she said, neatly wrapping me around her little finger. "Do you take requests?"

"For you, anything."

"How about Stardust?"

"Hoagy Carmichael," I crooned. "It goes like this." For the next fifteen minutes, I played *Stardust*, did some jazzy variations on the theme, and returned to the core melody at the end. I prefer that tune played softly on a trumpet, but it also sounds mellow on a sax. When I finished, her sweet smile was worth every note I played. "Can I ask you a question?" I said.

She waved a hand at me. "Of course."

"Do you ever worry about losing Ari? With all he's involved in, are you concerned that he could die?"

The corners of her mouth rose in a little smile. "No. No, I don't worry about such things. Worry is foolish. Better to treasure the moments we share. That's how I live my life with Ari. I take pleasure in every moment together. The rest is not for me to know, so I don't distress myself." She gave me a little smile. "Do you worry, dear boy?"

"Mac does."

She shrugged. "In every life, things will remain undone. Our work, our relationships, our plans? That's why I don't worry about Ari. I can't know what will be, so I can't tie a neat bow around my life with him. I can only cherish each moment."

"Even if it might be the last," I said.

She smiled. "There are no tidy endings. For most of us, life is an exquisite mystery that will end in mid-sentence."

She looked away, and I saw the lines around her eyes deepen, the shadows on her delicate, leonine face darken. It may have been a trick of the light, a cloud passing in front of the sun, or it may have been the passing of time compressed into an instant.

Later, I invited Ari and Catherine for brunch at Brenda's French Soul Food, a quaint Creole restaurant on Polk. They have a shrimp and grits dish Ari loves. After we agreed to meet at noon, I took a taxi to Pacific Heights to retrieve my car. Towering white clouds were billowing south and east of the City, their foundations turning grayer as they churned toward San Francisco. The wind was picking up, and the trees along Fell Street waved their arms, their leaves singing a warning. What had promised to be a bright spring day was turning blustery. There were already storm warnings on the bay.

I arrived at Golden Gate Park before ten and found a bench outside the boat house. The sun still shone on Stow Lake, but the wind blew ripples across the water, agitating the trees. Mac arrived a few minutes later. She was her usual fashion statement in black jeans and a black t-shirt under a chic gray jacket with studded lapels. Her dark hair fell around her shoulders in lazy waves, implying a more carefree mood than I knew she bore. She managed a slight smile when she saw me. We kissed, though it felt tentative, and she asked how I was. Okay, I told her. On the mend. We found a secluded spot with a park bench. Below us, two blue herons fished in the shallows at the lake's edge. They moved in unison, and we watched them before we spoke.

"I heard what they said on the news, but I want you to tell me. Why did they attack you?" I finally needed to be open with her, so I told her everything, beginning with Fetch's story about the girl in Green River. She watched my eyes as I told the story and gazed across the water when I finished. "I'm disappointed you didn't tell me this from the beginning."

"You wouldn't have approved."

"No. I would have tried to stop you before you went too far. You'll say you didn't go too far, but you were almost killed. Twice."

"I handled it, Mac."

She pointed to my bandages. "*This* is handling it."

"One of my attackers is dead. The other will never go free. Because I got involved, a group of pedophiles was exposed, and dozens will go to prison. Think how many innocent lives that will save."

"That's noble, Sonny, but you took a huge risk and didn't just risk your life. You risked mine, too. What would have happened if I'd been home when those men broke in?"

I looked away from her. "I don't want to think about that."

"I know you don't, but you have to. Your decisions have consequences. You can't just charge off and play the hero."

"That's not what I want."

"Yes, it is. You want to rescue this missing girl because maybe it will make up for not saving Aileen. You used to have nightmares about failing to save people."

"I still do."

"Can't you see them for what they are? You won't rest until you save the damsel in distress, even if it kills you and maybe kills someone you love."

"Mac, I don't want to put you or anyone else at risk, but if I don't look for this girl, I won't be able to live with myself, and that's the bottom line."

"If you find her, will that satisfy you? Will you be able to hang up your sword and shield and live a normal life?"

I looked away and watched the herons. She'd just asked one of the hardest questions anyone's ever asked me, and it deserved a thoughtful response. As the answer came, my gut tightened, and I felt the heavy weight of dread descending. When I looked at her, tears were already forming in her eyes. "Probably not," I admitted.

She breathed deeply and looked down. Tears rolled down her cheeks, and she whispered, "I was afraid you'd say that." She stood with hands on her hips and gazed across the lake. After a moment, she wiped her eyes and shook her head. "I can't do this. I'm sorry. For both of us." Then she walked away. When she disappeared from view, I slumped on the bench and spent the better part of the next hour mourning what I'd just lost. Shadows darkened the water, and trees grew more restless as the wind swept through them. Unlike poets, I couldn't grieve in words, but after my numbness passed, I heard blues in my head, one melancholy refrain flowing into another.

When it was time to leave, I walked through the thickening storm to my car and checked messages. I had two dozen from news agencies, which I erased, and one from Kat Hastings, which I returned as I drove.

"You doin' okay?" she asked.

"I'm pretty much at the lowest point in my life." I explained that Mac and I had just broken up, and a rock now sat where I once had a stomach. She commiserated and said she'd call me later, but I told her that discussing the case would take my mind off how I felt.

"Okay," she replied, not sounding sure. "Rayburn isn't answering questions, and the prosecutors aren't willing to deal with him. They have enough evidence to lock him away for a thousand years. The only thing Rayburn will say is that you tortured him, which is hysterical. His prints are all over the hammer, and none of your prints were on either weapon."

"Does Renicke know that?"

"Oh yeah. He's still puzzled by it. For the record, I don't care. What's new is that the task force found Luce's place in Oakland. In his driveway was a pickup with a camper shell. Inside it was an old comforter with dark stains, probably blood. The crime lab is testing it, but we're fairly certain he transported bodies in that camper. They also arrested Rayburn's wife, Renata Gonzalez, at a Holiday Inn in South San Francisco. She was waiting for Rayburn. They were headed to Costa Rica."

"Why there?"

"ICAC says there are enclaves of pedophiles there. Well-known to law enforcement but untouchable. A search of Rayburn's home in Danville uncovered evidence that Renata Gonzalez owns a small farm east of San Ramon. There's an abandoned house on it, along with a barn. Both pretty dilapidated. The FBI obtained a search warrant and has teams headed there."

"Rayburn didn't strike me as the farming type."

"It could be another porn production location, but from the surveillance photos, it doesn't look like anyone's used those buildings in years. They're falling apart. This is increasingly an FBI operation, so I'll be released from the ICAC task force tomorrow."

"Back to Sacramento?"

"Looks like it. Which is fine. I have my normal caseload there. But I'll let you know if I learn anything more about Erin Hightower."

"Thanks. Likewise."

I arrived at Brenda's before Ari and Catherine and waited outside in the wind for a table. While I stood there, I looked at the paper Fetch gave me. It was an intriguing clue—but to what, I wasn't sure. When my friends arrived, we found a small table inside. The restaurant was packed, and the air was thick with the aroma of roasted coffee, fried onions, garlic, and pepper. Ari and Catherine ordered Creole breakfasts, but I just had coffee and a piece of toast. I'd lost my appetite, and after I described what happened with Mac, they understood. When the food arrived, I told them about my conversation with Kat.

"Nothing new on the missing girl?" Ari asked.

"Not from the police," I said, "but I have one development." I told Catherine about the slip of paper that fell from the dark-haired woman's coat. "Turns out Fetch shoved it into a pocket."

I handed the paper to Ari.

"It's an ATM receipt from a Wells Fargo bank in Salem, Oregon. Someone withdrew five hundred dollars on April nineteenth, two days before Fetch saw them in Green River."

"The dark-haired woman?" Ari said.

"Presumably," I replied.

"Why were they in Salem?" Catherine said.

"I don't know. But if I'm right, they drove from Salem to Green River, a trip of about a day and a half. Then they continued on Eighty to Cheyenne and caught Interstate Twenty-five to New Mexico."

"ATMs have cameras," Ari observed.

I nodded. "This happened five weeks ago, so the bank should still have a photo of the person who withdrew the money. I need to confirm that."

Ari handed the ATM receipt back to me. "Wells Fargo will also be able to identify the account the money came from."

"And who owns the account," I added.

"You're taking time off from the band," Ari noted.

I nodded. "And I no longer have a girlfriend."

Catherine winced and reached across the table to squeeze my hand, but Ari offered no sympathy. He just crossed his legs and rested his chin on one hand. He looked thoughtfully at me and said, "You've had a tough week. I think you need to get away."

"You're right. I need a vacation, and I've never been to Salem."

Outside, the storm raged, sheets of rain sticking like glue to the windows at Brenda's. Fierce wind buffeted the front door, daring anyone to venture outside.

16

I arrived in Portland just after ten, rented a red Mustang, and drove south on Interstate Five. The storm raged over the west coast. A massive low-pressure system had parked on the edge of the continent, dumping rain from Vancouver to San Luis Obispo on the central California coast. It was expected to last three days and flood some areas. Moisture fell like a gray shroud, obscuring everything with sheets of rain that coalesced on trees and vehicles, ran in torrents into storm drains, and rose from the road like steam. Traffic on the interstate crept along at thirty miles an hour. I felt like I was trapped in a shower stall with the water running, but through beaded windows, I watched the Oregonian drivers around me patiently enduring the downpour. They were used to it.

I'd texted Mac from the airport and called her as I drove, but she wasn't responding. A bad sign. She gets tightly wound when the course she's on is not one she wants. She usually unwinds as her anger ebbs and decides that what happened wasn't as ominous as she feared. But the carnage in our home may have passed the tipping point. She's beautiful and intelligent but had a safe, middle-class upbringing. She's never confronted violence and death as starkly as she did two days ago with that horrific scene in her home. The thought of losing her gutted me, but I can't change who I am.

I crossed the Salem city limits just before noon. Salem is a sprawling, wooded city on the banks of the Willamette River. Built on gentle, rolling hills, it's a city of wide streets and low-rise buildings that feels more like a small town than a state capita l. From Wells Fargo, I learned that the ATM receipt came from Safeway on Lancaster. It was in a modern gray building with twin gables and a sleek, black metal roof. Inside, near a Wells Fargo satellite office, was a Starbucks, so I stopped for a cup of toasty Colombian while studying the bank's ATM and layout. Besides the camera on the ATM, I saw another surveillance camera in the bank and three more mounted on Safeway's ceiling.

I knew the bank wouldn't show me the video of the person who withdrew that money. Not without a subpoena. But I wanted to understand the place, see where it happened, and confirm what I thought was true. I showed a teller the ATM receipt and said, "I have some questions about the person who withdrew this money from your ATM."

"Is this your account, sir?"

"No."

"Are you a police officer?"

"No. I'm a musician."

Her eyes grew wide, and her mouth fell open. I guess that wasn't the answer she expected. I told her I wanted to know how long their bank kept ATM videos, and she said six months. I thanked her and left. You can't bluff your way into a bank's video records, and the only two cops I knew were in California. They couldn't show enough probable cause to justify a court order for an Oregon bank's ATM videos. I wasn't sure how to crack this nut until I stopped for lunch.

The Wild Goddess Cafe was in a quaint green building downtown. As I stepped into the alcove leading to the front door and shook the rain off my head, I saw a reward poster taped inside the window. In large red letters, it read, "Missing from Salem, Oregon. Angela Olivia Chang." The poster showed a photo of a beautiful Chinese-American child, five years old, with black hair and brown eyes.   She was last seen in her home wearing blue Scooby-Do pajamas. She went missing from her bedroom at approximately nine-thirty pm and may have been abducted by a Caucasian male about thirty-five years old wearing a Northwest Natural Gas uniform. Salem Crime Stoppers offered a $45,000 reward for information leading to Angela's whereabouts. Anyone with information should call Crime Stoppers, the Salem Police, the Marion County Sheriff's Department, or the National Center for Missing and Exploited Children.

I looked for the date Angela Chang went missing. April Nineteenth. *Holy shit*, I thought. On that same day, someone, presumably the dark-haired woman, withdrew five hundred dollars from the ATM inside the Safeway on Lancaster Drive. Two days later, she dropped that ATM receipt on the floor of a convenience store in Green River, Wyoming, where Fetch picked it up. *Holy shit.*

Salem's newspaper is the *Statesman Journal*. In their office, dozens of reporters sat at gray desks, hunched over their work, pecking at computers or murmuring on phones.

You could practically smell the next edition's deadline in the air. No one paid attention to me but a receptionist who had stacks of paper in front of her and was scribbling on a message pad. She was white as Elmer's Glue and hadn't brushed her hair since the Covid epidemic. When she glanced up, I said I wanted to see their newspapers for the past five weeks. She directed me to a visitor's desk with a computer terminal where everything was archived online. I began with the April Twentieth edition. As expected, Angela Chang's disappearance was the lead story.

The victim was taken from her home at nine-thirty Saturday night, the story said. Her parents, John and Alice Chang, had gone to the theatre and left Angela and her seven-year-old sister, Amy, and three-year-old brother, Nathan, in the care of a babysitter, seventeen-year-old Carolyn Reese, a neighbor who lives two blocks away. When Angela's parents returned at ten twenty, they found Carolyn unconscious on the sofa in their living room. They tried to wake her, but she was unresponsive. While John Chang stayed with Reese and called 9-1-1, Alice Chang went upstairs to check on their children. Amy and Nathan were asleep in their beds, but Angela was not in her bedroom. The frantic parents searched the home but found no trace of their daughter. When the Salem police and EMS personnel arrived, Reese remained unresponsive, but her vital signs were stable. She was taken to Salem Hospital in guarded condition after being treated for a suspected overdose, although police found no narcotics at the scene. Meanwhile, a search of the Chang home and the neighborhood that night failed to locate the missing child.

The headline in the April Twenty-first edition read, "Suspect arrested in child kidnapping." Nineteen-year-old Ronald Evan Case was arrested Saturday evening after police found him drunk and unconscious in the front seat of his 2008 Chevy Impala, parked against a curb one block from the Chang residence. Case, who'd been seeing Carolyn Reese for six months, had an empty bottle of whiskey beside him and a vial of Rohypnol in his glove compartment. A toxicology test of Carolyn Reese, the babysitter, revealed that she'd been given a high dose of Rohypnol. More commonly called "roofies," the date rape drug Rohypnol is known to cause amnesia and may be why Reese could not recall what happened to the missing girl. Case swears he was not drunk Saturday evening but can't explain how he and his car wound up near the Chang residence. He further denied having Rohypnol in his possession or giving it to Reese. Police are continuing their investigation, but one theory, attributed to a source in the Marion County Sheriff's Department, was that Case participated in the kidnapping with one or more individuals and became so intoxicated he passed out in his car. Police are still waiting for ransom demands from Chang's abductors. Meanwhile, a broader search of the area on Sunday failed to locate the missing child.

Later stories profiled the Chang family and Ronald Case. He had two arrests for possession of marijuana and one for assault and battery. Salem police indicated that Case was briefly a local street gang member, although his current ties are unknown. Meanwhile, Case continues to proclaim his innocence. Another story reported that Carolyn Reese had recovered some of her memory. After putting the three children to bed, she was watching television when the doorbell rang. A white male, mid-thirties, wearing a uniform, told her there was a natural gas leak in the neighborhood. She refused him entry but doesn't remember what happened after that. A canvas of surrounding houses indicates that no other homeowners were warned of a gas leak or were visited by a representative of Northwest Natural Gas. The utility confirmed that no gas leaks were reported in that area on April Nineteen.

The Angela Chang case was major news, but little additional information came to light in subsequent weeks. Ronald Case was charged with public intoxication and possession of a controlled substance but was not charged in the girl's abduction. Her whereabouts remained unknown, and neither the FBI nor the family had received a ransom demand. Like Erin Hightower, Angela Chang had vanished. The community rallied behind the Chang family and raised a $45,000 reward, which had produced no valuable leads. In the most recent story, dated yesterday, Special Agent Charles Iverson of the FBI and Detective Raymond Sobers of the Salem Police Department confirmed no new developments in the case.

I sat back in the chair and rubbed my eyes. I'd been reading for more than three hours and thought I'd learned all I could from the local newspaper, but on the chance I missed something, I returned to the April Twentieth edition and scanned it again—and that's when another story, buried in the middle of the paper, caught my eye. The headline read, "Stolen car found burning." The Marion County Sheriff's Department reported that a 2016 Ford Explorer, stolen from a shopping mall parking lot on the morning of April Nineteen, was found burning behind an abandoned grain mill near Hayesville at ten forty-five by a passing volunteer fireman, who called for assistance and helped put out the blaze but not before the fire destroyed much of the vehicle. Deputies and the fire marshal were investigating, but the initial report indicated arson.

Son of a bitch, I thought. Seven years ago in Sacramento, the people who kidnapped Erin Hightower had stolen a Chevy Malibu and burned it to destroy evidence. If the same people kidnapped Angela Chang, then burning the vehicle they stole for the abduction was part of their MO. Like the white van, their escape vehicle would be nowhere near the abduction site. The police in Salem hadn't made the connection between the Chang girl's disappearance and the burning Ford Explorer, but I was willing to bet they were connected. If I was right, the same people who kidnapped Erin seven years ago had just kidnapped Angela Chang. Why was Erin with them?

I found a room at the Grand Hotel in Salem. I told them I wanted their most soundproof room, and they put me in a suite on the top floor. I took a long, hot shower, re-bandaged my wounds, and put on a fresh t-shirt and pair of jeans. I called Mac but reached her voicemail and left a message. Then I called Kat and got her voicemail. While waiting for return calls, I played for half an hour, nothing special, just wandering around familiar tunes.

I never heard from Mac, but when Kat called me back, she asked how I was.

"Hanging in there," I told her. "What's happening with you?"

"A lot is happening here, though I'm no longer part of it. I'm headed back to Sacramento tonight. Remember the farm I told you about? East of San Ramon?"

"Owned by Rayburn's wife?"

"Yeah. Agents found an old well near the house that smelled foul. So they lowered a guy down, and he found human remains."

"Children's remains?"

"Right. The feds have already retrieved eleven bodies, but there are more. They don't know how many. The ones on top of the pile are decomposing. The ones on the bottom are just bones. They won't know how many victims there are until the water is drained. It's a pretty grim scene."

"Luce's dumping ground."

"So it appears. Forensic anthropologists will try to identify the victims, get photographs from the families, and match them to the children in Rayburn's porn films. If they can establish a link, Rayburn and his wife will be charged with murder. Still nothing new on Erin."

"They're not going to find her on Rayburn's videos. I think she was spirited out of California right after her abduction. I don't know where she's been since, but I'm convinced it was her in Green River. She was there on April Twenty-first when Fetch saw them, and two days before that, she was in Salem, Oregon."

"Whoa!" she said. "You lost me."

I told her about the ATM receipt and how that led me to Salem.

"You think the dark-haired woman used that ATM."

"Yeah. I was puzzled about what they were doing here, but now I know. They came here to kidnap another girl."

"What?"

"I think the people who kidnapped Erin seven years ago took another child in Salem on April nineteenth, two days before Fetch saw them in Green River. The victim's name is Angela Chang. Five years old. Abducted from her home while her parents were away. There's been no trace of her for five weeks and no ransom demand, just like Erin."

"You think Erin was with them?"

"She was with them in Green River. I don't have proof, but it stands to reason she was with them in Salem two days before that."

Kat was silent for a moment. "Maybe these cases are related. Maybe not. I hadn't heard about the kidnapping in Salem. What makes you think the same people did it?"

"The people Fetch saw in Green River were in Salem two days earlier. The ATM receipt proves that, although I want Fetch to see a photo of the person who withdrew the cash to confirm that she's the dark-haired woman. Then there's the MO. One, it was a clean, professional kidnapping done by a guy in uniform, someone people would trust. Two, no ransom demand. These kidnappers aren't after money. They're after something else. I don't know what, but the victims just vanish. And three, the same night the Chang girl was taken, someone torched a stolen car. Just like Sacramento."

"Son of a bitch," she said.

"Pretty much my take on it."

"All right," she said. "Granted, there are similarities. But why would they kidnap two girls seven years apart—and bring the first victim along on the second abduction? I don't get that."

"I don't either."

"I have a ton of questions." She asked for the name of the detective handling the Chang case and said she would call him.

"You need to come up here," I countered.

"I can't, Sonny. I have to get back to Sacramento. My caseload isn't getting lighter."

"No doubt. But as you told me, Erin Hightower is your case. We need a court order to see that ATM video. I'm a musician from California, and this local cop, Sobers, isn't going to take me seriously. But you're trying to solve another child kidnapping. You and Sobers together will have more weight with a local judge. If you discover who owns the account linked to that cash withdrawal, you'll get a lead on the kidnappers. In both cases."

After thinking about it for a moment, she said, "All right. I'll call Sacramento. If my boss won't authorize it, I'll take leave and fly there on my own nickel. I'll call Sobers and try to arrange a meeting tomorrow morning."

I told her to text me her flight details, and I'd pick her up. Afterward, I hung my sax from my neck. It was still raining. As I sat on the edge of the bed watching raindrops strike the windows, I thought about the children whose remains lay at the bottom of that well. Having no better way to give heartbreak a voice, I played the blues for hours, played as I thought about Erin and Angela, played for Catherine and Ari, who love my music, played as notes fell in familiar patterns to the beat of the rain striking the windows, played as I thought about Mac, remembering all the lovely things about her, wishing we would reconcile, where the man I am is a man she can accept, played until I my lips and fingers were numb, and I could no longer feel the hole in my heart.

17

I woke up Saturday morning with a head full of cobwebs and dust. A dream receded through the dark tunnels of memory, but I couldn't retrieve it. It had stopped raining. The sky remained overcast, and everything looked waterlogged, but it wasn't pouring. My shoulder ached. Everything ached. In the bathroom, I swallowed two Oxys and an antibiotic. The guy in the mirror looked as ragged as I felt. I took off the bandages, shaved, and stepped into the shower. Afterward, I decided against fresh bandages. A thin red line traversed my neck, and there were scabs on my wrists. But without the bandages, I looked less like a failed suicide.

My picture was on the front page of the *Statesman Journal*—alongside a mug shot of Billy Luce. I didn't want to go to the lobby and be recognized, so I ordered coffee, fruit, yogurt, and wheat toast from room service. While I waited, my phone rang. I smiled at the name on caller ID.

"What the fuck, man! You're a goddamn maniac," the caller cried.

"Hey, Garth."

"Jesus, partner. Guess you found some guys, huh?"

"They found me."

"Shit, dude. Knocked you out, tied you up, cut you, and you still killed one guy and fucked up the other one."

"I had 'em surrounded."

"Fuckin' A. Next time, call your brothers. Those were some bad motherfuckers, and you nailed their asses. I know a lotta bikers would eat that action up."

"I'll keep it in mind."

I no sooner clicked off when Xavier McQueen called with news that our albums were climbing the charts. Robbie Steffens, our manager, thought *Storm Warning* would go gold in a week. S'what happens, the X-man said, when your name's on the front page coast to coast. He asked when I'd be back, and I said give me another week.

Breakfast arrived, and I read the front page while I drank my coffee. The mug shot of Luce was from his arrest in Vegas for murdering a seven-year-old boy. The story was about the feds finding remains in that well outside San Ramon. They'd brought up seventeen bodies. Forensics linked Luce to the site, but they couldn't prove he murdered them. A sidebar profiled me, saying I'd uncovered the ring of pedophiles while looking into the disappearance of a friend's daughter, which wasn't true, but I wasn't going to call in a correction.

On the drive to the airport, I called Ari and told him what I'd learned in Salem. He said the police had released my apartment, and his crew finished cleaning it. Traffic ahead began slowing. Dark clouds were painted on the sky like daubs of thick gray paint applied with a trowel, and sheets of black were descending. The closer I came to the airport, the harder the rain fell. The pavement under the tires felt slippery, and raindrops danced on the hood like grease on a hot skillet. Outside baggage claim, I sat in the car, listening to rain pounding the roof until I spotted Kat. I rolled down the passenger window, honked the horn, and waved at her. She hurried over, nearly slipping on the wet pavement. She threw her bags into the back, jumped into the passenger seat, and slammed the door shut. Raindrops were beaded on her face, and her hair was streaked where water had soaked in. She wore a black suit, wet across the shoulders, and a shiny silver blouse. She smelled like wet gardenias.

"Thanks for picking me up," she said breathlessly. "I should have used my umbrella."

"It's just water. What time are we meeting the detective in Salem?

She glanced at her watch. "Eleven thirty. We okay on time?"

"We'll make it," I told her as I drove away from the curb.

She pulled down the visor and checked herself. After fussing with her hair and running a finger over her lips, she said, "How are you doing?"

"Better. No bandages."

"How's your girlfriend?"

That surfaced the heartache I'd been feeling. I didn't want to talk about it, but I said, "She's not returning my calls."

Her brows knitted. "I'm sorry to hear that. I hoped she'd get over it, but you know, if someone's not used to crime scenes, all the blood and the fact that someone died can be traumatic."

"Yeah. It freaked her out. She doesn't want me to get involved. That's the real problem. She thinks I should leave everything to the police."

"She has a point."

"She's worried about me bringing violence into our lives."

"As I said, she has a point."

I drove onto the interstate, reliving that awful moment when Mac walked into a crime scene that had once been our home.

"I'm accepting the fact that it's over."

She gave me a thoughtful look—maybe the kind someone gives you when their regard is more than casual, and I didn't know what to make of that. She was a nice-looking woman and had loosened up since I met her in Sacramento. The kind of woman you could be friends with. As I drove, I thought more about what had come between Mac and me.

"The bigger issue is that I can't avoid getting involved when something needs to be made right."

"That can get you killed."

"That's what worried Mac."

"Most women would worry. You always been like that?"

"More or less. After my legs healed."

"What happened to your legs?"

I told her about the home invasion and how I'd been injured trying to protect Aileen. "After that, I got into fights at school when I saw someone being bullied. I couldn't leave it alone. I got my nose bloodied a few times, but that stopped after I learned Aikido. When the bullies realized they couldn't beat me, they stopped bullying." We rode in silence for a while. When the rain came down harder, and traffic on the interstate slowed, I said, "If I stand by and watch it happen, I'm as guilty as the guy inflicting pain on someone else."

She glanced out the window at the rain beating on the pavement, the trees, and the houses beyond. I'd always imagined that rain washed everything clean, but the world outside the car looked drenched in misery. "I understand," Kat whispered. I could barely hear her above the pounding of the rain, but I thought she said, "It's why I became a cop."

The rain had let up when we pulled into the lot at Salem Police headquarters. Ray Sobers was a middle-aged, average-looking guy with medium-length salt-and-pepper hair that looked windblown. He had a pitted nose and bushy eyebrows, and yellow teeth, like an old wolverine. Sobers greeted us with a casual smile, stuck his hands in his pockets, and strolled back to a conference room with institutional green walls and a banged-up oak table and four chairs. A copy of his case file on the Chang kidnapping lay on the table. He told Kat she could hang onto it as long as she needed it. Sobers pulled out two chairs, sat in one, and crossed one leg over the other. He waved for us to sit in the other two chairs. He smiled at Kat, regarding her with an interested grin, casually glancing at her left hand. Kat filled him in on the Erin Hightower kidnapping, and I explained why I thought the two cases were related. While I spoke, he slowly cracked his knuckles.

"You want a court order for the ATM video?" he said to Kat.

"Also, the Safeway videos might show who used that ATM," I added.

He casually looked my way, a dawn of recognition on his face. He pointed a finger at me. "I've seen you somewhere."

"I have that kind of face," I said.

He turned back to Kat. "Well, that shouldn't be a problem. But I think you're off-base on this. Your kid disappeared from a shopping mall seven years ago. The Chang girl was taken from her home, and the low-life fuck-up who took her is in custody."

"Ronald Case," I said.

"Right," Sobers said. "This cretin's been on our radar a long time. He's your basic genetic mistake waiting for a place to go terminal. Ronny boy couldn't have done this alone. He's not that smart, but so far, he's not giving up his crew."

Kat said, "I read the sheet on Case. He's got priors for marijuana and assault. Going from that to child kidnapping is a major escalation for such a low-life fuck-up."

Sobers shrugged. "He didn't act alone."

"Why do you think he—or they—did it?" I said. "There hasn't been a ransom demand."

Sobers threw up his hands. "How the hell should I know? You want my two cents? Maybe the guys who have the Chang girl got cold feet when Case was busted. They figured Case would rat them out, so they buried the Chang kid someplace we'll never find, and they got the hell out of Dodge. Anyway, it's not my problem."

"Why not?" I said. "It's your case."

"Technically, but the feebies have taken it over. The guy in charge is out of the FBI office in Portland. Charlie Iverson. I'm the local yokel who's theoretically on their team because the crime happened in our jurisdiction."

Kat and I exchanged glances, and she said, "Should we ask Iverson about getting a warrant to see the ATM videos?"

"No, hell, we know the judges here. I'll take care of it. Won't be till tomorrow morning, though." He gave Kat a big yellow smile. "Speaking of which, I know some great places for dinner. Wanna join me?" His invitation was meant for Kat alone.

She smiled back. "I appreciate the offer, but I already have plans."

"Rain check?"

"We'll be back tomorrow morning. Nine o'clock?" Before he answered, she added, "Could I also see the case file on the Ford Explorer they found burning?"

He shrugged. "I'll have to dig it up for you."

"Could I get my own copy of that file, too? You've been a real help." We stood up, and he moved toward her like an electrical plug in search of an outlet. She deftly turned away, pretending to admire their facility.

Back in the car, I said, "Who are you having dinner with tonight?"

She gave me a smile that would melt ice in a freezer. "You."

"Thanks for reminding me."

It was late afternoon, and it was still raining. While I drove to the hotel, she called Sacramento and got the number for Charlie Iverson. We agreed to meet in the hotel's restaurant at seven. I worked out, favoring my shoulder, then showered and played my sax for an hour. I felt more ambitious, so I played some fast tunes in the spirit of Sonny Rollins. I didn't have a thumping bass and drums backing me up, but I could hear them in my head. When I came out of my reverie, it was five after seven.

The Grand Hotel's restaurant was called Bentley's. Kat was sitting in a corner booth, gazing into the distance, a glass of red wine poised just below her lips. I watched her for a moment and then slid across from her. "You're musing on something."

Her lips rose into that lop-sided smile of hers. She set down the wineglass. "Just thinking about today."

"Sorry you're not dining with Ray Sobers?"

"That dipshit."

I laughed. "I saw him checking out the ring finger on your left hand."

"Only after he checked out my chest. That's how men do it. Face, chest, ring finger. Or, if they're not discriminating, chest, ring finger, face. And if they're scumbags, chest, chest, chest."

That deserved a bigger laugh, and she joined me. A waiter arrived and asked what I wanted to drink. "I'll have the same," I told him. When he left, I said, "So did I check out your chest when we first met?"

"Just because I didn't catch you doesn't mean you didn't do it."

"Sorry to disappoint. Next time, I'll be more obvious."

"Don't be too obvious. I carry a gun."

"You're a crack shot, as I recall."

"Damn straight."

"All right. I've been warned." The waiter returned with my wine, and I raised my glass. "To finding Erin Hightower."

Her smile faded. "To Erin."

We looked at the menus. After deciding what I wanted, I said, "When we met in your office, I noticed a girl's photo."

That lit up her face again. "Sara. My daughter. She's eleven."

"I thought she was probably yours. Father?"

"Divorced three years. Typical cop marriage story. I worked the night shift too often, and his eye started wandering. He's still seeing the woman he slept with, the one I know about anyway."

"Was he a cop?"

"No. He owns a Sherwin-Williams franchise in Sacramento. Sara stays with him when I'm away." She took a slow sip of wine. "I miss her."

"I'm sure."

"Did you see the paper this morning?"

I nodded ruefully. "I have something like two hundred texts and voice mails from reporters and news agencies."

"You're the hero of the moment."

"Just a saxophonist with curiosity."

She gave me an understanding look. "Don't worry. It'll pass." The waiter returned to take our order. Kat ordered Oregon Rockfish. I had the pork rack chop.

Then she brought out a manila folder. "Before our food comes, maybe we can discuss the case." I nodded, and she pulled out some handwritten notes. "I called Charlie Iverson when I got to my room. I told him the scenario we're working on and learned that the toxicology report on Caroline Reese showed flunitrazepam in her system. The active ingredient in Rohypnol. She also had pentobarbital sodium."

"What's that?"

"Nembutal, a fast-acting sedative. A high-enough dose causes respiratory arrest. She had just enough to knock her out. Iverson thinks whoever attacked her injected Nembutal first. It would've put her to sleep within seconds. Then he injected Rohypnol to cause drug-induced amnesia."

"Sounds too complicated for Ronald Case."

She nodded. "Whoever injected it was trained and experienced. Beyond the skill set of a low-life fuck-up."

"That whole scenario is smoke and mirrors. The kidnappers staged it to divert local police from what happened."

"My thinking, too." She put her notes back in the folder and handed me an eight-by-ten photo. "This is a recent photo of the Chang family. Angela's the girl in the middle."

It was a family studio portrait with their names written on it. The parents, John and Alice Chang, sat in the rear, their faces composed and content. When this picture was taken, all was still right in their world. Five-year-old Angela sat in the middle of the front row. Her hair was in pigtails and she had elfin ears and two missing front teeth. Her impish grin conveyed the innocent delight of childhood. Seven-year-old Amy sat to Angela's left. Not as pretty a child, her face was rectangular, and she bore the serious expression of a child trying hard to be noticed. The responsible oldest sibling. Four-year-old Nathan sat on Angela's right. He looked bored.

"Something's bothering you," Kat said.

I glanced at her. "Why did they take Angela? There were three children in that house. The babysitter was drugged. The parents wouldn't return for more than an hour. They had time to do whatever they wanted. They could have taken the older girl. Or the boy. Or both girls. Or all three children. But they just took Angela. Why? Was this about made-to-order porn? Were they targeting a pretty Asian girl?"

"I don't know. When you arrived, you asked what I was thinking about. I was puzzled about the same thing. If you're right, these kidnappers drove hundreds of miles to snatch a child. They came a very long way. Of all the cities they could have chosen, why Salem?

Of all the families in Salem, why the Changs? And of the three children in that home, why Angela?"

18

The wind sounded like a two-hundred-ton locomotive roaring past—so loud it shook me to the marrow. The air beneath the door was sucked out and blown back in as though the house were attached to hell's bellows. Then came a ferocious rip-p-p-ping as pieces of siding sailed away, and the shingles flapped their wings like hundreds of startled ducks rising from a lake. The ground beneath the house rumbled, tremors cracking the walls, wrenching windows until they screeched. Above that, I heard a woman screaming from deeper in the house. The walls buckled as I hurried to find her, ceilings rippling as I ran from room to room, clawing past thresholds where pliant wood wrapped around my fingers. I found her huddled in a closet, curled in a ball, teeth chattering. As the storm bore down, I carried her into the cellar, the only place that seemed immune from the fury outside. It was musky, dark, and damp. I set her on the dirt floor, and she clung to me, her blonde hair wet and tangled around her face. I pulled her hair away and saw that it was Kat. Her eyes levied a terrible judgment upon me as she slipped from my hands and trembled in the fetid earth.

I heard a pounding on the floor above, a dreadful beating and crashing of timbers—the agony of the house being disemboweled. I flew up the cellar stairs and slammed the door, and when I turned back, Kat was gone. Leaping to the floor, I scrambled on all fours through the dark, trying to find her, but I touched nothing except cold, damp dirt. Then the house left its moorings and began spinning as it was sucked higher into the maelstrom. I sank onto my back, defeated, wishing all the tears of heaven could cleanse me, and then I woke up. I lay there, soaked, in a tangle of sheets, alone, in a room on the top floor of the Grand Hotel in Salem. Outside, the rain still fell.

I was still trapped in that nightmare when I met Kat for breakfast. I told her I hadn't slept well, and she asked if I'd dreamed about my girlfriend. I said yes before realizing I hadn't dreamed about Mac, but it was too late to correct my error. The thought of Mac dampened my mood even more than the endless rain. Kat finished her oatmeal and read the morning paper. I ate about half of my western omelet, but mostly I wanted coffee and drank three cups. My rain jacket was still damp from yesterday, but I had on fresh dry jeans and a t-shirt under it. Kat looked good in a black outfit with a gold blouse. When she saw me noticing, one corner of her mouth quivered upward, not quite a loopy grin but close.

We walked to my car under her umbrella. The air was heavy and cold, but I barely noticed. My nose was near the back of her neck, and she smelled like musk and amber and some floral scent, maybe plumeria. I opened her door and lingered in her scent as she slid inside and fastened her seat belt. Then I walked around the car feeling guilty about noticing anything about another woman and wondering if Mac and I had any shot at getting back together.

We met Sobers precisely at nine; he had the warrants we needed. Sobers looked dapper today. He wore a tweed jacket and brushed-wool slacks and had used gel in his hair. It held his hair in place, but now he looked like a high school lothario trying too hard at the prom. I caught him eyeing the top button on Kat's blouse a half-dozen times. I was embarrassed for the guy. If he asked me to be his romance coach, I wouldn't know where to begin. On the other hand, I've lost Mac, so what do I know about romance?

When we left, it had finally stopped raining, though it was still overcast, and the air carried that petrichor scent of rain. We arrived at the Safeway branch of Wells Fargo at nine-thirty. The manager who met us was a square-faced, frizzy redhead. When she saw me, recognition played across her face like ripples in a pond. She'd read the newspaper and remembered what she saw.

I held my hand out, and she took it. "Sonny Marshall. I was here on Friday."

She grinned like she was meeting a movie star. "Kaitlin Andrews. You're the guy who—"

"—is looking for a missing girl," I interrupted, "and the people who took her may have used your ATM. I brought the police with me," gesturing toward Sobers and Kat, "and they have a court order."

Sobers glared like I'd just yelled, "Who farted?" during a church service. I guess I'd stepped all over his prerogative, but Kat calmly produced her badge, and after a moment of hesitation, Sobers dug his out and handed her a business card. Then he pulled the court order out of his coat pocket.

"After your call this morning, detective," she glanced at his card, "uh, Sobers, I got here early and set everything up. If you'll follow me." After glancing at me, she led us to a desk with a large, gray monitor. She asked for the transaction number, and I handed her the ATM receipt. After a moment, she found the right location on the digital video and pressed play. But when the image came up, it was not a dark-haired woman. It was a young man with short, dark hair, thin lips, and a razor-sharp nose. He wore sunglasses and glanced around nervously after sliding his card into the reader.

"I thought we were looking for a woman," Sobers said in an amused tone.

"We are," Kat replied sharply.

The young man pressed the touchscreen a few times and retrieved what I assumed were his ATM card, receipt, and cash. I felt my heart sink. I was sure we'd see the woman who dropped the receipt on the floor in Green River. But as the young man turned away from the ATM, a woman stepped into view behind him, and although we couldn't see their hands, it looked like he had handed her the money. She had shoulder-length dark hair, a chiseled jaw, and a prominent nose. Like him, she wore sunglasses.

"Is that her?" Kat asked me.

"Could be. She looks like the woman Fetch described, but with the dark glasses, it's hard to tell." I asked Kaitlin Andrews if we could get some clear still shots of the young man and the woman. While she printed those, I told Sobers, "We need to see the Safeway videos. They wore dark glasses at the ATM, but it's rare to see people wearing sunglasses inside a grocery store. We need to see the woman's face without the glasses."

When Andrews handed me back the ATM receipt, I said, "You can tell from this receipt which bank the money was drawn from, right?"

"Yes," she replied, "and the account number."

"We need that information," Kat interjected.

"That wasn't listed in the court order . . . but, sure. Just a moment."

When she returned, she handed Kat a slip of paper. "I hope this is helpful."

Kat nodded and then studied it before handing it to me. Sobers read it over my shoulder. The money had been transferred to Wells Fargo from the Cayman National Bank Ltd.

"It's from an off-shore account?" Sobers said.

Kat looked at me. "These aren't your average kidnappers," she said.

I nodded. "They don't want their operating money traceable, and I'd bet the owner of the account is a shell corporation."

Kat nodded. "I'll call Charlie Iverson and see if they can trace the account." She looked at Sobers. "The feds will have more luck tracing an international account than we will." Sobers was silent, but his mouth turned down, and he looked away from her with a sour expression.

The Safeway videos were disappointing. We examined the tapes from the three ceiling cameras near the ATM, but none showed the two people without sunglasses. Then the store manager, a portly man named Von Drehle, suggested we watch their cash register cameras for the time and date in question. They were probably shopping for packaged snack items and drinks, which should not have taken more than fifteen minutes. We gave our estimate a five-minute margin of error, so we scanned the videos at every register from ten to twenty-five minutes after they left the ATM. We spotted them in line on the third register's camera eleven minutes after they withdrew the cash. Neither was wearing sunglasses. When the woman stepped up to pay for their purchases, we got a perfect look at her face, and Von Drehle was happy to give us prints when he learned we were working on the Angela Chang kidnapping case.

Back at Salem Police headquarters, Sobers asked a clerk to scan the photos. We had three good shots of the dark-haired woman, two without sunglasses, and two shots of the young man. Back in the conference room, Kat asked Sobers for the file on the Ford Explorer that had been found burning on the night of the kidnapping. Without a word, he left to get it. Sobers' mood had gone from happy-go-lucky and hopeful after drooling at Kat's gold blouse to sullen and surly. Instead of handing the Explorer file to Kat, he returned, tossed the report on the table, and abruptly wheeled around and walked out.

"I think you're frustrating him," I told her.

"He knows that eying the prize is as close as he's going to get," she said. "But there's wounded pride here, too. He abdicated responsibility for this case when the FBI got involved, and he knows we know he slacked off. We're showing him up in his jurisdiction."

"Professional pride is one thing," I said, "but he's not getting laid either. Double whammy." She laughed.

After the clerk brought us a thumb drive with the scanned photos, we borrowed a computer and emailed the images to Fetch. Then I called and asked him if he recognized the two people. While we waited, Kat opened the file on the burning Ford. The green Explorer had been stolen from the parking lot of the Lancaster Mall, not far from the

Safeway store. The owner reported his car stolen at ten fifty-eight am. When it was found that night, the plates on it had been stolen from another Explorer parked at McNary Field, Salem's municipal airport.

The car was found burning behind an abandoned grain elevator outside of Hayesville by Albert DeSilva, a volunteer fireman. He passed the elevator on his way home, saw smoke billowing behind it, and pulled into the access road. When he came to the burning vehicle, he called in the alarm and used fire extinguishers in his truck to begin dousing the flames. A fire truck arrived six minutes later and finished putting out the fire. What remained of a gasoline can was found inside the Explorer, along with the ashes of items piled on the backseat. Everything inside was destroyed except for two partially burned photographs under the front passenger seat. They may have fallen from the backseat and slid underneath the passenger seat, where they were somewhat protected from the fire.

Both photos were charred and bubbled, but the image on the first photo was clear enough to make out a white wall of a building with a cluster of low shrubbery that covered the lower right edge of the building. Above the shrubbery was a sharp-edged object that had one distinct ninety-degree angle, probably a window. The second photo showed a street with a curb on the right. A dark vehicle was parked along the curb, but I couldn't make out anything except the rear bumper and license plate. It was an Oregon plate, but the numbers were too dark and bubbled to read.

I asked Kat, "Would you indulge me in a hunch?"

"Why not? I'm on vacation. I can do whatever I want."

I smiled at her. "I'd like to see the Chang house."

"Okay. I'll see if Sobers wants to go with us." I nodded. It was better not to exclude him. It was his case, whether or not he gave a damn.

The Changs lived on a quiet, middle-class, tree-lined street in a neighborhood that looked like most other neighborhoods in small-town America. The houses varied in design, but not that much; the yards were green, neat, and trimmed; the trees were mature, their longest branches overhanging the sidewalks and streets; and nearly every house had flower beds and shrubs around its perimeter. The Chang home was a gray, split-level with stucco siding. There was a well-tended rose garden in front under a bay window and spirea bushes at each corner of the house, which softened the box-like effect of the structure. Next to the sidewalk on the front lawn was a huge maple tree, its majestic limbs arching out over the yard, the sidewalk, and the street. Beside the tree, a poster with Angela's photo was surrounded by flowers, stuffed animals, candles, cards, and yellow ribbons tied in bows—a prayer for Angela's safe return. All of it was a soggy ruin after days of rain.

Kat and I parked under the limbs of that enormous maple. Sobers drove a nondescript black sedan from the motor pool and parked behind us. The front of the Chang house faced south. Taking the photos from the burned Explorer, I faced the house and walked east. In the neighboring yard, an older woman wearing green coveralls and a wide-brim rain hat was pulling weeds from her flower garden. She kept her eyes on me. I walked until I could see the east side of the Chang house. I could hear Kat's and Sobers' footfalls behind me. When I reached the right vantage point, I crept toward the house, and the woman yelled, "Can I help you?"

Sobers replied, "Police business, Mrs. Bennett."

"Did you find little Angela?" Sobers shook his head. "We're all so worried. Such a little angel." Her voice was high-pitched and loaded with sugar.

"We're concerned, too, ma'am," Kat said. "We're doing all we can."

When I reached the right point, I held up the photo that showed the side of a building. Then I called to Kat and Sobers and asked them to compare the shape of the bushes on the northeast side of the Chang house and those shown in the lower right side of the photo. They matched. Exactly. The dark shape toward the middle of the image was the edge of a dark green window. I held what remained of a picture someone had taken of this side of the house.

"I'd be willing to bet," I said, "that this other partial photo is a shot of the street in front of Chang's house."

"I'll be damned," Sobers said. "Why would someone take these pictures?"

Kat took the photos and held up the one showing the bushes. After a moment, she said, "Surveillance. Before they snatched the girl. This wasn't the work of some local low-life fuck-up. These people are pros." She looked at Sobers, who had been listening with a blank look on his face. "This ties the stolen car to the kidnapping. Do you want me to call Iverson?"

"I'll do it," he said, snatching the photos from her. "Shit!"

My cell phone rang as Sobers trudged back to his car. It was Fetch.

"It's her," he said. "That's the woman I saw in the store."

I held the phone away from my ear and said to Kat, "Positive ID on the woman." Then to Fetch: "What about the guy?"

"I only saw him for a moment, but he looks like the driver. Oh, and the photo of the van? That was it."

I thanked Fetch and rang off. "The young man was the driver, and Fetch confirmed that the van was a Toyota Hiace," I told Kat.

I was startled by a high-pitched voice behind me. "Do you think you'll find her?"

Mrs. Bennett had walked up beside us. Up close, she looked older than at a distance. The skin on her face was gray and slack, and she had a scattering of small white patches on her cheeks and forehead. Her hands and arms were mottled with liver spots. This was a woman who'd spent a lot of her life in the sun.

"I hope so, Mrs. Bennett," Kat said. "We're following up on some leads."

"Everyone's so worried about John and Alice," Mrs. Bennett said. "And the other children. They're such a wonderful family. The children are so well-behaved."

"How long have you known them?" Kat said.

"Oh, my, let me see. They moved here just after Amy was born, so that would be, oh, well, it would be six years. Or seven. I forget. Amy was just a baby, and Angela hadn't come along yet."

"So you've known Angela all her life," Kat said.

"Oh, yes. Such a beautiful child. So good-natured. I never worried about her like I did Amy."

"Why did Amy worry you?" I asked.

"Amy's the oldest. She works so hard at being the best at everything. You know? Then Angela came along and did everything better than Amy without even trying. Whenever Amy was wrong, Angela would correct her. Not to embarrass her. But just because she knew the answers. Angela was reading when she was three and doing arithmetic at four. She was better at using computers than most adults. When my husband Frank was still alive, he liked to give Angela puzzles to solve—you know, those brain teasers—and she could always solve them. He couldn't fool her. She was truly the brightest child we'd ever known."

Out of the corner of my eye, I saw Kat's mouth rise in that lopsided grin she gets when she has an insight. I quickly thanked Mrs. Bennett and turned to Kat.

I took her arm and said, "What is it?"

She looked at me, wide-eyed in discovery. "That's what people told me about Erin. They said she was the brightest child they'd ever known."

19

We returned to our car, grappling with what Kat had just said. I stood silently at my door, and she at hers. Water dripped on us from the maple leaves towering overhead as we gazed at each other. Then she glanced at Sobers' car, and I nodded. While she spoke to him, I sat in our car listening to W. C. Handy's "Memphis Blues" in my head, drumming my fingers on the steering wheel to the beat. In Western music, the most popular musical form in the past century has been the twelve-bar blues, which Handy popularized. His simple song-writing formula has endured because it follows logical chord progressions and creates satisfying movement through the buildup and release of tension. The twelve-bar blues tells a story. We may not know where a song is going when it starts, but its chord changes are musically compatible, and the song ends in a satisfying, usually predictable way.

Mysteries have a lot in common with the twelve-bar blues. There is an underlying logic to them, although it's not evident at first. Each new fact you uncover is like another note in a song; the more notes you hear, the more of the melody you detect. As facts accumulate, patterns emerge, revealing the perpetrators' methods and motivations, how they've tried to cover up their crime or mislead pursuers, and what avenues a detective might take to illuminate what remains obscure. Discovering that Erin and Angela are both very bright was one of those facts, an important one because it could be pivotal in our understanding of the crime. But I wondered why people would kidnap two gifted five-year-old girls. That didn't make sense.

When Kat returned, she said Sobers was pissed and told her we're on our own from now on. "Asshole," she spit.

While her anger subsided, I said, "I've been thinking about music. The first note you play makes a statement. The second note creates an expectation. The third, along with tempo and duration, establishes direction. The fourth and fifth anticipate the melody." She looked at me with her head cocked to one side. "My point is that two instances of something don't make a pattern."

"No, but I don't believe in coincidences," she replied, calmer. "What are the odds that these two kidnap victims would be exceptionally bright?"

I considered that briefly. "One in ten thousand, assuming that exceptionally bright people make up no more than one percent of the population."

She looked at me quizzically and then burst into laughter. "How did you come up with that?"

"It's a simple joint probability calculation." She kept smiling at me, waiting for more. "Never mind. The point is that it's doubtful our two victims were chosen randomly."

She nodded. "You've made me a believer. There's a lot of similarity between these cases, beginning with the fact that both victims are very bright girls."

"Right. Girls, not boys. Five years old."

She brushed the hair away from her face, her smile fading, and looked past me. "The kidnappers came a long way to abduct them. That's a big investment in time and money."

"What else?"

She counted off more facts on her fingers. "The kidnappers are well organized. They work in teams. If these are not random victims, they're somehow targeting these girls."

"Which means they had to know them ahead of time."

"At least know of them."

"Right. Also, there were no ransom demands in either case."

"You thought they wanted Erin for sex."

"Yeah, but Fetch said Erin did not appear to be abused."

She shook her head. "ICAC didn't get a match when they ran her photo against the federal database. Something else. I had it for a moment." She lay her head back and closed her eyes. "A stolen car was used in both cases."

"Later burned. Both cars ditched close to entrances to interstate highways. They made the switch and got out of town fast."

"The victims were taken by men in trusted roles—a security guard and a gas company guy warning about a leak."

"Similar MOs but not exact. In Angela's kidnapping, they staged an elaborate diversion—the babysitter's boyfriend and that whole Roofies routine."

"As well as the Nembutal."

"Yeah. But in Erin's kidnapping, there were no drugs," I said.

"Actually, we think there were. It wasn't made public, but we think the guard gave Erin a Fentanyl lollipop. Do you know about them?"

"No."

"It's a mild sedative. Fast acting. They put it in special lollipops so kids will take it. Fentanyl lollipops are sold commercially and used by dentists and physicians to calm a child before a procedure. There's some controversy about using them, so they're not used widely today but are available. We think that's why Erin didn't struggle when the guard carried her out of the mall."

"So, in both cases, the kidnappers knew about pharmaceuticals."

"And had access," she said. "The more I learn about this crew, the more sophisticated I think they are."

I nodded. "Someone backs them. They draw operating capital from an off-shore account."

"Which requires planning and preparation. They're careful. They don't want to be traced. They wore sunglasses when they withdrew money from an ATM. And if they've done this twice," Kat began.

"They've done it more than that."

"Different places. Different jurisdictions." She shook her head. "If you hadn't come along, I would never have made the connection between this kidnapping and my seven-year-old case in Sacramento. Maybe there are more, Sonny. Maybe the pattern is so large we can't see it."

She turned and studied the Chang house. After a moment, she said, "But why five-year-olds? Why not ten-year-olds? What's magical about five-year-olds?"

"Because they're starting school? It's a transitional age. They're no longer toddlers. They're spending time away from their family. They're beginning to identify with a peer group."

She looked back at me. In the dappled lighting, only part of her face was well-lit—her right eye, the bridge of her nose, the yellow hair falling on her shoulder, the tip of her chin. The rest of her face was darker. "It's a mystery," I said, thinking about the case, but not entirely. "We need more." I looked beyond her at Chang's house. "I wonder if Alice Chang is home."

Kat followed my gaze. "One way to find out." We walked up to the front door. Kat pushed the doorbell. We heard muted scuffling inside a moment later, and then the door opened. The woman standing there was an attractive Chinese-American with large brown eyes set wide on her face. She had long, black hair and stood about five foot six. Although she was probably my age, the strain of the past five weeks had etched fine lines around her eyes and mouth, and her skin looked coated with a thin layer of wax. Her white blouse hung from her frame like oversized clothing on a JC Penney discount rack.

Kat presented her badge and said we'd like to speak with Alice Chang.

"I'm Alice," the woman said. Kat told her why we were there, and Alice said, "I don't understand. How could my daughter be connected to a kidnapping in California seven years ago?"

"There's a chance the same people may be responsible."

"Oh, my God. Do you think Angela's okay?" Alice said, her breath catching.

"We don't know, Mrs. Chang, but we're hopeful," Kat replied. "We have every reason to believe that both girls are still alive."

Kat told her about Erin Hightower and how she went missing. She added that a witness had seen Erin just over a month ago but did not tell her that we thought Erin had been in Salem when Angela was kidnapped.

When Kat finished, I said, "Mrs. Chang."

"Alice, please."

"Alice, your neighbor, Mrs. Bennett, told us how bright Angela is. We think that may have a bearing on the case. Can you tell us more about that?"

"I don't understand, but okay. Angela has always been exceptional. We knew from the moment she was born. She was a fast learner. As she grew, we tried to challenge her without slighting Amy or Nathan. It was difficult because Angela learned so quickly."

"Mrs. Bennett told us Angela was reading when she was three," I said.

That brought a small smile to Alice's lips. "When she was two, we gave her a chart of the alphabet. Within days, she had it memorized and could print all the letters. She practically taught herself to read. We did everything we could to help, but she needed more guidance than we could give. So we looked for special programs in Salem, and we joined a group called the American Society for Gifted Children."

"What's that?" Kat said.

"It's a national association that provides resources to parents and teachers of gifted children. They have tests for measuring a child's progress and create individualized programs for their advancement. Through them, we tested Angela's reading and math skills. ASGC told us her skills were at the fifth-grade level."

"So this group, ASGC, did the testing?"

"Yes. You register your gifted child with them and complete a questionnaire."

"What kind of questionnaire?" I said.

"Family information, date of birth, siblings, that sort of thing. Some medical questions, health, childhood diseases, our medical history."

"Why would they want that information?" Kat said.

"They create a profile of each child. Then they send you dozens of tests based on the profile."

"Like what?"

"Intelligence. Aptitude. Personality. That sort of thing. Based on the profile, they create a developmental program tailored to your child's gifts and interests."

Kat said, "When did you register her with this group?"

"When she was four. We knew by then we needed help."

Kat said, "Will you excuse me for a moment, Alice?" She walked back toward the car, digging her cell phone out. I asked Alice a few more questions, but my mind was on Kat. A few minutes later, she returned, her face intense and alive. "Alice, I apologize, but we need to go. We'll keep in touch and let you know when we learn something. Rest assured. We are working hard to bring both girls back safely."

I quickly followed Kat back to the car. When I climbed into the driver's seat, I said, "That was kind of a quick exit, detective," but she wasn't listening. She had a look of wonderment on her face, and she leaned back and smiled.

"I know how they targeted these two children," she said, turning to me. "I called Erin's mom and asked if she'd heard of the American Society for Gifted Children." She paused for a beat and said, "They registered Erin with ASGC, too."

20

"Iverson thinks the whole scenario is thin," Kat said. "It doesn't fit the FBI's paradigms for kidnappings." She'd called him as we left the Chang house and returned to our hotel.

"The fact that both girls were registered with ASGC can't be a coincidence," I argued.

"You don't get ahead in law enforcement by having an imagination."

I laughed. "Meaning what?"

"One of the lessons green detectives learn is to play the odds. Cops solve more cases by focusing on what typically happens in a crime."

"Man killed in the kitchen with a knife. Wife did it."

She nodded. "Nine times out of ten."

I shook my head. "No matter what the odds, ASGC is involved in this. I can feel it."

She nodded. "We need to learn more about them. Let's work on it over dinner." At the hotel, she went to her room to retrieve her laptop while I ordered room service in mine. Then I called Ari and told him what we'd learned in Salem. He hadn't heard of ASGC but said he would put some feelers out. Among my text messages, mostly from reporters asking me to call, I had one from Mac asking me to call her as soon as possible. Kat returned and sat at the desk, her legs crossed beneath it, as she booted up her computer and made a call. I gazed at her reflection in the mirror behind the desk while she talked. She absently twirled a lock of hair and made notes on hotel stationery.

I walked to the other side of the room and stood at the window, looking out at the parking lot and the trees and buildings beyond. After a few minutes of procrastination, I punched in the numbers. Mac answered on the fifth or sixth ring, and I asked how she was. She said she was fine, spending more time with her folks, which she hadn't done for a while, and it was nice to see them, and she was busy with work, a new show coming up, and she'd been looking at apartments but hadn't found anything yet, and she missed me, she wished things were different, and she'd been following the stories on the news, how awful it was about those children, and they were replaying Marcella Delgado's interview with me on CNN, and so on. She talked non-stop with a lightness in her voice that I recognized as anxiety. She had something on her mind she was afraid to say, something that felt like a confrontation, and she hated confrontations. So she had to work up to it using momentum as a surrogate for courage. When it finally came out, I was disappointed at her direction but not surprised.

"Oh, and, you know, I decided I just had to get out, so I went to dinner last night at Estiatoria Ornos, you know, love their petrale sole, and I saw some of our friends, David and Sherri, the Brewsters, and David looks like he's lost weight, which is great, because Sherri was worried about him, and I don't know if you've talked to them today, but anyway, I went there with a friend, and, well, he's more like a client, a guy I knew in college, and he's now a buyer for Nordstrom, and it's nothing serious, you know, but, just a night out with a friend, a client, but I didn't want you to hear it from David."

I let her ramble for a few more minutes before I said it was her life and she was free to spend time with anyone she wished. Only then did she ask about my injuries, and I said I was okay and not to worry about me. She told me to take care of myself. Then, her confession made, her anxiety purged, and her etiquette intact, she wished me well and said goodbye. I stared at the phone for a while and then gazed out the window at wispy clouds of scarlet and orange painted across the horizon as the setting sun gave way to the deepening gloom. So be it.

When I turned back to the room, Kat was off the phone. She gave me a sympathetic look and asked if everything was okay. I told her my shoulder ached a little, and I was hungry, but that was the extent of my complaints. She nodded, not believing me, and went back to writing notes. I walked to the bed and opened my iPad. The American Society for Gifted Children website revealed that the group was headquartered in Los Angeles but had branch offices nationwide. ASGC claimed to be the largest organization of its kind. Seventy-eight years old, it had more than one hundred thousand gifted children in its registry. Its mission was to advocate for the education of the gifted and talented, promote research on giftedness and gifted education, and be a resource for parents and teachers of gifted children. On the surface, that sounded benign. ASGC appeared to be a reputable group offering a valuable service. If ASGC was a façade for some darker purpose, they'd done a hell of a job disguising it.

There was a knock at the door—room service. We ate quickly, too quickly, and sipped our wine, mostly in silence. When we finished, I told Kat what I'd learned about ASGC. She typed while I talked.

"It's not much," she said, "but their website will paint the best picture. It's their face to the world, so blemishes will be air-brushed out."

I asked her what she had learned from her calls.

"Nada. They're not on police radar anywhere. No one's heard of them, and they're not on any watch lists. Squeaky clean."

"We have to dig deeper. What do we know about their director?"

Reading from her computer, she said, "Dr. Kaspar van der Heiden. Fifty-six. Born in Amsterdam. Undergraduate work at Erasmus University in Rotterdam. Then a medical degree from Harvard. Residency in neurosurgery at Johns Hopkins. Then, wait a minute." She scrolled down. "He spent a decade at the University of London Medical Center. Then went to an institute for brain research at Universität Leipzig."

"Brain research?"

"His bio says he's an anatomist and neuroscientist. Wrote a paper called 'The Anatomical Basis of Superior Human Intelligence: A Developmental Perspective.' For that paper, he dissected the brains of gifted children who had died before the age of ten. Here's another paper: 'Brain Architecture and Human Intelligence: The Structural Differences between the Brains of Average and Gifted Children.'"

"Maybe this whole thing is about medical research." I had trouble wrapping my mind around that. Child porn and pedophilia are horrible enough, but the thought of kidnapping children to dissect them was a depth of evil I couldn't comprehend.

"Think about it," Kat said, her voice flush with ire. "Through ASGC, he has a database of over one hundred thousand gifted children. He has test results and profiles. Remember what Alice Chang said. ASGC asked for the child's and parents' medical history. Why would they need that information?"

"If all they're doing is advising parents and teachers on educating gifted children, I can't see how their parents' medical history would matter."

Kat rocked back in her chair. "This is a sweet deal for him if he has no scruples. Instead of waiting for a gifted child to die and asking the parents' permission to dissect their dead child's brain, he can choose whichever child he needs for his research. He can pick the characteristics that matter to him: age, gender, race, medical condition—"

"How the child is gifted," I added. "Math, science, art, music, language."

"One possibility," she said, "is that the kidnap team works for him. He selects the target. They execute the kidnapping."

"Maybe Angela Chang was targeted not only because she's smart but because he needed an Asian specimen."

"But if what we're assuming is true, why is Erin still alive?"

I shrugged. "Didn't fit the profile he needed? Maybe he wanted to watch how she developed and will examine her brain later. Whatever the reason, he kept her alive."

"For now." Kat closed her laptop and stood up, and stretched. When she raised her arms and arched backward, the fabric of her gold blouse strained over her chest. If she'd caught me looking, I wouldn't have apologized.

I said, "Our plane is at eleven. We should be out of here by eight-thirty."

She looked at me with a little loopy smile. Something on her mind. "I see you brought your saxophone. Could you play something for me?"

It was late, but never too late for that. Not with a beautiful woman to play for. I opened with smooth jazz: *Feel Like Makin' Love* and *Try a Little Tenderness*. Then I played some Stan Getz, David Sanborn, and some Sonny Marshall improvs, playing around in A minor and D flat, catching melodic phrases and stringing them together with smooth bridges—the kind of pleasure I usually have by myself. Kat sat with her legs crossed, arms lying casually on her thighs. She rocked gently with the tempo of the music, head bobbing ever so slightly, eyes closed, a dream on her face. When I finished, I asked if she had any requests. She contemplated that and said, "I've always loved that Roberta Flack number. *Killing Me Softly with His Song*."

That one took me back to my college days. I hadn't played it since. I remembered how it went, then closed my eyes and let my musical memory guide me. I played it softly, as the song requires, sliding between some notes, hitting others crisply, and performing a gentle tremolo on longer notes. Now and then, I opened my eyes to watch her. Midway through, tears formed in her eyes, and I wondered if the song had some special meaning for her. When I finished, she wiped her eyes, gathered her things, and walked over to me. She put one hand on my uninjured shoulder and squeezed gently.

"Thank you. That was wonderful," she said, leaning in and kissing me on the cheek. "I'll see you at breakfast." She turned and walked to the door, pausing on the threshold to look at me again with a closed-lipped smile that lay somewhere between sadness and possibility.

I wiped down my sax and put it away. When I play, nearly everything leaves my mind except the music. But tonight, Kat occupied my mind, too, and I allowed that sweetness to settle in my blood, ferrying warmth throughout my body before the concerns of the day wormed their way back in. I was preparing for bed when my phone rang. I thought it might be Kat, but caller ID said Paul Fisher, and I answered it. "Sonny," he began. His voice was shaky, and he paused, catching his breath.

"What's wrong?"

"He did it," Paul managed.

"Who did what?"

"Annie's in the hospital. In a coma. He could have killed her. Nearly did."

"What happened?"

"He broke into her place. Sidwell. Kicked the door in. She's . . . she's hurt bad, Sonny. Ruptured spleen. Severe concussion. Broken hand. Her face is beaten to hell. He broke all the fingers in her right hand. Knocked out some teeth. She's on a ventilator."

"I'm sorry, Paul. I thought the guy got the message."

"I'm going to kill the son of a bitch."

"No, you're not. You can't touch him. You know that. Is he under arrest?"

"No. Insufficient evidence. There were no witnesses."

"But you know it was him."

"Yeah. She was still conscious when I got there. I asked if he did it. She nodded."

"Then arrest him for attempted murder."

"I don't want him in the system," Paul said with iron in his voice. "He'll be on the street again in twenty-four hours."

"So when she comes out of the coma, she can testify. Then you can arrest his ass. Put him away for ten years."

"I don't want him in the system. I want him permanently out of her life."

"I know you want to unplug this asshole, but you can't go near him. Are you listening to me?" When he didn't answer, I said, "Look, I'll be back in the City tomorrow. Early afternoon. I'll take care of it. I just want you to do one thing for me."

He struggled for a minute, his breathing ragged. Then he said, "What?"

"First, calm down. Have a drink. Go home. Get some sleep. Tomorrow, have someone locate him. Don't do it yourself. Have a cop find him and keep him under surveillance.

When I return to the City, I'll call you, and you tell me where he is. It'll be around one-thirty. Then leave the rest to me. Don't go near the guy yourself. Okay? I'll take care of it."

"All right," he said wearily. "I'm sorry."

"It's not your fault, man. Guy's a slimebucket. And a slow learner. He needs a lesson he won't forget."

"Don't kill him."

"Not my style."

"I don't want him near her again."

"Count on it. Now calm down and go home."

After I hung up, I called Ari and told him what had happened.

"What do you need," Ari said.

"Earl. For a couple of hours tomorrow afternoon."

"What time?"

"Maybe around two o'clock. I'll call his cell and tell him where and when to meet me."

"You got it."

21

I still grieved about Mac when we flew back to San Francisco the following morning. I felt like my heart was stuffed in my ears as Kat told me she would return to the ICAC task force to compare ASGC's registry of gifted children with the FBI's national database of missing children. She'd need a subpoena and wasn't sure Iverson would cooperate since he was skeptical about the connection between the two kidnapping cases. But it was worth a try. We agreed to meet for dinner that evening at Scoma's on Fisherman's Wharf and fly to LA tomorrow to scope out ASGC.

I punched in Paul Fisher's cell number while waiting for a taxi. He picked up almost immediately. "I'm here," I told him. "At the airport. Do you know where he is?"

"Yeah. He's in the Tenderloin at a bar on Larkin called Bixby's. He's been there for most of an hour."

"I know the place. Is he alone?"

"Yeah."

"Okay, pull your watcher out of there. Out of the whole area."

"All right. Call me later, okay?"

I told him I would. Then I phoned Earl and asked him to meet me in front of the Halston Hotel, about a block and a half from Bixby's. It was going on a quarter to two. My taxi got there in less than thirty-five minutes. I paid the cabbie and waited for Earl. He drove up a few minutes later in his black Chevy Camaro, and I stored my things in the trunk of his car. I told him who the target was and what I had in mind and then walked down Larkin while Earl parked his car. I was just blocks from the high-rise financial district in the City where the well-dressed and well-connected walked to charming little bistros for lunch and ate *steak au poivre* or *coq au vin*, but this stretch of Larkin was more like a third-world war zone. Ahead of me was a coin laundry with piss-yellow siding and dark windows. A forty-something black woman who looked sixty-something was parked outside the door. She wore a shapeless red jacket and a long brown skirt, and her hair spilled out in tangled braids of black from underneath a thread-worn knit hat. Her lips were sunken like she had no teeth. She smacked them as she stood watch. As I approached her, a young black man in a white t-shirt and black jeans stumbled out of the laundry and sank onto the sidewalk. A ragged residue of white crystals lay on the side of one hand, and he brought it to his nose and snorted. I paid him no mind, but the old woman gave me a defiant look anyway.

Beyond the laundry was a small grocery and liquor store. Three men loitered on the sidewalk outside the entrance. A long row of black plastic trash barrels lined the sidewalk next to the street, so passers-by had to walk between the barrels and the men to reach the corner. Two of them had bandanas around their heads, and they wore low jeans and black boots. They weren't talking to each other or doing anything in particular, just hanging out, and none paid attention to me as I drew near. But this was a classic trap. When the victim passed the first guy, that guy would fall in behind him. The middle guy would roust the victim while the other two pinned him between themselves and the trash barrels. No escape. No option but to give them what they want and pray they don't plant a knife between your ribs.

I feigned looking in store windows as I walked, but I had my hands at my sides, fingers curled, my arms taut, and a confidence in my stride that said I was alert and ready. I scanned the scene with studied nonchalance, not looking them in the eye but knowing where everyone and everything was around me. It's called situational awareness, and the slight relaxation of their bodies told me they noticed. Street people who will fuck with somebody won't fuck with you if you don't look like someone who can be fucked with. As I passed them, I glanced toward the door of the grocery, that glance giving me good peripheral vision of all three men, and I nodded slightly as if to say, "I know you know I know."

Bixby's was across the street and another half block beyond the liquor store. I arrived there just as Earl crossed the street before me and caught my eye. He was carrying a tire iron and had the kind of menacing smile on his face that I'd seen in films of hyenas stalking their prey. I asked where he'd parked his car. He told me and tossed me his keys. Next to Bixby's was an empty lot, a dented chain-link fence around it. The lot had seven cars parked in it. At the rear of the lot was a small brown van whose sides were dented and scraped. I nodded at the van, and Earl glanced at it and nodded in response. I knew Bixby's. At the back of the building was a door that opened into the lot on the far side of the van. It would be isolated there. Away from curious eyes and ears. Perfect.

Bixby's was a one-room shithole with a bar along the right side of the room as you came through the front door. There were booths and tables along the opposite wall. It was dark and old and hadn't been renovated or even cleaned in half a century. Whoever owned it didn't give a damn. Neither did the police or the City's building inspectors because nobody cared about the drunks, pimps, whores, and addicts who wasted their lives there. I saw Sidwell as soon as my eyes adjusted to the darkness. He sat at the bar with his back to me. He was hunched over a plate of something. Cigarette smoke curled up over his left shoulder, and he clenched a glass of beer with his right hand. Seven other people were in the place, including the bartender, and a few gave me a once-over to see if I was a cop. Then they went back to whatever misery they were nursing. The bartender was a lean white guy with hard edges on his face. He wore a filthy white shirt rolled up to his elbows and had prison tats on his forearms. He was drying glasses with a dish towel. He studied me momentarily and then returned to his work when he caught me watching him. In this part of town, steady eye contact is a challenge often met with violence.

I walked toward the bar like I was going to pull up a stool, but as I reached Sidwell, I came up quickly behind him, raised my right hand, fingers splayed, to the back of his head, and jack-hammered his face down onto the plate of whatever slop he was eating. He cried out as food exploded from the plate, brown goop splashing on him and all over the bar. Then I grabbed the collar of his jacket and jerked him sharply backward. His arms flew over his head, and his legs kicked out as his momentum carried him past the tipping point of the stool, and he and the stool pancaked in slow motion onto the hardwood floor with a loud whoop.

Blood spurted from his nose, and he screamed, "Muthafucka," as he clawed the slop out of his eyes.

Before the bartender could react, I pointed my finger at him and growled, "You didn't see a goddamn thing."

"Fuck, no, man," he said, averting his eyes and continuing to dry a glass. I glanced around the room. Everyone else in the place had quickly retreated into their own world.

"When that shithead comes to his senses," I told the bartender, "Tell him I went out the back door."

I turned toward the back of the bar but kept watch on the bartender in case he had a fit of heroics. In the background, Sidwell was cursing as he struggled to figure out what happened. I walked through the small office at the back of Bixby's and out the back door. After the darkness inside, the sunlight hurt my eyes. I shielded them with one hand while I surveyed the lot. The dented van we'd seen from the street was to my right. To my left were four galvanized trash cans and enough crap on the ground to fill twice that number if anyone bothered to pick it up. I walked to the back of the van and waited for Sidwell.

A few minutes later, he stepped through the doorway, looking like he'd lost a violent food fight. Brown gravy was splattered in his hair and on his face and hands and was smeared on his shirt and jacket. His nose was raw and red, blood still pouring down his chin. He squinted in the bright sunlight and rubbed his right arm across his face. As he did, I saw something shiny in his right hand. It was an automatic, nickel plated, with a small bore, probably a twenty-two, what street people call a double deuce.

"I warned you to stay away from Annie Porlier," I yelled. "You don't listen, shithead."

He waved the gun at me, his eyes struggling to make me out in the glare. "I'm gonna fuck you up, you fuck," he screamed. He started toward me but hadn't taken two steps before Earl hit him across the back with the tire iron. Sidwell went down hard, his chest and chin bearing the brunt of his fall. He still held the gun in his right hand, but Earl stomped on that hand and then kicked the gun under the van. Sidwell let out a guttural howl, rolled onto his side, and held his broken hand before him. He tried to leverage himself up with his left hand, but Earl was on his back instantly and muffled his cries by driving his face down onto the asphalt.

"Don't kill him, *guey*," I said when I reached them, using Mexican slang for *homie*. "He's a slow learner, but that doesn't warrant a death sentence."

"Sí, está bien, compa." Okay, partner.

"In English," I said. "He needs to know what you're saying." Earl looked at me and grinned. I fished his car keys out of my pocket and said, "I'll get your car."

As I walked away, I heard Earl say, *"Cabrón, puta."* Bastard, whore. "You like beating women, uh? Makes you feel like the big man. *¿Pues, puta?"* So, whore? "Why you do that?"

Sidwell responded by spitting a glob of something onto the pavement. Then I heard a snap, and Sidwell cried out sharply before sinking into a long, agonizing moan. It was almost hard to listen to. I tuned them out as I left the parking lot, walking past street people who took no more notice of Sidwell's cries than they would a barking dog, squealing brakes, or gunfire. In the Tenderloin, commotion is as common as smack. Twenty minutes after I sank into the driver's seat of Earl's Camaro, I saw him turn out of the parking lot. I fired up his car and picked him up.

"*Gracias, guey,*" I said.

We fist bumped, and then Earl stared through the windshield, rubbing the knuckles on his right hand. He had a fierce light in his dark eyes and sat there coiled as though he were simmering with the energy of a volcano about to erupt. "*Olvidate,*" he whispered. *It's nothing.*

I drove us to BiblioTech. On the way, I called Paul Fisher and told him Sidwell wouldn't hurt Annie again. He didn't ask for details. He didn't want to know. When we arrived, I got my things out of the trunk. Earl came around to the driver's side of the Camaro, and I handed him the keys.

"*Hasta pronto,*" I said. *See you soon.*

Earl gave me a steely look and said, "*La próxima vez lo mataré.*" *Next time I will kill him.* I'm not sure what demons inflamed Earl's temperament, but I nodded and went inside.

Ari and John were waiting for me at BiblioTech. I told them how it went with Sidwell but said we needed a more permanent solution. Not a grave but a relocation and an incentive not to return. As long as he remained in San Francisco, Porlier and other women he thought he owned would be at risk. After we tossed around some options and settled on a plan, Ari called Sana Houssian and put things in motion. I was about to ask Ari if he'd learned anything about Kaspar van der Heiden when someone knocked on the door and brought in coffee for us. It was hot, toasty, and rich, and it helped me calm down after the incident at Bixby's. While we drank it, Ari asked me to update John on what we'd learned in Salem, so I summarized it.

Afterward, John said, "You think the kidnappers selected these two girls because they were both registered with this association?"

"We think that's how they identified them. Both girls are brilliant. We think that's why they were chosen."

"But for what purpose?"

"I don't know. Given van der Heiden's background, the only plausible thing we could think of is that he wants them for medical research. He's a brain anatomist."

John sank back in his chair. "Dissecting the brains of smart children?" He took a sip of coffee and then tapped the cup with one finger. "Sorry. I don't buy it."

Ari gave him a curious glance. "Why not?"

"This group's been around for how many decades?" John said. "They've got a staff of hundreds. Well-developed systems and IT processes. That's a lot of record keeping, checking, and double checking, eyes watching what's going on, people who aren't in on the dark secret who would notice something out of the ordinary. And they're led by a mad doctor with a hidden lab somewhere?" He folded his hands and shook his head slowly. "Their offices are in Los Angeles, not Transylvania. If I were experimenting on children, I'd pick someplace remote where people won't notice and aren't asking questions. I'd have one or two trusted confederates, not a large staff who believe in the association's lofty mission and would blow the whistle on murder."

John's arguments made sense, and I had no other plausible explanation. I asked Ari if he'd learned anything useful about van der Heiden.

He shook his head. "I cast a pretty wide net, but nobody's heard of him. FBI. CIA. Interpol. Nothing. So I called a friend at the UCLA Medical Center, and he said van der Heiden is well respected in the medical community. I got the same response from the AMA and the Association of Clinical Research Professionals. If this man is Doctor Frankenstein, he's hiding it well."

I had the same sinking feeling I had in Salem while researching ASGC on the Internet. On the surface, ASGC and Kaspar van der Heiden looked clean.

John shook his head. "Van der Heiden has a lot of visibility. You need to consider the possibility that this guy had nothing to do with the kidnappings."

Ari asked about Mac, and I told him she was incommunicado at the moment, and I wasn't sure our relationship could be resurrected. They commiserated with me, having had good relationships end badly in their earlier lives. But who hasn't? I told them I was flying to LA tomorrow and wanted to investigate ASGC and talk to van der Heiden to get a feel for the man.

"You want company?" John said.

I shook my head. "Kat's going with me."

They glanced at each other. Then John's face lifted into a devilish smirk, and he said, "You still think she's an officious twit? Isn't that what you called her?"

"I'm revising my opinion on that. But don't get the wrong idea. She's good company, but she's a cop and is just doing her job."

"Okay," John said, still smirking.

My condo had been scrubbed clean and put back together. Ari's Armenian crew. No blood. No trace of the carnage. As though it never happened. But all Mac's things were gone, too, and it no longer felt like home.

I decided not to take my sax to LA. We wouldn't be there long enough, so I put it away. I sat in my music room for a while, listened to blues in my head, then checked my mail and paid some bills. I unpacked and threw fresh clothing into my canvas bag. Before leaving for dinner, I took two Oxys. My knee had a warm buzz, and my shoulder ached.

At a quarter to six that evening, I parked near Scoma's and walked two blocks to the restaurant. Although the day had been warm, a damp chill had arrived, a cool breeze blowing in from the bay. Tourists crowded the Wharf, some gathered before restaurants, pulling their coats tight, reading menus, and debating the merits of this place or that. I could smell the fishy odor of salt water, wet wood off the pier, and the spicy aroma of grilled shrimp and fish. Scoma's is on Pier 47 in an unpretentious white building with blue trim and awnings. Kat was already seated. She'd taken off a burgundy jacket. Her caramel-colored satin blouse reflected the ceiling lights, and she wore a gold chain around her neck. Warm gold and deep reddish brown, shifting as she moved. Caramel and gold looked good on her. It emphasized her moonstone eyes. But in my frame of mind, I suppose any colors would have looked good on her. She was drinking white wine and held her glass with both hands. When I walked up, she smiled and said, "I would have ordered for you, but I wasn't sure what you wanted."

I sat across from her and asked what she was drinking. A Beringer chardonnay. Good choice, but I needed something more potent, so I told the waiter Ben Nevis. Neat.

"You're a scotch drinker?" Kat said.

"Sometimes. This evening I'm in the mood."

"Are we celebrating something?"

I shook my head. "I wish. I don't have anything new. Kaspar van der Heiden appears to be spotless. If he's Catholic, we should nominate him for sainthood." She laughed. "How'd it go with you?"

"Better. I talked the FBI into comparing ASGC's list of registered children with their list of children who've gone missing. It took an hour on the phone with Iverson, but the subpoenas are in process. That's the good news. The bad news is that their tech people will need two or three days to do the comparison once the subpoena's been served."

"The wheels of justice turning slowly."

"Sometimes forensics takes forever. You wait weeks to follow up on a hunch because you don't have the reports. And sometimes you have all the forensics available, and every lead goes nowhere." She took a long sip of wine and gave me a rueful look.

"We're going to find her," I said. "Erin's still alive. I think both girls are."

When the waiter returned, we ordered dinner and talked about the City, the weather, the Giants, her daughter Sara and what eleven-year-old girls worry about. Afterward, we ordered coffee, and I asked if she'd discovered anything.

"Just something curious. It probably means nothing."

"What?"

"That white van your friend saw in Wyoming. You thought it might be headed to New Mexico."

I nodded. "Yellow rear plate. No front plate."

"I wondered if anyone in ASGC other than van der Heiden had a background in medical research, so I looked up the other members of their executive team and board of directors. No one else has a degree in medicine, but one board member has an address in New Mexico."

"Who?"

"Ruth Bellamy."

I shrugged. The name meant nothing to me.

"I hadn't heard of her either, so I looked her up. She's the daughter of Joseph Barnard."

"The billionaire?"

She nodded. Everyone had heard of Joseph Barnard. As I recalled, Barnard was an arms manufacturer. He made billions supplying munitions to the military during the wars in the Middle East. He was one of the wealthiest men in the country and, outside of Gates, Bezos, Buffett, King Charles, and some oil sheiks, probably in the world.

"Ruth Walsingham Bellamy is Barnard's youngest daughter. She—the whole family—they're real blue bloods. They trace their roots to the Mayflower. She has three brothers and one sister, and they're all on Forbes' list of billionaires."

"She lives in New Mexico?"

"Her principal residence is New York City. She and her husband own one of those grand penthouses overlooking Central Park. Huge art collection. Picassos, Monets, Renoirs. And they have an estate in Tuscany. Outside of Florence, near the Medici castle. But she also has a post office box in New Mexico."

"A vacation home?"

"That's what I assumed, but it didn't feel right."

"Why not?"

She set one elbow on the table and rested her chin on her hand as she thought about it. "I read a lot about her this afternoon. Ruth Bellamy was born in Connecticut. Graduated from Vassar and Yale. Strictly Ivy League. She's forty-six, married, sits on four boards—the Metropolitan Opera, Museum of Modern Art, New York Public Library—"

"And the American Society for Gifted Children."

"Right."

"Sounds more like Citizen of the Year than a kidnapping suspect."

She nodded. "It doesn't make sense that she'd be involved in crime. She's on the A list in New York society. There are scores of stories about her in the *New York Times* and other Eastern newspapers and magazines. *Vogue* profiled her a few years ago. I read an article about her in *The Atlantic*. Attends the most fashionable parties. Underwrote a new building on Yale's campus. A frequent guest at the White House and spends a lot of time in Europe. But in everything I read, I couldn't find a single piece of evidence that she had interests outside of New England and Europe."

"Except for that post office box. As I said, maybe she has a vacation home. Some place where she and her family can go and not be bothered. A lot of wealthy people have places like that."

She smiled at me, a cunning smile, and I felt like I'd fallen into a trap. "Exactly what I thought. Her post office box is in a town called Ruidoso."

"Which is where?"

"About two hundred miles south of Albuquerque. Remote. Surrounded by mountains, desert, forests, and lakes. There's a race track there. A casino. Lots of galleries and restaurants."

"Sounds like a great place to vacation," I said, continuing to play the straight man.

"Right. So I checked the Lincoln County Assessor's records to see if she owns property there."

"Let me guess. She doesn't."

Kat shook her head.

"Maybe the property's in her husband's name," I said.

"Ralph Bellamy."

"Like the actor?"

"Same name. Not an actor. He doesn't own property there, either. No one in Ruth Bellamy's family owns property in Lincoln County. So I checked the property records in all the surrounding counties."

"And you came up empty."

She nodded slowly and took another sip of coffee.

"That is curious, isn't it?" I said.

"It could be nothing."

"Probably is nothing. A corporation could own their place."

"Or a trust or an LLC."

"Or someone else, a family friend, lawyer, and they use it occasionally."

"But why would the post office box be in Ruth Bellamy's name?"

We gazed at each other, and I could sense the excitement in her eyes. It was the excitement I feel when I'm improvising and discover a catchy sequence of notes or a short riff with interesting possibilities. She leaned across the table, and I leaned in, too. Our faces were barely a foot apart. Hers was a lovely face, but behind that loveliness was energy, single-minded purpose, and the determination to make things right.

"I'm hoping there's more," I said.

"Oh yeah," she replied. "Her post office box in New Mexico is listed on ASGC's website, but it doesn't appear in any other literature on her. Not on the Barnard family's website. Not in her official biography. Nowhere else. Nothing I read about her mentions New Mexico."

"So," I said. "she doesn't own property in Ruidoso, at least not in her name, and as far as we know, she doesn't spend time in that New Mexico resort town, yet she gets mail there."

"Isn't that curious?"

"Very," I said. "I wonder if she owns a white van."

<h1 style="text-align:center">22</h1>

Musical improvisation is not like science. Science is logical, and music is based on the mathematics of sound and has a logical structure. But when you improvise, you sometimes take off on a familiar riff, experimenting with different intervals or tempos, playing free form, following wild-ass hunches, allowing your fingers to roam in ways that don't make sense, and listening for a musical phrase that sparks and crackles. Now and then, from somewhere beyond all the logic of musical theory and familiar musical forms, you hear something so unexpected and magical, it's like a seafaring explorer's first glimpse of land through a shroud of fog.

I thought of that as we drove a rented Prius into Ruidoso. We were following a wild-ass hunch. The main drag in Ruidoso, highway forty-eight, was a north-south winding touristy strip of motels, gas stations, galleries, real estate offices, mini-malls, cafes, souvenir shops, and rustic rental cabins. The south end of forty-eight connected with the town of Ruidoso Downs, which had sprung up along the east-west corridor of highway seventy to serve truckers and tourists. Commercially, it was Ruidoso's bigger cousin, featuring familiar fast-food joints and hotels, a casino, and the eponymous racetrack. As we cruised along seventy, we spotted the post office, a nondescript white building sitting back from the highway. It was late afternoon, and few people were in the lobby.

Ruth Bellamy's post office box was in the middle of a large bank of boxes along one wall in the lobby. Hers was large, which surprised us. People don't usually rent larger boxes unless they receive a lot of mail. Along a wall cattycorner to the post office boxes, thirty feet from Bellamy's box, was a narrow counter where people addressed letters or filled out forms. It would be a good place to watch Bellamy's box, but all the boxes had dark brass doors. We needed to mark the location of Bellamy's box so we could see it easily. At an office supply store along seventy, we bought a package of colored stickers.

Then we found a motel with vacancies up highway forty-eight. The Alpine Motor Lodge had a giant bronze statue of a bugling elk at the entrance to its parking lot. Half-wagon wheels marked each parking spot, and one lobby wall featured a collection of antique spurs. We got adjoining rooms, and while Kat went for a run, I phoned Ari and filled him in. Then I checked my email and found a lengthy response from Mac. She hadn't changed her mind. She had to accept that I would never change, she wrote, and while my impulse to protect others was admirable, she feared it would someday kill me, and she couldn't live with that dread. In the growing darkness, as night descended, my heart felt like the loneliness of a house in ruin, where dust lay on dead surfaces and airless rooms sat silent.

I remained in a funk when Kat knocked on my door an hour later. She was wearing white running shorts and a black sports bra and was beaded with sweat. Her hair hung in limp strands, and she peered at me with her weird loopy grin. Before I could peel myself away from my heartache, I blurted, "You know when you smile, one side of your mouth goes higher than the other?"

Her grin faded, and the warmth drained from her eyes. She wore the sorrowful expression of a girl at the prom no one asked to dance. "It's nerve damage. From a beating I took as a rookie. I arrested a three-time loser on a fugitive warrant, and my backup drove to the wrong address."

I don't know how you could feel worse than I did for the past hour, but now I felt like a complete shit and told her so. "Don't worry about it," she said. "Hungry?" I nodded. "Let me shower and get changed. I'll knock when I'm ready."

Over dinner, I told her about Mac and apologized again for being a jerk. She said her crooked smile was something she'd learned to live with, but it turned off a lot of guys. The doctors told her the nerves might regenerate in time, but it'd been nine years, and she wasn't hopeful.

When we returned to the motel, I stood outside her room while she fished the key out of her pocket. She unlocked her door, put her arms around me, and drew me close. I hugged her back and felt her chest pressed against mine, the softness of her back, and the aroma of her hair. Then she stood on her toes and gave me a light kiss on the lips.

"I'm okay," she said. "Thanks for asking about it. I hope we find something tomorrow. It's been seven years. I'm ready to close this case."

"Fingers crossed," I whispered.

She disappeared into her room. After lingering a moment, I returned to mine, got undressed, took some Oxys, and lay on the bed. I fell asleep, ashamed of myself and thinking about how good she felt.

The Ruidoso post office opened at eight. Before we left the motel, I bought twenty postcards. Then we drove to a Starbucks and got two large coffees. I backed the Prius into a parking space with a good view of the lot and the front door. The morning was cool and crisp. We sipped our coffee, which was hot and aromatic enough to dilate your nostrils. The sky was cloudless and deep blue. Outside, the air smelled like pine sap. It promised to be a nice day once it warmed up.

We did our surveillance in shifts, one in the car watching the lot while the other stood at the counter inside, pretending to write postcards. Kat hustled inside once the doors were unlocked. She took one sheet of the colored dots we bought yesterday and put a red dot on the door of the mailbox just below the box belonging to Ruth Bellamy. The dot would be visible from the counter, but it wouldn't alarm whoever checked Bellamy's box. Within minutes, the parking lot began to fill. While I waited in the car, I sipped coffee and settled in for what could be a long day.

As I sat, I noticed women gathering at a bus stop across the highway. They wore identical gray dresses and dark stockings. Some were older white women; the rest appeared to be Hispanic or Native American. All had lanyards around their necks. At eight-thirty, a bus from the east pulled up, and the women climbed aboard. Then the bus turned around and disappeared east on seventy. Hotel maids. Being bussed to work, not west to Casino Apache, more likely to a large hotel or resort east of Ruidoso. They must work outside of town, or they wouldn't need mass transportation to get there. Even something as mundane as maids getting on a bus is interesting when you're bored.

We passed the morning, taking turns watching Ruth Bellamy's post office box. Then at one thirty-five, while I was in the lobby, a young man walked in and opened her box. He was average height, slender but not thin, gray slacks, black shoes, yellow striped golf shirt. Short brown hair. He was turned away from me, but I saw his face when he left. White male, clean-shaven, thin lips, and a long, sharp nose. *Holy shit*, I thought. *The driver in Salem.* I felt my pulse quicken.

I kept scribbling on a postcard as he walked by. When I left the post office, Kat gave me a "What's up?" expression. I canted my head toward the guy, and she followed him with her eyes. As I reached our car, the guy climbed into a van across the lot. A white van, black across the bottom, the driver's side mirror mounted on the front. No license plate in front. "That's the van Fetch saw in Green River," I said.

"Or one like it," Kat mumbled. "I'll be damned."

"The guy driving is the one in the ATM photos."

"You were right," she whispered.

We followed the van east on seventy as it left Ruidoso Downs. About a hundred yards behind, steady at fifty-five. After three miles, the van began slowing, and we slowed with it. Then I caught flashing lights in the rearview mirror. I thought the cop would blitz past us, but he slowed and pulled in behind us, so I stopped on the shoulder and watched as the white van disappeared up the highway.

The officer who pulled us over was a stocky white guy wearing a Smokey hat. His face was clean-shaven and had all the character of a polished granite block. I rolled down my window. "Something wrong, officer?" I said. His name tag read "G. Thomas." The patch on his shoulder read, "Lincoln County Sheriff."

"You were speeding, sir. Eight miles over the limit. License and registration, please."

Kat dug the registration out of the glove compartment while I reached for my wallet and withdrew my driver's license.

"That's surprising," I said, handing him the documents. "Because I've been watching closely, and we never went over fifty-five. I'm pretty sure of that."

He leaned in and gave me a long, searching look. Then he stared at Kat and said, "I'm going to need to see your license, too, ma'am."

Kat looked surprised, and I thought she might identify herself as a police officer, but she reached into her purse, opened her wallet, and pulled out her driver's license. As she passed it to me, she said sweetly, "Since I wasn't driving, I didn't know I had to show you my license."

"Just routine, ma'am," Officer Thomas replied. He took our licenses and the vehicle registration back to his cruiser.

"Bullshit," Kat snarled. She turned and watched him. "If this bozo escalates this, I will flash my badge and raise holy hell."

When the cop returned, he handed me our licenses and registration. "What are you folks doing in Lincoln County?"

Kat leaned toward me and put her arm in mine. She snuggled close. "We're newlyweds, Officer. We're on our honeymoon and always wanted to see Ruidoso." There was so much honey in her voice I worried about it dripping onto my jacket.

"I don't see any wedding rings," the cop said.

"We both lost so much weight for the wedding we had to resize the rings," Kat explained. I looked at her and bit my lower lip, but she kept a straight face.

"Well, there's lots to see in Lincoln County," the cop said. "But it's mainly back in Ruidoso. Nothing out this way. Unless you're driving to Roswell, I'd suggest you head back into town."

"Good advice, Officer," I said. "We appreciate your help. So, are you going to give me a ticket?"

"No," he replied. "I've been having problems with my radar gun. Just a warning this time. You folks take care and have a good time in Ruidoso. Please drive carefully." He walked back to his cruiser and sat watching us until I started the Prius, glanced in both directions, and did a U-turn back toward Ruidoso.

"The guy in the van made us," I said, "and called in the sheriff. Whatever's going on, the county cops are part of it."

"I just . . . I don't believe it," Kat said. "That cop is part of it, whatever it is, but can the whole department be dirty?"

"It would be prudent not to trust any of them." I looked in the mirror. The county cop was following fifty yards back.

"Jesus Christ, Sonny. What the hell's going on?"

I shook my head and thought about that busload of hotel maids headed in this direction. The cop was right. It's desolate. Nothing to see. Nothing to do. So where were those maids going?

Back in town, we exchanged our Prius for a Jeep Wrangler. We stopped for a bottle of wine and drove back to the Alpine Motor Lodge. It was going on four. Kat went for a run while I called Ari and filled him in.

"So the sheriff's protecting them? Whoever they are?"

"Looks that way. We need a tracking device on that van."

"I'm sending John and Earl. They'll bring what you need."

"Tell them to come armed."

"Does Hastings have her weapon?"

"She didn't want the hassle of bringing it on an airplane."

"What does she use?"

"A Beretta. Twenty-round mag."

"I'll tell John."

At six-thirty, Kat knocked, and we went out for a pizza. When we returned, we camped in my room, ate pizza, and drank wine while I turned on my iPad and opened Google Earth. It took me less than a minute to locate Ruidoso. Then we followed Seventy east—to the next three towns, Glencoe, San Patricio, and Hondo—and saw nothing. I told Kat about the busload of maids headed east this morning.

"How many?"

"Forty. Maybe fifty. A normal-size bus, nearly full. I don't see any place they could have gone along Seventy. No resorts or large hotels. Nothing but isolated ranches and small buildings scattered along the highway."

"Wherever they went is off the highway."

"Yeah." I returned to Google Earth and expanded our search area, clicking on the map for more area and less detail. Again, I scanned the areas along Seventy from Ruidoso to Hondo. We saw only barren land, mountainous or hilly, a few ranches, and the straight lines of ranch roads. Then I scanned the areas farther north and south of the road. We kept that up for more than an hour, and I began to think that those maids had just disappeared, swallowed up somehow in the vast emptiness of the desert. But on my sixth or seventh pass, I saw an anomaly. Two or three miles southeast of Pajarita Mountain, about twelve miles southeast of the highway. We zoomed in on it. Whatever it was, it was huge, easily the size of a small city, but it had no name and was not on our map of New Mexico. There appeared to be no major roads leading to it, only one long ranch road.

I zoomed in on the site as closely as possible without losing much detail. On the periphery were dozens of buildings. In the center was a massive circle of white. Kat asked how large it was. I used the scale of the map to gauge the area's size. "About two square miles. Twelve hundred acres."

"What do you think it is?"

I shrugged. "Government installation? Military? I don't know." I navigated around the site. There were buildings along the entire perimeter of the white area, and on the western border between two buildings was what appeared to be a huge parking lot. The resolution was not great, but the lot seemed to be about half-full of vehicles, and maybe twenty of them were white and rectangular, like vans.

I positioned the map along the northwestern boundary of the site and followed a ranch road north. "This road leads to Seventy. Assuming the van turned off the highway and went to this compound, this is probably the road it took." I paused at the junction of the ranch road and Seventy, trying to figure out where that turn would be. Kat leaned in over my right shoulder. Her hair was touching mine, our faces so close I could feel her warmth.

"If you're right, the county cop stopped us about two miles before the van turned off," she said.

While we finished our wine, I navigated around the area of the compound and found a mesa a half-mile away and another ranch road that came within about a quarter mile of its summit. "Look at this," I said. She huddled next to me again. I was not so absorbed in the map that I didn't think to appreciate how close she was. "We can hike from the end of this road to the top of this mesa and get a good vantage point to check out this place."

"We'll need binoculars," she said.

"I saw a Walmart on Seventy."

After she returned to her room, I called Ari and told him what we'd discovered. I gave him the coordinates and told him we would get a closer look from that mesa tomorrow.

"What you're describing sounds major."

"Looks it. We're assuming that's where the white van went. I think that's where the maids were headed, too. There's nothing else out there that would require that many maids."

"Okay. John and Earl are on the way. They'll arrive by noon. You want me to send Sana?"

"Not yet. Let me scope it out tomorrow."

"You think that's where the kidnapped girls are?"

"No clue. Whatever it is, it's huge, not on any maps, and in the middle of nowhere, New Mexico."

Next, I called Garth Wyman and caught him before he left the shop.

"How's it going, brother?"

"Fine," I told him. "Hey, man, when we talked last week, you said to let you know if I needed help."

"Check."

"Turns out I might." I explained what we discovered. He was ready to roll out the troops tonight, but I asked him to wait until I had a better idea what's there.

"I'm gonna call a few guys, anyway," he said. "See what we can line up. Where'd you say you are?"

23

When I was eight, my parents took us to a magic show in an old theatre in Los Angeles. Outside, the gutters were clogged with trash, and cracked streetlamps were so grimy you couldn't tell their original color. We sat before a small stage in rows of seats whose threadbare red cushions sagged. The magician, who billed himself Godwin the Great, looked about eight feet tall and older than grandfather Marshall, which meant he was ancient. He wore a shiny black suit with a hundred pockets and a blue cape that swirled when he turned as though it were always a half-step behind him. His first trick was to pass a deck of cards to the person sitting at one end of the front row. He told that person to select one card from the deck, any card, not show it to anyone, and then pass the deck to the next person, and so on. Godwin had everyone in the first two rows—about forty people—select a random card. Then he went person by person through both rows announcing which card each held—and he was right on every count.

I remember being so amazed I could barely pay attention during the rest of the show. I kept marveling at how he'd done that. To this day, I don't know. But what I took from that experience was more than a boy's fascination with a magic trick. I learned that the quality of your life is only as great as your capacity for wonder. If you can marvel at a flower's intricate design, the sensations of an artfully crafted hors d'oeuvre, the beauty of a masterful piece of music, or the brilliance of a magician's illusion, then your soul will remain nourished and your life enriched. Ironically, that's how I felt about what occurred on this day of my life—not that I wouldn't have prayed for a different outcome. But when your capacity for wonder is met with equal measures of genius and evil, you can feel your mind expanding with each heartbeat.

We left early, stopping at Walmart for binoculars and a backpack and at Starbucks for large coffees. The ranch road to Pajarita Mountain was fifteen miles out of town. Covered with gravel, it was wider than a ranch road should be. We rattled over a cattle guard and then came to a small clearing where the road split. A narrower road led west. Rutted. Low weeds and grass were growing in the middle—a road infrequently used. The main road led east past a small pond surrounded by tall cottonwoods. This branch veered south toward the mountain but was barred by a barbed-wire fence and a metal gate with signs: *Gate Access Call (575) 555-4732. No Trespassing. Private Property. Violators will be prosecuted.* Kat backed down the narrow road until the gate was just visible and waited for a vehicle to come along and open it. Twenty minutes later, a dark blue pickup pulled up. After it passed through the gate and headed south, Kat sped forward and caught the gate just as it began to close. She skidded to a stop on the other side and waited five minutes for the blue pickup to get far enough ahead.

"What will we say if we meet somebody coming the other way?" Kat wondered.

"I kind of like your honeymoon idea." She gave me a frisky smile as though saying, "Aren't you a bad boy?" While we waited, I opened Google Earth on my iPad and traced the road we were on. "About eight miles ahead, a road on our right will circle north around Pajarita Mountain and turns south toward the mesa."

Kat eased forward. The road was long and straight. Pajarita Mountain loomed ahead, nearly eight thousand feet high. A long line of cottonwoods wove its way east of us, probably following a creek bed, but the terrain to the west was hilly and barren except for scattered scrub oaks and junipers, dry grass, and sagebrush. After several miles, we saw a dust cloud looming in the distance. Another vehicle, just a speck but coming fast. Then we spied a gap in the barbed-wire fence ahead on our right. The vehicle approaching us was white and had just begun to take shape when we reached our turn. Kat pulled onto that road and raced ahead. I watched as the truck behind us reached the crossroads—but kept going north, as did the truck behind it and the ones behind that. A small convoy. Two pickups, three semis, then another pickup. Whoever they were, they had no interest in us.

"That's heavy traffic for a ranch road," I said.

Kat nodded, pulling to a stop. "Probably why the road is wider. Built for heavier loads."

"I wonder what they're moving."

By now, the sun was laying some serious heat on the desert. My t-shirt was damp, so I unzipped my leather jacket and shrugged it off. Two or three miles ahead, we stopped in the mountain's shadow, and Kat pulled off her sweatshirt. "Some isolated buildings out here," I said. "Probably old homesteads. We're clear to the mesa." Kat nodded and started driving again. A bank of dark clouds began forming on the southwest horizon. Overhead, the sky remained blue, but that front expanded by the minute.

"It's going to storm," Kat said.

After we passed the western slope of Pajarita, the road gradually rose to the mesa. Sparse grasses and cacti clung to the crumbly slopes. The road was scarred by ruts, not from traffic but erosion, and rocks, some as big as a basketball, lay scattered in our path. During the last hour of our journey, we bounced out of ruts and over rocks, Kat weaving every few feet to avoid the larger ones. I got out a dozen times to lift or push impassable boulders out of our way.

We stopped at a wider spot where we could turn the Jeep around. Then we stuffed our things into the backpack and trekked to the top. The sun beat down on us relentlessly. As I pulled my soaked t-shirt away from my body, I began wishing for those storm clouds to hurry. The vegetation was scraggly and tough, as it needed to be to survive in this environment.

We caught our breath when we reached the top, and I pulled out my iPad to get a bearing. The best vantage point was two miles away, so we walked quickly. The cloud bank was nearly overhead when we reached the mesa's rim. The compound was below us, still a half-mile away. It covered a larger area of the valley than I'd realized. We walked along the rim and found a spot where a notch in the rock dropped three feet to a small platform shaded by a large juniper. We stepped into it and got some protection from the sun. I took off the backpack and retrieved the binoculars. Kat opened her cell phone, zoomed in on the site, and began taking pictures while I examined it through the binoculars.

The buildings on the perimeter were uniform—adobe colored, many windows, and flat gray roofs, most four-to-five stories tall. The large white object I'd seen on Google Earth was in the compound's center and covered half its total area. I could see that white object from the side through the gaps between buildings. It was open underneath and looked like canvas but much thicker. Faint borders between sections of the object appeared to be seams. It looked to be forty feet off the ground, so it must have been supported by sturdy columns, but I couldn't see far enough under it to divine its purpose. Maybe it provided shade. But for what?

A tall wire fence topped with concertina circled the compound. Just outside it, on the southwest side, was a large white water tower and tank. Within the fence was a perimeter road, and I could see a gated entryway far to the left where the wide ranch road entered the compound. I watched as several semis drove into the site and proceeded around the perimeter road to the large lot on the west side. A massive building at one end appeared to be a warehouse. There were loading bays behind it where ten or eleven semis were parked. A building across the lot had vehicle entry bays like a garage—two fuel pumps in front of it. Among the vehicles parked, there was a fleet of white vans. I passed the binoculars to Kat.

"What do you think?" Kat said as she peered at the site.

"Whatever this is, it's a major operation. It took serious money to build this place."

"And operate it. Government?"

"Your tax dollars at work? But it's not on any maps."

"A secret base like that one in Nevada?"

"Area 51? Roswell's not that far away." It made as much sense as any other explanation. There were no signs on the road leading to it and nothing else identifying it or suggesting its presence.

"This must be where those maids went."

I nodded.

As we observed the site, we ate lunch and watched a shadow slowly pass over the compound. Then it passed over us, and the air was instantly ten degrees cooler. We were now in the shadow of that vast, dark, roiling cloud bank. Its bottom was a dark gray and black swirl, threatening a downpour.

Kat sat up sharply and peered into the sky around us.

"What are you doing?"

"Did you hear that?" she said.

"What?"

"I don't know."

"What's it sound like?"

She shook her head, puzzled. "Buzzing. High pitched. Like an electric razor, but far away. I might have imagined it."

"I didn't hear anything, but I have hearing loss," I told her. "Playing in a band for ten years."

Moments later, we heard the whop-whop-whop of helicopter blades, faint at first but steadily growing louder. I crouched on my feet, raised my head over the notch, and looked back across the mesa.

"Chopper," I said. "Headed this way."

I sat back down. We looked at each other and laughed. "You think our honeymoon excuse is still viable?" she said.

The chopper landed on the rim above us, dust blowing over our heads. It sounded like it was three feet away. Dust blew into the notch, so I stuffed everything into the backpack. "We need to give it some authenticity," I yelled. "Let's get undressed and fool around."

Kat laughed. "You are so bad," she yelled back.

Then two men appeared above us. They wore dark helmets and desert camo uniforms, and pointed assault rifles at us. Black. Lightweight. Semi-automatic. AR-15s.

"Hands up," one of them yelled. As we complied, he ordered us to stand. "You," he cried, pointing his rifle at me, "toss me the backpack. Then climb out slowly. I want to see your hands at all times."

I handed him the backpack and climbed into the rotor wash dust storm. A soldier patted me down and took my wallet and cell phone. Then he ordered Kat to climb up, patted her down, and took her things as well—all but her badge, I noticed. She carried it in her back pocket, and he didn't touch her there. Two other soldiers joined him. One asked for the Jeep keys.

"In the backpack," I yelled. With the rotor and engine noise, it was nearly impossible to hear. "Be careful," I added. "It's a rental, and I didn't take the collision coverage."

He might have punched me if another soldier hadn't cuffed my wrists behind my back. They handcuffed Kat, too, and then lifted us into the chopper. As the soldiers piled in, the one with our backpack fished for the keys.

Kat leaned in and put her mouth to my ear. "I guess we'll be guests of the U.S. Air Force."

"I don't think so," I replied, looking at the soldiers sitting opposite as the engine revved and the helicopter became airborne. They wore no insignia, no unit patches, nothing but name tags. According to his tag, the guy across from me was Smith 26. His buddy was Smith 14. The chopper touched down on the other side of the mesa, and the soldier who'd taken our keys jumped out. He was Smith 38. Then the chopper was airborne again, swung across the mesa, and headed for the compound. We landed at a helipad on the eastern perimeter. The soldiers lifted us from the chopper and marched us toward a two-story building.

Inside was a small room with a table, several chairs, and a holding cell. They told us to enter the cell and turn our backs toward them. I felt one of them unlocking my handcuffs. Then he shoved me deeper into the cell before removing Kat's handcuffs. Two soldiers stood at the cell bars guarding us. The cell had a bench but no sink or toilet. People weren't meant to stay here long. We sat on the bench, and I rubbed my wrists where the handcuffs had chafed against the scabs. While we sat, another soldier entered the room with our backpack and emptied the contents onto the table.

Fifteen minutes later, a door opened, and a man entered with an open dossier, which he was reading. He was about my height, muscular and solid, with the massive biceps you get by pumping iron. He had gray-blonde hair and strong features—a rectangular face with a sharp jawbone, wide-spaced eyes, and a nose that had been knocked out of place once or twice. He wore khaki pants, desert boots, and a black t-shirt, and he had a holster clipped to his belt with what looked like a Colt .45.

He closed the dossier and then poked through the items from our backpack. After a few seconds, he looked up and said, "Sonny Marshall. Why are you here?"

I opened my mouth, but he cut me off. "Don't bother to lie." He turned and said, "Sergeant Katrina Hastings."

"If you know who I am," Kat said defiantly, "then you know I'm a police officer. You are guilty of kidnapping by holding us here against our will."

He regarded her with a smirk. "So arrest me."

"Don't think that won't happen," she snarled.

He cocked his head and stared at her. Then he nodded at a soldier and said, "Come with me."

One soldier unlocked the cell door while two others covered us with their weapons. As we left the cell, we were ordered to empty anything else in our pockets on the table. My pockets were empty. Kat shook her head, but the leader wasn't satisfied. "Don't force us to do a strip search," he growled. She paused, reached into a back pocket, pulled out her badge, and set it on the table. We followed him out, two soldiers behind us, climbed into a black van with *Security* written on its door panel and were driven north on the perimeter road. I was seated on the left side of the vehicle, so I could see into the compound. I took in as much as I could before we pulled into a driveway that sloped down and ran underneath one of the tallest buildings on this side of the perimeter.

The van stopped in a sally port beneath the building. The soldiers hustled us out and led us to an elevator that opened with a key card. The leader jerked his head at us, and we stepped in, the soldiers behind us. We rode to the top floor and then walked down a long, wood-paneled hallway whose walls displayed a collection of paintings I'd never seen. I'm no art expert, but these looked exceptionally fine. We came to a set of tall wooden double doors, which the leader opened, waving us inside. Then he called someone with his cell and said, "They're here."

We were in a grand library in the style of an English manor house. The mahogany bookshelves had brass-grilled covers. There must have been a thousand books on those shelves. The room's centerpiece was a Persian carpet with two long, black leather sofas, matching easy chairs, and end tables. A wet bar sat along one wall, and there was a large mahogany desk beneath a huge, four-by-six array of flat-screen monitors, which were off. After a minute, a side door opened, and in walked a handsome man in his mid-fifties wearing a black suit, white shirt, and dark gray and black striped tie. He had gray hair parted in the middle, a pleasant face, a small mouth, and prominent black eyebrows.

"I see you've met my brother, Martin," he said, gesturing to the leader. "You'll have to forgive his abrupt manner. Martin is our head of security and is very good at what he does, though he's not the affable sort."

Martin looked at him impassively.

"I'm Henry Barnard," the man announced as he strode up to Kat, smiling, and shook her hand as though he were genuinely happy to meet her. "Detective Hastings. You are even more beautiful in person," he said warmly. Then he turned and offered me his hand. As I shook it, he said, "And Mr. Marshall. Torran, I'm told, is your first name, but you go by Sonny. You're quite handsome, too. We hadn't planned on guests today, but I'm delighted you've come to visit."

He gestured for us to sit on one of the sofas. As we did so, he sat on the sofa opposite, smiling broadly, and said, "Welcome to Paragon."

24

"Have you had lunch?" Henry asked us.

"Yes," I replied.

"Then something to drink? I'll have iced tea and water brought up." He went to the desk and picked up the phone, then turned back, an apologetic look on his face. "Or would you prefer something stronger?"

His gracious host routine was a con, but I didn't know the game, so I played the gracious guest. I said iced tea was fine, and he called someone. Martin had positioned himself beside the sofa, so Kat was between him and me. Henry puzzled me, but I had no doubts about Martin. He was a warrior and would kill us when ordered, but I couldn't move on him while we were seated, and Kat was between us. Besides, two guards were outside, and we didn't have what we came for.

One of the doors behind us opened. A soldier brought our backpack and handed it to Henry, who emptied our things onto the desk and examined them before returning our wallets.

"These are yours, I believe."

I accepted mine as though thankful to have it returned, but Kat remained stone-faced and hesitated before taking hers. Henry smiled at her, but a flicker of annoyance crossed his face. He recomposed himself and sat opposite, smoothing the folds in his suit coat and straightening his tie. He was a compact man with neatly trimmed hair and manicured nails. He carried himself like a Wall Street banker, but beneath the groomed façade, he reminded me of a game-show host whose shtick had become second nature.

"We don't have many visitors," he said, "so I'm always thrilled—"

"By calling us guests, you infer that we are free to leave," Kat said, cutting him off.

"I'm afraid that would not be possible," Henry said, as though he truly regretted it.

"If we're not free to leave, we're your prisoners."

"That's such an uncivil word."

"If we're not free to leave, it's the fucking truth. How's that for uncivil?"

"Miss Hastings," he sputtered, his game-show persona in full retreat. "Can I call you Katrina?"

"No, you can call me Sergeant Hastings." Her face had turned florid. "And I want my badge back. Now."

Henry's face turned to stone. He glared at her and nodded to Martin, who retrieved her badge from the desk, tossed it on the sofa beside her, and resumed his post. She fumed for a moment before returning the badge to her back pocket.

"Sergeant Hastings," Henry said. "In my experience, anger rarely results in a satisfactory outcome." He turned to me. I must have looked more agreeable. "I see you are interested in our endeavor. I'm sure you have some questions for me, and I have some for you."

Kat inhaled sharply, but before she could speak, I laid my hand on her arm and said, "You welcomed us to Paragon. I've never heard of it."

"Excellent," Henry said, rubbing his hands together. He couldn't have been more delighted if I'd just won the new car behind door number three. "Paragon is a research institute. A laboratory. A think tank. We are creators and inventors. Scientists. Engineers. And artists."

"I noticed the paintings in the hallway," I said agreeably.

"Beautiful work, aren't they? Our people are extraordinarily creative in the arts as well as the sciences. Here's an interesting fact. We hold more than two thousand patents. Our people are doing cutting-edge work in robotics, medicine, bioengineering, microelectronics, materials science, energy, optics, low-temperature physics, information technology, and many other fields. We have technologies so advanced we haven't shared them with the world."

"Why not?" I said.

Henry smiled at me. "All in good time. It wouldn't be wise to flood the market. Paragon is an idea-generating engine, Mr. Marshall, and the growth of new ideas here is nearly exponential."

"It's a huge facility," I said, playing the awestruck tourist.

"And we have manufacturing plants in a dozen states. More in Mexico, Brazil, Japan, Korea, Malaysia, and Eastern Europe."

"Impressive," I said. "But if your organization is that large, you should be high on the Fortune 500 list, and I've never heard of you."

"A fair point. The only part of our operation called Paragon is this research facility. You would know the names of our sister entities if I mentioned them. But we've segregated our organization so no one can grasp our scale. A legion of government accountants couldn't put the pieces of the puzzle together, but if we were to combine the annual gross revenues of our operations, they would be greater than the GDPs of all but nineteen countries. Much of our revenue comes from licensing intellectual property, but we also manufacture numerous products."

There was a knock at the door, and a woman entered, pushing a cart with refreshments. She was a diminutive Native American. No more than five feet tall, she had the raisined complexion of a farm worker. She wore a gray dress with black stockings and an ID tag on a lanyard. Kat and I glanced at each other as we accepted glasses of iced tea. Then Henry said, "Now I have some questions for you. Let's begin with what brings you here, and while I appreciate entertaining fiction, you should know that we've thoroughly checked your backgrounds since you met that deputy sheriff yesterday."

"He's on your payroll?" I said.

"They all are," Henry responded. "The sheriff works for Martin. We got him elected so he could look after our interests. Now, Mr. Marshall, we know you are a musician. You were investigating child pornography, although we're not convinced the media are correct about how that occurred. You and Sergeant Hastings were instrumental in exposing child pornographers in the San Francisco area. The two of you are not on your honeymoon. You are single, and Sergeant Hastings is divorced and has a daughter named Sara."

Kat winced at the mention of her daughter's name.

"You followed one of our vans yesterday and switched vehicles last night, presumably to deceive county deputies. As you can imagine, we have good sources at the car rental agencies. We tracked you to the mesa, where you were photographing our facility this morning."

"If you tracked us," Kat said, "why didn't you stop us before we reached the mesa?"

"We were curious about what you were up to," Henry replied.

"Tracked us how?" I said. "We were in open country and didn't see anyone."

He smiled at me. "Drones, Mr. Marshall. We have extraordinary drone technology. It's an area of special interest to some of our scholars. Our site is under constant drone surveillance. Had you ventured out here at night, we could have tracked you as easily with drones that detect heat signatures."

"That's what I heard on the mesa," Kat said in an aside.

"We've developed solar-powered, self-guided drones that investigate anomalies in their search area and can remain airborne almost indefinitely. They can also electronically paint a vehicle of interest and follow it. One of them followed you the moment you left your motel this morning. Now, back to my question. What brought you here?"

"We're looking for two missing girls," Kat told Henry point-blank.

"Are you?" he responded, a look of surprise on his face, though it might have been contrived. "What makes you think they're here?"

She looked at me, and I decided the truth was less risky than a lie, which they might see through. So I told him the story, beginning with Fetch seeing Erin at that convenience store in Green River. As I told it, he sat back on his sofa in rapt attention.

"Remarkable," he said when I finished. "Absolutely remarkable. You deduced that she was in New Mexico based on the absence of a front license plate?"

"It was a stretch," I admitted, "but it led us to Salem, Angela Chang's abduction, ASGC, and Ruth Bellamy's post office box in Ruidoso."

"An oversight we will correct immediately."

"My turn," I said. "Is Erin Hightower here?"

He gave Martin a quick look, then shook his head. "Not by that name. We call her Rachel. Rachel Nine."

"Rachel *Nine*?" Kat said.

"Paragon is not merely a research institute. It's also a school, principally in fact. However, I prefer to think of Paragon as one arm of a grand experiment in human engineering. What we are doing here represents nothing less than the salvation of humanity."

In the few seconds it took this to sink in, I realized how much trouble we were in. I've heard other men claim to represent the future of humanity, but they were usually staggering along the Embarcadero holding a bottle of whiskey in one hand and their junk in the other. Maybe it was the word *salvation*. I wondered if Paragon was a religious cult.

Kat ignored what Henry said and asked if Nine was Rachel's new surname.

"No," he replied. "Nine is her level. Think of it as a grade. Our levels represent degrees of intellectual accomplishment. She is now a Level Nine. When she advances, she'll be known as Rachel Ten."

"How many levels are there?" Kat said.

"Twenty."

"What is her surname?" Kat said.

"She doesn't have one. None of our scholars do until they reach Level Eighteen. Then they choose the surname they want the world to know them by. It's an important rite of passage here, and we treat it ceremoniously." Then he surprised us. "Would you like to see Rachel?"

Kat held a breath and nodded.

Henry rose and said, "Give me just a moment." He walked to his desk and clicked buttons on a remote. A few seconds later, the array of monitors on the wall behind him came to life. He did a quick search, and then a single live image, broken into twenty-four screens, came up on that array. He waved us over. Martin followed at a careful distance. We stood by Henry at the desk and watched a group of scholars, as Henry called them, at work around a large table. Six, ranging in age, I guessed, from eight to thirteen. They studied a large screen that lay flat in the middle of the table. On the screen was an image of a rotating whirlpool galaxy. One girl typed something into a tablet, and instantly the image accelerated, the arms of the galaxy stretching outward.

"What're they doing?" I asked Henry.

"If I'm not mistaken, they are simulating the evolution of galaxies."

"Erin," I heard Kat whisper. Her face had grown pale and still, a portrait in alabaster except for the mist in her eyes. She pointed to one panel, and I followed her gaze. The girl on the laptop spoke to the others, although we couldn't hear her. She had long, dark hair, a delicate chin angled sharply back to her throat, high cheekbones, and a strong nose. After a few seconds, she faced the camera, and I recognized Erin Hightower. She looked poised, beautiful, self-confident, and engaged. Whatever she was now called, that was Erin.

"I've been searching for her for seven years," Kat said, turning her misty eyes toward Henry. "Seven frustrating years."

"And in that time," Henry said, "she has accomplished more than most students will in their academic careers. At twelve, she is doing college-level work in astrophysics."

"Very impressive," I said. "As the head of Paragon, you must be very proud."

Kat flared. "She was kidnapped, Sonny. That's nothing to be proud of."

"Rescued," Henry said. "We rescued her."

"Rescued?" Kat said. "Rescued from what? You stole her from her family."

"We rescued her from a life of mediocrity," Henry insisted. "We rescued her from an environment where she could never thrive as she has here. The gift we've given her is priceless." Then he turned to me. "And I must correct one misperception. I'm not the head of Paragon. That would be my brother Gordon. He leads the Paragon Academy, which we refer to as our Environmental Accelerator. I am the chair of the HEAD Project. Why don't we return to the sofas, and I'll explain."

Before we did, I noted the number of Henry's desk phone. When we were seated again, Henry refilled our iced teas. He'd left the monitors on, so we could still see Erin/Rachel and her fellow students as we continued talking.

"HEAD stands for Human Evolutionary Acceleration and Differentiation. That's a lot to absorb. Have you heard of Eugenics?"

I shook my head. Kat sat in silence beside me.

"Eugenics was well-known and debated among educated circles a century ago. It was practiced in many countries. Eugenics was a movement aimed at improving human populations through selective breeding on the one hand and sterilization and euthanasia on the other. Its founder was someone you may have heard of, Sergeant Hastings: Sir Francis Galton, who invented the science of fingerprint analysis. Galton was Charles Darwin's cousin. He believed that the genetic quality of the human species could be improved through selective, rather than random, reproduction methods. Rather like dog breeding."

"Who does the selecting?" I asked.

"As the interest in Eugenics grew, governments began classifying which people were fit and unfit to reproduce. The unfit usually included the mentally ill and developmentally disabled or those with very low IQs, but some governments included people who were blind, deaf, or poor, as well as gays, lesbians, promiscuous women, and racially inferior groups."

"The Final Solution," I said.

Henry nodded. "Nazi Germany implemented the most extreme practices of Eugenics, but in the early decades of the twentieth century, Eugenics was a widespread social concept. By 1930, there were hundreds of courses on Eugenics in American colleges and universities. Many states adopted programs of forced sterilization for people who were feeble-minded or otherwise deemed unfit. North Carolina's sterilization program did not end until 1977."

"Is that your plan?" Kat said, the defiant tone in her voice unabated. "Sterilizing the unfit?"

"Goodness, no," Henry replied. "We're not monsters. The goal of the HEAD project is to create a new breed of human beings, a genetically superior race with the intelligence, creativity, breeding, and resources to lead humanity away from its current course, a course that will inevitably lead to our destruction."

"You are insane," Kat hissed.

"Quite the contrary," Henry said, smiling at her. "The HEAD project may be the only hope humanity has."

"What does Erin Hightower have to do with this?" I asked him.

"Ah! On point as always, Mr. Marshall," Henry said as though I were his star pupil. "Human beings are a product of genetics and environment: nature and nurture. So to accelerate human evolution, we are maximizing both. Paragon is our Environmental Accelerator. Here, every aspect of the child's environment is rigorously controlled. They eat only the healthiest foods. They get the right amount of exercise. They have no access to alcohol or tobacco, and none of our staff are allowed to smoke. Our scholars live and work in cohorts looked over by emotionally supportive guardians, and our faculty, the world's best, act as mentors, not drill sergeants. Our scholars have no exposure to the distractions of television, video games, recreational drugs, or the destructive influences of lesser peer groups. No Tiktok, Instagram, Twitter, Snapchat, or Facebook. They live in a controlled environment and have the finest education in the world. We spend over four million dollars educating each scholar."

"You kidnap brilliant children," I said, "and use them as subjects in your experiment in human engineering."

"We rescue them, Mr. Marshall, and give them the guidance, support, encouragement, and resources to maximize their intellectual development."

"How does that result in genetically superior humans?"

"By itself, it doesn't. Our Genetic Accelerator program does that. My wife, Stephanie, who has a doctorate in genetics, is responsible for breeding. She identifies men and women worldwide with superior genetics, people who are exceptionally bright, healthy, athletic, and physically attractive, and we approach them, confidentially, of course, to acquire the men's sperm and the women's eggs. As you might guess, we pay handsomely for that. The eggs are fertilized and implanted in the wombs of surrogate mothers, who spend the terms of their pregnancies in our facilities under close guidance. When they're born, the babies are raised in other special facilities, and at five years of age, they are enrolled in Paragon. We refer to our program enrollees as alphas, and when they become sexually mature, we teach them that alphas must only mate with other alphas."

"Do you distinguish between kids like Erin and those you breed?" I asked.

"No. They are all alphas. But as our population of purebreds grows, we have a declining need for genetically superior children acquired from other sources. We now have one hundred and twenty purebreds in our academy."

Kat perked up at that. "My God," she said, "how many students do you have?"

Henry smiled. "Scholars, not students. Currently, the answer is three hundred forty-two."

It was a stunning admission. "You've kidnapped more than two hundred children?" I said.

"Rescued," Henry insisted.

"And you targeted them through ASGC?"

"ASGC is one source for our American acquisitions. About a hundred, in total, from this country. The rest we've acquired around the world. We have sources like ASGC in other countries."

"White Christian children?" Kat asserted. "Your new master race?"

"Oh, no," Henry replied. "We're not racists, sergeant. Our scholars represent a good cross-section of humanity. Our only criteria are superior intellect, health, attractiveness, and sound genetics.

"How do you know they are genetically acceptable?" I asked.

"We genetically test each acquired child before we accept them into our program, and we use organizations like ASGC to select only the finest specimens in the first place."

"What happens to the ones who aren't suitable?" Kat said.

"We test them immediately after they are acquired. If the tests reveal markers for genetic disorders like cystic fibrosis, hemophilia, muscular dystrophy, and the like, our people find a safe way to return them to their parents. The children are kept sedated, so if they're unfit, they don't remember enough to compromise our program."

"And you keep the perfect ones. I can't believe this," Kat mumbled.

"Does Kaspar van der Heiden target the children to be taken?" I said.

"No, my sister Ruth does that. Kaspar is involved in our genetic research but knows nothing about Paragon."

"If you're breeding superior children, why do you kidnap others?"

"Rescue, please. When we began our program, we believed we had sound ideas for our Environmental Accelerator, but we lacked proof of concept. So we built a smaller version of Paragon and acquired subjects to test our theories. Our acquisitions have all been in the top one-half of one percent intellectually, so we were confident they would eventually become good breeding stock if our environmental controls proved effective. Our initial subjects are now out in the world leading companies and establishing themselves as future world leaders."

"Would we know any of them?" I asked.

"Oh, yes. Some have become famous in a few short years. They are young luminaries in Silicon Valley, Tokyo, Wall Street, Washington, London, Paris, Madrid, Copenhagen, and Beijing. Eventually, they'll be rising stars in politics, and we'll support them as they attain higher and higher office."

"So that's your goal?" I said. "To rule the world?"

Henry gave me a wide, self-satisfied smile. "Of course, Mr. Marshall. We can't very well leave the world to amateurs. Look at what's happening throughout the world, at what's been happening for centuries—wars, genocide, fanaticism, religious intolerance, economic inequities, overpopulation, famines, failed social systems, rampant pollution, terrorism, the proliferation of nuclear weapons, and implacable enemies deadlocked in conflict. At the core of it is the absolute inability of human beings and governments to solve a myriad of problems that threaten our existence. We are hell-bent on our destruction and are poisoning our planet as we do it. Tell me now, honestly. Are you content with the direction of the human race?"

My silence confirmed what he knew my answer would be.

"Then it's time for a better solution. If we don't accelerate the evolution of human beings, if we can't create a race that is intellectually superior, more gifted at solving problems, and powerful and influential enough to implement solutions, then the human race will perish through catastrophes of our own making."

25

Henry interlaced his fingers in his lap and observed us with smug satisfaction. What makes true believers so dangerous is not only the force of their convictions but their suspension of moral restraint. Having kidnapped more than two hundred children, they would have no compunctions about murdering us or anyone else who threatened Paragon.

"What about Angela Chang?" I said. "Is she here, too?"

"Certainly," Henry replied. "Although her new name is Hwei-ru. She's a Level One, so her full name is Hwei-ru One. I'm told she's quite the firecracker."

"Giving your people fits? I'm glad to hear that," I said.

Henry laughed. "The assimilation process is never smooth, Mr. Marshall, but the outcome is inevitable. When she advances to Level Two, she will have adapted completely to her new name, home, and family."

"New family?"

"Her guardians and fellow scholars."

Angela would recover quickly if we could rescue her soon enough, but it would be challenging for Erin. She's been assimilating for seven years. I asked Henry about the enormous white object in the center of Paragon. We learned it was a solar magnifier, a solar power generator a hundred times more efficient than the best commercially available solar panels. It was invented by three of their Level Nineteens and supplies all of Paragon's energy needs. Excess power is stored in an underground facility for stormy days like today.

"Your solar magnifier has one other benefit," I said. Henry cocked his head and raised his eyebrows. "Satellites can't see beneath it."

A smile spread across his face like cold butter in a hot skillet. "We prefer not to be observed," he said.

"By our government or any other."

Henry nodded.

"You can't keep this place secret forever," Kat said.

"We don't intend to."

"Some of your graduates are already out in the world," she said.

"And doing very well. We continue to provide the resources they need to achieve their goals. And ours."

"You buy their silence?"

"You misunderstand us, Sergeant Hastings. By the time our scholars leave, they are very loyal to Paragon. They embrace our mission and are grateful to have been chosen. They appreciate what their lives could have been were it not for us."

"Are they allowed to leave before they reach Level Twenty?"

Henry shook his head. "We couldn't permit that."

"So they're prisoners just like us. Despite everything you give them, you deprive them of freedom."

He regarded her sadly. "If they'd stayed with their birth parents, would they have been free to leave their homes before they reached maturity? Let's be realists, Sergeant; freedom is illusory, especially for children." He glanced at his watch and added, "Please wait here for a moment." He returned to his desk and picked up the phone. While he spoke, I studied a map of Paragon on the wall beside the sofa.

The site was circular, like a wagon wheel. The perimeter buildings were organized around the solar magnifier, and now I saw a large building beneath the magnifier at the hub of the wheel labeled *The Commons*. There were walkways leading to it from various points on the perimeter. All the perimeter buildings had numerical designations. The motor pool we'd seen from the mesa was *265*; the warehouse beside it was *275*. I realized that the building designations represented the degrees on a compass. The main entrance to the compound was north and labeled *357*. The helicopter that brought us here landed at a helipad on the east side of the compound, and the security office beside it was *Building 88*. It was a simple system. Once you knew a building's number, you could quickly locate it in the compound. When we left *Building 88*, we were driven north around the perimeter road. The map showed that we were now in *Building 20, Paragon HQ*. East of the compound, outside the perimeter fence, was a large square object labeled *90 Power*

Station. It was shown in dotted lines, meaning, I guessed, that it was underground. But I was most interested in two buildings on the southeast side of the perimeter. *Buildings 135 and 145.* The former was labeled *Scholars Dormitory*; the latter, *Masters Dormitory.*

When Henry returned, I said, "What is *The Commons*?"

"Our dining hall," Henry explained. 'It's what other colleges would call a student union, a place for meetings, activities, and the like."

"And the *Masters Dormitory.* Who are the masters?"

"Our senior scholars, Levels Sixteen and above. Each level mentors the scholars two or more levels below them. When they reach Level Sixteen, we consider them master teachers, and they have more privileges at the master level."

"Like what?" I said.

"More autonomy. The freedom to choose special areas of study. Cohabitation privileges. Greater access to the omega world."

"Omega?"

"The last letter in the Greek alphabet. Our scholars are alphas. Leaders. Superior human beings. Normal humans are omegas, and we teach our alphas that their role in life is to lead the omegas out of the self-destructive path they're on. We are breeding our alphas to be smarter, taller, stronger, healthier, and more creative than average humans. We're breeding them to be the world's future leaders, and when we've succeeded, they will stand out as a superior breed."

"You expect us omegas to stand by and let them rule us?" Kat said.

"You won't have a choice, Sergeant. Our alphas will also command much of the world's wealth and resources. That's what we're creating here. Paragon is not only a superior human gene pool; it's also a wealth engine that will enable our alphas to attain positions of authority and power where they can make the decisions that will save the human race as a whole."

"A plutocracy?" I said.

Henry shook his head. "No, plutocracy means rule by the wealthy. The correct word for what we will accomplish is geniocracy, rule by geniuses. Of course, they will also command great wealth."

"When I listen to you," Kat said, "I don't know whether to laugh or cry. You believe this bullshit."

Henry scowled at her. "Have you kept up with world events since you've been in Ruidoso?" he said. "Islamic radicals are slaughtering more innocents. Russian troops have occupied another country and are massing along the borders of the Baltics. Israel and Hamas are fighting again in Gaza. The US Navy is tracking four Chinese nuclear missile submarines patrolling along the California coast, early wildfires have burned more than a million acres in the western US, Congress is hopelessly deadlocked, and scientists report that the polar ice cap is melting at a rate nearly twice as fast as their worst-case predictions. Shall I go on?"

Kat was silent.

"Someone has to do something, Sergeant, because you omegas are incapable of making and implementing the decisions we desperately need to save ourselves and this planet."

I said, "Just how smart are the kids here?"

"Their average IQ is one hundred seventy-four. We have twenty-six with IQs above two hundred."

"They would do well on Jeopardy," Kat said. I suppressed a laugh while Henry glanced sourly at Martin. His patience with her was wearing out.

"I'm curious about one other thing," I said. "When we asked you earlier about Erin, you found her quickly. With hundreds of scholars, keeping track of their schedules must be difficult. How did you locate Erin?"

"Rachel," Henry insisted.

"Sorry, Rachel."

He told us that everyone except day workers like the maids has GPS locators surgically implanted behind their right ear. Powered by the warmth of the human body, they enable Paragon's security team to track everyone all the time.

"You guys have nailed big brother," Kat said. "You've got it down to a science. Is there anything you don't watch?"

A flash of anger crossed Henry's face. "We're not voyeurs," he admonished. "But we have one hell of an investment to protect, and the future of the human race depends on our ability to track everyone involved in the HEAD project."

"What about you, Henry?" I said. "Do you have an implant?"

"We make no exceptions," he said. Henry glanced at his watch. "I have a proposition for you. I was intrigued by your story of how you found us. We are having a dinner this evening for our family members responsible for the HEAD project and Paragon. I'd like you to join us and share your story with them. They would find it as fascinating as I did."

It was late afternoon, and we needed to buy more time. Heat-sensing drones or not, we were better off trying to escape at night than during the day. Putting on my best convivial face, I said, "We'd be delighted to join you, wouldn't we?" I gave Kat a look and nodded.

"Wonderful," Henry said. I smiled at him like we were old friends. I smiled at Martin, too, but he wasn't buying any of this bullshit.

Kat looked haggard, and I needed to get her alone, so I said, "Maybe we could freshen up before dinner."

"Certainly," Henry replied, ever the gracious host. "Martin will direct you to a place to do that. We'll see you at seven."

We followed Martin into the hallway. Two more soldiers joined the ones stationed at the door, and Martin led us all to the elevator. Kat and I stepped to the rear, and the four soldiers followed, positioning themselves around us. One of them, whose name tag read Smith 7, kept his eyes on me as the elevator descended. He was powerfully built, like Martin, and had short-cropped red hair and a fat-lipped sneer. He reminded me of a bartender at Durty Nelly's Irish pub in San Francisco who always looks one insult away from a fistfight. Another of the soldiers, Smith 39, tried to appear disinterested but kept stealing glances at Kat. He was a homely, mid-twenties kid with big floppy ears and a pimply face. I doubt he'd had much seasoning. He probably hadn't had female company for a while—or maybe ever.

When the elevator stopped, and its doors opened, Martin stepped out. There was a large room behind him. I caught only a glimpse but saw scores of wall-mounted monitors and a hive of activity. Their command center, I guessed. After descending to the first floor, Seven motioned us out, and we followed him down the hall. He paused before a door and unlocked it with a card key. It opened into a monastic room with a single bed, dresser, nightstand with a lamp, easy chair, and small bathroom. Two sets of towels lay on the bed, and four water bottles sat on a silver tray atop the dresser.

We entered, and as Seven began to close the door, I said, "Hey, why are all you guys named Smith? What's up with that?" His sneer morphed into a slivered smile as he closed the door and latched it.

Kat opened her mouth, but I quickly shook my head, pulled her close, and kissed her lightly on the lips. She was too startled to kiss back. Then I hugged her, my mouth beside her ear. "Assume they can hear and see everything," I whispered.

I felt her nod, and then she pulled back and gazed at me. Anxiety had drained the color from her cheeks and deepened the lines around her eyes and lips. She put her arms around me and pulled me close, her mouth going to my ear, and she whispered, "I'm worried about Sara. I can't stop thinking about her."

I held her tight for a long moment. Then I nudged her head aside with my cheek and whispered into her ear, "I know." As we hugged, I felt the pressure of her fingers on my back and the rhythm of her breathing. Her shirt was soft, and she was warm, but the muscles in her back were tense. After a few minutes, she pulled back and gazed at me again, her eyes exploring my face as though she were seeing me for the first time. Her face was pinched with worry, but it softened as we held each other. Her eyes began to moisten, tears welling on her lower lids. She brushed the tears away with one crooked finger, then leaned in and kissed me fully. Her lips were warm and soft and wet. We kissed for a long moment, and my heart quickened. Finally, she broke away, slid her soft cheek along mine, and whispered into my ear, "We picked a hell of a time to become romantic."

26

We were locked in a small room in a hard place, watched by people who will kill us tonight.
I had no doubt. We'd bought time this afternoon, but our hours, like our options, were
running out. Between dinner and our execution, there had to be some moment when
the odds tipped in our favor. I worried about Kat. She was capable but a cop, not a street
fighter. She'd play by the rules, and street fights have no rules.

I whispered to her that we'd be taken away after dinner and guarded. I said I would
act quickly when I saw an opportunity—and I didn't think there'd be many. She grew
anxious and found my ear, urgently whispering, "What are you planning?"

We couldn't let them see us whispering, so I kissed her again, snuggled against her ear,
and whispered, "I won't know till it happens. Trust me."

She turned to my ear and whispered, "This is scaring the hell out of me."

I held her close enough to feel her heartbeat. "I know. But you have to trust me. I'll
get us out of this."

She nodded and went into the bathroom. She returned a few minutes later, pulled me
close, and whispered, "Microphone under the sink, but I couldn't find any cameras. I'm
going to get cleaned up." She returned to the bathroom and closed the door. A minute
later, I heard the toilet flush and the shower running. I thought about where I would
mount cameras in this room and searched casually, knowing they'd be watching me. I
spotted one tiny camera lens in the lamp's base and another in the bathroom door below
the doorknob. I couldn't find the listening devices, but they were there.

When Kat left the bathroom, I hugged her, whispered where the cameras were, and
then got in the shower. While the hot water ran over me, I thought about how they'd

dispose of us. I know how I'd do it, and I was reasonably sure they'd do the same. If I was right, we'd have one chance to escape. Just one. When I opened the bathroom door, Kat was sitting on the bed looking pensive. She'd removed her badge and stared quietly at it, the gold shield gleaming. Then she glanced up with a determined look, which softened when she saw me and returned the badge to her pocket. We had about an hour until they came for us, so I walked over and sat on the bed beside her. Her hair was damp and smelled freshly shampooed. Her skin was soft and clean. I put my arm around her and kissed her on the cheek. As she hugged me, I whispered, "I think I know how they'll do it. After dinner, watch my eyes and follow my lead." I felt her nod, and I put a hand under her chin, pulled her face toward me, and kissed her on the lips again. I could feel the worry on her face, but this kiss was a warm promise like the ones before it. Again at her ear, I whispered, "Did you see that guard eying you?" She nodded. "If he's part of the detail taking us away, you need to distract him. I'll let you know when."

We played kissy face a little more, and she whispered, "Don't worry. I'll have him drooling."

"It's working on me," I whispered.

"Good," she said, giving me another long, warm, wet kiss that left my face flushed and warmth spreading in my groin. Then she whispered, "I'm sorry about losing it with Henry. I couldn't help it. What they're doing is evil."

"It's okay," I whispered back. "They were always going to kill us. You didn't do any harm. I was playing the good cop to your bad cop."

"These people have violated federal law. I don't have any authority outside of Sacramento, but this is an emergency, so the hell with it. I'm a police officer, and I'm deputizing you. In case something happens."

I laughed at the idea of being deputized. "Something will happen," I said.

"I'll be ready," she whispered. "I'm pissed off and really fucking motivated."

When the knock came at the door, I glanced at my watch. It was seven on the dot. The door opened, and Martin stood there with that same blank look. Chances are he'd been watching us, probably with a leering crowd of soldiers hoping we'd do more than kiss. "Come with me," he said. We followed him to the elevator. Two soldiers escorted us, redheaded Smith 7 and pimply-faced Smith 39, still carrying AR-15s. Seven's sneer annoyed me. I hoped they'd be around after dinner.

We took the elevator to the fourth floor and the most exquisite dining hall I'd ever seen—polished cherry walls, opulent crystal chandeliers, and a massive stone fireplace at one end. The table was large enough to seat forty and was beautifully set on the end nearest the fireplace. The outside wall had a bank of tall windows with long white lace curtains pulled open. It was now dusk, and the storm clouds muted the light, but I could still see drops of rain hitting the windows and caught an occasional flash of lightning. It would be dark in an hour. The storm was upon us.

Henry stood at the fireplace talking to a middle-aged man of medium height. That man wore dark slacks and a white shirt under a gray tweed jacket. He had a trimmed white beard and mustache. When we approached, Henry said, "Ah, here you are. Let me introduce my brother Gordon, head of Paragon." Gordon shook our hands. "These are our guests this evening," Henry told his brother. "Sonny Marshall and Katrina Hastings. Sonny is a musician from San Francisco, and Sergeant Hastings is with the Sacramento Police Department." Gordon said he was delighted to meet us, and Henry asked if we'd like some wine, a fine cabernet, he promised. Two other men entered the room and were introduced as Ralph Bellamy and David Montgomery Barnard.

Bellamy was a lanky man with short-cropped gray hair and wire-rim glasses. He had thin lips and a nose whose tip drooped like a parrot's beak. Henry told us that Bellamy was the intellectual architect of the HEAD project. He glanced at us briefly after shaking our hands, but his eyes flitted with restless energy. After half a beat, he turned to Gordon and spoke to him, but his eyes were restless even with Gordon. His attention seemed about a quarter step ahead of whomever he was talking to. David Barnard was Henry's youngest brother, a dashing fellow in his mid-forties with a long face, short brown hair, and a patchy growth of hair on his face. He smiled broadly and told us he was head of the guardians. Paragon was indeed a Barnard family affair.

As Henry handed us wine, a young man and woman entered the room. The man was thirty-something and had a dark goatee. But where I have a long face with a square jaw, Lawrence Livingston Barnard (one of Henry's sons and known to everyone as "Livingston") had a round, pudgy face like Mr. Potato Head with bushy dark eyebrows that looked glued on. But if his appearance was comical, nothing was funny about his purpose, which I understood when I saw his wife. I recognized her instantly from her photograph. She was the dark-haired woman in Green River, the one at the ATM in Salem, the female member of their kidnap team. She was introduced as Laura Wilson Barnard, Livingston's wife. Then I realized that Livingston had played the security guard in Sacramento. Seven years later, he was the gas company representative in Salem. He snatched the children. I felt my pulse quickening when I saw them—that shock of recognition. I could imagine what the sight of them did to Kat. When Henry introduced us, I shook their hands, but Kat refused, creating an awkward moment. She would rather have been slapping handcuffs on them.

Henry suggested we move to the table. He sat at the head and told us to sit by him. Three more women entered as we approached the table, and Henry quickly introduced us. His sister, Dorothy Richmond Barnard, ran administration for Paragon and was head of their intellectual property rights division. She was a pleasant woman of about fifty with pale skin and the heavy makeup women of her age sometimes use. She greeted us warmly and then spoke to Gordon. Henry's wife, Stephanie Louise Barnard, was a tall, beautiful woman with long, grayish-blonde hair. She wore a dark green suit with a black pearl necklace and had small eyeglasses with tortoiseshell frames. She's a physician, Henry told us, and head of their breeder program, the Genetic Accelerator. She affected warmth but could not disguise her contempt for us. She was too aloof to coddle children, but I could imagine her designing babies with little regard for them as human beings. The third woman was Henry's other sister, Ruth Walsingham Bellamy. She had short blonde hair and a face that would once have been pretty but was now showing wear. As I shook her hand, I wanted to say she was why we were here. *We don't know you, Ruth,* I thought, *but we know your mailbox. Thanks for helping us locate those two missing girls. And hundreds of other missing children.*

Dinner was served by white-coated Asian waiters, petite men who were polite and well-groomed but spoke no English. The head waiter wore a red sash and gave them directions mainly with his hands and eyes. I had no doubt they were paid well for their service, but the gulf between them and our hosts made me wonder what this new world order the Barnards envisioned would be like for us omegas. Dinner was simple, healthy, and would compare with meals in the finest five-star restaurants. I couldn't have asked for a finer last meal.

Before the dessert was served, Henry told us that we'd come at a propitious moment because they were holding the quarterly meeting of their leadership team. Then he asked for silence and said to everyone, "I asked our guests to join us this evening because they told me the most entertaining story earlier today. They've come from California, and I think you'll be fascinated by how they found Paragon."

I looked at Kat, but she shook her head, wanting no part of this charade. So I told the story, pausing now and then to clarify this point or that. They were curious about how we traced them to New Mexico and how the ATM receipt helped us link the two kidnappings and led us to ASGC. Ralph Bellamy found the story implausible, arguing that we'd made unwarranted assumptions and our logic was flawed.

"They're here, aren't they?" Henry said dryly.

When I finished telling them how we discovered Paragon, Stephanie Barnard said, "The two of you did this on your own? It wasn't part of an official investigation?"

"It's part of my investigation into the kidnapping of Erin Hightower," Kat asserted.

Stephanie cast a concerned look at her husband, and Henry said, "They came to Ruidoso by themselves. We don't see any other activity."

You missed John and Earl, I thought. *They're now in Ruidoso, and when you see them, you will know it.* But what I said was, "Henry's right. We came here on our own. We had no idea Paragon existed until we stumbled upon it, and even then, we didn't know what it was. Now we can't wait to return home and show our friends the photos from our trip."

Everyone except Martin looked at me like I'd told an off-color joke. Martin looked amused. An uneasy silence followed, then side conversations erupted, so many I couldn't follow them, but the gist was recognizing that they had to scrutinize how they'd been operating and increase security to protect themselves from people like us. Livingston and Laura Barnard bore most of the criticism, which was unfair because they'd kidnapped children for years and hadn't been caught. Ruth Bellamy got her share of grief for being careless enough to open a post office box in her name.

"None of this was my idea," she snapped. "Henry told me to get a mailbox so ASGC had an address for Paragon. Don't blame me!"

"It seems you've stirred up a hornet's nest," Henry said as an aside. "Exactly what I wanted. We've become complacent, it seems, and need to reexamine operational security."

"Glad we could help," I said. "Now, fair's fair. I have some questions."

"Okay," Henry said, smiling at us. Gordon sat at the corner of the table next to Henry, and he smiled, too, immune from the soul-searching around the table.

"Why are all the soldiers named Smith?"

"We don't use real names among our staff," Henry said. "Our security people are called Smith. The maintenance workers are Jones. The professors, or mentors, are named Escalante. It helps our younger scholars, like Rachel Nine when their mentor is called Escalante Thirty, or just E Thirty. It makes them feel normal. As they reach higher levels and prepare to transition to the omega world, full names become important."

"Why do you insist on changing their names?" said Kat.

"After we acquire them, we want them to adopt their new identity as quickly as possible. Who they were with their birth family is no longer relevant."

"It is to their parents," Kat said. Henry turned away and signaled the head waiter to refill our wine glasses.

"If your educational system is so superior," I told Gordon, "why don't you go public and open real schools?"

He shook his head distastefully as though I'd offered him caviar on a saltine. "Our system depends on having brilliant, motivated scholars. We have a demanding program. Like Montessori schools, all our learning is project-based, and our learners work in cohorts with mentors. But we have a rigorous curriculum and set very high expectations."

"From the beginning," Henry added, "we teach them that they are special and are meant to rule the world. They hear that message every day."

"Sounds like you're developing a group of narcissists," I said.

"Healthy narcissists," Henry replied, holding one finger up to emphasize his point. "Narcissism is healthy if it's warranted; unhealthy if it's not. Self-pride is essential for achievement. Pride is the prerequisite for self-confidence, which is a prerequisite for effective leadership and command. We don't want braggarts and bullies, Sonny. We want superior people who know their superiority and employ it wisely."

No, you want to create a master race and subjugate the rest of humanity to them, I thought. "Fetch saw the girl you call Rachel Nine in Wyoming. She was with your kidnap team in Salem, too. What was she doing there?"

"She was on an excursion," Gordon replied. "At Level Six, they begin traveling through the omega world to see firsthand what it's like. Of course, they always go with guardians and are closely supervised, but we need them to experience the omega world and see how flawed it is. With each increase in level, they earn more privileges like omega excursions."

Kat looked alarmed. "She wasn't part of the kidnapping, was she?"

Henry laughed at the thought. "No, no," he said. "And we call them acquisitions, by the way. No, she was along to further her omega studies."

Gordon said, "We teach them omega history, psychology, sociology, and religion so they can better understand what's wrong with humanity and why omegas make bad decisions and act irrationally. Understanding omegas is critically important when they assume commanding roles."

I turned to Henry. "You called Paragon a wealth engine," I said, "but your goal isn't to create wealth. Your goal is to create a master race and to do that, your alphas should breed only with other alphas, as you said. Wouldn't you corrupt the superior gene pool if they left Paragon and screwed around with ordinary omegas like us?"

"Absolutely," Henry replied. "They would fall out of the program and lose their shares of the wealth if they did that."

"We encourage them to mate," Gordon added. "When our alphas become sexually mature, we educate them on sexual relations and encourage them to experience it with each other when they're ready."

"When they become sexually mature? Did I hear that right?" Kat said. "That can happen when girls reach twelve or thirteen. Do you encourage it then?"

"If they are psychologically ready, yes," Gordon replied. "But only sex with other alphas. Never anyone else. And we arrange some couplings based on their genetic profiles."

Kat's mouth hung open, her breath caught in her throat. Her daughter was that age. "Are you aware that that is child abuse?" she said, loudly enough that it hushed the table. "If the girls become pregnant? What then?"

Gordon looked smugly at her and raised his chin. "We encourage it, absolutely. Their progeny are the next generation in creating a superior race of human beings. In fact, I believe more than forty of our female alphas are pregnant."

"Forty-six," Stephanie said, looking pointedly at Kat, then turning to Gordon. "Three more last week, including Clarissa Thirteen. She had trouble conceiving, if you recall. Happily, we've solved her difficulties."

Kat looked stricken, so I ran with it. "What happens to the babies?"

"Naturally, we raise them," Stephanie said. "And when they are five years of age, if they meet our other criteria, we enroll them in Paragon."

"You must have some failures," Kat said. "You can't be right one hundred percent of the time. Even as selective as you are, there must be some children who don't measure up. What happens to them? What happens to the rejects?"

I looked around the room, scanning each of their faces, and the only person who wasn't uncomfortable with that question was Martin. He casually picked at his dessert as though nothing had happened. No one spoke for a long moment. Then Henry said, "You are correct, Sergeant. Some don't advance through the levels as rapidly as they should or show themselves to be unfit for behavioral reasons. Obviously, they can't remain in our alpha population."

"So what happens to them?" she insisted.

Henry looked to the others for help, but no one came to his aid. Finally, he said, "They are reassigned."

"That's a new one," Kat said. "I've never heard it called that before. You can't return them to their families, and you can't release them. So by reassigning them, you mean handing them over to Martin and his stormtroopers? Does he bury the bodies in the desert?"

Stephanie gave Henry a scathing look and said, "Must we listen to this drivel?"

Kat glared at her and cried, "I'm through playing nice with you people. You've kidnapped more than two hundred children. You've sexually abused them, no matter how you justify it, and if they don't measure up, you've murdered them. I don't give a damn how lofty your aims are; what you've done is morally repugnant and criminal."

The silence in the room was so complete you could hear distant thunder rumbling. The waiters froze, too, maybe not comprehending what was happening but sensing they shouldn't move. Then Ralph Bellamy said, "Are you familiar with the Heinz Dilemma?"

I shook my head.

"It's a moral dilemma developed by psychologist Lawrence Kohlberg to elucidate stages in moral development. Heinz lived in a small town, and his wife became ill with cancer. A local pharmacist had developed a drug that doctors said would cure her, but the pharmacist wanted more money for the drug than Heinz had or could borrow. The pharmacist was unwilling to sell the drug at a discount, even knowing it would cure the woman's cancer. So Heinz broke into the pharmacy and stole the drug. The question is, was Heinz right or wrong? People who believe in law and order say Heinz was wrong; he should not have committed the crime and should be penalized for it. But people at a higher stage of moral development argue that Heinz was justified because saving a human life has more moral value than the pharmacist's property rights. We certainly recognize that some of our decisions violate the letter of the law. But what we will accomplish by doing so has far more value to humanity than avoiding the conventional crimes you think we've committed. What we are doing is morally justifiable because it will save humanity."

Kat stared at him as the silence in the room deepened. Then she said, "I don't buy it." She pushed back from the table and stood up. Taking her badge from her back pocket, she held it up and said, "You're all under arrest."

<h1 style="text-align:center">27</h1>

Kat's announcement left the Barnards dumbfounded. People of their economic and social station had never heard those words. I chuckled at their shocked faces and nervous glances. Then Martin barked a laugh, startling everyone. Head thrown back, eyes wrinkled shut, he shook with laughter that spread like a virus to the others. Even the waiters began tittering. Kat glared at the Barnards, her neck corded. "I am fucking serious," she screamed, and the room was again shocked silent.

Then Henry nodded at Martin and said to Kat, "So are we."

No longer the gracious host, he now had the deathly demeanor of a judge passing a mortal sentence, but Martin couldn't suppress a smile, which I appreciated because I didn't think the guy had a sense of humor. He opened the door and waved Smiths Seven and Thirty-nine inside. Then he ordered us to stand and waved us toward the door. Kat stood her ground for a tense moment before returning the badge to her pocket and complying.

Before we left, I turned to the family and said, "Well, this has been fun. Let's do it again. How about our place next time?" No one responded. I guess they didn't want to encourage a wiseass. In the hallway, Martin led us to the elevator. He wore a black sports coat, which fell awkwardly because of a bulge on his right hip. His Colt. He walked with the surety of a man who embraced his mission. Solid, rugged, well-trained, and undoubtedly quick. A gladiator. The Barnard family's Heinrich Himmler.

At the elevator door, I glanced at our guards. Seven looked at me like he would enjoy pulling the trigger. I was his manhood challenge for the day, and he could count coup by killing me. In the elevator, Seven held his rifle with a firm grip. Thirty-nine was more relaxed. Seven was the cautious one. There'd be no grabbing that rifle away from him, which gave me an idea.

I told Martin, "This has been a wonderful visit, but we would appreciate it if you could return our things and take us to our car."

That provoked another smile, and he said, "Just what I had in mind."

"I thought that's how it would go down. An accident? But not close to Paragon." When he didn't respond, I said, "At least give me the satisfaction of knowing if I'm right."

He looked smugly at me. "Eighty miles from here. North of the highway. A ravine with a steep drop from the road. They won't find your bodies for months. But we'll leave the windows open, so the coyotes will find you." Seven observed Martin like a fawning puppy and smiled. I wanted to ask Seven if he was Martin's Mini-me but decided against it. I needed Seven to be cocky, not angry. Martin left the elevator on the second floor, telling our guards he'd meet them in the sally port in two minutes.

When the elevator reached the sally port, Seven backed out and waved with his rifle for us to follow. Then he told us to stand by the driveway. *We have two minutes.* Seven stood a few feet from me, keeping a close watch. Thirty-nine stood next to Seven, facing us, about five feet away. He kept staring at Kat while trying to be nonchalant. I saw a door I hadn't noticed when we arrived. Farther into the sally port tunnel with a sign that read *Danger—High Voltage.* An electrical utility room. The only avenue of escape was up the sally port drive. Then I heard a vehicle and saw a black van easing down the driveway into the sally port. Our ride.

I caught Kat's eye and glanced at the approaching van, canting my head slightly. She saw it and turned back. I gave her a slight nod, and she returned the gesture, indicating, I prayed, that she understood what I wanted her to do. I dropped my eyes to her chest and held them there for a beat. Then I looked into her eyes and saw that she understood. She raised her hand to the spot between her breasts and began pulling at her bra as if it needed adjusting. I casually turned and saw that Thirty-nine had developed tunnel vision. He had only one thought on his hormonal mind.

Seven stared at me defiantly as the van drew near, daring me to give him an excuse. When the van stopped beside us, I said quietly to him, "You aren't tough unless you've survived a night in the Tenderloin." His eyes narrowed as he strained to comprehend what I'd said. Then the van driver's door began to open. We now had just over a minute.

Guys like Seven are junior psychopaths willing to inflict pain, given the license to do so. When they're guarding prisoners, the worst thing that can happen is to lose control of their weapons. That's what I counted on. While his mind was distracted by my Tenderloin comment and the arrival of the van, I quickly spun and grabbed his rifle with both hands, my feet planted. I pulled back sharply, and he instinctively resisted, holding onto the gun with every ounce of his arm strength. Then before Thirty-nine could react, I launched a swift, stiff-legged kick at his throat. My boot heel crushed his windpipe, and he dropped his rifle and staggered backward, hands flying to his throat. He clawed for air, a stricken look on his face, and collapsed. He would suffocate within minutes.

Behind me, Kat threw herself into the partially open door. The driver bellowed in surprise, and Kat kept slamming the door into him. With my right leg back down, I pulled at Seven's rifle, and he pulled back hard, eyes wide, face ashen. We played a deadly tug-of-war, his rifle midway between us, and he was a strong son of a bitch. I'd surprised him, but he was hell-bent on winning this battle. One of the fundamental principles of Aikido is to use your opponent's energy against him. If I wrestled with Seven over the rifle, one of us would tire, and it might be me. So I clung to the rifle but instantly stopped trying to pull it away from him. The force he continued to exert made the rifle fly back toward his body, and as that happened, I thrust the butt end of the rifle upward. It was a motion he hadn't expected, and before he could counteract it, the rifle's stock caught him squarely on the side of his face. His head snapped sideways, blood, saliva, and broken teeth spewing from his mouth. He yelped, and I threw my body downward, trying to use my weight to wrest the rifle from him while he was in agony, but the stubborn bastard refused to let go.

Then the air was split by the thunderous roar of gunfire, amplified and echoing in the confines of the sally port. Someone behind me was firing an assault rifle on automatic. As I sank lower, Seven let go of the rifle. I dropped to the pavement and saw him jerking backward against the wall, a line of bullet holes stitched across his chest and shoulders. As the roar of firing continued, Seven slumped, his body deflating, blood forming a connect-the-dots pattern across his chest. Bullets ricocheted off the wall, exploding fragments of the stone wall flying with them. Clutching Seven's rifle, I rolled onto my stomach and spun around on the pavement. Kat crouched against the van's door, straining to hold it closed.

The rifle fire came from the other side of the van. A fourth guard, riding shotgun. I saw his boots beneath the van on the other side. He kept firing over the top of the van, not the smartest tactical maneuver. He inched toward the van's rear, trying to circle it, and before I lost sight of his boots behind a tire, I aimed at his feet and fired a three-round burst. He collapsed, shrieking in pain, his body a wriggling dark mass under the van. I fired another burst into his core, and the movement and shrieking stopped.

Jumping to my feet, I saw Kat still struggling with the driver. The side of the van was splattered with blood, the driver's mangled head hanging outside. Rivers of red ran down his face, and his broken left foot dangled beneath the door. His eyes were wild with rage. He had both hands out of the door and was wedging it open. I raised the rifle and butted him in the forehead. He grunted and yelled, "Fuck, fuck, fuck." So I hit him again, harder, and heard a vicious crack as his forehead split open. He slumped and fell out of the van as Kat released the door.

The smell of blood, metal, and sulfur permeated the sally port. Smoke hung in the air. We were both out of breath, and Kat had blood splattered on her face and hands. My ears rang. "We don't have much time," I yelled. She nodded, sucking in breaths, and we pulled the unconscious driver away from the van. He wore a tactical duty belt with a pistol, a knife, and other gear. Kat quickly undid his belt, threw it into the van, and then jumped into the driver's seat while I ripped open the van's side door and jumped inside. Then I spun and looked at the elevator. As Kat put the van in gear, the elevator door began to slide open. I fired a burst through the door. I could see nothing inside but a shadow reflected on the elevator's back wall. Probably Martin, and now he'd be hugging the wall beside the control panel. "Get us the hell out of here," I screamed, firing into the elevator until the clip was empty and the van lurched away.

Water poured down the driveway as we raced up toward the perimeter road. We were enveloped in pouring rain when we left the sally port. Kat cranked on the windshield wipers and yelled, "Which way?"

"South," I stammered. "To the right."

Our tires spun on wet pavement as we accelerated through the downpour. "Where are we going?"

"Building One Thirty-five," I said. "That's where Erin and Angela will be." My knee throbbed severely and felt like a basketball. Though painful to touch, I massaged it. We saw the flickering lights from buildings and streetlamps on our right through the rain-beaded windows as we rushed past. To our left was the perimeter fence and immense darkness beyond, lit fleetingly by flashes of lightning as the storm raged.

"How are we going to get out of here?" Kat cried.

"I don't know. But those girls are why we're here. We have to find them."

"I know, but God, Sonny," Kat said. Her voice was wound tight. "We have to get out of here."

"We will." I scooted up and looked around at her. She was trembling. A near-death experience and a massive dose of adrenalin will do that to you. I put a hand on her shoulder and squeezed it. "Thanks," I said. "You saved my ass back there."

She looked at me warily, her face tight with anxiety and freckled with blood. "Can they see us?" she said.

I kept patting her shoulder. "Yeah, but not well in this rain. They'll be confused for a few more minutes, trying to piece together what's happening. But they'll have cameras inside the dormitory. They'll see us then. We have to be quick."

"What time is it?"

"Why? You have an appointment?"

"No, I just . . . I'm just . . ."

"It's okay," I said, squeezing her shoulder. "I'm wired, too." I checked my watch. "Just after nine."

"Do you still have your rifle?"

"The clip's empty."

As we passed the helipad, Kat slowed, and I saw figures scurrying around one of the choppers. There was movement, too, at the edge of the helipad.

"Did we kill that guy? The driver." Kat said.

"No, but he'll have a hell of a headache when he wakes up."

"What about the other three? What about them? The other guards?"

"Dead."

I kept rubbing her shoulder, and she wasn't trembling as much. "Good. They would've killed us."

"That was the plan." I strained to make out the numbers on the buildings as we passed them, but the rain and our speed made it difficult.

"I feel sorry about that kid, though."

"Thirty-nine? Me too. But he signed up for this. He should've stayed on the farm. For all we know, he pulled the trigger on some of their rejects. Okay, slow down. I think I just saw the sign for Building One Twenty." The buildings we passed were sizable, four or five stories. Their numbers were engraved on stone blocks at the right corner of each building. "One Thirty," I read as we came to that building. Kat slowed more. The rain obscured the building ahead, but many windows were lighted, particularly on the higher floors. There was a small parking area in front of the building. Empty. Kat turned into it, and I could see the cornerstone. Building 135.

As we coasted to a stop, Kat cut the lights. We didn't see anything except rain. No soldiers. No vehicles. No guardians. Nobody. It was eerily quiet except for the pounding of rain on the van's roof and the pavement outside. Kat took the pistol from its holster, racked it, and thumbed it back. Then she removed the clip and checked it. "Glock Fifteen," she said. "Full clip and a spare on the holster." She looked over the duty belt. "Handcuffs. Knife. And keys. On the belt. You want any of this?"

I shook my head. "We won't have much time inside. Need to find Erin quickly and evacuate her."

"Back here?"

"No. This'll be a trap. They'll put up roadblocks. Have to find another way out."

"Dammit! What about Angela?"

"Let's find Erin first."

"Okay," she said. She scooched forward and fastened the duty belt around her waist. "Let's go."

The rain had slackened a little, but we were still soaked when we reached the door. It was oversized, wooden, with a glass window. We peered through it and saw a reception desk in a foyer. A young blonde man wearing a black shirt sat behind the desk. A guardian. He was in his late twenties, clean-shaven, with neat, short hair. Kat said, "They haven't sounded the alarm, or this place would be locked down. I'll take the lead. Okay with you?"

"You're the cop."

She turned the doorknob and found the door unlocked. She looked at me and nodded. Then she burst through it and sprinted to the desk, the Glock and her shield held high. "Police," she yelled. "Hands up. Now, now, now, now." The guy recoiled when he saw her coming. He jumped up, stumbling backward, face wide with fright. His chair was on wheels. It skittered across the room and slammed into the wall. He was a tall kid, lanky, and stood with his arms raised, shaking.

I slammed the door and ran to the desk, searching for a cell phone. There was a black desk phone, but I didn't trust it. "Do you have a cell phone?"

He shook his head. "They're not allowed," he said.

I pointed at the desk phone. "Can you get an outside line on this?" He shook his head again. "Down on your knees," I told him. When he didn't move, I walked behind him and pushed him down. His hands shook, and his face was white as chalk. "We're looking for Rachel Nine," I said. "Where is she?"

"I can't tell you that," he managed—the good boy scout. But I didn't hear a firm resolve.

I said to Kat, "Let's just kill this asshole." She tapped him on the side of his head with the Glock, but he stayed silent.

I faced him and said, "Look, man. There's an easy way to do this and a messy way. You've got nothing to prove. They'll know you had a gun in your face. So let's avoid the drama. Where is she?"

He looked at me, and I saw his resolve crumble. "Third floor. I don't know which room. It's on the list." He pointed at the desk, and I found a laminated list of names and room numbers beside the phone. "Three forty-two," I told Kat. She handcuffed him to the desk. While she did, I scanned the list and found Angela's room number. Then Kat cut the cord on the desk phone while I bounded up the stairs. Pain shot through my left knee, but I kept moving, Kat half a stairway behind me. The building was like most collegiate dorms: institutional gray walls, tile floors, modern furniture, bulletin boards, and common areas with sofas and chairs. We scrambled onto the third floor and hurried to Room 342. A camera was at the top of the stairs and more along the long hallway. We were being watched and didn't have more than three or four minutes, but I waited for Kat to reach me. Erin was her case. She should be the first one through the door.

She knocked, and a girl inside said, "Come in." Kat holstered the Glock and pushed open the door. The room was cozy and warm. There were two girls inside. A dark-skinned girl was lying on a bed reading a book. She glanced up in alarm, and I didn't blame her. We were wild-eyed and soaked. The rain had washed off some of the blood, but we still must have looked like freaks. Erin had been sitting at a desk working on her tablet. When we came in, she dropped the tablet and stood, body frozen. Both girls were frightened. What was happening was so far outside their experience that they couldn't comprehend it.

Kat approached Erin cautiously. "Don't be afraid. It's okay. I'm a police officer." She showed them her badge.

Erin backed away. "What do you want?" she cried. She looked prettier in person than she did in Bai's photo. Her eyes were perfectly shaped, emerald green, with long lashes. Her lips were fuller and lusher, and she had long, lustrous brown hair. She'd be a knockout when she grew up.

"Rachel," Kat said. "When you were five, you were taken from your parents and brought here. The people who did that committed a crime. I'm the police officer responsible for solving that crime and bringing you home. Do you understand?" Erin shook her head. "Your real name is Erin Hightower, and you were born in Sacramento, California."

The girls glanced at each other but were mute.

"I know this is overwhelming, but we must leave quickly."

"No," Erin pleaded. She backed farther away.

"Rachel," I said. "A little over a month ago, you took a trip with Livingston and Laura Barnard. Remember? You were with them in Salem, Oregon. On the way back, you stopped at a convenience store in Green River, Wyoming, and you went inside the store with Laura. A friend of mine recognized you. He called you by your real name, Erin, and you looked at him. You looked at him because you recognized your name."

"My name is Rachel," she insisted.

"I know, honey," Kat said. "The people here have called you Rachel, but they had no right to do that. Your parents named you Erin. Erin Hightower."

"We have to get out of here," I whispered to Kat.

"I know," she said. Then to Erin: "I'll explain on the way, but we need to leave."

Kat walked around the desk and took Erin's hand. She said, "Please trust me," and led her toward the door.

The other girl looked terrified, and I said, "It's okay. Don't worry." I went to the door and cautiously peered out but didn't see anyone. I turned and nodded to Kat, and she brought Erin to the door.

Then Erin jerked her hand away from Kat's and looked at us as though we'd brought the plague. "You're omegas," she spat, hitting a red button beside the door, a fire alarm I hadn't noticed. A siren wailed as Erin fled behind her desk. The other girl joined her, and they hugged each other. The siren grew louder, its wailing infuriating, and my heart sank. It felt like my recurring nightmare had become real, that I could not put out the fire, save the drowning swimmer, or rescue Teagan from a madman dragging her into an empty house. It felt like I was twelve again on that awful night in Pasadena when I couldn't rescue Aileen.

I felt Kat tugging at my arm, but I couldn't take my eyes off those two terrified girls holding each other as though we meant them harm. Then she pulled harder and jerked me down the hallway, opposite the way we'd come in. "Hurry, Sonny," she screamed. "We have to get the hell out of here."

28

With the siren wailing, we ran down the long hallway. The racket had roused the students. They spilled into the hallway, bewildered by the sight of two strangers racing through their sanctuary. A sea of frightened faces parted as we drew near and closed behind us like we were surfing through the hallway on a wave of apprehension. Kat kept the Glock holstered until we reached the top of the stairs but pulled it out as we started down. Halfway down, a door across the stairwell banged open, and a guard rushed through it. He wore black body armor and a black helmet over camouflage fatigues and carried an assault rifle.

Kat yelled, "Police! Stop!" but the guy was too startled to think and raised his rifle. Kat leveled the Glock and fired two quick shots. The soldier managed to spray the stairs below us with a burst on automatic. Then he did an awkward back flop, legs still moving forward while his torso slumped backward. One hand flew to his throat, but he couldn't staunch the flow of blood. I raced down and grabbed the AR-15. He'd been hit twice in the throat and gurgled blood as he struggled to breathe. I looked down the second-floor hallway. Most students had run back into their rooms, but half a dozen craned their heads out of their doors. A camera was mounted on the ceiling in the middle of the hallway, and another directly above us. I aimed at the one overhead and fired a quick burst, shattering the camera, pieces raining around me. Then I aimed at the camera in the hallway, and the students ducked back into their rooms as I destroyed that one.

Then three deafening shots overhead stunned me. I hit the floor and rolled. Kat stood over me in a shooter's stance. She'd fired those rounds into the room the guard had come out of. "He's down," she yelled. I clambered to my feet, my left knee on fire, and peered into the room. It was a small office with a body slumped against the far wall. Another guard, this one half-in and half-out of his body armor. His head had fallen unnaturally, and he lay still. I ran to the door and scanned the room. There were no other threats.

When I turned back, Kat looked stunned, gazing at the guy she'd shot. He lay still, having bled out through the neck. His face was ghostly white, and the floor was awash in red. She still held the Glock with both hands. I hurried to her.

"Help me pull this guy inside." She looked stricken but nodded. We grasped the guy under his arms and pulled him into the office, and I slammed the door.

Kat stared at the body against the far wall. "He was aiming at you," she said. "He raised his rifle. He wasn't even dressed."

"You had no choice. Give me the knife." I told her to put on the guy's body armor as she did. "Hurry. We don't have much time."

While she removed his breastplate, I hurried to the other guy. He'd been hit squarely in the face and had a baseball-sized exit wound in the back of his head. Blood and bits of flesh and bone were splattered everywhere. I shook out his body armor, shrugged it on, and slipped the bloody helmet over my head. Then I rotated his head until I found his right ear and felt the lump behind it. I drew the knife across the lump, opened the wound with the blade's tip, and fished out his locater. Underneath the blood, the device was light gray, the size of a small hearing aid. Kat was fastening the straps on her guy's body armor when I reached her. She'd already put on the helmet and tucked her hair under it. I handed her the locater.

She looked at it like I'd handed her a dead roach. "This what I think it is?"

I knelt beside the body at my feet and cut out his locater. "Yeah. We have to make them think we're these two soldiers. Put it in your mouth. Under your tongue. They're powered by body heat." This guy's name tag read *Smith 31*. I wiped the blood off his locater, popped it into my mouth, and rolled it under my tongue. The coppery taste was strong, and I suppressed the urge to retch. When enough saliva formed, I spit out the foulness. Then I picked up the AR-15, grabbed Thirty-one's radio, and opened the door. A clump of soldiers was busy at the other end of the hall, and I heard shouting upstairs. When I turned back to Kat, she was spitting on her locater and wiping it off. "Hurry!" I cried. She slapped the bitter pill into her mouth and grimaced before joining me at the threshold. The hallway floor was puddled with blood, a long red smear running toward the door. "Don't slip on that," I warned as we left the office.

The soldiers at the other end of the hallway saw us. One of them waved us toward them, but I pointed a finger toward the stairway to the first floor, and we hustled down the stairs. "What're they doing?" Kat said behind me.

"Searching the students' rooms," I called over my shoulder. More soldiers scurried around the first floor, but they were preoccupied, and we eased out the door without a confrontation. With the body armor and helmets, we looked enough like soldiers to pass inspection at a distance. We were on the side of the dormitory that fronted the solar magnifier but weren't under it yet, so we were battered by heavy rain.

It was hard to hear anything in the cold, pounding rain, so I held the radio to my ear and listened. As rain soaked my clothing, I began to feel the chill. I nudged Kat, and we stepped under the solar magnifier. It was warmer under the canopy and mostly dark. Scattered lights illuminated the walkways. "What are they saying?" Kat said.

"They're setting up roadblocks on the perimeter road and sending reinforcements to the main gate. They think we're still in One Thirty-five. But they're checking vehicles, too. That's how they expect us to flee. They have orders to shoot us on sight."

"What are we going to do?"

"Get away from this building. They'll expand the search area when they discover we're not here." I nodded north, and we trotted in that direction, still under the cover of the canopy. We passed Building One Thirty and then One Twenty-five when I spotted a camera mounted under the canopy pointing directly at us. "Shit," I muttered. I'd forgotten that this whole area was under surveillance.

A moment later, a voice on the radio said, "Thirty-one, what's your twenty?" Asking for our location. *They should know that.* I pushed the transmit button and said, "Uh, building one two five. Over."

"Why did you and Forty-seven leave your posts? Over."

"Thought we saw movement outside. We're checking it out. Over."

"All right, Thirty-one. But back on station pronto. Over."

"Roger that. Give us five. Out."

"What's up?" Kat said.

"They're tracking us. Told us to return to One Thirty-five. We need to duck back into the rain. They'll be able to follow the locators, but they can't see us in this downpour." A curtain of rain fell from the edge of the canopy. Stepping through it was like walking through a waterfall. The brisk water ran off my helmet and soaked into my shirt around the collar and down the sleeves. Tiny rivulets ran down my chest and back, and I shook involuntarily from those cold currents.

"How the hell are we going to get out of here?" Kat said.

"This way." I began running north through the rain, north past more buildings, north toward the helipad and the security building, whose lights I could see ahead. It hurt every time I came down on my left knee, but I swallowed the pain and kept running with Kat behind me. Most of the columns holding up the solar magnifier were eight-by-eight steel posts, but as we ran, we came upon a thicker column on the edge of the canopy. It was three times the size of the other columns. We were close to the easternmost point of the compound. At the base of that thicker column was a concrete pad, five by five, with a padlocked metal hatch. I pulled Kat close and said, "If I'm right, this hatch accesses a utility tunnel. The thicker column houses electrical lines that transmit power underground to their substation. On the map, that was the large, buried structure outside the perimeter fence where they store solar energy. If we can get there, we'll be outside the fence."

"If we get there, how do we reach the surface?"

"There'll be access to the surface. An emergency hatch, if nothing else. They wouldn't have built it without that."

"What if you're wrong?"

"Then we're screwed. But it beats waiting in the rain for them to kill us."

She looked around warily. Beads of rain on her helmet reflected lights from the compound, making her head appear studded with stars. Some of her hair had fallen under the helmet and hung in sodden clumps around her neck. Rain coursed down her face like a dozen trails of tears. Even with that, she looked beautiful to me. I angled my head down and kissed her on the lips. When I pulled back, she gave me one of her loopy grins, which I now felt was endearing. I spat my locater into my hand and pressed it into one of hers. "Run to the far side of this building," I said, nodding at the building beside us, "and drop both locaters there. Someplace warm if you can find one. I'll open the hatch."

She clutched my locater and sprinted off while I turned to the hatch. It lay flush with the concrete. The padlock was a serious piece of business—large and thick, hardened steel. I angled the lock's body away from me and placed the rifle barrel two inches from it. I closed my eyes and squeezed the trigger. The rain muted the sound of the shot, but my ears were still ringing when I opened my eyes and saw the lock blown in half. I brushed the broken lock pieces away and pried open the hatch as Kat ran back.

"Heating vent," she panted. "They'll stay warm for a while."

"What building was that?"

"One Ten."

"Let's go."

A metal ladder descended ten feet to a dimly lit tunnel. Opposite the ladder were vertical PVC conduits. Kat started down the ladder while I keyed the mike on the radio and yelled in a panicked voice, "This is Thirty-one. Shots fired! Shots fired!"

"Where are you, Thirty-one?" said a steady voice on the radio. It was a voice I recognized. Martin.

"I'm sure you know where I am," I calmly replied.

"I do," he said. "And we'll be there soon."

"Are we still playing hide-and-seek?"

"We're through playing games."

"You're going to take more casualties. Maybe you this time."

"I don't think so," Martin said.

"I thought you might have been hit in the elevator." He didn't respond, so I said, "Sorry about the mess in the sally port."

"You left one in the dorm, too."

"We're leaving messes everywhere. Were they good men?"

"I have better."

"You'll need them."

"I'm going to enjoy killing you," he said.

"People should enjoy their work. So long, asshole."

Assuming they could track us from the radio's location, I threw it as far toward Building 110 as I could. Then I slung the rifle over my shoulder and climbed far enough to close the hatch. The utility tunnel was concrete, about five feet high, so we had to crouch. One wall was lined with warm conduits. Lights were recessed into the walls about every ten feet.

"Martin and his stormtroopers are on their way," I said. "We don't have much time."

"You keep saying that," she said. She scooted north along the tunnel, moving faster than I could manage. The crouching position hurt my knee. When I put weight on it, I had to push on the knee with my left hand to avoid collapsing. I carried the rifle in my right. We'd gone maybe a hundred feet when we came to another ladder to a service hatch. We stopped and listened for sounds behind us but heard nothing.

"What's keeping them?" Kat said.

"They'll worry about an ambush. That'll slow them down."

"Could be," she worried. "Or maybe they know exactly what we're doing and will be waiting for us when we pop up on the other side."

I shrugged. "We don't have many options."

We took off down the tunnel, Kat in the lead. After several hundred feet, we came to a larger tunnel running perpendicular to the one we were in. Turning right should take us east, and that's where Kat headed. This tunnel was closer to six feet high, so I could walk through it by lowering my head. There were thicker conduits in this tunnel. I could hear the hum of electricity coursing through them. We scampered down this tunnel for ten minutes, pausing now and then but still not hearing anyone. Then we came to a white metal fire door. Kat tried the lever, and the latch retracted. She held up the Glock and her badge and said, "Ready?" I nodded, and she swung the door open and burst into the room beyond. It was a small control room. The console occupied one wall and was filled with gauges, switches, and monitors. Two men sat at the console. They wore tan coveralls and were drinking coffee. On the opposite wall were personnel lockers. When Kat burst in, she yelled, "Police. Raise your hands. Now!" While she ran to them, I slammed the door shut.

Startled, the men wheeled around in their chairs and raised their hands. Their name tags read Jones 16 and Jones 35. While Kat held the Glock on them, I said, "Anyone else in here?" When they didn't respond quickly enough, I pointed the rifle at the lockers and blew a hole in the closest one. In that confined space, the gunshot was deafening.

"Jesus Christ!" Sixteen yelled.

"Same question," I said, pointing the rifle at them.

"One guy," Sixteen said urgently. "Working in the electrical room."

"Is he armed?" I said.

"No. We're— We don't carry guns."

A door at the other end of the control room led to a small hallway. Beyond it was a massive electrical room, which held long banks of industrial batteries, transformers, and a generator the size of a minivan. The batteries were black, six feet high, arranged in rows. Standing at the end of one row, I yelled, "I know you're there. We won't hurt you, but you need to come out right now, arms raised." A moment later, another guy wearing tan coveralls crept forward, holding a large crescent wrench in one hand. "Drop the wrench," I said, and it clattered to the floor. His name tag read Jones 11. He was an average-sized guy with straight black hair, and his hands shook. I yanked my head toward the control room and led him there.

Eleven sat in a chair beside his buddies. "How do we turn off the power to Paragon?" I said.

"Why would you do that?" Sixteen said. He must have been the senior guy. "There are critical systems in there."

I tapped myself on the chest and said, "This is a critical system, too. Answer my question." They looked at each other, wondering who would get blamed.

I pointed the rifle at them, and Thirty-Five said, "Fuck this." He showed us which switches controlled the power to the complex.

"See how easy that was?" I said to him. "Now you're coming with me. We're going to disable the backup generator."

He shook his head disgustedly and said, "Fine. Whatever. I'll need a screwdriver."

"Get it," I told him. I followed him to a tool bin in the electrical room. While he found the tool, I glanced around the room and saw a ladder attached to the wall beside the battery vault. It disappeared through the ceiling. "Where does that go?"

He glanced at it. "The surface." Then I followed him to the generator and watched him disconnect several heavy wires. He handed them to me, and I coiled them and put them in my pocket. Then I told him to back away. I raised the rifle, butt first, and slammed it into the generator's control panel. After a half dozen swings, the panel was destroyed, switches torn off, glass shattered, and a circuit board underneath smashed beyond redemption.

Thirty-Five looked pissed. "That cost a lot of money," he said.

"Have them bill me," I replied.

We returned to the control room. I nodded at Kat, and she asked for a flashlight. Thirty-Five found a large flashlight in the locker I'd shot and handed it to her. I herded them through the fire door and locked it behind them as Kat stepped to the control panel and followed the sequence Thirty-Five showed us. After a few seconds, the lights went out, and we could hear machinery shutting down. "We have to disable these controls," she said.

"Yep. Give me some light." She pointed the flashlight at the console, and I raised the rifle butt and smashed the monitors. Glass fragments exploded all over the console. Then I smashed the gauges and switches. Finally, I pointed the rifle at the control panel and sprayed it with bullets until the clip was empty. Afterward, the room had that acrid metallic smell of gunfire, and clouds of smoke swirled in the flashlight's cone of light. "Let's get out of here."

We hurried to the ladder. I climbed first, aiding my knee by pulling up with my arms instead of putting weight on it. When I reached the hatch, Kat snapped off the flashlight and let it fall. Then I edged up the hatch and peered out. It was still raining hard, and I could barely see anything in the darkness. *What the hell*, I thought, and I pushed the hatch all the way open. Beyond my getting drenched, nothing else happened. So I pulled myself out of the hole, and Kat followed. We lay in the mud for a moment. Then I eased the hatch shut. Paragon was a few hundred yards to the west, black except for moving cones of light—vehicles and people with flashlights.

"When they see what we did to their power station," I said, "they're going to be pissed."

"Go figure," Kat said as she leaned over and kissed me.

When she pulled away, I said, "Can I get a rain check on that?"

She smiled, rain pouring from her helmet onto my neck, and said, "Absolutely." Then we got to our feet and peered into the blackness to the east.

"Now we run," she said.

I nodded. "Now we run."

29

We ran. Kat darted ahead, and I struggled to keep up, explosive pain in my knee making every step agony. Sometimes we slogged through glop sticking to our shoes, but mostly we ran through water pooling in dips and depressions. Streams crisscrossed the terrain like blood flowing through arteries and veins. The water slowed us, but we ran. On a night as black as coal, with the desert growing colder and more water washing over us than I've had in some hotel showers, we ran, clumsily when a dip surprised us, and we lurched one way or another, barely keeping our feet, or when we crashed into sagebrush and wet grass that whipped our legs. We ran, unsure of our direction, it was so dark, but we ran.

After fifteen minutes, I held up my watch and pushed the button to illuminate the face. Ten thirty-seven. My knee burned with a hundred fires, but still we ran. Then a flash of lightning showed a dark mass ahead, a large, bushy tree, a scrub oak. Their dense, unforgiving dead branches end in spikes that would impale you if you careened into them. Kat stopped abruptly less than two feet from the oak, and I nearly slammed into her.

"Shit!" she screamed in a high, tight voice.

"What?" I said breathlessly.

"Tree. Didn't see it. Scared the hell out of me."

I put a hand on her shoulder. "We need to slow down. They won't have to kill us if the desert does it for them."

"How far have we gone, do you think?" she panted.

I looked back at Paragon. It was smaller but still discernable when lightning showed its silhouette. "A mile," I said. "Maybe a mile and a half."

Kat rested her hands on her hips and caught her breath. We were both in reasonably good shape, but this wasn't a daylight run on a good trail, and my knee felt like it was nearing a hard stop.

"Can they see us?" she said.

"Not without electricity. And their drones won't be effective in this storm. But we must put more distance between them and us before they restore power."

"Okay. Just a moment." She filled her lungs and let the air out slowly. "Erin was terrified of us."

"I know."

"To her, we're the kidnappers."

My clothing was sopping wet. Fresh rain hitting it dripped like water pouring from an open faucet. My boot leather was soggy. I could feel water squishing in my socks. The chill settling into my bones made me worry about hypothermia. We needed to get someplace dry and warm.

"How are we going to get Erin out of there?" Kat said.

"I don't know. Not by doing what we just tried."

"We need more time with her. Convince her she doesn't belong at Paragon."

"Maybe she does."

"No," she said, wiping a soggy sleeve across her face. "None of them do."

"My point is, she's been here so long, Kat. This is all she knows."

"That doesn't make it right."

"Course not. At least we know where she is. Angela, too."

She waited for another flash of lightning to illuminate the scrub oak. Then she circled to the side and looked back. "You ready?"

I lied by nodding. When I put weight on my knee, it hurt so badly it felt like my thigh and calf were disconnected, but I followed her, and we ran on a dizzying course, weaving around trees and bushes that were nearly invisible in the rain and dark. Then Kat tripped on a rock and plunged headlong into the muck, helmet flying. She slid five or six feet and lay in the water. I ran up and turned her onto her back.

"You okay?" I cried.

I felt her nod, but in the flash of distant lightning, I saw that her face was black with mud, and she was trembling. I sat her up and tried to wipe the mud from her face. What I couldn't remove, the rain did. Finally, she laughed and said, "If there's a God, I'd like to know what I did wrong."

"That's easy," I said. "You're hanging out with me."

"I knew you were trouble when you came to Sacramento."

"Should've shot me then."

"Would've been easier." She leaned her head back and opened her mouth, filling it with rain. Then she swished it around and spat it out. "Now I'm waterlogged and drinking mud."

"You can't say I don't know how to show a woman a good time."

She laughed and raised her arms for me to help her up. When she was on her feet, she tugged at the straps on her chest plate. "I never liked wearing body armor. This contraption is just slowing me down." While she took it off, I waited for another lightning flash and spotted a large scrub oak about twenty yards away. "If they find us," she said, "it won't matter if we wear armor."

"Right." I took mine off, too. When she found her helmet, we headed for the oak and heaved everything underneath it. Then we set out again, the dark compound at our back, the rain relentless. I was so drenched my skin was pruning. As we ran, I wanted to see a ranch house. They wouldn't have Oxy, but any pain meds would do. Anything. The pain in my knee was so intense it made my ears ring. Then lightning struck nearby, instantaneous thunder so startling it took my breath. But in the flash of light, I saw a gully ahead on our left, and I worried about falling into it, and then I did.

When I woke up, Kat was talking to me. My head was in her lap, and she was leaning over me, sheltering me from the rain. Nothing she said made sense, but it was comforting to hear her voice. I watched the rain dripping from around her head, then remembered falling, remembered the excruciating pain in my knee. But it wasn't as bad now. I was lying on my back in muck, my feet uphill. Kat said, "What happened?" I told her about the motorcycle accident that nearly killed me and told her I'd be okay if I could take some Oxy. "You're on Oxycodone? How long have you been taking that?"

"I don't know. A long time."

She said, "Wait here," and laid my head in the mud and left. I couldn't see the rain. It was dark, and my eyes were closed. But I felt it on my face. It was cool and soothing. Minutes later, when I opened my eyes, the heavens were glowing.

Kat yelled, "We have to get out of here." She handed me a piece of wood, long, tough, a dead branch, oak, a walking stick. "They've got power!" I turned onto one elbow and wheeled around. Paragon was ablaze with light. The complex was lit up like a floating oasis in the middle of an ocean. It was as though they'd harnessed all that collective brain power to illuminate the clouds. Kat took my elbow, and I used the stick to get to my feet and watched as a helicopter took flight.

"I didn't know choppers could fly in the rain," Kat said.

"I guess they can. How long was I out?"

"Twenty minutes? I elevated your feet to get more blood to your head."

"Took the pressure off my knee. Thanks." I gazed around us. I could see what I'd thought was a gully in Paragon's faint glow. It wasn't. It was an arroyo that wasn't deep here but looked deeper farther east. "They'll have night vision gear. Maybe heat sensing as well. We need to get below ground." I sat on the edge of the arroyo and slid about four feet into it. My boots sank into cold water. I planted the walking stick and shoved away from the bank. Kat slid down behind me, and we began slogging through the muck. My knee ached, but the pain was tolerable with the walking stick as a crutch. Every minute or so, I peered around at the chopper. It was too far south, so they hadn't tracked us from the power station's emergency hatch, and their drones hadn't spotted our heat signatures. Our salvation was this heavy rain. Then I saw a second chopper taking off from Paragon. This one banked in a northeasterly direction. Toward us.

"Shit!" I said.

"What?"

"Another chopper. Coming our way." While she peered around at it, I started walking faster, using the stick like an oar to propel myself forward. I could hear Kat sloshing behind me. The arroyo became deeper the farther we ran into it. The walls were now above my head. The glow from Paragon was no longer providing even dim light. The darkness was welcome, but we had to move slower. Occasional flashes of lightning helped, but it was like seeing a photograph for a split second and having to move forward based on what you recalled from the image. Then in a flash of lightning, I saw something that sent a chill through me, and I stopped abruptly.

Kat came up and put her hand on my shoulder. "What is it?"

"A snake. Swimming. Five or six feet long."

"What kind of snake?"

"I don't know. I only saw it for a second. Probably a rattler, though. They're common in this desert. And they can swim."

"Oh, great. That's all I need. I hate snakes. And that chopper's getting closer."

"Well, hell," I said. "We have to keep moving." I started forward again, using the stick to sweep the area before me. After ten minutes, we came to a bend in the arroyo. The wall was higher on the inside of the curve, and I walked close to the wall, putting out a hand to steady myself. But about halfway around the bend, I put out my hand and felt nothing. I couldn't see what it was in the darkness, so I stopped and felt along the wall. There was an indentation of some kind. I used the stick to probe it and discovered a shelf about four feet off the ground, not high and not deep, but long enough for us to lie in it.

Kat hurried up. "That chopper's not far behind. It's following the arroyo."

I heard the whop-whop-whopping of its blades. I put the stick back into the indentation and banged it up, down, and side to side.

"What are you doing?"

"There's like a little cave here. I'm making sure there're no snakes in it." Then I climbed up onto the shelf and rolled onto my back. It was no more than three feet deep and narrowed toward the inside. I scooted as far in as I could. With my left arm pressed against the wall, I didn't think the chopper could see us. I told Kat to climb in. She unbuckled the duty belt and slung it onto the shelf below my feet. Then she climbed into the cave. There wasn't enough room for her to lie next to me, so she turned onto her stomach and climbed on top of me, her head on my cheek.

"This is cozy," she said.

"I've stayed in smaller hotel rooms."

"When you made this reservation, didn't you ask for the honeymoon suite?"

"I did. This is it."

"Well, I'm not staying in this place anymore."

"It's a pretty good deal for the money."

She laughed and turned her head so we were both facing out. Rain fell in torrents past the opening of the cave. Then we heard a more ominous sound, the deadly deep whirring of the rotor blades as the chopper drew closer. We couldn't see the chopper, but a brilliant cone of light swept through the arroyo from its searchlight and stopped mercifully at the edge of our hideout. Light and sound hovered over us as they swept the arroyo outside. Air whipped up by the rotor blades blew rainwater on us, pelting our skin and forcing our eyes shut. Then the sound slowly grew fainter and the air calmer. After a while, we were alone in the darkness and the falling rain.

"They're gone," I said, wiping the water off my face.

"For now," Kat replied. "But I think we should wait a while in case that helicopter circles back."

"Yeah."

"You okay down there?"

"I'm fine," I said. "Better." My knee wasn't hurting as much, and I wasn't as cold with our bodies pressed together.

"How's the bed?"

"Lumpy."

"That does it," she said. "I'm filing a complaint with management."

"Good luck. I don't think management cares."

"Shame on them." She inched her way up my body, and I turned my face toward hers, and we kissed. Long, slow, warm, and wet. It was a kiss I would not have traded for any other kiss at any other place or time. The warmth of her lips spread through my body like wildfire in a windstorm, filling my chest and spreading to my loins and down my legs, all the way to my toes. When it ended, I felt for her waist, slid my right arm over her back, and squeezed gently. She snuggled into me, wriggling in a way that set my soul on fire, and we kissed again and again, our lips woven so tightly we had to break now and then to catch our breath.

Then Kat said, "You sure there're no snakes here?"

"I'm pretty sure there aren't."

"Cause I can feel one. On my leg." She reached down, rolled as far to the side as she could, and rubbed my erection under my jeans.

"God," I whispered. "You shouldn't do that."

"You're right," she said, continuing to rub me. "It's not fair."

Then she slid down, and I felt her put more weight on my stomach. She was fumbling with something. "What are you doing?"

She began wriggling and said, "Sliding down my jeans." While she did that, I tried to unbuckle my belt but didn't have room. "Let me do it," she said. When she was ready, I could feel her pulling my belt. Then she pulled my zipper open and tugged my jeans down, which was a struggle because they were sopping wet. I tried to help by raising my butt and felt the soggy material sliding down my legs. Then she tugged down my soggy underwear. When she wrapped her hand around me and began stroking, I groaned, and she said, "We could die tonight."

"If we do, I'll die happy."

"Me, too." With that, she inched her way up again and straddled me as best she could in this confined space. Then I felt her pushing aside her panties, and she pulled me into her. We held each other and rocked together slowly and then faster, oblivious to everything outside. I tried to push myself as far inside her as I could, and we moved as one, flushed and breathless and joined in intimacy, and when my urgency reached its peak, I felt myself release. At that moment, I wanted nothing more than to spend the rest of my life with this charming creature. "You are beautiful beyond words," I whispered to her.

"You're a handsome devil yourself," she whispered back, "and a sweet man," and we clung to each other as the storm outside raged. After we caught our breath, she kissed my neck and said, "You have a knack for two-part harmony."

"I'm a musician. You know what they say about us?"

"No, what do they say?"

"Musicians have more rhythm."

"If you need a testimonial, I'll gladly provide one."

"Thanks," I whispered. Then I felt a slight tremor, and an alarm bell went off in my head. The ground was vibrating, slightly at first, but the tremor grew more intense as I lay there feeling it on my back. I heard something, too. I wasn't sure what. "Do you hear that?"

"Yes," she said. "It's not a chopper. What is it?"

My heart leaped when it came to me, and I scooted over and stuck my head through the curtain of water falling over the opening to the shelf. I looked down and saw the white froth of water coursing through the arroyo. "Oh fuck!" I yelled.

"What?" Kat cried.

"Flash flood!" She scrambled off me and slid into the arroyo. I followed her, pulling up my underwear and jeans and buckling my belt. She was pulling up her jeans, too, as I looked behind us. I couldn't see anything, but the roar grew louder as the ground shook harder. The rushing water in the Arroyo was bouncing as the earth trembled. I grabbed my walking stick with one hand and Kat's arm with my other and turned us downstream, back toward Paragon, and we trudged through the water that began sweeping us from behind. I looked desperately for a way to climb out of the arroyo but saw only black walls. Then I felt something wriggle past my leg, but I couldn't worry about it. The snakes must have been as terrified as we were. I yelled at Kat to run as fast as she could, to go ahead without me, but she refused.

"If that water catches us," I yelled, "we'll be dead within seconds."

"Run faster," she screamed. She grabbed my arm, and we moved as though the devil himself was at our back. When the roar grew so loud that I couldn't hear anything else, I looked back and saw a wall of water careen around the bend where our little cave had been, no more than a hundred yards behind us. The tidal wave looked like an angry god, merciless and chaotic, and it bounded toward us like the end of time itself.

30

Paragon's lights spared our lives. As we ran through the muck with the tidal wave bearing down, Paragon's glow lit the heavens, and we saw the silhouette of a tree growing at the arroyo's wall. Some exposed roots were thicker than a garden hose. Kat clutched them and pulled herself up, five feet, then ten. She clung to the tree's thick lower branches. I thrust the walking stick toward her, and she grasped it while I pulled myself up. The ground shook as that monstrous wave came roaring like a jet engine, and I saw the agony in Kat's eyes as I strained to reach her.

I had just touched her outstretched hand when a surge of water blasted me. Flung through the turbulent water, I tumbled and corkscrewed endlessly, holding my breath but still catching mouthfuls of muddy water. Then I hit something hard and bounced, was carried away, and bounced again and again, finally coming to rest on a mud-filled creosote bush. I lay on my back, covered with filth. My stomach felt like I'd swallowed a five-pound cheese ball. The mass forced its way up as I rolled over, and I retched, grit coating my teeth. After the worst passed, I stood up, dripping mud and shivering in the cold desert night. The flood had thrown me fifty yards from the arroyo. I could see Paragon—miles away but its lights radiant. My walking stick was a silhouette stuck in the mud like a javelin. I retrieved it and looked for Kat but saw no sign of her. One of the choppers was circling an area far south. The other was hovering northwest. They had no idea where we were. I scraped the mud off my watch. It was twelve forty.

I hoped Kat still clung to those roots, so I headed toward the arroyo. Paragon's lights dimly illuminated the landscape. The ground was strewn with boulders, broken branches, and uprooted trees and bushes. In some pockets of water, I sank to my knees.

When I reached the arroyo, I followed it east until I came to the tree whose roots Kat had climbed—but there was no sign of her, only broken branches and mounds of mud, some large enough to cover a body. I called her name, softly at first and then more urgently. The only other sound was the pummeling of the endless rain.

When she didn't answer, I felt the leaden taste of fear creep up my throat. I searched in widening semicircles from the tree, using the stick to probe mounds of mud large enough to cover her body, but I felt nothing underneath except rocks and plant debris. My search pattern was not exact, but as misery settled into my heart, it was the best I could do. When I'd made a dozen sweeps and hadn't found her, I decided to search all night. Giving up on her was not an option, even if Martin's stormtroopers found me, and if she'd died, I at least wanted to find her body. I owed her that.

After four more sweeps, I saw two pinpoints of light in the darkness, something reflecting Paragon's lights. It wasn't Kat, but I couldn't tell what it was. Then it shook its body, flinging mud, and I could make out pointy ears and a long snout. It was a coyote. Or a wolf. A big male, maybe sixty pounds.

We stared at each other, two feral creatures in the darkness. Then he huffed. One sharp exhalation of breath. A warning. He was guarding something. His den may have been near. Maybe his mate was buried in this muck. Or his pups were close. Maybe he didn't know if they were dead or alive. I took a cautious step forward, and he huffed again, backing away just a half-step. He wasn't going to give much ground.

"It's okay," I whispered. "We're searching for the same thing. If your family's here, I'll help you find them." One muddy desert shrub was just to my right. I probed it with my stick and felt nothing but branches and mud soup. Another shrub was five feet away, closer to the animal. I edged toward it while he watched. When I'd nearly reached it, he raised his snout and howled—one long, forlorn cry. I waited, and he watched me warily as I probed that shrub with my stick. Something was in there. I took another slow step towards it and knelt but couldn't see into the muddy mass. So I put out my hand and lowered it into the shrub until I felt something solid. Bone, covered with mud. Curved. A head, covered with fur, only not as dense as fur. Hair. Long hair. Then I felt cold fingers on a cold hand.

Instantly, I dropped the stick and reached in with both hands to pull Kat out. She groaned and coughed violently as I wrenched her free of the shrub, and we fell together into the slop. I shook her, and she opened her eyes and began trembling uncontrollably, so I removed my sodden jacket and pulled it around her, holding her tight. When I glanced up, my feral companion had disappeared. Having helped me find my mate, he was now searching for his own.

Kat and I clung to each other. She couldn't remember being thrown. I was so relieved that I failed to notice an ominous change during the half hour we sat holding each other. It had stopped raining. Paragon's helicopters were still no closer, but if their heat-sensing drones found us, those choppers would make a beeline for our location, and this would all be over in minutes.

"We have to get back into the arroyo," I told her. She nodded. "You still have the Glock?"

She shook her head. "I forgot it . . . when we ran . . . from our love nest. I was too busy pulling up my pants."

I chuckled. "Okay. It is what it is. I'm sure it's gone, but we'll check. Before we move, we have to reduce our heat signatures, or the drones will spot us."

"How?"

"Mud."

"It fucking figures."

"On our heads, faces, necks, arms, hands, any exposed skin. Anyplace their sensors could detect areas hotter than the environment around us."

She nodded, and we scooped mud with our hands and piled it on ourselves and each other. The mud was cold, but the air was colder—and death colder still. We had to move. I helped her to her feet, and we walked back to the arroyo, careful not to move quickly or dislodge the mud piled on us. "I'm sorry I don't have my camera," she said as we slid back into the arroyo. "This would be a moment to remember."

"If we get out of this, maybe we could do some naked mud wrestling and take pictures then."

"I'll keep your offer in mind. You're such a romantic."

As we trudged east through the arroyo, we had a plentiful supply of mud to keep ourselves covered. The water was ankle-deep in many places but knee-deep in others, and trudging through it was exhausting. As I thought, Kat's duty belt was no longer on the shelf in our cave. It would be buried in the muck downstream. My knee was aching again, but the walking stick kept the pain manageable. We made our way east in the arroyo for over an hour, stopping only to slather on more mud and listen for choppers. Eventually, we arrived where branches opened up in the arroyo, one smaller branch heading northeast and another south. The main artery turned southwest and appeared deeper ahead of us, so we took the northeast branch, which began climbing slowly and then grew shallower several hundred yards ahead. The ground there was muddy, but we saw fewer standing pools of water, and the arroyo walls were no longer over our heads.

Then I saw a pinpoint of light to the north, and we hunkered down and watched. As the light grew, it resolved into the headlights of a vehicle moving on a road in front of us. As the vehicle approached, we dug more mud and painted our faces with it. My hands, my whole body, smelled like old shoes and wet wood, but beyond that, I sensed something else—the smell of decomposing grass and something sharp and sulfury. When the vehicle drew close enough, I saw it was one of Paragon's black security vans. It passed slowly by, about half a football field away. In its headlights, I could see a barbed-wire fence on the far side of the road and caught a glimpse of disembodied white faces beyond.

When the van was a mile or so down the road, I whispered an idea to Kat, and she nodded. Then we walked quickly to the road and climbed the fence. The field reeked of manure and wet grass, but considering what we'd just endured, walking through cow shit was like a day at a spa. The herd appeared to be more than a hundred strong—brown with white faces, some with white patches on their chests and legs. I had no idea what kind of cattle they were, but they were big and seemed docile enough. Dozens of calves loitered amongst them. We walked carefully toward the nearest individuals, either munching on wet grass or gazing at each other—whatever cattle do in the middle of the night. Our presence didn't spook them, so I thought my idea might work.

"We need to go north," I told Kat. "Toward Highway Seventy. Follow me and try to find a nice, sweet cow that won't mind if you stand close to her." We slowly wound our way through the herd, careful not to let our presence alarm them. I reasoned that to Paragon's drones, our heat signatures wouldn't look significantly different from the cattle's. Ours would be smaller, so we might look like calves. As we walked, we brushed as much mud off of ourselves as we could, and when we reached the cattle at the northernmost point in the herd, I gently tapped a half-dozen of them on their butts and flanks with my walking stick to get them moving north. It took twenty minutes of insistent prodding before they decided walking north was preferable to putting up with me. Kat and I followed them, and the rest of the herd followed us. Soon we were one big happy herd ambling north across the soggy, manure-filled prairie. Paragon security vans drove down the road twice, but when we saw their lights, we just stooped on the other side of our bovine escorts and stood again when the vehicles passed. Herds of cattle were a common sight out here, so they didn't arouse suspicion, which confirmed that Paragon's security forces were not as bright as the children they were guarding.

I gently prodded the leading cows to keep them moving north and, after a long while, began to see the tall, dark shadows of trees ahead on our right. Those would be the cottonwoods we saw as we drove in, which meant we were nearing a creek. In the deep shadows ahead, I also saw a small flickering light and, now and then, several other small cones of light. The flickering light was stationary, but the cones were moving. A campfire, I guessed, and two people with flashlights. I told Kat I thought the lights were about a half-mile away. Moments later, the cattle I'd been driving stopped abruptly with some grunts of consternation. Several turned right and began walking toward the creek, and the others followed. Then I noticed barbed wire in front of me. We had reached the northern boundary of the pasture. The wire was all but invisible in the darkness.

Kat had turned with the cattle and followed them along the fence line. I caught up with her and said, "That's got to be a campfire up there. I don't think Martin's men would have built it. I don't know why they would. When we reach the creek, let's follow the tree line north and check it out."

She nodded. "We need to find water. I'm getting dehydrated."

"Me, too. If it's a Boy Scout troop up there, they'll have water."

She gave me a weary look, either tired of my jokes or just plain tired. She was tough, but the night had taken more out of her than she wanted to admit.

The eastern side of the pasture was flooded with overflow from the creek. We could hear the faint but persistent rush of flowing water. Some of the cattle lowered their heads and drank. While the rest of the herd hurried forward to the water, Kat and I climbed over the fence and hurried to a cluster of cottonwoods. The trees towered over us, and we were ankle-deep in cold running water, which would wash the cow shit off our shoes. I don't know how invisible we were to the drones, but we had to head north using the trees for cover. It was tough going in the dark. We kept running into fallen logs and thickets. I walked in front, trying to locate obstacles with my walking stick, and I guided us a few hundred yards before stepping out of the trees to get a better glimpse of what lay ahead.

It was a campfire with thirty or forty people sitting in a circle around it. I checked my watch. It was three thirty, an odd time for people to sit around a campfire telling stories or whatever they were doing. Beyond the campfire was a small moving van, maybe twenty feet long, with some lettering on the side I couldn't make out. One man stood by the truck, smoking a cigarette. I slipped back into the cottonwoods and told Kat what I'd seen. I said I wanted to get closer and asked her to follow me but stay in the tree line. Then I moved in the darkness along the trees, and as I got closer, I saw we'd come upon an old ranch. A small, dark ranch house stood near the trees and looked like it had been abandoned decades ago. In the faint light of the fire, I could see that the wood siding was warped and bleached, and one long roofline dipped in the middle. There were a few small outbuildings, a shed maybe, or an outhouse, and what might have been a chicken coop. Behind the truck was the dim outline of a small barn. Someone's dream until the harsh reality of living in this desolate place ruined it.

Then another pair of headlights came down the road. This vehicle slowed and turned in toward the ranch. It was a dark-colored pickup that looked shiny and new. The man who climbed out of it was short and had a mop of black hair falling over his forehead. He walked over to the guy standing by the truck's hood and spoke to him. That guy was taller and had a thick beard and a mass of dark hair on his head. Then I saw a third man walking towards them. Bald and clean-shaven. He was large but looked blubbery and carried a rifle or shotgun. Everyone else sat around the campfire, their backs hunched over. I decided to call the guy from the pickup Moe, the hairy guy Larry, and the bald guy Curly. Perfect. Whoever they were, to me, they looked like the Three Stooges.

The carcass of an old car sat in some tall weeds between me and the fire, and I got low and crept to it, close enough that I could hear the crackle of the fire and smell its smoke. As I scrunched down behind the rusted carcass, Moe walked into the circle and began speaking Spanish to the people sitting there. In a loud, menacing voice, he told them he needed more money. It cost more, he said, to smuggle them into the country. They'd had problems and had to spend more to bribe the police. He said if they didn't give him more money, he would leave them there, and the Border Patrol would find them and send them back across the border. I heard murmuring among the illegals around the campfire, and a few brave voices protested. I couldn't hear them distinctly enough to know what they were saying, but imagining their response to this extortion wasn't difficult.

I crept back into the tree line as Moe kept haranguing them, and I found Kat and told her what I'd heard. "These illegals are our ticket out of here. We need to find a way to get into the truck when they leave."

"What about the coyotes? Aren't they armed?"

"Yeah, but they're extorting more money from those people. I don't think the illegals will give us up. They'll despise those assholes."

"What about Paragon? What if they stop the truck?"

I shrugged. "It's a chance we'll have to take. The coyotes are paying off somebody. Probably the cops and Paragon. Otherwise, Paragon wouldn't allow them to use this ranch. This is our best shot for getting out of here tonight."

She nodded uncertainly and said, "Okay. What the hell."

I led her in the dark to the side of the fire closest to the pickup truck. Larry was collecting money from the illegals while Curly kept watch. Moe stood off to the side, talking on a cell phone. I got us in position at the back of the pickup and waited for Larry to finish. We still had dirt all over us, so our skin looked darker than usual. When Larry left the campfire to give Moe the money he'd collected, Curly joined them to see what the take was. While they were counting their money, I tossed my walking stick into the darkness, and Kat returned my jacket and threw away the dead man's shirt she'd been wearing. Then we scooted over to the campfire and plopped down among the illegals sitting outside the circle. Some of them watched us sneaking in. They glanced around at each other, but none spoke. To those closest to us, I whispered in Spanish that we were friends, that some people were trying to kill us and we needed help, that we had to get on the truck with them when it left. I said we would help them if we could, that I'd heard the bad coyote demanding more money, and that wasn't right. When I finished, those who heard me turned to the neighbors and spoke quietly, passing on what I'd said.

Sitting beside me was an older woman who quietly sobbed into a handkerchief. She had gray hair with black strands and wore a brown headscarf, a red blouse, old jeans, and sandals. A small black leather purse hung on a strap around her neck. Her feet were cracked and blistered. It must have hurt her terribly to walk. I leaned down and said, "*Madrecita, ¿por qué llora?*" *Mother, why are you weeping?*

She said the coyotes had taken all her money, and she was anxious to reach her son in America. She was afraid she would never see him and his family again.

"*¿Dónde está su hijo?*" *Where is your son?*

"*Está en Albuquerque,*" she said.

"*¿Cómo se llama Ud.?*" *What is your name?*

"*Juliza Morales,*" she told me.

"*Me alegro de conocerte. Mi nombre es Sonny. No se preocupe, Señora Morales. Hoy verá a su hijo. ¿De dónde es Ud.?*" *I'm glad to meet you. My name is Sonny. Don't worry, Mrs. Morales. You will be with your son today. Where are you from?*

"Guatemala," she replied.

"*Guatemala es un país hermoso. Como Ud.,*" I said. *Guatemala is a beautiful country. Like you.*

She held out her hand, and I took it and squeezed it gently. Then she removed her headscarf and handed it to me. "*Para tu hermosa mujer rubia,*" she whispered. *For your beautiful blonde woman.*

"*Gracias, mamacita.*" *Thank you, mother.*

I passed the scarf to Kat. She smiled at Señora Morales and nodded a thank you as she put it over her head and tied it beneath her chin.

A few minutes later, people in front of us passed something to me. It was a cream-colored, long-sleeve shirt. The man who sent it sat in the first row and had taken it from his backpack. He was about forty, had black stubble on his chin, and was missing several teeth. He grinned widely at me, gesturing that I should put on the shirt. I told him it was too nice for me, but he shook his head and gestured at me again, so took off my jacket and slipped his shirt on over my t-shirt and said, "*Gracias, señor. Gracias.*" Another man sitting nearby introduced himself as David Martinez and asked if we wanted water. Martinez looked to be about my age. He had a broad, pleasant face and thick black hair that fell over his forehead and nearly covered a long, white scar caused, I thought, by a knife. I said yes and shook David's hand when he spread the word, and several bottles of water made their way to us. I could still taste mud, but I drank the fresh water eagerly, as did Kat, and was happy when several more bottles were passed to us.

After counting their money, Moe ordered the illegals back onto the truck. David Martinez and other people sitting near us gathered around and made sure we were in the middle of the pack climbing into the truck. Curly and Larry watched over that process, and when we approached them, Martinez spoke to the two coyotes, distracting them while we climbed aboard. Once we were safely on the truck and the doors were shut, I thanked everyone for their kindness. Nothing happened for a few anxious moments. Then the truck's engines roared to life, and we pulled onto the road. Kat and I sat with our arms around each other, weary but relieved.

"Do you know where we're going?" she said.

"No, but I know where we've been, and whatever happens in the morning, at least we've escaped from Paragon tonight."

It was as black as Martin Barnard's soul inside that truck. We sat shoulder to shoulder with our fellow travelers, forty sardines jammed into a can meant for twenty, trying to fit legs and arms together in a jigsaw of limbs. We pitched and weaved, bumping heads and elbows with murmured apologies as the truck bounced along a rough road. Kat sank into my body and fell asleep within minutes. I held her close and kissed the scarf on her head, trying not to think about how pungent the odor was inside the truck, how hard it was to breathe, how much my knee ached, or how my feet were rotting inside these waterlogged boots.

I drifted off, thankful for these simple people who'd protected us, and wondered if raising supremely intelligent children in a moral vacuum was possible. Without parents, without familial bonding, without faith in something beyond their intelligence, without the mercy that comes from seeing others harmed and learning the value of helping, without the judgment that arises from making bad decisions in the real world and learning from the consequences, without understanding the whole tapestry of humanity with its virtues as well as its vices, how could these brilliant children solve the world's problems? Henry Barnard envisioned his new breed of superhumans leading the world to a bright and shining future, but I believed that if his vision came to pass, we would instead be marching into the abyss.

31

Like everyone else in that hot cargo box, I'd been jolted awake when the brakes squealed, and the truck bounced to a stop on some rutted road. My watch read a quarter to five. We hadn't been traveling long, which was good. We'd still be close to Ruidoso. Someone unlocked the doors of the cargo box, and the doors screeched open. Then a coyote ordered us to get out and wait in the barn nearby. My knee was hurting from a night of fighting and running and from it being jammed in the same position for too long inside a cramped cargo box. Pain can be good; it's nature's way of telling you when something's wrong. But prolonged pain, unbearable pain that settles in like a visiting cousin you never liked—who mooches from you, capitalizes your time, and blathers endlessly about nothing—that kind of pain is like an elephant hanging by meat hooks from your soul. I needed painkillers and woke up worrying about where to find them. I massaged my knee and moved my leg back and forth to restore circulation. Then I hobbled to the back of the cargo box and saw Curly on the ground directing traffic. He had slung the shotgun over his right shoulder, the barrel behind him. It was early in the morning. Curly was tired and wasn't expecting trouble.

Kat and I jumped down and passed him without incident, and I glanced around. We were in the barnyard of another ranch, one still in use but somewhere remote. In the dim light before dawn, I could see the outlines of tall trees in every direction around us. The air was cool and smelled wet from the dew on the grass and puddles of water remaining after last night's rain. Five or six horses stood in a misty corral next to the barn, like images in a painting. I heard a rooster crowing and could smell the acrid, musty stench of a chicken coop somewhere close. The ranch house was forty yards away—a single-story log structure with smoke curling from the chimney, its windows ablaze. Moe and another man stood talking at the front stoop. The barn was close to the truck, and Larry was just inside the barn door. I didn't see anyone else, but two cars were parked outside the house, three vehicles, including Moe's pickup. I couldn't be sure more armed men weren't inside the barn, but it was a chance I had to take. I leaned into Kat, passed her my jacket, and said, "I'm dropping back. Go on ahead of me. I'll disarm the guy in the barn when I pass him. Look for something to stuff in his mouth and tie his hands and feet. If shooting starts, tell our friends to hit the ground. Yell *tirense al suelo ahora*." She nodded and walked hurriedly away. She was well inside the barn when I planted my left foot.

I was just past Larry's center of mass, and he held the revolver in his right hand. I swiftly grabbed the barrel and pushed it to my left, pointing the barrel away from me and hyperextending the fingers on his right hand. At the same time, I brought my right knee up into his groin. The secret to kneeing someone in the groin is not to aim for his balls but for a spot about six inches farther back. That way, you're still accelerating when you make contact, and the force delivered is much stronger. The blow knocked Larry backward and immediately dropped him to the ground. I sank with him and planted my right knee on his neck, preventing him from crying out. With the explosive pain in his balls and the fingers of his right hand, he released the revolver, and I now held it in my left hand, my firing hand. I glanced out the door and waved the remaining illegals into the barn. They hurried in uncertainly, and then I said, *"Todo está bien. Vamos a ayudarles. Por favor, quédense aquí y quédense callados." It's okay. We are going to help you all. Please stay here and stay quiet.*

Then I leaned down to Larry and poked the barrel of the revolver in his side, hard enough for him to feel it, and whispered that I would kill him if he made a sound or resisted me in any way. He lay curled in the fetal position with his hands cupping his crotch and nodded weakly. Kat ran to me a minute later with some rags and a large roll of gray duct tape. "They have a shop in here," she said.

I gave her the revolver and told her to watch for Curly and anyone else. Then I stuffed a rag in Larry's mouth and secured it with duct tape over his mouth and around his neck. His face and head were covered with thick black hair. "Sorry about the tape," I whispered to him in Spanish. "It'll be a bitch to get this off." He mumbled something inarticulate into the rag. I looked up into the crowd of anxious faces and found David Martinez. I waved him to me and asked him to help me with Larry. We picked him up by his arms and walked him through the anxious crowd of illegals to the rear of the barn, where I found some straw-filled stalls that smelled like horseshit. Larry was still doubled over but was recovering from the initial shock and gave me a calculating aside, so I pulled his hands behind his back and wrapped them tightly with duct tape. Then I made him lie down in the straw and bound his ankles securely.

Kat was standing to one side of the barn door when I returned. She peered out, the revolver in her hand, and said, "The bald guy went to the house. He's walking back to the truck now. Still has the shotgun."

I nodded and took off the shirt the man at the campfire had given me. "Give this back to that nice gentleman. I'll go take care of Curly."

"Be careful," she said, handing me my jacket and the revolver. She took the shirt from me and began pulling off the headscarf Señora Morales had given her.

I watched from the barn door as Curly ambled across the lot to the back of the truck. He leaned the shotgun against a rear fender and began closing and locking the doors to the cargo box. As the doors were screeching shut, I ran up behind him and planted the barrel of the revolver in his ear while I grasped the other side of his neck. He froze and peered around anxiously at me. "*Sí, es pistola,* I said. "*Ven conmigo. Sin palabras.*" *Yes, it's a pistol. Come with me. Keep quiet.*

I don't know if Curly was naturally acquiescent or just the dimmest bulb in the chandelier, but he didn't require much persuasion. As he trudged ahead of me toward the barn, I picked up the shotgun and led him back to the stall where Larry lay. Kat held the revolver on him while I bound Curly's hands behind his back with duct tape.

"*Voy a matarte,*" he said to me. *I'm going to kill you.*

"*Tú y quién más,*" I replied. *You and who else?*

When his hands were secure, I taped his mouth shut, told him to lie on the straw, and then taped his ankles. Before we left the barn, I told the illegals we would get their money, and they would soon be on their way. David Martinez volunteered to help us, but I said it would be dangerous and he should stay here and assure his fellow travelers that everything would be okay. Then I took the duct tape and the shotgun, Kat took the revolver, and we headed for the ranch house.

First, we did a cautious circuit around the house to ensure no other men were outside. We peered in the windows as we stole around the house and saw Moe with two other men sitting at a table in the dining room. There were piles of money in front of them. The younger of the two men was Hispanic. The other was an older Anglo, as was the woman we saw in the kitchen cooking breakfast. Her gray hair was piled on her head like a turban, and she had thick gray veins on the backs of her hands. She wore a shapeless black dress and a stained yellow apron. The kitchen window was open, and the aroma of frying eggs and bacon made me realize how hungry I was. When we reached the front door, Kat took out her badge, and we pulled the door open and rushed into the dining room.

"Police!" Kat yelled, pointing her badge and the revolver at them. "Get your hands up!"

I leveled the shotgun for Moe's benefit and said, "*Policía, póngan las manos arriba!*" I was sure Moe understood English, but I wanted him and the others to appreciate the shotgun.

They froze. Moe gave us an "oh shit" look and stared at the piles of money on the table. He seemed to deflate as he calculated his loss. The old Anglo glared at us as though we'd landed from another planet, his face an absolute portrait of surprise. Then he chucked up a lugie, spit in on the floor, and drawled, "Who the fuck are you people?"

I pointed at Kat's badge and said, "You're busted, asshole. Now, all of you, put your hands on the table." They did, and while Kat watched them, I got the woman from the kitchen and sat her beside them. Then I taped their hands and feet to the chairs. When the indignant old guy repeated his question, I said, "We're guardians of the oppressed, defenders of the weak, avengers of those who've been wronged. Now shut the fuck up." I wrapped tape over his mouth and around his neck and said to the rest of them, "I need a map of New Mexico. Quickly! Before this gets ugly."

The old woman had a resigned look on her face. She sighed, canted her head toward a sideboard beside the dining room table, and said, "In the top drawer." The old guy grunted displeasure at her, but she gave him a disgusted look and said, "Oh, fuck you, Harold."

I dug through the drawer until I found a frayed state map. Then I turned back to the old woman and said, "And a cell phone."

"Mine's on the kitchen counter," she said.

"Do you need an access code to unlock it?"

She nodded and gave me the code. I walked into the kitchen, found her cell phone, opened it, got a dial tone, saw that it had plenty of power, flipped it shut, and stuck it in my front pocket. I saw a pile of brown paper grocery bags in the pantry next to the kitchen. I took one and scooped the money on the dining room table into it. It was a shitload of money, tens of thousands by the look of it, so I counted out three hundred dollars and shoved it into my front pocket. Moe gave me a hateful look as I pocketed his cash, but he was smart enough to keep his mouth shut. I leaned over and said to him, "I need to borrow your truck. Is that okay?" He gave me a look that would frighten NFL linemen, which I interpreted as permission, so I patted his front jeans pockets and found his keys.

My roll of tape was wearing thin, but I had enough left to tape their mouths. Then I covered their eyes with strips of tape. It's harder to escape when you can't see what you're doing or make eye contact with fellow captives. While I was taping their eyes, Kat walked behind the men and pulled wallets from their back pockets. "You are all under arrest," she said, and I chuckled. *She must enjoy saying that*, I thought. She removed their driver's licenses from their wallets, put them in her front pocket, and tossed the wallets on the floor. Then she said, "I'll notify the Border Patrol later this morning, and they'll be by to pick you up."

In a bathroom next to the kitchen, I found a bottle of ibuprofen and swallowed four of them with water I pooled in my hands and slurped into my mouth. Then I went to the kitchen, found a spoon in a drawer, and ate four big mouthfuls of scrambled eggs. Kat said she wasn't hungry, so we scanned the area between the house and the barn, saw no threats, and walked quickly to the barn. David Martinez was right inside the door. I handed him the paper bag of money and the map. I asked him if he could drive the truck, and he nodded. "Load up everyone and drive to Albuquerque," I told him. "Follow the map. When you get there, find the house of Señora Morales' son. He will be able to reach the right people to help everyone else get where they're going. Divide up the money equitably. And drive the speed limit, not too fast or too slow. You'll be okay. But don't stay here too long. You need to leave right away." He looked in the bag with his eyes wide. I hoped I hadn't made a mistake, but you have to trust someone to do the right thing, and Martinez had been a decent guy so far.

Before we left, I found Señora Morales. I held her hands, looked into her eyes, and said, "*Madrecita, ahora podrá ver a su hijo. Vaya con Dios.*" *Mother, now you go see your son. God be with you.*

She put her arms around me and kissed me on the cheek. Then she whispered, "*Eres un ángel.*" *You are an angel.* I thought, *not really, but if you think so, that's okay.*

Kat and I jumped into Moe's truck. It was a new Dodge Ram with all the bells and whistles. It must have cost Moe more than fifty grand. I guess smuggling illegals into the country is lucrative. The truck purred like a lioness as we bounced down a road as gray and broken as the veins on the old woman's hands. The sky overhead looked clear, but the eastern sky glowed like a curtain of orange fluorescence, promising a clear morning but the possibility of storms later.

Kat looked weary. She lay back in the seat, her head bouncing off the headrest with each bump. "Why did you take some of the money?" she said.

"Everything in my wallet is waterlogged, and we can't use plastic," I told her. "We need a little cash until we hook up with John and Earl. Besides, there was a lot more money on that table than they took from the illegals."

"Maybe they're also running drugs."

"Seems likely."

"God," she said. "Do you have any idea how many procedures I've broken? Not to mention laws? That money was evidence."

I shrugged. "Those people helped us escape."

"I know."

"They have hope in their eyes but smell of desperation, Kat. They're trying to better their lives and be reunited with their families. They need that money more than the assholes who took advantage of them."

"I know. But, Christ, Sonny. I'm a police officer. We just destroyed evidence and took part in the trafficking of illegal aliens. We killed men last night. We just stole a truck."

"He gave me permission to borrow it," I said.

She smiled, despite herself. "Yeah, right. I heard you. That's called coercion. When this is over, I will face a review board."

I looked at her. "If we live through the next few hours, you mean. If we escape the drones overhead right now, in a clear sky, looking for us. If we evade Martin's stormtroopers, the county cops, and the Ruidoso police working for Martin."

She shifted the revolver in her lap. "Right. If we can do all that."

"If they catch us, we'll be killed on sight." She looked away from me out her window. "We'll be safer when we reach my friends. Then we need to figure out how to rescue Erin, Angela, and the other children at Paragon."

She looked back at me and said, "Okay, I agree. But when we reach your friends, we start going by the book. I need to call Charlie Iverson in Portland and tell him what we've discovered. We need to involve the feds because there'll be many arrests and much evidence to be collected, and what the Barnards and their accomplices have done violates federal law. This has to be done right, or the people at Paragon won't be brought to justice."

"Do you regret what we had to do last night?"

"No," she said quietly. "I don't regret any of it. We did what had to be done. And at least one part of it was delightful." She put her hand on my arm and squeezed it. "But now it's time to follow procedure if we're going to make a prosecutable case against the people responsible for these crimes."

"Fine," I said. "But first things first. I'm going to call John."

"We need to get cleaned up. Find a change of clothes. Some decent food. And get some sleep. Even if it's just a couple of hours."

I pulled up my soiled t-shirt and sniffed it. "Cleaned up? I don't know. I'm beginning to enjoy the smell of swamp gas."

She laughed. "Yeah, well, if you want to do more than sleep when we find a bed, you'll have to shower."

"Only if you join me."

She smiled at me. "Deal." Then as she gazed at the brightening dawn we were driving into, her smile faded. "We can't go back to our motel."

"They'll already have cleaned out our rooms."

"We can't go to Ruidoso either. They'll be looking for us there."

I nodded. We'd been driving out of the mountains on the muddy old gravel road that led to the ranch, and we came to an intersection with a paved road. I stopped and looked both ways, trying to get a bearing, and I saw a sign indicating that Fort Stanton was just a few miles north.

"Do you know where we are?" Kat said.

"Yeah. This must be Highway Forty-eight. We're north of Ruidoso." I glanced at my watch. It was going on six o'clock. I took the old woman's cell phone out of my pocket, entered the code, and dialed John's cell phone. He answered after three rings.

"Shipping and receiving," he said. His standard greeting when he didn't recognize a caller's number.

"Can I speak to Torran?" I was telling him it was me and our conversation might be overheard.

"Sorry. He's not in."

"Too bad. I have a lot to tell him about the last shipment. How about Dad? Is he in?"

"Your unlucky day, I'm afraid. He and his buddy are headed to the race track." I held the phone to my chest and said to Kat, "John and Earl are staying in a motel near Ruidoso Downs."

"I hope they have better luck than I'm having," I said into the phone.

"When we're not betting on the ponies, we're watching old Andy Griffith re-runs. I love Barney Fife, and we're seeing a lot of him in the episode on now."

I held the phone down again and looked at Kat, "John says there're a lot of cops down there." Back on the phone, I said, "Is that the episode where Barney pulls over a black van?"

John said, "Yep. That van's all over the place. A regular parade."

"My favorite episode is when Opie spots a satellite in the night sky. As I recall, he sees a lot of them."

"I don't know that episode, but I'll look for it."

"I need to go. Been on the road all night. Need to clean up. Get some rest. Maybe you know of a good place north of your warehouse."

"How far north?"

"Oh, four miles, I guess. Could be eight."

"Four or eight? Give me a minute," John said. When he returned, he said, "Have you done any climbing in Yosemite?"

"Yeah, I've been there."

"Then you know that famous peak."

"Know it well."

"It's about twenty miles north. There was a forest fire at Yosemite last year.

"I remember reading about that."

"Careless campers. The bear was unhappy about them."

"I don't blame him."

"Well," John said, "gotta go. A John Wayne movie's coming on our TV. One of the best westerns I've ever seen. Tell you what. We'll call you back later this morning."

"I'll look forward to your call," I said as he hung up.

"What was that all about?" Kat said.

"The cops and Paragon's security forces are thick in Ruidoso. I told John about the drones and asked him to find a motel to meet at later.   He found one up Highway Forty-eight, a Best Western called Smoky something. It's in the town of Capitan."

"Where's that?"

"North about twenty miles."

The sky lightened as we drove toward the Sacramento Mountains. Mist floated between layers of pine forests and mountain ranges, their peaks glowing yellow. After a while, we saw low buildings ahead and passed a sign that read *Capitan Village Limit*. Just past the sign was the Smokey Forest Inn, a U-shaped motel that looked about five years away from being torn down or remodeled. I pulled in by the office. Two cars were parked in front of the rooms. All the rooms were dark. I gave Kat the money and said, "When you check in, tell them you're by yourself. Ask for the room farthest from the office. Leave the lights on. I'll ditch the pickup and walk back. Shouldn't take more than twenty minutes. John and Earl will be here later this morning."

She nodded, leaned over, and kissed me. "When you get back, I'll be in the shower," she whispered.

"In that case, I'll run the whole way."

I watched her walk into the office. Then I drove through Capitan and found a crowded campground. I left the pickup between a silver Airstream and a supertanker-sized Winnebago. I limped back, my knee again threatening a total shutdown. It was dawn, and few people were up and about. I followed Capitan's main drag, staying inside the trees and close to the buildings. The same two cars were parked in the motel's lot, but I didn't see lights in any rooms, including the one farthest from the office. I peered through the curtains, but it was too dark to see anything inside.

My stomach grew tighter as I walked to the office. The clerk was a forty-something beanpole of a man with thinning salt-and-pepper hair and wire-rim glasses perched low on the bridge of his nose. He looked anxiously at me and said, "Can I help you?"

"I'm looking for a woman who checked in about half an hour ago."

His eyes grew jittery behind his glasses, and he looked like he'd swallowed his tongue. "I'm sorry, sir," he managed, "but we haven't had any check-ins since last night."

"I know you had one," I said. "I dropped her off twenty minutes ago."

"Don't move," said a voice behind me.

I slowly raised my hands and turned and saw a familiar face. Beneath that face was the business end of an automatic. "Officer Thomas. How nice to see you again," I said. I sensed someone else and kept turning and saw another county trooper with his gun drawn. They'd flanked me, and while it's possible to defend yourself against one gun, it's exponentially harder against two.

"Your girlfriend's in custody," said Thomas. "She's on her way south. Put your hands behind your back." I did, and the other cop handcuffed me. As he turned me toward the door, Thomas said, "Martin's gonna be real happy to see you, but you're not gonna be happy to see him."

32

Once I was handcuffed, both cops holstered their weapons. The one who handcuffed me was named McClary. He was short and too fond of pancakes. They grabbed my elbows and were hustling me outside when the door swung open, and a man walked in wearing a bulky fisherman's vest and a soft hat with a wide brim. The vest and hat were cluttered with lures, hooks, and patches. "What time does your restaurant open?" he yelled. Then he noticed the deputies and backed away, saying, "Oh, jeez, excuse me." Eyes wide and mouth screwed tight, he tipped his hat. But as McClary passed him, the fisherman gave him a swift karate chop to his neck, and McClary dropped like a stone. I fell on him as the fisherman whipped out an automatic and pressed it against Thomas's nose.

"Hands up," the fisherman yelled.

Mouth agape, Thomas quickly raised his hands. The fisherman whirled him around and shoved him against the wall while pulling the pistol from Thomas's holster and shoving it into one of his large vest pockets. Then, ordering the clerk to raise his hands, he removed Thomas' handcuffs and cuffed his hands behind his back. After that, he knelt beside me and unlocked my cuffs. I slipped the cuffs onto McClary's wrists, ratcheted them tight, and removed his service belt. After patting him down for backup weapons and finding none, I got to my feet and raced behind the counter with McClary's Sig Sauer. I held it to the clerk's face and yelled, "What happened to her?"

His mouth opened, but the look forming on his face spoke of denial. There was a clock on the wall behind him. I pivoted the Sig Sauer and blew the clock to hell. The clerk blanched and shrunk backward, air fluttering from his mouth like a punctured tire. I pushed him against the wall and yelled, "Once more. What happened to her?"

He gasped for air, his eyes turning weepy. "They took her."

"Who took her?"

"The sheriff. Two deputies."

"When?"

"'Bout ten minutes before you came in."

"Shit!"

"They faxed your pictures," he said, tilting his head toward the counter. I glanced over and saw our wanted posters. They'd made them from our driver's license photos. "They said you were wanted for murder. I called nine one one when I recognized her. Like I was supposed to."

The fisherman led Thomas into the office behind me. I held the clerk by the neck while my anger dissipated. He was a cog in their machine, but I was royally pissed. Then the fisherman returned and laid a hand on my gun arm. "Easy, *compa*," he said. "This guy's not a player."

"I know, *padre*," I responded.

John looked at me with a rakish grin. "We gotta keep moving, partner. And get you cleaned up. You smell like a high school wrestling team's dirty laundry."

I smiled despite myself as John handed me a pair of handcuffs and told me to cuff the clerk to the desk in his office. I did that as he dragged McClary into the office and dumped him on the floor. The motel looked like it had been built forty years ago. Veneer was peeling from the desk's edges, and the paint on the window sill was as cracked as an old man's face. Along one wall was an old-fashioned radiator. We cuffed McClary to the radiator as Thomas watched with murderous rage.

When we turned to him, he spit out a "Fuck you" but was resigned to his fate. John held the gun on him while I cuffed him next to McClary.

Before I rose, I shook one finger at him and said, "This is what happens when you harass honeymooners."

My knee throbbed as I pushed myself up. While John smashed the cop's radios and cell phones and threw the pieces into a toilet next to the office, I searched the desk and found a bottle of ibuprofen, dry swallowing four more. John flipped the sign on the front door to Closed, locked the door, and turned off the lights. We left out the back door. A sheriff's cruiser was parked there, all its tires flat, jagged tears in the rubber where the tires had been cut. Beside the cruiser was a dark blue Chevy Suburban, Earl Zepeda behind the wheel. He was wearing a white wife-beater t-shirt under a black leather jacket. His face was filled with menace, but when he saw me, the corners of his mouth turned up in the briefest of smiles. I walked up to his open window and gave him a fist bump.

"*Gracias, guey,*" I said. *Thanks, homie.*

"*Si, compa. De nada.*" *Yeah, partner. You're welcome.*

As we headed south, John turned on a portable police scanner, and we heard radio calls from the local police and sheriff's offices. They were coordinating their hunt for me while reporting that the female suspect was in custody. Several cars were ordered to the Smokey Forest Motel in Capitan. Unit six-four had not checked in and was not responding to calls.

John said, "We've been listening to their radio traffic most of the night. They started a sweep of local motels about an hour ago, so we dashed up here. We were too late to keep them from apprehending Sergeant Hastings."

"Kat."

"Kat. Missed her by minutes. But we saw the cruiser pull up behind the motel and the deputies getting into position to arrest you."

"Where'd you get the costume?"

"Brought it from home. Thought I'd get in some fishing while we're here."

"Wiseass," I said.

John laughed. "It was in a closet of a vacation home we rented. When we arrived yesterday, we rented two safe houses, one near the regional airport and the other east of Ruidoso in the mountains. We were in a motel by the racetrack when you called us. That place may be compromised now, so we're on our way to the safe house by the airport."

"They own the cops," I said.

John nodded. "What I assumed." He removed the goofy hat and ran a hand through his hair, pushing it off his forehead. His neck and cheeks were carpeted with curly black hairs. He hadn't shaved in three or four days.

"I need to call the people who took her," I said.

John peered around at me and nodded. "Do it while we're moving."

As I took the clerk's phone from my pocket, I heard sirens, increasing in volume. Coming at us were two sets of flashing lights, moving fast. I ducked until the wailing of their sirens faded. Then I opened the phone and punched in Henry's number. It rang six times before someone picked up. But there was silence on the other end. He didn't recognize the number.

"Hello, Henry," I said.

After a beat, he said, "How did you get this number?"

"I memorized it while we were standing by your desk."

"You continue to amaze me."

"Is she there?"

"She's on her way."

"I'll be really unhappy if you harm her."

"That's more a function of your behavior than ours. You need to return to Paragon, Mr. Marshall. We need to continue our discussion."

"I thought we were all talked out."

"Oh, no. I was hoping to convince you to join us. I must say your escape last night, while unfortunate, revealed the kind of initiative and ingenuity we value. We could use a man with your resourcefulness. You could be a huge asset to us and would be rewarded handsomely."

"I'm flattered. I've always just thought of myself as a musician."

"You are hardly just that, and now you're patronizing me."

"I want her back," I said. "Unharmed."

"You will need to come to get her, I'm afraid. And quickly. I can guarantee her safety today, but today only. If you don't return, Martin tells me he will begin delivering parts of her to you. That could take a while and would not be pleasant."

"What makes you think I care?"

He laughed. "I saw a video of you and her together before dinner. You care."

"That was an act, Henry. I'm a musician. Women throw themselves at me all the time. What do I need with some self-righteous bitch with a badge?"

"You're lying. I know you better than you think I do."

"Whatever. I'll think about it. Meanwhile, give some thought to what it's going to take to buy me off."

"Buy you off? A simple cash payout?"

"Plus guarantees of my safety. You are flush. You can afford to buy my silence."

"Do you have a figure in mind?" Henry said.

"I'd rather hear what you think my silence is worth. Meanwhile, all bets are off if any harm comes to Sergeant Hastings."

"If you don't care about her, why does that matter?"

"Because if you harm her, I have no guarantee you won't try to harm me. If you don't harm her, I'll know you're a man of your word. She's just a pawn in this negotiation,

Henry, but if anything happens to her, you can multiply by ten whatever settlement figure we reach. You're good at math. Run the numbers. Or, hey, what the hell? Maybe I don't need the money. Maybe I'll just skip town."

"You can't walk away from us, Mr. Marshall."

"Sonny, please. We're friends now, aren't we?"

"You can't walk away, Sonny."

"Sure I can, and I can write one hell of a story and get it published if Katrina Hastings is harmed and Martin and his goons pursue me. You saw my press clippings. CNN, Fox, BBC, ABC, CBS, NBC, Washington Post, New York Times—they all want to talk to me. A Pulitzer is waiting for the reporter who cracks this story. They'll be lined up down the block."

"I can't guarantee that Martin won't act alone."

"Now you're lying," I said. "You have baby brother on a short leash. He won't do anything without your blessing. You can't bullshit me, Henry. If anything happens to her, I'm holding you accountable. You personally and you alone."

He paused for a moment and then said, "I find these kinds of discussions distasteful. Threats and counter-threats. Tell me what you want."

"I'll call you back later today. Stay by your phone, and be prepared to make me an offer too extravagant to pass up."

I ended the call but left the phone on. We were behind a white pickup, and I told Earl to pass it when he could. I lowered the window and tossed the phone into the bed of that truck as Earl drove past.

The safe house was a split-level with wood siding and a three-car garage. Inside, it was all hardwood floors, Navajo rugs, pine cabinets, stone fireplaces, and leather furniture—rustic mountain décor. I needed fresh clothing, and we needed throw-away phones. Before Earl left for those supplies, I told him I also needed Oxy. My knee wouldn't calm down without it. He said he would score the Oxy, too. *No hay problema.*

We made coffee, and I briefed John on what had happened yesterday. Then I drew a map of the compound and told him where I thought they'd hold Kat and where the students were housed. We considered our options and came up with a plan. The priority was rescuing Kat and the two missing girls, but we had a chance to crash the whole party. After Earl returned, I popped two Oxys, took a long, hot shower, and put on fresh clothing. Then we called Ari and discussed the plan with him—all but the part involving

Earl. I needed to talk to Earl *mano a mano* about that. It was the perfect role for him if he would do it.

I lay my head back on the sofa, let my eyes drift shut, and tried to clear my mind. The room smelled like pine and smoke. Beyond the crackling of the fire, the only sounds were distant static and chatter from the police scanner. I tried to listen to the scanner, but the words flew in and out of my mind.

I felt like I was floating in the eye of a hurricane, the leading wave of the storm having been weathered, the trailing wave looming and monstrous in its appetite for destruction. I saw Kat being pushed along in the wind, out of reach, her arms flailing as she tried to find her balance. She whipped in circles around me, faster and faster as the storm gathered strength until she was nothing more than a blur, a black streak against dirty white clouds being shredded like a flag torn apart in a gale. The rain stung my face, forcing my eyes shut. All I could hear was the howling of the wind and the roaring of water as I was wrenched from my mooring and flung into an abyss of such energy and anger that I lost all sense of direction, felt only the ferocious force of nature's breath and the piercing sting of rain. I tumbled and corkscrewed through the air, disoriented and weightless, lost in heavens grown cold and dark. Then something latched onto my arm, and I began shaking. I tried to pull away, but whatever it was clung to me, and I thought it might be Kat, that she'd found me somehow in the cyclone.

"Wake up, partner," John said. He was gently shaking my shoulder. I opened my eyes but couldn't understand what I saw. Then I recognized John's face looming over me. "You have a call," he said. "Your friend Garth."

I thought he'd still be in Oakland, but when I picked up, he said they were in Flagstaff. "What the hell you doing there?" I said.

"Road trip. I called some Angels, and, what the fuck, we hit the road. If nothin' happens, hey, we're on the road, and that ain't bad."

"How many guys with you?"

"'Round twenty."

"Armed?"

"Shit, yes."

"Can you be in Ruidoso tomorrow morning?"

"Count on it."

"Only thing is, I need more guys."

"How many?"

"As many as you can get."

"I'll call around. There're chapters in Phoenix, Albuquerque, Las Cruces, Santa Fe. Places like that. What's going down?" I told him about Paragon and what I had in mind. "Fuckin' A," he said. "You want an army, you'll get an army."

"Call me when you get close."

My ass was dragging, so I walked back to one of the bedrooms and collapsed on a bed. I was asleep before my head hit the pillow. When I woke up four hours later, it was early afternoon. I took another hot shower, shook the cobwebs out of my head, and swallowed two more Oxys. While I waited for the kick, I closed my eyes and tried to clear my mind, but I kept seeing Kat's face and the faces of those kids in the hallway as we raced down it, saw Erin's green eyes and Henry's smug self-assurance and the leering evil behind Martin's cold countenance, and that whole table of Barnards—preened and plump with conceit, so confident they were humanity's salvation they could already hear the accolades—the arrogance of the few deciding the fate of the many.

John and Earl sat in the kitchen listening to the police scanner. Hours ago, they'd found McClary and Thomas and were now looking for a man who might be dressed as a fisherman. They hadn't seen the blue Suburban and weren't aware of Earl.

"Sana Houssian's on the way," John told me. "He and five Armenians are on a private jet, landing in about an hour. They're bringing the supplies I requested, including explosives."

"They'll need vehicles," I said.

"Already taken care of," John replied. "Earl will take them to a rental place far from here."

"The rental people could be on Paragon's payroll."

"Noted."

I looked at Earl and said, "We'll need fireworks. They're legal in New Mexico. You can find them at stands along the roads and in some stores."

"Why we need them?" Earl said.

I explained and added, "We need enough fireworks to fill four large containers. Have Sana and his guys buy them, not too many at one place."

"*Entendido*," he said, telling me he understood.

"One more thing, Earl. What's going down tomorrow will be dangerous. These people are well-armed and have eyes everywhere. We can't pull it off unless you do something special for us. But you're not going to like it."

He shrugged his shoulders and said, *"Lo que sea."* *Whatever.*

I wasn't sure he'd be so agreeable when I explained. I showed him the map of Paragon and told him what I wanted him to do. His face turned dark as I spoke, but the worst he called me was a fucking whore, which, given my request, wasn't so bad. I've been called worse. He crossed his arms and did a slow burn, but in the end, he nodded. We discussed what else he needed from Wal-Mart, and he left to pick up the Armenians.

"That could have gone worse," John observed. "At least he didn't kill you."

"If he'd come after me, I would've told him it was your idea."

"Bastard."

We both chuckled, but I was relieved. Only Earl could pull this off. I borrowed John's laptop and spent the next two hours writing everything I remembered about Paragon and the Barnards. Then I emailed the document to myself, Fetch, and Ari. When it was gone, I called Fetch.

"We found the girl," I told him.

"Erin Hightower? Holy cow, Sonny. I can't believe it. She's alive?"

"I talked to her last night. I just sent you an email with the whole story. I need to make sure you got it."

"Okay, hold on," he said. A moment later, he was back. "It's here."

"Good. Now I need you to promise me something. You can read this, but don't show it to anyone else, especially Marcella Delgado, until tomorrow at noon."

"What's happening at noon?"

"I'm going to shove a rocket up somebody's ass and light it. If they know the story's out, they'll kill me, Fetch. You're my insurance. I'm counting on you to keep this to yourself until noon tomorrow."

"Okay. Will do. How else can I help?"

"Just give it to Marcella at noon. Tell her this is the exclusive she wanted."

"Can I share this with Stephanie tonight?"

"No. Your eyes only until noon tomorrow."

Earl returned a few hours later. He walked by without speaking, carrying two Wal-Mart bags with the supplies he needed. After he disappeared into one of the bedrooms, Sana walked in from the garage, followed by his fellow Armenians. They carried three trunks, which they set on the living room floor. John opened them and inspected the contents while Sana introduced his friends. They were a ragtag assortment of social misfits—like everybody else in this operation. Azad Bedrossian was a kid with short black hair, five o'clock shadow, and eyebrows so thick they bridged his nose. Hovig Gregorian was a mid-forties guy with a thick black mustache and long black goatee. When he smiled, his eyes crinkled shut. The oldest was Davros Hakimian, who had long black hair, unfashionably long sideburns, and a chin as sharp as an anvil. Easily the scariest of the bunch was Shiraz Torosyan. He had a bald head like a watermelon and big flat ears with diamond earrings. His swollen, misshapen knuckles bore witness to every punch he'd ever thrown. The fifth guy was Taniel Zakarian, a mid-twenties pretty boy with brown hair that swept over his forehead, pale green eyes, and a thick lower lip. His gaze was as penetrating and creepy as a psychopath's, but these were Ari's guys, and I could trust them with my life.

John and I briefed the Armenians on their roles, and then John asked if they had any questions. A couple of them shook their heads. The rest gazed at the fire with lazy eyes. They were unnaturally calm for what lay ahead, but I knew I was projecting my fears about what might happen. These guys were as cool as a mountain stream.

They'd rented two GMC Yukons. The fireworks were in the backs of those vehicles. We sat around the dining room table looking over maps of Ruidoso and my hand-drawn map of Paragon as John and I laid out the plan. Sana and the Armenians were reviewing the details when the bedroom door opened, and Earl walked in. We all looked at him and fell silent. The effect was spellbinding. He wore a long, black wig. The hair, parted in the middle, cascaded over his shoulders and down onto his chest. The bangs softened his forehead, and the hair at the sides of his face hid his ears and made his face appear longer and more feline. He was shaved clean, and with rouge, pink lipstick, black eye shadow, and mascara, he had transformed himself into a vision of the girl he once was. No one made any stupid remarks, but I'm sure the other men were thinking what I thought—that Earl had once been a beautiful young woman.

"That'll do," John said. "Let's take your picture."

While they were busy, I grabbed a throwaway phone and asked Sana to take me for a ride. He drove one of the Yukons while I sat in the backseat, where I was less visible. We found a residential area southwest of our current location, and Sana drove randomly around it while I phoned Henry.

"I wasn't sure you'd call back," Henry said when he picked up. "It's late."

"Sorry if I made you anxious. I needed some sleep after my adventure last night. I'm sure you understand."

"None of us slept much last night."

"Which is a shame. Sleep is important to your health."

"Why don't we have this conversation another time?" he said.

"A man who gets to the point," I replied. "I like that."

"We insist on absolute non-disclosure in any agreement we reach."

"Okay."

"We are prepared to offer you a position at Paragon, but if you're not inclined to accept, and I assume you're not, then you'll be free to live your life as you choose—with the proviso that you remain silent about Paragon, the HEAD Project, and the Barnard family."

"There goes my front-page story in the *Enquirer*." He didn't find that remark funny. "Just kidding, Henry. Lighten up. Why don't we talk cold, hard cash."

"I was getting to that. We are prepared to offer you twenty million dollars for your cooperation. We think that's quite generous."

I paused for effect and then said, "I have to say I'm disappointed, Henry. I was thinking fifty million. Your family's worth billions, and with all the money you're making off your students, you could come up with much more than twenty mil. That'll barely pay for my yacht."

"I'd urge you not to push this, Sonny. Greed will kill this deal. Nonetheless, we thought you might not agree to the initial figure, so we are willing to increase the offer to thirty million—and that is absolutely the final figure."

"Well, as figures go, that's a much nicer one. Of course, this deal includes Sergeant Hastings. She and I will split the money."

"So long as she also agrees to the terms."

"Understood. Now, speaking of Sergeant Hastings, how is she?"

"Fine. I told you we wouldn't harm her until—"

"Tomorrow, yeah" I said. "But if you don't mind, I'd like to talk to her today. I want to hear it from her."

"I'm sorry. That's impossible."

"Oh, I think it is. I know you guys. You can have her on the phone in minutes."

"You need to trust me when I say she's okay."

"I'd like to, Henry, but trust has to be earned, and after last night you can't blame me for being skeptical. I'll give you five minutes to have her on the line. After that, the settlement figure increases by a million dollars every minute. And if she's been harmed, the settlement figure is three hundred million."

"Goddammit," he barked. "Wait a moment."

I heard him yelling for someone and checked my watch. In three minutes and forty-two seconds, I heard Kat's voice.

"Sonny?"

"Kat."

"Are you okay?"

"Yeah," I said. "How about you?"

"Tired but okay."

"They haven't hurt you, have they?"

"No. They say they will if you don't return."

"They sang that song to me, too. I told them what would happen if they harmed you. I know they're listening, so you won't have to repeat this. I'm coming for you. I'll be at the front gate before ten tomorrow morning. If anything happens to me along the way, or if anything happens to you, they'll be featured on the six o'clock news and will never recover from the shit storm that follows. I've worked out a deal for us."

"What deal?"

"I'll tell you tomorrow."

"Okay," she said, and then she was gone.

33

John Sebastiani and I sat on the concrete steps leading from our safe house into the garage watching Sana, Azad, Hovig, and Shiraz repack the fireworks into four large plastic bins. On the floor beside them were backpacks, industrial smoke pots, sealed quart Bell jars of gasoline, and cell phone-activated triggers. They handled the fireworks carefully, tried different packing arrangements to minimize empty space, and then placed a fuse on top. When they were satisfied with the bins, they locked their lids in place and lifted them into the backs of the Yukons. I thought of the police investigation following the havoc we meant to cause tomorrow morning. "Won't their fingerprints be on the packaging?" I said.

John sat with his right hand perched on his chin, his index finger on his lips. He shook his head and said, "They're wearing the latest in criminal hand wear—skin-tight, latex gloves with someone else's fingerprints etched onto the fingertip surfaces."

I peered closely at their hands and saw the gloves. They were nearly transparent.

"When the crime scene techs run the prints," John said, "they'll discover that the culprits were Al Capone, Ted Bundy, Frank Sinatra, people like that. Taniel is the genius behind it. He finds fingerprint cards online and copies the patterns to a gadget he invented that etches the patterns onto the gloves. After they put them on, they spray them with jojoba oil, so they leave prints. Taniel's also an excellent forger."

I smiled at him. "Like I said, for an ex-priest, you know some interesting people."

John took a sip of coffee. "These guys are loyal to the core. They have an unconventional view of right and wrong, but they look after their own, do what they're asked, and wouldn't betray you if their lives depended on it. I'd rather be around them than crooked cops or pedophiles."

"Or people who kidnap smart kids to create a master race?"

"Them, too." John put his hand on the back of my head and felt my wound. "You still have a staple in your scalp."

"It's supposed to come out tomorrow."

"I wondered what held you together."

"Staples, baling wire, and duct tape."

He laughed. "If you don't make it to the hospital tomorrow, I can pull that staple out. I'm sure there are rusty pliers around here somewhere."

The Armenians walked over with a smoke pot and a trigger, and John showed them how to rig them. "Each burns for thirty minutes and puts out two million cubic feet of smoke. Three pots at each site will generate enough smoke to simulate a disaster covering eight square city blocks. The fireworks and burning trash in the dumpsters will make it look and sound like a war zone, but other than causing panic, no real harm will be done."

"Four sites. Four fires. Four smoke clouds," I said. "That'll keep the cops busy."

"It'll seriously mess with their heads. The cops won't know piss from Pepsi, and calls from citizens will jam their coms. They won't be able to help the crew at Paragon."

I nodded but wasn't optimistic. "They say your battle plan never survives first contact with the enemy."

"That's right, partner. But you still plan. You execute as well as you can and adapt as things unfold. That's the best you can do. I know you're worried about her."

I nodded.

"Don't worry about it tonight. They'll keep her alive until they have you. Show Henry what you wrote. He'll want to know who else has it. They'll use torture to get that out of you—but they'll torture Kat, not you. They'll make you watch until you talk. Then they'll kill you both."

"I know."

"I worry about you, Sonny. You're too tough to be afraid but not too tough to die."

"You're wrong, John, but I'd rather die on my feet than on my ass. Vincent van Gogh said, 'Fishermen know the sea is dangerous and the storm terrible, but they've never found these dangers sufficient reason to remain ashore.'"

He thought about that for a moment. "Yeah, well, if this all goes to hell tomorrow, some of the wrong people might get killed."

The door behind us opened, and Davros told us to come for supper. While the other guys were making bombs, Davros and Taniel put together a meal of lamb kebobs, pita, and a mezze platter with tabbouleh, hummus, roasted red peppers, olives, tzatziki, dolmas, baba ghanoush, and cubed feta cheese. John filled a plate and ate by the police scanner, listening to the traffic. The rest of us sat at the dining room table. I thanked the Armenians for their help and raised my glass in a toast. "Whatever happens tomorrow, may every man's character be his fate," I said.

During the meal, Earl and I talked about what he would do tomorrow. The Armenians spoke among themselves, but after they broke into laughter, Hovig said in accented English, "I was telling about an Armenian woman who envies her neighbors. One night she says to her husband, 'Every night he makes passionate love to his wife, and every morning when he leaves, he sweeps her into his arms and kisses her and then blows more kisses to her as she watches him from the window. How come you never do that?' And her husband says, 'I hardly know the woman!'" Hovig's face lifted in an impish grin, a white glob of baba ghanoush smeared in his black goatee. With his thick eyebrows and curly black hair, he looked like a demonic circus clown.

"Hey, quiet, guys!" John yelled, waving a hand at us. He turned up the volume on the police scanner, and we heard a flurry of static-filled radio traffic.

"What's up?" I said.

"They're desperate. Doing neighborhood sweeps now," he said. "Telling people an escaped murderer is somewhere in town. Roadblocks. House-to-house searches. They've cleared the areas east of town. They've got units coming our way. We need to move. Sonny, you're with Sana. Earl, with me. We're out of here in ten."

Sana barked something in Armenian—and his men sprang into action like firefighters hearing an alarm. Before climbing in the Yukon with Sana's guys, I pulled John aside. "You've got one more call to make tonight. You got the number?"

"I can get it. No problem." Then he said to the others, "Azad, when you guys hit Forty-eight, turn south and head into Ruidoso. At Seventy, head east to safe house two. Call me when you get there. Sana, you guys go ahead of us. Turn north at Forty-eight. Drive to Capitan, then east on Three Eighty to Hondo, then west on Seventy to the safe house. Earl and I will be a hundred yards behind you. We're your backup if you run into trouble. Remember, they have eyes in the sky, so drive the speed limit and blend in with the tourists. We're on vacation, planning to hit the casino and the race track. Any questions? No? Okay, go!"

It was dark as we pulled out of the garage and left safe house one behind us. As big as Yukons are, riding on the floor in front of the backseat was like being folded into a portable dog cage and riding over railroad tracks—only not as comfortable. My left knee was cramped and painful from the start, and I felt like I was smothering beneath the blanket. I took my mind off it by playing some jazz in my head, which helped, but not much. Taniel and Hovig sat in the backseat, their feet perched on my left leg and arm. In the front passenger seat, Davros got a call on his cell and answered it in Armenian. Then he said, "Police ahead. Azad and Shiraz are at the checkpoint." Above me, Hovig and Taniel racked their weapons, chambering a round. I heard the guys in the front seat rack theirs, too. We were screwed if a firefight erupted. I knew these guys could take out the cops, but that would put us on the wrong side of this equation. Killing cops, even crooked cops, was something the law wouldn't forgive. I was thinking that I didn't have a weapon when I felt a tap on my shoulder, and Hovig passed me an automatic. He told me it was racked and ready, and I thought *it was a hell of a firing angle from down here. If the shit starts, the best I can do is lay low and hope I don't catch a stray.*

After a few minutes, I felt the Yukon slow down and come to a stop. The guys were speaking quietly to each other in Armenian. A long minute later, we inched forward and stopped. Then I heard the front windows rolling down. Again, we rolled along slowly, a few feet at a time, and stopped. "Four cops," Hovig whispered to me. Sana said something to the other guys in Armenian. I couldn't understand him, but I'm sure he told them which cop each was responsible for taking out if things went heavy.

Then a voice outside the car said, "Good evening, sir."

Sana usually speaks good, unaccented English, but for the officer's benefit, he sounded like he'd just stepped off the boat when he said, "Ello, ese problema?"

"There's a fugitive on the loose, sir, and we're checking all vehicles."

I saw moving lights through the blanket as the cops shined their flashlights into the car. Hovig and Taniel rolled down their windows, and I thought, *oh fuck*, but they began talking to each other and the cops in Armenian mixed with very broken English. Through the noise and confusion, I heard Hovig say, "We go to cashino. Yeah? To cashino. Win big money, yeah? You know cashino?" I could imagine the goofy grin on his face. When Hovig didn't look evil, he looked like an idiot, and I hoped the cops were buying his routine.

Over the continuing Armenian patter, one of the cops spoke louder. "Have any of you seen this man?" They quieted a moment while they peered at what I guessed was my photo. Then there was a chorus of denials before they erupted again in Armenian. "He's wanted for murder," the cop shouted. "He's armed and dangerous. If you see him, call the police."

"H'okay, h'okay, we calla," Sana assured them. "We calla. H'okay." Then the car inched forward, and I heard the windows being rolled up. I'd been holding my breath so long my lungs ached. I let out it and sank to the floor. A minute later, I felt the Yukon turning to the right. We were on Highway Forty-eight. Hovig pulled the blanket off me, and they moved their legs out of the way and helped me up to the seat. Sitting between them, I stretched out my left leg as much as I could in the cramped confines of the Yukon, but anything was better than the floor.

"Goddamn," I muttered, massaging my knee in a futile attempt to rub the pain away. "We got any water?" Taniel reached around behind him and passed me a bottle. I leaned back and dug through my front jeans pocket for an Oxy, which I eagerly swallowed. When I could get my mind off my knee, I said, "You guys should take your comedy act to Vegas." Hovig appreciated that and said he'd consider it.

The drive took more than an hour. We stopped in Capitan for ten minutes to ensure we weren't being followed and to confuse anyone watching feeds from the drones. John called Sana fifteen minutes later to say he'd heard from Azad. He and Shiraz had arrived at the safe house and cleared it. When we reached the Hondo intersection, John and Earl passed us in the Suburban and parked in the shadows of an abandoned building, their lights off. Sana pulled into a copse of trees, and we also went dark. When we left again, we followed the Suburban to safe house two. It was an older, block-like house with tan siding, square windows, and a red, corrugated roof. It was in the forest about half a mile uphill from Highway Seventy. The nearest house was several hundred yards away. Lights burned in some of its windows, but we saw no other activity. When he entered the safe house, John swept the place with a portable bug detector and found none. Then he set up the police scanner and listened to it while we moved our things inside. It was nine o'clock, and the air had turned chilly and damp. Shiraz got a fire going in the fireplace while Azad brought in two cases of cold beer they'd bought in Ruidoso. We sat around the fireplace for the next hour, drinking beer and shooting the shit until John joined us.

"They don't have a clue," John said, sitting beside me on the sofa. "They think you might have left the immediate area. But they'll continue searching all night, so we need to post guards."

Then John went over the timetable for tomorrow. When he finished, I told the Armenians, "You're going in with the bikers. Hovig, Azad, and Shiraz to the right as you reach the main gate. Your target is due west in the complex. Sana and Davros, left at the main gate. Your target's due east. Their security force wears camo, and they're well-armed. The guardians are in black. If possible, we need to neutralize their security without inflicting casualties and protect the students. Once you arrive, no one leaves."

"We're up at five," John said. "Out of here at six. Questions?"

A couple of them shook their heads. I laid back on the sofa and closed my eyes. I heard the occasional tinny snap of a pull tab, swampy belches from Shiraz, and low conversation in Armenian. The police scanner burped now and then, but it soon became white noise as my mind sought a truce with my anxiety.

Hours later, John shook me. "Wake up, partner," he said. "You have a call. It's Garth."

I roused myself as he handed me a cell phone. "Yeah," I said.

"Hey, Asshole."

I pushed the cobwebs aside. "Where are you?"

"Carrizozo. Fuckin' beat, man."

"Long day on the road."

"It still happenin'?"

"Fuckin' A."

"All right. We're shuttin' down here. What time do you want us there?"

"Six-thirty. At the rendezvous point."

"Count on it."

"How many guys d'you round up?" When he told me, I said, "Holy shit, man."

"Comin' from every fucking direction, brother."

"Ciao, bro."

I found John in the kitchen listening to the police scanner. "Any news?"

He shook his head. "Same old." He canted his head toward one of the bedrooms. "Better catch more zzz's."

I nodded. "You make the call?"

"Yeah. He busted my chops for twenty minutes." He was drinking another cup of coffee. The rest of us might catch some sleep tonight, but John would be up all night listening to the scanner.

"Will he come through?"

"Oh, yeah," John said. "Big time."

I dragged myself to one of the bedrooms, found a bed, and lay there thinking about tomorrow. I passed out during my third or fourth pass through our plan. I woke to the toasty aroma of coffee. John sat on a stool in the kitchen with a big white bra on the counter. He was stuffing cotton balls into the enormous cups. Beside the bra were two explosive charges, each about the size of a baseball.

A door opened down the hallway, and Earl came out wearing a long white cotton slip, black pantyhose, and women's black flats. He wore the black wig and had shaved and made up his face. I was again struck by how attractive a woman he made. Earl sat on the stool beside John, pulled the slip's straps down, and let it fall to his waist. There were thin, white, horizontal scars across his chest where Earlene's breasts had been removed. John held up one of the charges.

"These are the explosives," John told him. "The timers are set to go off at ten o'clock, but they won't be armed until you slide this green switch. There are two adhesive strips on the back of each one. Pull off the plastic tabs and push the charges firmly onto the surface. *¿Comprendes?*" Earl nodded. "Then slide the green switch on both devices and get the hell out of there." Earl nodded again, and John carefully put one charge into each cup of the bra, packing cotton around them and putting thick cotton pads over the ends of the charges. Then he picked up the bra and helped Earl put it on.

"The Beretta?" John asked.

Earl opened the bathrobe, pulled up the bottom of the slip, and spread his legs. A small, black Beretta was strapped to the inside of his right leg; a knife in a sheath was strapped to his left.

"*Hombre*," John said, patting Earl on the shoulder, "with bombs in your bra and a gun and knife between your legs, you are one lethal mama." Earl flickered a smile, no doubt at the part about being lethal.

Azad, Shiraz, and I left in one of the Yukons at six o'clock. At the bottom of the hill, we fell into a line of RVs headed west—early risers from the campgrounds east on Highway Seventy—and although we passed some troopers parked along the highway, none attempted to stop us. At twenty after, we pulled into the casino's parking lot and drove to the west end, where about fifty Harleys were lined up in two rows, their riders milling around. I found Garth and his crew of angels, did the ritual high-fives and fist bumps, and then met guys who'd arrived from Phoenix, Albuquerque, Roswell, and other towns around the southwest. They were a scruffy-looking bunch—chop shop owners, grease monkeys, survivalists, and guys in biker clubs, including Hell's Angels. For the next half hour, more bikes roared down Seventy and turned into the lot. When most of this ragtag army had arrived, we had around a hundred and fifty souls in black leather and camo. Three casino security guards and a handful of sheriff's deputies watched from a distance but weren't about to crash this party.

Shiraz carried over bolt cutters and cable ties and set them by the bikes. I told Garth we needed teams to simultaneously hit the place from four directions. I gave him a map of Paragon and explained what I wanted them to do. To them all, I said, "Thanks for makin' it, brothers. We're here to liberate more than two hundred kidnapped children. Garth'll fill you in on the details. The security force at this place wears camo and packs AR-15s. Try not to kill any of 'em. Don't want to see you guys up on murder beefs when this is over. So scare the shit out of 'em. Take their weapons. Tie their hands and keep 'em down. If you see any kids, round 'em up and keep 'em safe. You with me?"

A couple of guys nodded, but otherwise, the response was anemic.

Garth whispered, "Need to work on your leadership skills, brother."

So I yelled, "You motherfuckers with me?"

Laughter burst from the group, and a dozen bikers yelled, "Fuck, yeah, man."

Garth patted me on the back. "More like it," he said.

"See you in hell," I told him.

"See you in hell, bro," he replied.

At six-fifty, traffic was picking up through the heart of Ruidoso as RVs, campers, and SUVs pulled into places like IHOP and Denny's for breakfast. The police were out in force, threading their way through traffic and parked along the highway, scanning passing vehicles, but we made it safely through the phalanx using tourist traffic as camouflage. At ten after, we were back at safe house two. I swallowed another Oxy and put two in my front pocket. Then I jumped into the Suburban with John and Earl. Earl sat in the back with the terrycloth robe pulled around him. We followed Azad and Shiraz in their Yukon as they headed into town.

Ruidoso looked busy and peaceful, just a small tourist town waking up on a summer morning. I glanced at Earl. He stared out the window, his mouth turned down. *"¿Estás bien?" Are you okay?*

"Pinche que, sí," he replied. *Fuck yes.*

"Gracias, carnal." Thanks, cuz.

His eyes bore into me, and then his mouth turned up in a parody of a sweet smile, and he said in a chillingly light voice, "*Como no, señor.*" *Of course, sir.* A chill ran up my spine as I thought about the capacity for harm behind the smile on that beautiful face.

At seven thirty, I spotted Sana and Taniel in one of the Yukons parked just off the highway. They fell behind us as we inched toward a red light. On the other side of the light were twenty motorcycles headed east. The guttural roar of their engines disturbed the morning like battle tanks arriving at a wedding reception. When the light changed, John turned onto a residential street. Sana followed about half a block behind. We cruised the streets for a while until we saw a likely candidate. She was about five-six and a little stout. More importantly, she was busty and wore a gray dress that buttoned up the front and black pantyhose. She looked Hispanic and wore a lanyard around her neck. I glanced at Earl, and he nodded, so I called Sana and said, "At our three o'clock." We drove on slowly, and I peered around and saw Sana's Yukon stop as the woman walked toward them. Taniel stepped out of the Yukon and approached her.

We drove to an isolated area north of town and waited. Moments later, Sana's Yukon pulled in beside us. I opened the side door on our Suburban, and Sana hustled the terrified maid into the seat beside me.

"*No te preocupes,*" I said to her. *Don't worry.* "*No vamos a lastimarte.*" *We are not going to hurt you.* Her lanyard identified her as Maria Alvarez.

"*Por favor. Tengo familia,*" Maria cried. *Please. I have a family.* Her lips trembled, bulging eyes welling with tears. She was in her early twenties and wore a thin gold band on her left hand. Behind the fear on her face, I saw a young woman who had resigned herself to a life of service but had a young family and was trying to understand what was happening to her.

"*No vamos a lastimarte,*" I repeated. "*Todo estará bien. Tranquila.*" *It will be okay. Be calm.*

She brought a shaking hand up to her face and wiped her eyes. "*¿Qué quieres?*" she said. *What do you want?*

"*Por favor. Necesitamos tu vestido,*" I said. *Please. We need your dress.*

"*No, no, no,*" she cried, backing into Sana.

"*Quítate el vestido rápidamente. Hazlo ahora,*" Earl snapped at her. *Take off your dress quickly. Do it now.* She turned to him in surprise, trying to reconcile that womanly face with his harsh, male voice.

"*Por favor,*" I said. "*No vamos a lastimarla, pero necesitamos su vestido. Ahora.*" *Please. We are not going to hurt you, but we need your dress. Now.*

She cried, tears streaking down her face, but she unbuttoned her dress with trembling fingers and struggled out of it. Earl took off the bathrobe and tossed it to her while he put on the dress. John gave me an envelope, and I handed it to her.

"*Esto es para Ud.,*" I told her. *This is for you.* The envelope contained fifty one-hundred-dollar bills. She peered cautiously inside. As Sana reached for her arm, she stuffed the envelope in her purse, and I said, "*Por ayudarnos a exponer a gente muy mala. Gracias.*" *For helping us expose very bad people. Thank you.*

While Sana led her back to the Yukon, Taniel handed me the maid's lanyard. Earl hung the lanyard around his neck. He'd pasted Earl's maid photo on the ID tag and re-laminated the card so artfully I couldn't tell it'd been tampered with.

"You ready?" I said.

He nodded, and John drove away. We returned to the bus stop as maids were climbing aboard. John pulled to the curb thirty yards away, and Earl stepped out. He smoothed the dress and looked at me with the fierce expression I usually see on him. Then his face magically grew softer as he got into character, and he walked away looking no different than the other fifty maids on that bus. We watched as the bus pulled away, our Trojan horse having begun his journey.

John drove to Enterprise Rent-A-Car and walked inside with a driver's license and credit card identifying him as James G. Talbot from Springfield, Missouri, and rented a Dodge minivan. It was eight-fifteen. Back at the safe house, Maria Alvarez sat in the main room, the white terrycloth bathrobe snug around her. Taniel sat opposite, drinking coffee. I asked Maria if she was okay, and she nodded. I told her that Taniel would look after her until this afternoon, and she could not contact anyone. She looked at me warily but had dried her eyes and was no longer shaking. She folded her arms around her black purse and held it close. I assured her the money was hers and no one would take it.

At eight forty-five, Sana called 911 and told them he'd planted a bomb at the Apache Casino. We listened to the police scanner as the report was radioed to units in the area, and four units were dispatched to that location. One minute later, Sana phoned the igniters on the devices planted in a dumpster behind the casino. Within moments, the airwaves went viral with reports of shots fired and an explosion, fire, and smoke at the casino. People were being evacuated into the parking lot as other police units were ordered to the scene along with the fire department and two ambulances. At eight-fifty-five, police radio traffic again erupted as reports came in of another explosion and fire behind a vacant building off Highway Forty-eight. Citizens in the area reported hearing gunfire and seeing billowing clouds of smoke. Some units heading to the casino were diverted to the new location.

The situation was still chaotic at nine-ten when another explosion and fire were reported behind a large superstore off Seventy a mile east of the casino. I walked outside the safe house and looked toward Ruidoso. Three pillars of smoke were visible above the town, the one above the casino highest and spreading over a large area. The black smoke, curling and snaking its way through mushrooming clouds of white, reminded me of images on television of towering oil field fires in Iraq during the Gulf War. I walked back inside and heard reports of a fourth explosion west on Seventy. The cops now thought it might be a terrorist attack and called on neighboring communities for first responder support.

Amidst this chaos, I pocketed a copy of my Paragon report, shook hands with John and Sana, and walked outside to the Suburban. John followed me and offered me a handgun, but I told him they would confiscate it when I arrived at the gate.

"Okay, partner," he said. "Go save the world."

I drove down the hill. At the intersection onto Seventy, I sat for a moment surveying the scene in town. It looked like hell had come to Ruidoso. While I watched the smoke, seventy or eighty motorcycles thundered past on their way east. I took a deep breath and followed them.

34

We can predict the future only if we can change the past, and I was powerless to do either, so I had to trust that what I'd set in motion would end well. If it ended badly, I'd have only myself to blame.

Within minutes of turning onto Paragon's road, I picked up an escort, one of Paragon's black vans. It hung thirty yards behind me all the way to the gate. I arrived at Paragon at nine-thirty-five. A half-dozen guards covered me as I left the Suburban, hands raised. Martin emerged from the gatehouse dressed in the camouflage uniform of the security guards. His name tag read *Smith 1*. "Are you responsible for the fires in town this morning?" he said.

"What fires?" I sounded as innocent as Julie Andrews in *The Sound of Music*.

He gave me a "fuck you" look as he handcuffed me. He had a bandage on the left side of his neck and less mobility in his left shoulder. I canted my head toward his neck. "Did I do that?" He looked at me with such hatred I almost felt bad about myself. "In the elevator? A ricochet? I'd apologize, but it wouldn't be sincere."

Martin wheeled me around and searched me. He smashed my throw-away phone under his boot before taking the written report from me and stuffing it into his pocket. Then with two guards in tow, he took me to Henry's office. He told me to sit on the sofa facing Henry's desk and posted the guards on either side six feet away. I was dangerous, he told them, and had to be watched carefully. These two guys were Smith 4 and Smith 9, veterans with the hardened faces of men who'd dug graves and buried people. They regarded me with empty eyes.

Henry and Gordon Barnard walked in through the side door. The wall clock read 9:44. Henry wore a chic black suit with a white shirt and silver tie. He was well groomed but had worry lines under his eyes. Gordon wore a brown corduroy blazer over black slacks and a blue shirt with a button-down collar. Very Ivy League. All he needed was a pipe. As they sat opposite me, Henry smoothed his suit coat and tie.

"You've given us quite a turn, Mr. Marshall."

"Sonny. Remember?"

"Where have you been?" Henry said.

"I spent yesterday in Roswell at the UFO museum. If you haven't seen it, you should go. It's pretty cool."

Silence. I guess they didn't appreciate alien kitsch.

Martin said, "He told me he wasn't responsible for the fires in Ruidoso."

"I find that hard to believe," Henry said coldly. "The authorities are now aware that the fires were a prank. But it tied up all their resources."

I smiled at him. "Probably some kids having a little fun."

Gordon crossed his arms over his chest. "Tell us about the fisherman who helped you escape from the motel yesterday morning," he said.

"I was sure glad to see him," I said. "I have no idea who he was, but I asked him to friend me on Facebook."

Their scowls said it all. The wall clock read 9:47.

"Clearly, we underestimated you," Henry said.

I gave him a disappointed look. "Again?"

His eyes flared, but he contained his anger. "You have underestimated us as well," he continued. "This morning, one of our drones saw your van at the gate, and we ran the digital recording back and traced your vehicle to a house in the foothills east of Ruidoso. Sheriff's deputies are on the way there now. If your fisherman is there, he'll be in custody momentarily." I tried to look worried, but my smirk may have betrayed me. Martin passed my report to Henry. He scanned it, shaking his head as he read. He passed the report to Gordon and studied me with cold, flat eyes. "Who else has seen this?"

"First things first," I replied. "We have a deal. I have a confidentiality agreement to sign, and you owe me thirty million dollars."

Henry's jaw tightened. "Who else has seen this document?"

I glanced at the clock. It was 9:50.

Turning to Gordon, I said, "You're the head of the school. What grade would you give me for my report? I think it deserves an A, but I'd like your opinion."

"Answer me!" Henry shouted.

"Henry, the last time we were here, you told us that anger rarely results in a satisfactory outcome. Remember saying that? Let's remain friends and conduct our business cordially. Back to my question. Gordon, what do you think of my paper?"

Gordon tossed the report aside and regarded me with a frown. I would have flunked his class. "I'm sure you know how damaging this could be," he said, "so don't play games with us. Who else has seen this?"

"Okay, if you insist. You have something to write on?"

Martin went to Henry's desk and returned with a pad of paper and a pen, which he handed to Henry.

"Okay, let's see," I said. "I sent it to Jimmy Cobb and Paul Chambers, two old friends. And Bill Evans. Hmmm. Also, Julian Adderley and John Coltrane. I call him Trane. Oh, and to Miles Dewey Davis, the third. So that's what? Six guys?"

"Did you say John Coltrane?" Gordon said.

"Yeah, Trane."

Gordon looked at me angrily. He turned to Henry. "John Coltrane was a jazz musician. I think he's dead."

"He died in the late sixties," I said, "so I guess he won't read my report."

It was 9:53.

"Goddammit," Henry said. "What are you trying to pull?"

I laughed. "Your legs, guys. Come on! It was a joke. The names I gave you were the musicians who recorded the album *Kind of Blue* with Miles Davis. Some of the best modal jazz ever recorded."

Henry seethed, beads of moisture appearing on his temples and hands. He looked like he'd gotten dressed too quickly after a workout. I hoped the sweat wouldn't ruin his suit. "This is not a joke," he said. "We need to know if anyone else has seen this report."

"And I want to see Kat Hastings. I need to know she's okay."

"In good time," he replied.

"No, now. Then you can show me my thirty million dollars."

"I have lost all patience with you," Henry said. He nodded at Martin, who went to Henry's desk and picked up the remote. He punched a few buttons, and the bank of monitors on the wall lit up. A moment later, Kat came into view. She was sitting in a cell in their security building. She sat on a bunk wearing the same clothes she'd worn yesterday. She leaned against the wall and looked haggard.

"I find this exceedingly distasteful," Henry said, "but you are giving me no choice. If you don't start telling us what we need to know, I will allow Martin to make the remainder of her life an absolute hell."

Martin appeared beside me with a black object and held it before me. It was a two-foot-long black rod with a silver tip and a thick black handle. "Do you know what this is?" he said.

I shook my head.

"It's like a cattle prod, but it's meant for crowd control. It delivers five million volts, not just at the tip but all along the length of the rod," he said, running his fingers along it, "so if a protester grabs the rod, he gets a jolt that can melt his hand and turn his brain to custard. Lose the attitude and tell us the truth, or I will have my men rip off your girlfriend's pants and strap her down. After they've taken turns with her, I will ram this inside her and give her a fucking that will make her eyes glow in the dark."

The clock read 9:56.

I saw in Martin another child killer like Billy Luce. I knew he would do to Kat what he described. Psychopaths like them have no boundaries.

I pointed at Martin but asked Henry, "Is this the fine new world you envision? Torture, rape, and murder sanctioned by those in power?"

"It's an unfortunate expedient," he replied.

"Bullshit, Henry. Committing these crimes is as much a part of your moral code as the good you see yourself bringing to the world. Rape and murder are the dark sides of your vision, and you think your students don't know that? You think they don't know what happens when one of their friends disappears? Some kid who isn't keeping up? What you're teaching them is that the end justifies the means. You're not creating a superior generation of leaders. You're creating people who will have the intelligence, money, and power to rule the world but will be morally bankrupt. You're creating monsters."

Martin's cell phone rang. It was 9:57.

He looked at the screen and stepped away to take the call. As he listened, his eyebrows knitted, and a shadow passed over his face. Then he clicked buttons on the remote. Instantly, the bank of monitors showed a new image, a drone's eye view of the road leading to Paragon. On the screen was a long line of motorcycles, three abreast, and two SUVs, all streaming toward Paragon at sixty miles an hour. The dust cloud billowing up behind the bikes nearly obscured the caravan, but they flew relentlessly down that straight road like an arrow shot into Paragon's heart.

Gordon and Henry spun their heads around. "What is this?" Henry said. He stood and faced the monitors, Gordon following. "What's going on?"

"I don't know," Martin said. He turned on his cell again and speed-dialed a number. To the person answering, he said, "I'll be right down." As he hurried toward the door, he said to his guards, "If he tries anything, shoot him in the feet, but don't kill him."

The wall clock said 9:58.

Gordon rushed to the desk and picked up the phone. Henry stared at the monitors a moment longer, marveling, I imagine, at how his empire was unraveling so quickly. Then he regarded me with contempt, the lines on his face drawn deeper in the last few minutes. He stood absolutely still while Gordon spoke on the phone behind him. Henry's face had gone gray, his skin sunken like dried leather, as though a taxidermist had stuffed his dead body and dressed it in a suit. Then he said, "You did this."

The clock said 10:00.

I waited. But nothing happened. I could sense the guards on either side of me growing anxious. They could see the threat looming on the monitors, and they were torn between keeping their eyes on me and watching that long line of motorcycles on the road. Like soldiers waiting as an invading army approached their lines, they knew a reckoning was imminent.

The clock said 10:01.

And still, nothing happened. Henry continued to stare at me. His fingers twitched. "Do you know what you've done?" he finally said.

"Yes," I responded. "Do you know what you've done?"

The clock said 10:02.

Henry joined Gordon at the desk. I studied the wall clock and wondered what the hell had happened to Earl. If he'd been caught, our plan would quickly unravel.

The clock said 10:03.

Then, abruptly, the lights went off, and I heard the muffled sound of an explosion below us. Earl had blown up the electrical lines serving this building. The room was dark except for the light from two windows. The monitors were black, and Gordon stared at the telephone receiver as though it were playing a trick on him. The guards riveted toward me and leveled their rifles.

I laughed softly. "Henry," I said. "Your clock is three minutes fast."

"What?" he said. Then to the guards, "One of you go find out what happened."

Four, the guard to my left, said, "We were ordered to stay here with him."

"I don't care, goddammit," Henry replied. "We have to know what's happening."

Just then, the door to the hallway opened behind me. The hallway was dark, but a ghostly figure emerged from the darkness. It was a maid.

"Perdónenme, señores," she said. *"Debo limpiar la habitación, y apagaron las luces."* *Excuse me, gentlemen. I must clean the room, and they turned off the lights.*

I could barely suppress a smile. Gordon said, *"Fuera de aqui, más tarde puedes limpiar la habitación."* *Get out. Later you can clean the room.*

"Tengo que limpiar la habitación ahorita," the maid insisted. *I have to clean the room now.*

"Dammit," Henry muttered. Then he told Smith 4, "Get her out of here." Four walked briskly toward the maid. She backed away as he approached. He grabbed her arm and marched her into the dark hallway.

I looked at Henry and said, "I have a confession. I haven't been negotiating with you in good faith." Henry raised his eyebrows. "I never wanted your money."

We heard muted scuffling in the hallway. Then silence, and a moment later, the maid reappeared by herself. She held something small and dark in her right hand. *"Debo limpiar la habitación,"* she said. *I must clean the room.*

Henry began to bark something, but before he got it out, the maid pointed her automatic at the remaining guard. As Smith 9 wheeled his rifle around, Earl fired three quick shots, and Nine collapsed. Earl swung the pistol toward Henry and Gordon, and I said, "Put your hands up." They reacted with stunned silence, and then both raised their hands.

"Gracias, guey," I said as I hurried to Nine's body and felt on his service belt for handcuffs. I found a pair and keys, which I used to unlock the cuffs on my wrists. Then I took Nine's AR-15 and walked over to Henry and Gordon. I told them to move in front of the nearest window, where I could see them better. Earl came up behind them and held his gun on them. I set down the AR-15 and quickly searched them for weapons. Then I gave Earl both pairs of handcuffs and told him to take the Barnards into the bathroom off this office and handcuff them to the toilet.

While he did that, I walked back to Nine and knelt beside his body. I found one extra magazine, which I stuck in my back pocket. Then I ran to the window and peered outside. On the perimeter road below, two black vans raced toward the main gate, and I could hear the growing roar and rumbling of motorcycles. A moment later, the first motorcycle raced past in the desert about fifty yards outside the perimeter fence. First one, then two more, then a dozen, and then a blur.

Gordon was lying on the floor in the bathroom with his arms wrapped under and around the toilet seat. His hands were cuffed over the lid. Henry was lying on his back on the other side of the toilet. His left armed snaked behind the toilet and up between Gordon's arms. He was cursing as Earl pulled his wrists together and handcuffed him. The Barnard brothers looked like a contortionist act. "Get used to this view," I told them. "Where you're going, you'll be cleaning many toilets."

"These are two of the bosses," I told Earl. "Stay with them and make sure no one tries to free them." I handed him the AR-15 and an extra magazine. "They need to answer for their crimes. Don't listen to anything they say. They're devils and may try to tempt you."

"No te preocupes," Earl said. *"No escaparán a menos de que les corte las manos."* Don't *worry. They will not escape unless I cut off their hands.* I don't know if Henry understood Spanish, but Gordon did, and his face blanched.

I found Four's body slumped against a wall in the hallway. His throat had been cut, and his body lay in a large pool of blood. The coppery scent of it was nauseating. It was dark, but I could see enough to make out his rifle. I picked it up and found one extra magazine, which I wiped on my jeans and stuck in a pocket. On the dark stairway at the end of the hall, I heard people walking below. I eased my way down and brushed past people in the dark.

Outside, I sprinted toward the security building. Motorcycles roared past the perimeter fence, and I heard scattered gunfire around the compound. People stood outside the buildings south of me, lips buzzing, but they quickly ducked back inside when gunfire erupted nearby. As I reached the corner of the next building, I saw a black security van hauling up the perimeter road toward me, so I cut between buildings, running toward the solar magnifier. When I reached it, I turned south again and raced ahead. The lights under the magnifier were on, and scores of people were running here and there. Adding to the confusion of motorcycle engines and sporadic gunfire were screams and shouts, although sound reverberated under the magnifier, making it impossible to tell where the sounds were coming from.

When I reached the corner of the building next to security, I stopped to watch the building and catch my breath. My left knee began to throb. The Oxy was wearing off. I had two more in my pocket and dry swallowed one. The back doors of the security building stood open. Behind me, I heard the distinctive "potato-potato-potato" rumbling of Harley engines. I looked back into the magnifier as those engines revved into a throaty roar and saw six Harleys streaking across the area under the magnifier. The bikers had breached the fence, and at least six were inside the compound. Before long, they would all be.

I sprinted to the security building and wheeled into the doorway with the rifle poised, but the anteroom was empty. I started down the hallway, trying to remember where the holding cell had been. I found it in the center of the building, but it was empty.

Then the air was split by a thunderous explosion several buildings away. I ran outside and saw a roiling cloud of smoke and flames climbing skyward. Then a second explosion rocked the ground, followed by another expansive ball of smoke and fire. Sana and Davros had reached the helicopters and blown them up. Hovig, Azad, and Shiraz would disable Paragon's vehicles at the motor pool. The plan had been for the Armenians to eliminate all means of escape. If Martin had planned on flying away with Kat as his hostage, he would now have to go to Plan B, and with no vehicles to drive, his best option would be the utility tunnel.

I cut between buildings and raced toward the hatches that led to the tunnel, but when I came within thirty yards of the solar magnifier, Martin and Kat appeared ahead, running north, Martin pulling her by the arm. Kat was closest, and her body kept me from having a clear shot at Martin. Her hands were cuffed in front of her, and she had a gag over her mouth. She saw me and gave a frightened look of recognition. Then Martin saw me. He stopped, pulled her in front of him, and raised his rifle behind her. Before I could react, he fired on automatic, sweeping the space before me.

One round stung my left arm, and another punched my right side, spinning me around. I kept turning as he fired and then collapsed onto the grass. The firing stopped, and they were gone. I pushed myself up and looked at my arm. I'd been hit on the outside of my bicep. An ugly groove in the flesh was raw and red, blood seeping down my arm. I rolled over and looked at my right side. A hole had been punched in my t-shirt. I raised it and found an entry wound in my side, just below my ribs. I couldn't see the exit wound, but it felt hot and wet and stung like a son-of-a-bitch. The wound wasn't mortal, but it was bleeding steadily. A wave of nausea washed through me.

I forced myself to my feet, picked up the rifle, and hurried to the corner of the building. Peering around it, I saw Martin climbing down the ladder, pulling the hatch closed behind him. Once again, I'd failed to save someone I cared about. I leaned against the building, my mouth like lead, and felt defeated. *I could slide down,* I thought, *just sleep for a while. Someone will come along. How much longer can this fight last?* I held my hand against the wound in my side. Blood poured over my fingers. It looked like rain dripping from eaves and pooling in the grass. I closed my eyes, felt heavy darkness descending, recalled the look of terror on Kat's face, and whispered, "Forgive me, Aileen."

35

In the darkness, I heard Lijah Washington's gravelly voice singing, "Woke up this mornin', ain't feelin' no pain. Then you walk out, baby, blues comin' down like rain." Lijah Monroe Washington playing slide, singing *Blues Comin' Down Like Rain*. I felt the rhythm of those mournful St. Louis blues, felt my blood pumping with the beat, sticky fingers tapping my side. I don't know how long I listened—the darkness was ageless—but it lifted my soul like coming home. Then I remembered where I was. When I opened my eyes, dazzling light reflected off the wall, and I heard the deep rumbling bass of throaty engines. Closing my eyes, I saw Kat swallowed by the earth, disappearing like Alice down a rabbit hole pursued not by the Mad Hatter but by a white banshee wearing camouflage. I pushed away from the wall, opened my eyes, and steadied myself.

I dragged myself to the security building, holding my stinging side. The building was still empty. In their main office, I found a first aid kit and water. I dug out compresses and a thick roll of white tape, then saw clotting agent in a brown packet. I quickly washed my wounds, poured on the clotting agent, and bandaged myself as best I could. Both wounds stung like a bitch. Then I dug the remaining Oxy out of my jeans and swallowed it. I found body armor in a locker, put on the bullet-proof vest and helmet, and hurried back to the hatch. The interior of the compound swarmed with Harleys. Their engines were deafening, but I could still hear sporadic gunfire. I pulled the hatch open, cradled the rifle, and climbed down. I could see Martin and Kat far ahead.

"Martin!" I screamed and lurched back into the ladder well as he turned and fired. Bullets zipped past, ricocheting off the sides of the tunnel. When the firing stopped, I yelled, "I'm coming for you, asshole." He fired again, a dozen rounds spitting past me like meteorites. When the firing stopped, I peered around and saw Martin's back as he pushed Kat ahead. The tunnel walls had conduits on my left, but there was no cover until about forty yards ahead, where I saw a small alcove in the tunnel wall. *I have to try.* Taking a deep breath, I stepped out and ran bent over. I prayed the son of a bitch wouldn't turn around too soon, and I nearly made it to that alcove before he spun and fired. Bullets whizzed over my head, but one struck me in the chest and knocked me flat. I lay on the floor, gasping for breath. The body armor stopped the bullet, but it felt like a sledgehammer had slammed into me.

"I'll kill her," he yelled before running again, pushing Kat ahead.

I clambered up and ran for cover in the alcove. "She's the only thing keeping you alive," I yelled. "You hear me, asshole?"

He responded with a volley, bullets punching into the conduits beside me. My wounds throbbed where bullets had carved tunnels in my flesh, but fuck it. I pushed out and reached the next alcove before Martin realized I was moving. He spun and fired, stopping abruptly after four shots. I ran again while he changed clips and ducked into the next alcove before he could fire another burst. He waited for me to expose myself, and while he did, my mind retreated to Washington's song.

"Gotta hole in my soul," I said to myself. Then screaming: "I got a hole in my soul."

"Stay back, you son of a bitch!" Martin screamed.

"Blues comin' down like rain," I sang at the top of my voice. Now I was fully inside Washington's blues number. "Ain't no place that's safe," I sang, "Ain't no place to hide."

"You're fucking crazy," Martin yelled, scrambling down the tunnel.

I poked my rifle out of the alcove and fired a burst in the opposite direction, away from Kat. The noise was as loud as if I'd been firing at Martin, and he responded with another long burst of fire. Some bullets gouged the walls near me, but most whipped by.

"Wind blowin' through leaves," I sang as loud as possible. "Devil callin' my name."

I peered out and saw him disappearing down the tunnel. He should be nearing the intersection of this tunnel and the central passageway leading to the electrical room. I ran hunched over for the next alcove, but Martin turned and let loose another burst of fire. Although I threw myself aside, another round caught me in the chest and knocked me backward. *Oh, Lord, that hurts*, I thought. *If I live through this, I'll have bruises on top of bruises, but if I die here, it won't matter. Fuck it.* Picking myself up despite the pain, I began running again.

"Since I lost my sweet woman," I sang. "Blues comin' down like rain." Fifty yards ahead, Martin and Kat turned the corner. I knew he'd stop and step back for a shot, so I knelt and braced myself. When his rifle appeared, I fired a long burst at it. I don't think I hit him, but his rifle slammed against the tunnel wall and landed on the floor. I leaped up and ran, continuing to fire until my clip was empty. Then I ejected the clip and rammed home a fresh one—the only one I had. Martin stepped out to retrieve his rifle as I ran, so I fired single shots to drive him back.

Then his arm appeared around the corner, and he started blind-firing with his Colt. I was too far from any alcove to find cover, so I kept firing and running, and one of his rounds hit my helmet and spun my head around. I stumbled and fell as his firing abruptly stopped. "Don't matter it stop rainin'," I said to myself. Then I sang aloud, "Don't matter it stop rainin'." I picked myself up and took off the helmet. It was creased on one side, the silver undercoat showing where the black exterior was grazed. I tossed the helmet aside and kept running. "Devil comin' just the same," I sang.

When I reached the junction, I hugged the wall. I could hear them a distance away, nearing the electrical room. I remembered that it wasn't far from this intersection. "Hey, Martin," I cried.

"Stay the fuck back!" he screamed.

"Martin?" I yelled. "Don't matter it stop rainin'," I sang, "Devil comin' just the same."

He fired another volley, shots reverberating through the tunnel, and then I heard metal clattering on metal. Peering around the corner, I saw them disappearing through the electrical room door. I lunged toward it, singing, "Gotta hole in my soul since you went away. Like lookin' for sunshine on a rainy day."

Before I reached it, the door swung open, but it wasn't Martin who emerged. It was two maintenance guys in brown coveralls, eyes wide, mouths agape. When they saw me, they raised their hands and pressed against the wall. I still had the rifle but was out of ammunition. Lurching to my feet, I dropped the rifle and ran toward them. "Get out of here," I yelled, and they side-stepped as I passed and scurried down the tunnel away from me. About twenty feet from the door, I saw Martin's Colt, its slide racked open. He was out of ammunition, too.

When I reached the door, I yanked it open. In the control room, panel doors lay open, and wires and equipment lay all over the console. They'd jerry-rigged the controls, so the power functioned. Now they were replacing the components I'd destroyed. Open boxes lay on the floor, along with tools, spools of wire, and replacement parts. Martin stood in the center of the room facing me, holding Kat in front of him, his left arm around her neck, his right holding that black cattle prod against her head. Her eyes looked bloated and red. Her hands were cuffed in front of her and clasped as though in prayer. Martin's arm forced Kat's chin up, and he held her tight.

"Come closer and I'll kill her," he warned.

"Martin, it's over," I said. "By now, the FBI is topside. Paragon is finished. The only reason you're still alive is that she is, too. If you kill her, I will make your death long and painful."

I inched toward them, and he backed up. Then he snickered as he saw blood seeping down my arm and soaking the right side of my t-shirt, oozing down onto my jeans. "I hit you," he laughed.

I nodded and inched forward. "Yeah, you got me. But I'm still here. Still standing. Still coming for you. I may stop you with my dying breath, but I will stop you."

As he dragged Kat backward, I inched forward again and saw a long screwdriver on the floor near my right foot. Its steel shaft was a foot long. I picked it up, singing, "Don't matter it stop rainin'. Devil comin' just the same."

"Stop saying that," he screamed, his eyes wide.

No matter how determined I was, my strength waned as I lost more blood. I felt like a tire with a slow leak. You can't run hard and smooth when you're deflating. If this fight dragged on, I'd grow weaker. I stepped forward again, and Martin backed away, dragging Kat.

Then he backed into a large, open box on the floor behind him. He stumbled, and his right arm flailed as he fought for balance. With the prod no longer pressed to her head, Kat arched her back and swung her left elbow into the soft, meaty part of Martin's wounded left shoulder. He yelped when her elbow made contact. Then he lurched backward, stepping over the box and dragging Kat. As she tried to wriggle free, he plunged the cattle prod against her rib cage, and with a resounding electric pop, the prod delivered its punch. Her body was thrown sideways into the control panel. She slumped, dead or unconscious, onto the control panel and collapsed. I yelled and lunged at Martin with the screwdriver. Startled and off-balance, he tumbled backward through the doorway. He scrambled to his feet and backed farther into the electrical room. While he did, I bent down, eyes on him, and felt Kat's neck. She lay still but had a weak pulse.

I stood and stepped through the doorway, facing my enemy. I breathed deeply, using Aikido, and rooted myself as though connected with the earth. But Martin's black prod was formidable. If he zapped me with it, I'd be unconscious, and he'd kill me. Simple as that. But the prod had limits. The more he used it, the more voltage it bled. He couldn't dissipate too much of the charge., and the prod could only be held underhand; otherwise, he couldn't operate the ON switch, couldn't shift it like a knife to the overhand position, and stab downward, so his moves were limited. If I could shove it into him while it was on, he'd zap himself.

His vulnerable areas were his neck and left shoulder. He was right-handed, and as long as he held the prod in his right hand, he couldn't use his entire arsenal against me. If I'd been him, I would've held the prod in my left hand and kept my stronger, better-trained right hand as another weapon.

"I'm going to kill you here," he said.

I regarded him calmly. "Don't talk about it. Do it." Holding my hands out, palms up, I wiggled my fingers for him to come at me.

He studied me with cold eyes but hesitated. That flicker of uncertainty meant he wasn't sure of the outcome, despite my blood loss. My skills in the sally port fight had eroded his confidence. "You can't sucker me in," he said.

"Oh, man, I already have."

His eyes tightened. He was worried now, which impaired his combat effectiveness. But that prod was wicked at close range. He could reach me with it before I reached him, so I had to stay out of its striking distance and neutralize it.

I wasn't surprised when he lunged and swung the prod at me, but he was faster than I expected. I jumped backward, but the prod's silver tip grazed the canvas on my chest plate, and I could smell burning cloth as I lurched to my left and spun around. When he lunged again, I threw the screwdriver at him. It struck him blade first in his left shoulder but didn't strike his wound. As the screwdriver bounced harmlessly away, Martin grinned. Then he lunged again, and I threw my left arm straight and up into his right forearm, blocking his thrust and deflecting the prod. I ducked and punched him twice in the throat. Then I leaned in, forcing him backward while kneeing him in the groin. He staggered away, eyes watering.

I circled farther to my left, and he matched my movements, which put the bank of batteries at his back. Then his eyes narrowed, and he launched himself, trying to stab me in the stomach with the prod. I side-stepped, ducked, and kicked him in the ribs as he rushed past. He stumbled sideways, swallowing a bucket of air. I'd caught his ribs with the sole of my boot and must have broken some. It would hurt like a bitch and restrict his movements.

As I straightened up and faced him, my vision spun from the loss of blood. He watched me warily, holding his ribs with one hand, but he noticed my unsteadiness. He gave me a predatory smile and stepped forward. I surveyed the room and saw what I needed. Circling to the right, I backed away, trying to look wearier than I felt until I was within arm's reach of a wooden broom leaning against a wall. I grabbed the broom and quickly broke off the head over my right knee. I was left with a four-foot broom handle with one splintered end. I deflected the prod with the broom handle when he came at me. Wood doesn't conduct electricity, so he couldn't zap me unless he got inside the defensive perimeter of the broom handle. We danced around the room like swordsmen, him swinging the prod while I blocked it with the broom handle and kept circling.

When my back was to the batteries, I said, "I can do this all day, Martin. The FBI will be down here sooner or later, and you'll be fucked."

He lunged again, and I batted away the prod, but this time he kept coming. I backed farther away, and he came again, and then I backed into a large battery, and he swung with his hand and hit me in the jaw with a fist the size of a cantaloupe. My head snapped back into the battery casing, and sharp pain radiated through my skull. I stumbled to my right but kept focused on his right hand. He raised the prod and pushed the switch. It sparked and crackled as he thrust it toward my left shoulder. I rotated away as the prod drove home, and it missed me but hit the battery. With a thunderous snap and explosion of sparks, the prod burst from his hand and was flung across the room. The smell of ozone was acrid and thick. I fell away and rolled several times with the broom handle clasped to my chest. Martin turned toward me, an outraged look on his face, and came at me again, arms raised, fists clenched. As he closed the distance and fell toward me, I rose on one knee, planted the smooth end of the broom under the toe of my boot, and aimed the splintered end at him. It penetrated him just below his armpit. His weight forced the broom to sink several inches into his body, and he howled in agony, twisting away and collapsing, blood spurting from the wound.

He was still bellowing as I got to my feet. I kicked him in the face, pulled the broom handle out of his side, and smacked him on the head until he lay still. I was out of breath and nauseous, the room spinning as I struggled to stand upright. I leaned on the broom until my head cleared. My jaw ached, and I spit blood as I stared at him. A wave of hatred pulsed through me, and I raised my right foot to stomp on his neck and break it, bringing an end to this evil son of a bitch. But I held the foot there.   He was defenseless, and I couldn't do it. A moral code isn't a code unless you live it. So I walked away. In the control room, I found duct tape and returned. His face was battered and bloody, but the damage was repairable, and the wound under his arm bled but not profusely. I taped his ankles, elbows, and wrists together behind his back.

Kat was unconscious but had a steady pulse. I knelt beside her, pushed the hair from her face, and kissed her cheek. My arms were weary, but I slid them under her, struggled to one knee, and lifted her. She wasn't heavy, but the wounds in my side and arm had begun bleeding again, and my left knee throbbed. I didn't know what reserves I had left, but I carried her into the tunnel, cradling her head on my shoulder, and was okay while I could walk upright. But at the intersection, with the longest stretch ahead, I carried her bent over. For fifty yards, I soldiered on. Then the pain in my back and knee made the trek unbearable. I lowered her to the floor and caught my breath several times before reaching the shaft to the surface.

I lay at the bottom of the ladder, defeated and empty. Then I sang softly, "Blues comin' down like rain. Blues comin' down like rain. Don't matter it stop rainin'. Devil comin' just the same. Devil comin' just the same. He comin' just the same." Hefting her over my shoulder, I climbed, one god-awful step at a time, finally breaching the surface. Lowering her to the concrete, I bent over and lay still, my head swirling. Later, I heard a voice say, "Show me your hands."

I turned my head and opened my eyes. A young man wearing black FBI body armor stood over me. I said, "She's a cop." He looked at me quizzically, so I slowly moved one hand to her back pocket, found her badge, and showed it to him. "We're the ones who called you guys. We discovered this place."

He stayed with us until a golf cart arrived, driven by a medic who examined my wounds and asked what had happened to Kat. I told him, and he examined her, gave her a shot of something, and held something else under her nose. Her head snapped back, and she opened her eyes. After a few minutes, the medic helped Kat sit up and gave us water. While we drank, he tended my wounds. He said I'd be all right, but we needed to go to the hospital.

Kat said before we go anywhere, we have to go to Building 135. That's where the girls are that we'd come to rescue. The FBI was now everywhere throughout the compound. The bikers laid their arms down and stood in clusters under the solar magnifier. At

Building 135, Kat told an agent why we were there. A few minutes later, he led Erin Hightower outside.

"Do you remember us?" Kat said.

Erin nodded but looked bewildered. We were in even worse shape than the last time she saw us.

"We've come back for you, honey. I'm Katrina Hastings. I'm a police officer from Sacramento, where you lived until you were kidnapped. And this is Sonny Marshall. He's the reason I'm here. He's the reason you're free."

She looked at me uncertainly.

I said, "I promised myself I would find you, and I did, but Sergeant Hastings is the real hero here. She's been looking for you for seven years and never gave up."

Erin looked into Kat's eyes, and Kat pulled her close and hugged her.

"What's going to happen to us?" Erin said.

"I don't know, honey, but it will be all right," Kat replied.

Another agent brought out a feisty five-year-old who looked more self-possessed than many adults around us. She was a beautiful Asian child with shiny black hair in pigtails and the brownest eyes I'd ever seen.

"Hi, Angela," I said.

She smiled at hearing her name and said, "What's the matter with you?"

"I'm not sure where to begin. I met your mom. She and your dad will be happy to know we've found you."

"I want to go home," she said. "And I'm hungry." The agent who'd brought her out chuckled and led her and Erin back into the building.

"What the hell?" I heard behind me. It was John Sebastiani wearing FBI body armor. Another agent stood beside him. "I throw a party, and you disappear. Chicken out when the fighting began?"

"You know me," I said. I told him about chasing Martin through the tunnel and rescuing Kat. "You'll find that psychopath trussed up in the electrical room. He's their security chief. He killed some kids here. Earl's been guarding Henry and Gordon Barnard. They're the money and brains behind this operation."

"We have them in custody," said the FBI agent. He stuck out his hand, and I shook it. Then he shook Kat's hand. "I'm Charlie Iverson."

"Happy to finally meet you," Kat said. "We have a lot to talk about."

Iverson nodded, looking around the compound. "It's going to take a while to sort this out."

Then Earl walked up, still wearing the wig and dress, although, without the bombs in his bra, he wasn't so buxom.

I gave him a fist bump and said, "*Gracias, hombre. Muchas gracias.*"

John looked Earl over, a smile lifting his face, and said, "You know what I just realized, Earl? You look really good in a dress."

Earl laughed, despite himself. Then he gave John the finger and said, "*Puta.*"

36

John Sebastiani's role had been to coordinate everything from outside Paragon. He called Charlie Iverson, the FBI agent responsible for the Angela Chang kidnapping, the night before our raid and told him we'd found Angela and two hundred other kidnapped children at a compound in New Mexico. He asked Iverson to bring the FBI in force the following day. Iverson was pissed at not being notified earlier, but John explained why that wasn't possible and told Iverson to meet him at the Sierra Blanca airport at ten. At that hour, Iverson and twenty-six other agents arrived in six helicopters with more agents on the way by car.

Curiously, when the dust settled at Paragon, the Armenians had vanished. All six. Gone as though they'd never been there. I meant to ask Ari about that but never did. Weeks later, when I saw Sana, he nodded and returned to work. Some people are an enigma. Taniel whisked Maria Alvarez away from the safe house before the crooked cops arrived, and she returned to her family later that day five thousand dollars richer, although she had to find another job.

Paragon had a small hospital onsite. Kat and I were driven there but separated, and I didn't see her again while I was in New Mexico. Doctors cleaned and stitched my wounds, which weren't serious, pumped me full of antibiotics, gave me more morphine—and removed the staple from my scalp. When I awoke that evening, Ari and Catherine stood by my bedside, Ari looking relieved and Catherine looking as beautiful as ever. She kissed me on the cheek with those luscious red lips. Then John and Earl ambled in. John was no longer wearing the FBI armor, and Earl had lost his maid disguise. It was good to see him looking like himself again. We discussed what happened, and then a nurse said I had other visitors—CBS's Marcella Delgado and David Fetchenheir. They'd chartered a flight the minute Marcella read my letter. Marcella interviewed me for the next hour while Fetch videotaped. Marcella had her exclusive, but within a day, Paragon was besieged by news vans, tents, satellite dishes, generators, food trucks, and RVs as the world press descended.

Charlie Iverson and a federal prosecutor cornered me when I was released from the hospital. They interrogated me in one of Paragon's classrooms. Iverson had many questions, primarily about why I involved the bikers. I told him the local police and sheriff were compromised, and I didn't know how far Paragon's influence extended. With Henry threatening to torture and kill Kat Hastings, I enlisted the aid of men I knew I could trust. That didn't turn out so well, Iverson said, because nineteen bikers were injured, two critically, six of Paragon's security guards were killed, and nine wounded. I asked if all the children were safe, and he said yes. Then I'm happy, I told him. If you don't like what I did, arrest me.

But he couldn't do that. John provided cover for me in whatever role he had with the FBI. More importantly, Kat told Iverson that she'd deputized me, and I was acting on her behalf. The federal prosecutor said technically she didn't have that authority, but I reminded them that we'd rescued two hundred and twenty-four children kidnapped over fifteen years. They couldn't easily arrest one of the key people responsible for finding those children—and saving a police officer's life. The issue was optics. The media were spinning a story that made Katrina Hastings and Charlie Iverson the heroes in the dramatic rescue. The FBI hadn't had press this good in decades. So they agreed to a cover story that minimized my role and swept any charges against me and my biker friends under the carpet. The one condition was that I tell them exactly what happened, which I did except for small details like who disabled Paragon's vehicles, who caused the chaos in Ruidoso that morning, and who killed the two guards watching me in Henry's office. To those questions, I pleaded ignorance.

I later learned that Kat notified Ray Sobers in Salem. He called Angela Chang's parents, told them he'd found their daughter, and the three of them were on the next flight to New Mexico. When Kat was interviewed, she gave Sobers more credit than he deserved, but I understood how that worked. Law enforcement people looked out for each other. I didn't care if Sobers looked like Detective of the Year; I didn't like how he leered at Kat.

Hundreds of family members descended on Paragon from around the world—so many that the feds sent another hundred agents to gather evidence, conduct interviews, and coordinate family reunions. Because so many Paragon students had been kidnapped from other countries, the State Department also became involved. Scores of their people showed up to deal with the international ramifications of the return of abducted children.

Henry and Gordon were arrested on multiple counts of kidnapping and murder. Paragon's records revealed that twenty-two students had been murdered when they couldn't meet Paragon's high-performance standards. Martin and four of his lieutenants executed them and buried the bodies in the desert. After the bodies were recovered, dental records identified the deceased.

Dorothy Barnard, the administrative head of Paragon, and Henry's son David, director of the guardians, were captured onsite, but Ruth Bellamy and her husband Ralph fled, as did Stephanie Barnard, Henry's wife and head of their genetic accelerator, as well as Laura and Livingston Barnard and Jonathan Curtis, the kidnappers. They were arrested in Argentina months later and extradited. Ruth Bellamy was arrested by Dutch police while attempting to cross the border into Belgium. She'll be tried in The Netherlands because three Dutch children were among those kidnapped. But Ralph Bellamy and Stephanie Barnard remain missing. The current speculation is that they are in China attempting to restart their human genetic accelerator program.

Federal marshals took over the local sheriff and police departments until the feds could determine which authorities were on Paragon's payroll. That investigation continues, but the press reported that shake-ups extend to the Governor's office. Paragon kept good records, which are now in the hands of federal prosecutors.

Paragon's genetic accelerator sparked renewed interest in eugenics. Some people argued, as Henry did, that creating a superior breed of human beings was humanity's only hope for survival. Eugenics societies emerged around the world, and money began pouring into research. Others protested human genetic engineering and attempts to pervert natural law. Their opposition prompted a global debate on the ethics of human genetic manipulation and designer babies. I left all that intellectual breast-beating to others.

The most challenging issue was what to do with the children. People agreed that the kidnapped children should be returned to their parents, but that wasn't so easy. The youngest Paragonites re-assimilated with their families without much distress, but the older ones had no connection with their parents or homelands. Like displaced refugees, some adjusted, but many felt like they'd been cast from a luxury liner into a leaky rowboat. There were behavioral problems, some suicides, and others who fell into drugs, alcohol, and violence as they acted out their feelings of dislocation and disenfranchisement. After being told throughout their young lives that they were unique and privileged, they could not cope as alphas living among omegas.

The purebreds, the products of Paragon's genetic accelerator, had no families to return to. They had no parents, and the government could not easily determine what to do with them. Adoptions and placement in foster homes failed because the purebreds were not suited to those environments. Eventually, most became wards of the state and were placed in emerging Paragon-like boarding schools.

Another dilemma was the pregnancies among Paragon's girls. Those unborn children had parents, but three pregnant girls were just thirteen, and none of the expectant mothers—or teenage fathers—were ready for parenthood. The youngest of the pregnant girls were adopted by couples who were a good match for them intellectually and culturally, so they could raise their babies in a supportive household. In the end, the solution came down to money. Paragon had amassed a fortune in the hundreds of billions. The patent on the solar magnifier alone was worth ten billion dollars. The question was, who owned it? The feds argued that it was federal property, having been seized as the fruit of a criminal conspiracy. However, legions of lawyers soon lined up to represent the interests of the Paragonites. They argued that the money had been promised, in effect, to the students of Paragon and was rightfully theirs. That debate continues and will take years to resolve in the courts. Meanwhile, the federal government set aside funding to care for the babies.

Martin recovered and will soon stand trial, along with his senior staff and surviving security guards. Henry, Gordon, and the other Barnards have the best attorneys money can buy, but their legal fate seems inevitable. The evidence against them is overwhelming. The FBI arrested scores of Paragon's guardians and mentors. Their standard defense was that they didn't know the children had been kidnapped—an excuse that brought the wrath of the world and the legal system down upon them. We heard that from the Nazis in Nuremberg, people cried. Their trials start in a few months.

After Iverson interrogated me, Ari and Catherine drove me to dinner in Ruidoso. They said Earl and John were joining us, and they'd brought another of my old friends with them. I thought they meant Mac and felt conflicted about seeing her, but when we reached our table, I found my saxophone sitting in my chair. I was never so happy to see anything in my life. I cradled it in my arms for ten minutes while everyone else talked, and John made some wiseass comment about sax porn. That night I played it for hours before I slept. I haven't parted with it since. I have parted with Mac. I've accepted that what I had with her is over, and we're both better for it.

Angela Chang was reunited with her parents the night of the raid on Paragon. She had no trouble re-assimilating with her family. To her, it had been a scary but exciting adventure. A month later, FedEx delivered a large box to me from Angela's parents. Inside were a letter of thanks and a 1960 vintage Selmer Paris Mark VII alto sax with its original lacquer finish. It was beautiful, a classic. I knew better than to refuse their gift but told John Chang it wasn't necessary. He said Kat had told him the truth about Angela's rescue, and no gift, however grand, could compare with having his daughter home.

Erin's homecoming was not successful. She'd been away from her family for too long and had no connection with them. Nor were her mother or father comfortable with her, especially when she insisted that her name was Rachel. She called me within days of her homecoming and begged me to come and get her, which I did after conferring with her parents and social services. Rachel stayed with Ari and Catherine for a week, which coincided with my parents' visit to San Francisco. They'd come to care for their wayward son and discover how much trouble I'd gotten myself into. My siblings came, too, so we had one big family reunion, which Rachel joined. During that week, Rachel and my mother spent a lot of time together, and my mother made plans for Rachel to live with them in Pasadena, an arrangement Rachel welcomed, and her parents and social services approved. Rachel and my math professor mother had far more in common than Rachel did with her own mother, and before long, my parents became Rachel's foster parents. When the next school year began, thirteen-year-old Rachel was enrolled as a freshman at Cal Tech, where my mother teaches, and is doing well in college. When I talk to her, she calls me Uncle Sonny.

The band reunited at our studio within days of my return to San Francisco. The X-Man brought wine and beer, and we spent hours talking about the raid, Garth and I regaling them with (mostly) truthful stories of our escapades. Then we picked up our instruments and got back into the groove. The Storm Lake Blues Band became more popular with my and Garth's notoriety, and soon we had a national tour put together. I was thankful for the distraction of music because I was on my own again.

I didn't see Kat for more than a month following our trip to the hospital on the afternoon of the raid. We called each other, but she was busy with debriefings, interviews, and awards presentations. The media portrayed her as a dedicated detective whose tireless search for a kidnapped girl led her from California to Oregon and New Mexico, where, with her FBI counterpart, Charles Iverson, and Salem detective Raymond Sobers, she brought down the worst kidnapping conspiracy in history and rescued more than three hundred children being held captive by twisted megalomaniacs bent on taking over the world. It was a good story. Except for Marcella Delgado, the media downplayed my role in the rescue. Marcella, bless her heart, claimed to have the inside scoop on Paragon and tried to paint me as the story's real hero. She reprinted the letter I sent her, and that story played for several weeks, although I kept insisting to anyone who asked that Katrina Hastings deserved all the credit.

Kat was named Law Enforcement Officer of the Year and spent weeks traveling the country, telling the story she and I agreed upon and receiving accolades. I was happy to see her get them. I wanted no part of it. I occasionally caught her on television, speaking with a talk show host or giving an interview. She and Iverson received the Presidential Medal of Freedom at the White House and had dinner with the President and First Lady. Meanwhile, I happily played with the band. Record sales were soaring, and we felt on top of the world.

After her whirlwind journey around the country, Kat returned to Sacramento and was reunited with her daughter. Then she called and asked if she could see me this weekend. Sara would be with her father, and Kat wanted to drive over on Friday afternoon and spend the weekend with me. I canceled my gigs for those nights, made other arrangements, and then felt my heart surging all week as I waited for Friday. I told her to dress for dinner that evening, and she arrived at my condo late Friday with an overnight bag. She wore a slinky, black satin dress that showcased her figure and risked causing heart failure in every man who saw her, and she smelled like plumeria on a warm tropical morning. I wore a black suit with a lavender shirt and a deep purple silk tie. We held each other for a long moment and kissed until we ran out of breath. I told her she was as beautiful as I'd ever seen her.

She gave me her loopy smile, which raised my temperature by twenty degrees, and said, "Where are we going for dinner?"

"Someplace special." I picked up my saxophone, and we took the elevator to the garage. I drove us to Cactus Jack's. While a valet parked my car, I took my sax and Kat's hand, and we walked inside. I'd reserved the place for the evening, so it was empty except for Joe Warfield at the bar and the Storm Lake Blues Band on stage. The lights were low, and a single, candle-lit table with two chairs sat in the middle of the room. I escorted Kat to it, and Joe brought a nice bottle of Bordeaux. After we toasted each other, the guys in the band introduced themselves.

While Kat chatted with them, I carried my sax to the stage and got ready. Then the band joined me, and we played some smooth jazz we'd been practicing for this moment: *Naturaleza Muerta, Unbreak My Heart, Let's Stay Together, Have I Told You Lately That I Love You*—songs like those. I was not so lost in the music that I didn't notice her arms lying together in her lap, her body swaying gently, eyes closed. In between numbers, she looked at me as though I was the only person in the room. When Joe signaled that dinner was ready, I rejoined Kat, and the band serenaded us while we ate a dinner prepared by the finest caterer in San Francisco.

Afterward, Kat said, "I'm ready to return to your place. We have some unfinished business."

"Oh, I don't know. Wouldn't you rather find a rocky ledge in a downpour and make love while people try to kill us?"

She smiled, her eyes crinkling, and touched my arm. "That was a memorable first time, wasn't it?"

"I'd say it was one of the more memorable first times in history."

She kissed my ear with moist lips, "The second time will be just as wonderful." Her warm breath caused a sensation throughout my body.

"I have just one question," I said. "Are you wearing a badge under that dress, officer?"

"You'll have to take it off and find out."

"With pleasure. But I want to play one more song before we leave." Returning to the stage, I picked up my sax, turned to her, and with the band's sweet sounds behind me, played the tune I knew she loved best: *Killing Me Softly with His Song.*

About the Author

Terry R. Bacon is a poet, playwright, and award-winning author of over a dozen professional books, including *The Elements of Power*, *Elements of Influence*, and *What People Want*. *Executive Excellence* named him one of the Top 100 Thinkers on Leadership in the World. He has a Ph.D. in Literary Studies from the American University and a B.S. in Engineering from West Point. A world traveler, he now resides in the mountains of southwest Colorado with his wife.

He was the sax player in a rock band in his youth and today plays the alto and tenor saxophone, guitar, and baritone ukulele. He studies history and cosmology in his spare time and is an active blogger when he is not working on another writing project. *Storm Warning* is his first novel. His next novel, *The Cerulean Ark*, will be published in 2024.

For more information on the author, see www.terryrbacon.com.

Read more about Sonny Marshall at www.sonnymarshall.com. On Sonny's website, you can subscribe to receive a Sonny Marshall short story, "The Pickled Man," and have access to future Sonny Marshall mystery stories.

Also By Terry R. Bacon

The Cerulean Ark (forthcoming in 2024)
Ex Terminus (a play)
The Elements of Power
Elements of Influence
What People Want
Effective People Skills
Selling to Major Accounts
Effective Coaching
Leadership through Influence
Leading for Empowerment
Adaptive Coaching, 2nd Ed. (with Laurie Voss, PhD)
Winning Behavior (with David G. Pugh)
The Behavioral Advantage (with David G. Pugh)
Power Proposals (with David G. Pugh)

ISBN 979-8-9880748-0-9
$16.99
51699>